HEAT

STUART WOODS

HarperTorch
An Imprint of HarperCollinsPublishers

This book contains an excerpt from *Imperfect Strangers* by Stuart Woods. This excerpt has been set for this edition only and may not reflect the final content of the hardcover edition.

This is a work of fiction. Names, characters, places, and incidents are products of the author's imagination or are used fictitiously and are not to be construed as real. Any resemblance to actual events, locales, organizations, or persons, living or dead, is entirely coincidental.

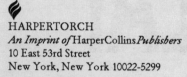

HARPERTORCH
An Imprint of HarperCollins*Publishers*
10 East 53rd Street
New York, New York 10022-5299

Copyright © 1994 by Stuart Woods
Cover illustration by Kirk Reinert
ISBN: 0-06-109358-0

First HarperTorch paperback printing: July 2002
First HarperPaperbacks printing: March 1995
First HarperCollins hardcover printing: June 1994

HarperCollins®, HarperTorch™, and ◆™ are trademarks of HarperCollins Publishers Inc.

Printed in the United States of America

Visit HarperTorch on the World Wide Web at
www.harpercollins.com

20 19 18 17 16

ACKNOWLEDGMENTS

I am grateful to my editor, HarperCollins Vice President and Associate Publisher Gladys Justin Carr, and to her staff for their hard work in the editing and preparation of this book; to all the other people at HarperCollins who have worked for the book's success; to my agent, Morton Janklow, his principle associate, Anne Sibbald, and their colleagues at Janklow & Nesbit, who have been so important to my career; and to my wife, Chris, for her help, understanding, and love.

CHAPTER

1

Atlanta Federal Prison swam slowly out of the smog as the helicopter beat its way south from Fulton County Airport. Kip Fuller was transfixed by the sight.

In his three years in law enforcement Kipling Fuller had never been inside a prison of any sort, and Atlanta held a place in his imagination on a level with Alcatraz and Leavenworth—especially Alcatraz, since that was a prison of the past, as was Atlanta.

Alcatraz was permanently closed, though, while Atlanta had been partly reopened to handle the overflow of federal prisoners. At its peak the prison had held a population of nearly four thousand, but the current number was closer to eight hundred. The prison had been a temporary home to Cuban refugees, Haitian boat people, Colombian drug lords and the occasional special prisoner. It was a special prisoner that Fuller would meet today—or, rather, meet again.

To avoid breaking the FAA regulation prohibiting flights over the prison yard, the pilot made a turn that took him parallel with the wall, a few yards out. They were at five hundred feet now, aiming for the big H painted on the prison roof, and Fuller could see into the yard. As he watched, two figures met in the middle of the open area, and the other prisoners immediately rushed to surround them, leaving a small circle free for the two men, who were now swinging at each other. At the outskirts of the crowd, uniformed guards could be seen trying to push their way to the center, but Fuller thought they weren't trying very hard. He brought the microphone of his headset close to his lips.

"What's going on down there?" he asked the assistant warden sitting next to him.

"That's your man," the official replied.

"What, you mean fighting?"

"That's right. Every time he gets out of solitary, he gets in another fight, and back in he goes."

"How long has this been going on?"

"Fourteen months; the whole time he's been inside."

"Jesus," Fuller said.

Jesse Warden sat on the edge of the examination table and watched through his swollen left eye as the male nurse pulled the thread tight, knotted it and snipped it off with the surgical scissors.

"There you go, Jesse," the man said. "How many stitches is that I've put in you the last year?"

"I've lost count," Warden said in his native hillbilly twang. It hurt when he moved his lips.

"So have I," the nurse said, placing a large Band-Aid over the cut under the eye. "That's it," the nurse said to the guard.

"Let's go, Jesse," the guard said. The guards didn't call him by his last name, as they did the other prisoners; "Warden" was a term of address saved for prison management.

Warden let himself down slowly from the table and preceded the guard through the door, trying not to limp. The guard gave him plenty of room; no guard had touched him since the first fight.

Fuller jumped down from the helicopter and followed the assistant warden across the prison roof toward a door; shortly they were walking down an empty corridor, their footsteps echoing through the nearly empty building.

"It's kind of spooky, isn't it?" Fuller said.

"You get used to it," the AW replied. "In the old days this place would have been full of noise, like any prison, but with the population out in the yard for exercise right now, it's dead quiet."

Fuller followed the man through a door, across a waiting room to another door, where the AW knocked.

"Come in!" a voice called from behind the door.

The AW opened the door, let Fuller in and closed it behind him.

The warden stood up from behind his desk and offered his hand. "J. W. Morris," he said.

"Kip Fuller, from the U.S. Attorney General's office," Fuller replied.

"I've been expecting you, Mr. Fuller. Have a seat; what can I do for you?"

Fuller sat down and took an envelope from his inside pocket. "You have a prisoner named Jesse R. Warden here."

"We do," the warden replied.

Fuller handed the envelope across the desk and waited while Morris read the paper inside.

"This is unusual," the warden said.

"Is it?" Fuller had no idea.

"Normally, when a federal prisoner is released to the custody of the attorney general, it's by court order and a reason is stated—like the prisoner is needed to testify in court."

"Not in this case," said Fuller, who had read the document during his flight from Washington in the Gulfstream government jet.

"Could I see some ID?" the warden asked.

"Certainly," Fuller replied, offering his identification card.

"'Special Task Force,'" the warden read aloud. "What does that mean?"

"Just what it says, sir," Fuller replied. "That's all I'm at liberty to tell you."

The warden nodded. "I see," he said. "I wonder if you'd mind stepping out into my waiting room for a moment?" He didn't return the ID to Fuller.

"Be glad to," he replied. The man was going to call Washington, and Fuller didn't blame him a bit. He left the room and closed the door behind him. The waiting room walls were bereft of pictures, and there were no magazines lying around. Fuller paced the floor slowly, measuring the dimensions of the little room. About the size of a cell, he guessed. The door opened, and the warden waved him back into the inner office.

"Looks like you've got yourself a prisoner," Morris said. "When do I get him back?"

"The AG's order says 'indefinite custody,'" Fuller replied.

"Does that mean he's not coming back? The man's serving two consecutive life sentences; with the most favorable consideration he's in for twelve, thirteen more years, and his conduct so far has not been such to warrant favorable consideration."

"I'm afraid I can't answer your question, Warden," Fuller said. "I'm just a pickup and delivery man." He was more than that, but the warden didn't need to know.

The warden took a form out of his desk and rolled

•

it into a typewriter at his side. He filled it out, hunting and pecking, then whipped the paper out of the machine and pushed it across the desk with a pen. "I'll need your signature," he said.

Fuller read the form and the paragraph at the bottom:

Received a prisoner, Jesse R. Warden, no. 294304, at the personal order of the Attorney General of the United States, from the Federal Penitentiary at Atlanta, Georgia, this date, for indefinite custody.

Fuller signed and dated the document. "Where is Mr. Warden now?" he asked.

"In solitary confinement," the warden replied, "where he always is."

CHAPTER

2

Jesse walked into the punishment cell, and the door was slammed and locked behind him. This time, though, he wasn't alone in the dimly lit room. Just as the door swung shut he caught sight of a man sitting on the bunk, and he wasn't a prison official. Jesse knew him; his name was Charley Bottoms, and he was major trouble. Bottoms was the leader of the Aryan Nation group inside the prison; they were racist, anti-Semitic and extremely violent.

"Come on in, boy, and sit down," Bottoms said.

Bottoms was a biker type, six feet five or six, three hundred pounds and covered in tattoos. Jesse had no intention of sitting on a bunk with him. "I'm all right where I am," he said.

"You know," Bottoms said in a southeastern drawl, "them's the first words I ever heard you say. What kinda accent is that? Where you from?"

No need to be hostile to the man; Jesse wanted to leave this cell alive. "North Georgia," Jesse replied. "Up near the Tennessee border."

"Tennessee was my guess," Bottoms said.

"Yeah, even folks a little farther south in Georgia think my accent's kind of crazy."

"A real hillbilly."

"The real thing." Jesse was a preacher's son and he had three years of college and two of law school, but his childhood country accent had never changed a whit.

"I hear you're heat," Bottoms said.

Now they were on dangerous ground. "Used to be."

"Why ain't you still?"

Jesse thought about it for a moment. Hell, why not? "They found half a million dollars and my dead partner in the trunk of my car."

"You did all that?"

"I couldn't convince them I didn't."

"Come on, boy, I want to know what you did."

"I'm not making any jailhouse confessions; they have a way of turning up later on."

"You think I'd testify in court against another con?"

"Maybe against a con who used to be heat."

Bottoms shook his head. "You got a bad opinion of me."

"Not at all," Jesse said. "I just try to run a tight mouth."

"So you're doin' two big ones, back to back, huh?"

"That's what the judge said."

"How many fights you been in since you got here?"

"A hell of a lot more than I was looking for."

"Yeah, I guess cons just naturally don't like heat," Bottoms said. "You're one tough son of a bitch, though; I'll give you that. You took on some of the hardest guys in this joint, and you're still alive. Don't appear to be punchdrunk, either."

Jesse wondered how long it would be before he was.

"Word in the block is, it's not gonna change," Bottoms said. "Every time you get out of solitary somebody's gonna take you on." He grinned. "There's a long line."

Jesse shrugged. "Nothing I can do about that."

"Sure there is," Bottoms said. "What you need is some friends in this joint."

"Yeah?"

"Yeah. If you're a nigger in the joint, you join up with the niggers; if you're a spic, you join up with the spics. But you're a white man, so you oughta join up with white men. That's us."

"It's real nice of you to think of me, but I don't buy your rules," Jesse said. "Thanks, anyway."

"Just what is it you don't buy?" Bottoms asked.

"I don't hate anybody."

"Shit, man, you gotta hate *somebody* just to live, so we picked niggers and Jews. What's the big deal?"

"Every time I ever hated anybody, even for a little while, it did more damage to me than him. Besides, I know some real good black people and some real good Jews. In fact, in both cases, I've known a lot more good ones than bad ones. Trouble with you people is, you've got to hate somebody else so you can feel worthwhile. That's what I don't buy."

"Look, Warden," Bottoms said, and he sounded exasperated, "you got a lot of time to pull in this joint, and every time you walk out in the yard, somebody's gonna try and beat the shit out of you, because you used to be heat. Now so far, nobody's been able to do it, but I'll tell you something, my friend, you're not looking so good."

"Well," Jesse said, "I've got thirty days of solitary to rest up."

Bottoms stood up, and his full stature was awe-inspiring. "You're gonna need your rest, buddy, because if I don't hear by the time your solitary hitch is up that you're ready to join up with us, then the next guy you meet in the yard is gonna be me." Bottoms looked him up and down. "What're you, six-three, two-twenty?"

"That's close enough, I guess. It's been a while since I got measured and weighed."

"Most places, that's big. Not in here." Bottoms rapped on the steel door. "You better be in touch, you hear?" The door opened, and Bottoms strode out of the cell, then the door slammed shut again.

Jesse sank onto the bunk and stretched out his aching limbs. The guy he had just fought had kicked him, hard, in the thigh, and it hurt worse than his cut eye. He had another thirty days to do in this cell, and he was looking forward to the rest. Still, with no radio or TV and no reading matter it would be hard. Once again, he was alone with himself, and the company was lousy.

Whenever Jesse closed his eyes the same picture came back to him: it was the best year of their marriage; Beth was healthy after losing a breast to cancer five years before; Carrie, named after his mother, was nearly four, smart and pretty; they had the little house in Coral Gables, and he was moving up in the Drug Enforcement Agency.

Jesse had never thought of being a cop; he'd had his life all planned. It was college, law school, a few years in an Atlanta firm, then back to north Georgia to set up a practice. Then Beth got pregnant and sick at the same time. Jesse's parents were dead, and Beth's weren't rich; she had to quit her job, and the part-time work he had in the admissions office wasn't enough to support them. There was nothing to do but leave law school and look for a job.

The DEA was recruiting on campus, and they

made working for the government look attractive and secure. Beth recovered, the baby was born healthy and things started looking up.

That year was the best—not just because they were comfortable and happy, but because the future looked so bright. Jesse had enrolled, part-time, in law school, and once the degree was his, he could rise to new heights in the Justice Department. His assignment to the South Florida Task Force had been a plum; it was where the action was, where promotions happened and careers were made. He was twenty-eight, smart, hard-working, making big busts on a regular basis, and his superiors, once they got past his hillbilly drawl, thought of him as a comer. Then Beth had gotten sick again.

Her first illness had been covered by her parents' medical insurance, but when they got married, that lapsed. Then, when he had joined the DEA, her cancer was excluded from his insurance as a preexisting condition. Suddenly, all the money was going to doctors, medical laboratories and hospitals. Beth took fourteen months to die, and meanwhile Jesse was left thoroughly in hock, with nearly $400,000 in outstanding medical bills. That was when he had started to think about the cash in the evidence locker.

He was startled by the opening of his cell door; he hadn't expected it to open for another thirty days.

"Jesse, you got a visitor," the guard said.

Jesse sat up and blinked in the bright light. A prisoner in solitary wasn't allowed visitors, and since his lawyer had died a couple of months back, there was nobody left to visit him. He got up and followed the guard.

He was led upstairs, in the direction of the warden's office, and shown into a small conference room.

A man who had been sitting at the table stood up. A cardboard box was in front of him on the table.

"Hello, Jess," Fuller said. "You look awful."

Jesse blinked at this apparition. "Hello, Kip," was all he could think to say. Kip Fuller had been with the South Florida Task Force for less than a year when Jesse had been arrested. The young officer and his new wife had been out to the house a couple of times for barbecues, and Jesse had liked them. When Jesse had been arrested, Kip had been sympathetic, had brought him things in jail, had tried to help inside the agency. "Seems like a long time," Jesse said.

"It does, doesn't it?"

Fuller reached into the cardboard box and took out a set of chain restraints, then shoved the box down the table toward Jesse. "Your clothes are in there," he said. "Get dressed; you and I are going to take a helicopter ride."

CHAPTER

3

J esse had trouble climbing the stairs to the roof, because of the chains. Fuller helped him.

"I'm sorry about the rig, but I've got my orders," Fuller said.

As they stepped through the door onto the roof the helicopter started up with a whine, drowning out Jesse's question. Fuller helped him into the machine, fastened his seat belt, then took the facing seat. He clamped a headset on Jesse, then put one on himself.

Jesse reached for the switch that isolated the passenger compartment intercom from the pilot, then adjusted his microphone. "What's going on, Kip?" he asked. The dull whine of the two turboprop engines made conversation noisy, even with the headset on.

"There's not a lot I can tell you," Fuller said. "Barker will explain."

"Dan Barker?" Jesse asked, surprised. Barker had been his last superior on the South Florida Task Force. They had never liked each other. "What the hell does he want with me?"

"Barker is no longer DEA; he's a deputy assistant

attorney general now, and he took me with him to Justice. He's in charge of a new special task force."

"What kind of task force?"

"Barker will explain." Fuller looked out the window; he seemed embarrassed.

"How've you and Arlene been, Kip?"

"We've both been very well," Fuller replied. "Arlene likes living in Washington; she says she needs a place with seasons." Fuller smiled. "There's more good news: Arlene is pregnant."

"That's wonderful, and after trying so long. Always happens when you least expect it."

"Thanks," Fuller said. "I don't think I've ever been so happy." Then he looked embarrassed again. "Jesse, you look like absolute hell. What's been going on?"

"Cons don't like ex-cops," he said.

"The assistant warden said you'd been in a lot of fights."

"I didn't start any of them."

Fuller looked out the window again. "I tried to get them to put you inside under another name, so nobody would know. Barker killed that little effort. I'm sorry, Jesse; I did what I could."

"I appreciate that, Kip," Jesse replied.

"If this thing today doesn't work out, I'll try to get you moved to Leavenworth and work up a new identity. Now that I'm at Justice I have a little more clout, and maybe I can do it without Barker hearing about it."

Jesse leaned forward in his seat. "Kip, was it Barker who hung me out to dry?"

Fuller shook his head. "I honestly don't know, Jesse. I combed through all the paper on your case, all the depositions and testimony, and I couldn't find a thing to hang on him. Certainly, he was in a position to do it, but so were half a dozen other people. I'm damned if I could ever find a motive."

Jesse sat back. "Kip, there's something I never told you, something important."

"What's that, Jesse?"

"I wasn't entirely innocent."

"What do you mean, exactly?"

"I was going to steal the evidence money; Bobby was going to help me. Beth's medical bills were out of sight, and my only other alternative was bankruptcy. I wish I'd taken that route now, but it was something to do with the way my old man brought me up. A man who couldn't pay his bills was worse than dirt to him, and bankruptcy was the worst possible shame. I even went to see a lawyer about it, but I just couldn't do it. Then Bobby, who was the sweetest guy I ever knew, brought up the evidence locker and what was in it."

"That doesn't sound like Bobby Dunn," Fuller said. "He was the straightest arrow I ever saw."

Jesse nodded. "I know he was. And when he brought it up he made it sound, I don't know . . . almost like I was entitled to the money. He even volunteered to move the cash from the locker to the car, while I was upstairs in a meeting. He said nobody would ever suspect him, and he was right; nobody ever did."

"What about the coke and Bobby's death?" Fuller asked.

"I had nothing to do with either one," Jesse replied. "What I think happened is, when Bobby went to the evidence locker for the money, he got caught by somebody and that somebody cleaned everything out of the locker and stuffed some of it into my trunk, then shot Bobby and put him in there. There was about a million and a half more in that locker, and a ton of coke."

"And they nailed you for all of it," Fuller said.

"They did. And somebody walked away with the rest of the money and the drugs and never got caught.

I always thought my best chance was that the guy would do something stupid and get nailed. But he didn't; whoever he was he played it very smart. Barker is that smart."

"He is," Fuller said, "but I always thought it was one of the other agents. I never had a line on who, though."

They rode in silence for a few minutes, then Jesse asked the question he had wanted to ask all along. "Did you ever get a line on Carrie?"

Fuller shook his head. "I tried again when I knew I was going to see you, but it was the same as when I wrote to you last year. I got hold of the woman in charge of the adoption agency a couple of days ago, tried to use a little Justice clout, but she wouldn't budge. All she said was that the people were very nice, ideal adoptive parents. She said Carrie was very happy, and that if you knew the people, you'd be pleased. I hope that helps some."

Jesse nodded. "Some. I just wish I could write to her and that she could write to me. There's so much I want to tell her, and if I could hear from her then at least I'd know something about how she was being brought up."

"Carrie's young, Jess, and she'll adapt very quickly. I know it's hard for you, but I really think you should try to put that out of your mind. There's absolutely nothing to be done about it. Believe me, I tried everything."

Jesse looked out the window and saw an airport. "Where are we going, Kip?"

"That's Fulton County Airport; the locals call it Charlie Brown. We're going to a meeting there."

"With Barker?"

Fuller nodded.

"Any advice, Kip?"

Fuller looked uncomfortable, but he seemed to be

thinking about it. Finally, he looked up. "Barker needs you pretty bad. You're not in much of a position to negotiate, but you might remember that." He looked out the window again. "I won't be able to help you, Jess; remember that, too."

The helicopter was hovering over the tarmac outside what looked like an office building. Finally it set down, and the pilot cut the engines. Fuller helped Jesse out of the aircraft and across the tarmac to a door at the end of the building, then up a flight of stairs.

Finally, Fuller opened a door and ushered Jesse into a conference room. A soft drink machine sat in a corner beside a coffee pot. Sitting at the table was the man Jesse held responsible for his incarceration and the loss of his daughter, the man he hated most in the world.

"Hello, Jesse," Barker said.

"Hello, Dan." Barker was the epitome of civil service smoothness, Jesse thought.

"Have a seat. Would you like a cup of coffee or a cold drink?"

"Some coffee, please."

Fuller went to the coffee pot. "Black, as I remember."

"That's right," Jesse replied.

"It's not great coffee," Barker said, "but I expect it's better than what you've been getting."

"I expect."

Fuller handed Jesse the cup, and he raised his cuffed hands to receive it. "You think I could take the restraints off now, Dan?" Fuller asked.

"I think not," Barker replied. "So, Jesse, how are things in prison?"

Jesse had still not sat down. "Dan, I'm not talking to you while I'm wearing this." He held up his cuffed hands. "So you can either get this stuff off me right now or go fuck yourself." Jesse knew he was flirting with a trip back to prison, but he was angry.

Barker waited a beat before he turned to Fuller. "Kip, get this piece of shit back to the pen."

Jesse turned and hobbled toward the door.

Fuller caught up with him in the hallway. "That was a mistake, Jesse."

"The hell with him," Jesse said.

Barker's voice came down the hall after them. "All right, all right, come on back in here and let's talk."

Jesse turned and held his hands out to Fuller, who began unlocking. First the handcuffs came off, then the leather belt that buckled in back, then the chain that connected the cuffs to the leg irons and, finally, the leg irons. Jesse walked slowly back into the conference room, rubbing his wrists and stretching his legs, then he sat down. There were some pencils on the table; Jesse wondered whether he could plunge one into Barker's neck before either he or Fuller could shoot him.

CHAPTER

4

Barker took a seat at the opposite end of the table. "How would you like to get out of prison?" he asked.

"I'm already out of prison," Jesse said. "Now why don't you just cut to the chase and tell me what I have to do to stay out?"

Barker nodded at Fuller and the younger man placed a briefcase on the table, opened it, took out an eight-by-ten photograph and put it in front of Jesse.

Jesse saw a head and chest shot of a young man in the uniform and green beret of the Army Special Forces. He was rail thin, handsome, deeply tanned, square-jawed and his chest displayed many ribbons. Master sergeant's stripes adorned his sleeves.

Barker opened his own briefcase and took out some papers, glancing at them as he spoke. "This man's name is Jack Gene Coldwater; that photograph was taken in 1972, and, as far as we know, it was the last picture ever taken of him. Christ only knows what he looks like now. He was born in Ship Rock, New Mexico, in 1949, to a Navaho father and a white mother;

he attended the local public schools, played football and was good at it. He turned down a football scholarship when he graduated from high school; instead, he joined the army; he was good at that, too. He was big, smart and tough as nails, and Special Forces got hold of him right out of boot camp. His service record says he was a natural. He pulled *four tours* in Vietnam and led missions all over the country, north and south, in Cambodia and Laos, mostly infiltration with only a few men; he rose to the rank of master sergeant faster than it should have been possible, and by the time the war ended he was the practical equivalent of a company commander. There were bird colonels who were scared shitless of him, and his commanding officers, his platoon leaders and company commanders, *always* did what he told them to. He won just about every decoration the army had to offer, except a Medal of Honor, and he was recommended for that. Word is, his regimental commander—one of those colonels who was scared shitless of him—blocked it; I wasn't able to find out why.

"Coldwater didn't want the Vietnam war to end, and when Saigon fell, he passed up a seat on the last chopper out, then fought a rear guard action for another week. He finished up at Vung Tau, southeast of Saigon, with his back to the sea and two men left. Then he stole a boat and sailed it down the South China Sea, past the mouth of the Mekong River, fighting a running battle with Vietnamese craft, around the cape called Mui Ca Mau, then northeast along the Cambodian coast to Trat, in Thailand, right on the Cambodian border.

"From there he and his merry band took a bus to Bangkok and reported to the military attaché at the American Embassy, who got them onto a plane back to the States before anybody knew they were there. Once home, he took discharge, and that was the last we heard of him until a couple of years ago."

"So what's he doing now?" Jesse asked. "Dealing drugs?"

"The DEA can be happy he's not," Barker said. "The truth is, we're not exactly sure *what* the hell he's doing, but we think it involves a lot of weapons. He's living in the Idaho panhandle, on a mountain just south of the Coeur d'Alene Indian reservation, next to a little town called St. Clair; he has at least four wives, numerous children and no visible means of support. He's the titular head of something registered as an official religion in the state, called the Church of the Aryan Universe."

"Funny," Jesse said, "I had a meeting with a fellow from Aryan Nation just this morning."

"This isn't Aryan Nation; it's an entirely separate organization. Aryan Nation is mostly made up of convicts and ex-convicts. The people around Coldwater are apparently model citizens. They do seem to share a view of the world with Aryan Nation, though—the idea that the white man is God's supreme creation and that everybody else is inferior."

"Sound like a delightful bunch of people," Jesse said.

"Yeah. A couple of years ago the Bureau of Alcohol, Tobacco and Firearms began to get reports of somebody buying large amounts of small arms on the West Coast; then the reports got to be of bigger stuff—anti-tank weapons, recoilless rifles, that sort of thing. They put a couple of men on it; one of them got close and got a bullet in the brain for his trouble, then the trail went cold.

"About fourteen months ago—just about the time you went away—we got a snitch who said that Coldwater was the guy buying the weapons. ATF sent two men up there, undercover. One went in as a life insurance salesman—they actually trained him to sell insurance. The other got a job as a shoe salesman. Both of them simply vanished."

"Did they report anything before they went up in smoke?" Jesse asked.

"Only what I've told you; that's everything we know up to now. When the new administration came into office, some people at Justice began to take an interest in cults and white supremacist groups, and somebody at ATF, which was backing away from this real fast, passed on the Coldwater file, such as it was, to us. All of it is in Fuller's briefcase; you can memorize it at your leisure, then destroy it. A special task force was authorized to investigate cults in general and Coldwater's in particular, and I was picked to form it and lead it."

"And naturally," Jesse said, "the first person you wanted aboard was good ol' Jesse Warden."

Barker managed a tight smile. "The last person, actually. But I didn't want to follow the ATF example of bureaucratic stupidity and lose a couple more men."

"So you decided to lose me?"

"Christ knows you're expendable, Jesse, but you also have something to gain from all this."

"I was hoping we'd get to that," Jesse said. "Just what do I have to gain?"

"Your freedom, if you bring off the assignment. We're talking about a presidential pardon."

"Oh, I love that," Jesse said. "I suppose you have a letter from the president in your briefcase, confirming all this."

"Of course not," Barker said irritably. "You'll have to take my word for it."

Jesse leaned forward. "Dan, before we go any farther there's something you'd better understand: I'll go back to prison before I'll take *your* word for a goddamned thing. Now let's stop wasting time; you tell me what you want done, and I'll tell you what you have to give me to do it. If we can't agree, then the hell with it."

The hell with it, indeed. Jesse figured he could disable Kip, kill Barker and disappear before anybody knew it. The two of them probably had enough money on them to get him started, and he no longer resembled any existing photograph of himself. He'd have a better chance than he would back inside Atlanta Federal Prison.

"All right, let's get down to brass tacks," Barker said. "As you'll see when you read the ATF reports, Coldwater appears to have two principal lieutenants: their names are Casey and Ruger, both ex–Special Forces. Both were on that boat with Coldwater, and a distillation of both their service records is in Fuller's briefcase. I want to know what this organization is doing, where they're getting their funding and what other organizations they're connected with. And I want hard evidence for at least one serious felony conviction—I'm talking twenty-five to life—for each of the three top men—Coldwater, Casey and Ruger. I intend to break up this outfit, and when you get the evidence, I want to *personally* make the arrests."

"All right," Jesse replied, "and here's what I want: I want a written agreement that guarantees me, first: an unconditional recommendation by the attorney general for a presidential pardon for *any* crime committed up to the actual date of the pardon; second: I want a hundred thousand dollars in cash; third: I want a completely new identity, tailored to *my* specifications and entry into the Justice Department's witness protection program; and finally: I want a package delivered to the adoptive parents of my daughter, *immediately*, which will contain a letter from me to my daughter, and you will secure their written agreement to give it to her no later than her twenty-first birthday. The agreement is to be *personally* endorsed, *in writing*, by the attorney general herself, and my obligations will be satisfied when Coldwater, Casey and Ruger are either dead or indicted for a serious felony."

"Why dead?" Barker asked.

"So that, if you try to take these guys and you kill one or all of them, you won't be able to weasel out."

Barker looked at Fuller. "Can we do this thing about the letter to his daughter?"

"I've spoken with the head of the adoption agency," Fuller said. "I think she would be amenable to passing the package to the parents, but I don't think there's anything in the world we could do to force them to give the girl the letter. They might, but they might not."

"All right," Jesse said, "I'll settle for a letter from the head of the adoption agency swearing that she has passed the package to the adoptive parents."

"I think I can get that," Fuller said.

"And I can swing the rest," Barker replied. "It's going to take me a couple of days, though, and you'll have to go back into the joint while I work things out."

"No deal," Jesse said vehemently. "There's a hotel in this city called the Ritz-Carlton Buckhead; Fuller and I will wait there in a suite, and I want my own bedroom."

Fuller chimed in. "Dan, it'll give me a chance to brief Jesse on the new background we've got worked out for him, and that'll save us time."

Barker turned back to Jesse. "I used to think of you as an honorable man. Will you give me your word that you will remain in Fuller's custody until I get back from Washington?"

"I give you my word on that," Jesse said. "But no more chains." There would be time enough later to kill Barker if he came back from Washington empty-handed.

"All right, you've got a deal," Barker said. "But I'm damned if I'll shake your hand on it."

That was just fine with Jesse.

CHAPTER

5

J esse sat at the dining table of a twelfth-floor suite
at the Ritz-Carlton in Buckhead and polished off a
large cut of prime rib. Elsewhere on the table were
the remains of a loaded baked potato, a Caesar salad
and a bottle of Mondavi Cabernet Sauvignon (the
reserve). He took another swig of the wine, then
turned his attention to a large dish of macadamia brit-
tle ice cream.

"Prison hasn't improved your table manners," Kip
Fuller said from across the table.

"You'll have to forgive me, Kip, but it's been a
while since anybody cared." The ice cream was sensa-
tional. "Why aren't you eating?"

"Because it's three o'clock in the afternoon, and I
had lunch," Fuller replied. "Are you sober enough
after all that wine to start absorbing some detail?"

"Shoot."

"Ordinarily, I'd just build you a legend for this
job, but last week I got lucky." He handed a large
newspaper clipping across the table.

Jesse picked it up; it was from the Toccoa,

Georgia, newspaper: LOCAL BUILDER'S FAMILY WIPED OUT IN DUI CRASH.

He read a few paragraphs, then looked up at Fuller. "Okay, so the guy's name is Jesse; what else?"

"His wife and three daughters were killed in a head-on car crash."

"I read that much."

"What's not in the article is that the husband, one Jesse Barron, lived through the crash and was hospitalized with head injuries. When he recovered enough, he checked himself out of the hospital and disappeared. I talked to the local sheriff, who knew the man well, and he reckons he's a suicide; they just haven't found the body yet."

"What else do you know about him?"

Fuller took a file folder from his briefcase and opened it. "Born in a place called Young Harris."

"I know the town; not far from where I was born."

"He's two years older than you are; went to North Georgia College, in Dahlonega, flunked out the first year. Single for a time, then married in his early thirties to one Sally Terrell, had three kids close together— daughters, Margie, Becky and Sherry, ages seven, five and four. The guy worked in construction in Atlanta for half a dozen companies, then moved to Toccoa a little over a year ago and started his own business. He was having a tough time of it, apparently—on the verge of bankruptcy, so the loss of his family wasn't his only reason for suicide."

"He could have just taken a hike," Jesse said.

"The sheriff doesn't think so. Barron had been drinking heavily, was depressed and had talked about suicide before the accident."

"Sounds good. Anything unusual about the guy?"

"Very little. A high school football knee injury kept him out of the military, and he was too young for Vietnam, anyway. There is one delicious little detail, though; something we'd have been hard put to invent."

"What's that?"

"He was arrested nine years ago in a fight; he was one of a group of hecklers who were badgering a black couple who had bought a house in a white neighborhood."

"I like it," Jesse said. "A nice little credential. Was he a member of the Klan or anything?"

"I checked with the FBI—they've got a man in just about every Klan organization. He was actually on a list of people approached about joining, but he never did. It shows that the guy must have had a reputation for bad talk around town."

"Good. What did he look like?"

Fuller handed over a small color photograph. "This was his driver's license picture. A little smaller than you, and fatter, but you could be him after a car crash."

Jesse nodded. "Does he have any family?"

"A grandfather in a county nursing home—in his nineties and ga-ga. That's it."

"How'd you come across this guy? You don't read the Toccoa, Georgia, newspaper."

"No, but researchers at Justice do; they keep an eye out for identities that could be used in the witness protection program. I've also got a name from Alabama, but he's not nearly as good—too many relatives. The nice thing about Jesse Barron is that he's from your part of the state, so your accents are probably similar."

"If he's from Young Harris, they certainly are. What happens if Barron's body turns up?"

"The sheriff has agreed to keep it quiet," Fuller said. "There's nobody to notify, no heirs, nothing to leave them if there were any. The guy was living in a rented trailer." He pushed the file across the table to Jesse.

Jesse looked through it; it was complete down to Barron's failing grades his first and only year in college. "Sold," he said. "Now let's talk about this town in Idaho. What was it called?"

"St. Clair. It's a one-industry town—a chipboard manufacturing company called St. Clair Wood Products. Family-owned, employs around four hundred people. We've been subscribing to the local weekly newspaper, the *Standard*, for a while and, apart from jobs in the local stores, county government, the sheriff's office, that sort of thing, Wood Products is about it."

"Any black people in town?"

"None. A few Indians."

"If this guy Coldwater is half Indian, what's he doing as head of something called Aryan Universe?"

"Apparently, they consider the Indians as some sort of racially pure strain; I know, it's bizarre."

"What sort of ideas have you got about infiltrating?" Jesse asked.

"Maybe you, as Barron, could set up some sort of small business, maybe remodeling of houses, like Barron? You had some construction experience in your past, didn't you?"

"I worked summers at house building when I was in high school and college. I'm fairly handy, but God help the person whose house I tried to remodel."

"Well, then."

"I don't like it; two guys have already gone in there in regular middle-class jobs. If Coldwater is recruiting, I doubt it's from that bunch. He's likely to want a more disappointed kind of recruit, I would think; somebody who's pissed off at the world. Certainly Barron, if he were alive, would have a lot to be pissed off about—he's lost his family and his business. Tell me, was the drunk who hit his family black?"

"I'll find out. I think you've got a good idea about the guy being disappointed. How would you infiltrate?"

"Maybe just drift in there, look for work, drink at the local beer joint, see who's who around St. Clair. If Barron suddenly turned up, would the local cops want to talk to him about anything? Did he do anything illegal?"

"Nothing like that in the record."

"So I could use Barron's name with no fear of his name ringing alarms if he got busted for speeding or something?"

"Why not? That way, if somebody did some checking on him, we'd know exactly what they'd find. He's got a social security number and that's helpful, if you're going to look for work—and we could have a word with some of Barron's former construction employers in Atlanta, alert them for requests for references."

"Okay, let's do it that way. What about a driver's license and credit cards? I'd like to have one working credit card in my pocket."

Fuller looked through some papers. "His credit report says he's got a Visa, but it's tapped out and way overdue. I'll fix something up with the bank and have them issue a new card. As for the driver's license, I can get one made up with your picture on it. Hang on, I've got a Polaroid camera in my luggage." Fuller got up and went to his bedroom.

Jesse wiped off the hefty steak knife the Ritz-Carlton had furnished with the prime rib, slipped it under his belt in the small of his back and tucked his shirttail in over it. He had still to hear from Dan Barker, and he meant to be ready if he didn't like what he heard.

CHAPTER

6

J esse stood at the bathroom sink and looked at himself in the mirror. The face that stared back at him was still unfamiliar; there had been no mirror in the solitary confinement cell where he had spent so much of his prison stay.

The nose was the worst; it had been broken twice and badly repaired in the prison infirmary. It was flat across the bridge and distorted at the tip, but at least he could breathe through it properly. There was scar tissue around the eyes, and the right ear had begun to cauliflower at the top. He looked like nothing so much as a punchdrunk fighter. The face would scare anybody; it certainly scared him.

The doorbell of the suite rang, and Fuller knocked on the bathroom door. "Barker's here," he said. They had been in the suite for three nights.

"Be right there," Jesse said. He tightened the knot of his tie, slipped into his jacket and looked at himself. The suit and shirt had been finely cleaned by the hotel, and, except that his clothes were a bit loose on him, he thought he looked quite well. He wrapped the blade of the sharp steak knife in two sheets of hotel stationery, making a kind of scabbard, then tucked it into his belt at the small of his back. In a few minutes, he knew, he would either have preserved his freedom or stolen it by killing Barker. He hoped Kip would not force his own death by resisting. Since the day he had been arrested Kip had been the only person who had treated him decently.

Jesse buttoned his jacket and walked into the living room. Barker sat at the dining table, and a catalog case rested on the floor beside him. "Sit down, Jesse," he said.

Jesse took a chair two down from Barker, so he could reach him easily.

Barker took a sheaf of papers from an inside pocket and handed them to Jesse. "See if that's what you want," he said.

To Jesse's surprise, it was, including the letter signed by the attorney general. "It looks just fine," Jesse said.

Barker reached into the case and removed an automatic pistol and a box of ammunition. "I wouldn't send anybody, even you, up there unarmed," he said. "It's a brand new, Hechler & Koch 9mm automatic; takes fifteen in the clip and one in the chamber. It was bought this morning at an Atlanta gun shop in the name of Jesse Barron, and all the proper forms were filled out, so it can't be traced to any government agency."

Jesse nodded and removed the weapon from its holster.

"No need to load it now." Barker handed him a card. "Here's an eight hundred number; memorize it; Kip will be on the other end of it."

Jesse glanced at the number, committed it to memory and returned the card to Barker. "I'm not going to report in every day," he said. "I don't want people noticing the calls."

Barker reached into his magic case again and produced a small cellular phone in a leather pouch. "This is a very special cellular phone," he said. "Press this button and your conversation is scrambled. Hide it somewhere. The eight hundred number is programmed in already; just hit zero-one and S-E-N-D. The cellular coverage in the St. Clair area is good."

Jesse accepted the phone and its recharging accessories. "Anything else?"

"Yes. Remember that you have absolutely no law enforcement authority. Whatever happens, this is not going to be your bust. I want you to work this so that you get evidence, then call us in for the climax, is that clear?"

"Perfectly."

Barker handed him a well-worn wallet; inside were a driver's license, a credit card, social security card and some business cards from Jesse Barron's business.

"These look good," Jesse said, shoving the wallet into his hip pocket.

"Kip tells me you've got your cover down pat, and I've arranged to have Barron's name put on your fingerprint record, so if you get printed for any reason, you're okay."

"It sounds like we're all buttoned up, then," Jesse said. "Except I'm going to need a good bit of cash."

"How much?"

"I'm going to need a vehicle and a little nest egg; say, thirty thousand?"

Barker turned to Fuller. "Get him twenty-five, and get a receipt."

"I've got that much now," Fuller said.

"Give it to him."

Fuller produced some banded stacks of bills from his briefcase and handed them to Jesse; he wrote out a receipt, and Jesse signed it.

"I want you on a plane to Boise today," Barker said, "and in St. Clair tomorrow."

Jesse shook his head. "I'm going to buy a vehicle here, register it in Barron's name and drive across country, picking up motel receipts and buying stuff I need. I'll be in St. Clair in a week or ten days."

Barker leaned forward and put his elbows on the table. "I guess you think I'm just turning you loose," he said. "I guess you must think I'm a blithering idiot."

Jesse smiled. "That's pretty close to my personal opinion of you, Dan, but I know very well you wouldn't let me out except on a leash."

"I've got better than a leash," Barker said. "You're to report to Kip daily on your way to St. Clair and every chance you get once you're there. If you go too long without reporting in, I'll fall on you from a great height."

"Sure, Dan."

"Get something straight, Jesse; you haven't been paroled; you're still serving your sentence. You're just going to be doing your time in St. Clair."

"Right up until you get your indictments," Jesse said.

"That's right, pal; right up until the president signs your pardon. Until that day, you're nothing but an escaped federal prisoner. You got that?"

"Sure, Dan."

"I can press a button, and there's a nationwide manhunt for you in full swing; the Immigration and Naturalization Service already has you down for arrest if you try to cross any border, so don't get it in your mind to tool on up to Canada or down to Mexico, got it?"

"Sure, Dan."

"And something else you'd better know, boy; if this doesn't work out—for *any* reason—if I don't get good busts on those three men, then you're going back to Atlanta, and you'll *never* see the light of day again. If the cons don't kill you, then you'll never make parole; I'll *personally* see to that."

"I know you will, Dan," Jesse replied. He stood up and turned to Fuller. "I'll need a ride to a used car lot," he said.

Barker stood up and turned to Fuller. "Call me when he's on his way." He picked up his catalog case and walked out of the room.

Fuller sighed. "I'm glad that's over," he said.

"Let's get moving," Jesse replied.

"Jesse," Fuller said, "you've got a gun now; can I have the steak knife, please? The hotel would just charge it to my bill."

CHAPTER

7

Jesse found what he wanted at the third car lot; it was a two-year-old Ford pickup with four-wheel drive and a camper box filling the truck's bed. He made the deal and counted out ninety-six hundred dollars. When he had the paperwork, Kip walked back to the vehicle with him.

"Are you driving West now?" Kip asked.

"I've got a few things to pick up—the license tag, some clothes, a sleeping bag. No need to come with me; I'll be on my way by tomorrow."

"Call me when you're on your way," Kip said. He looked embarrassed again. "I wish I could have done more for you, Jess. I wish I could have fixed it for you to be with Beth when she died. I know it must have been hell, locked up at a time like that."

"You've done a lot more than anybody else, Kip, and I'll always be grateful to you."

"You understand that Barker thinks what you're about to try to do can't be done," the agent said.

"Sure, I understand that; he always underestimated me, though."

"That he did," Kip said, smiling.

Jesse started to offer his hand, then surprised himself by hugging Kip.

"You take care of yourself, Jess," Kip said. He handed over a card. "This is my home number; if you can't reach me at the office, don't hesitate to call."

Jesse handed Kip a thick Ritz-Carlton envelope. "You'll see that this gets to the adoption agency?"

"I'll FedEx it before the day's over."

"I'll be seeing you," Jesse said, climbing up into the truck.

"I hope so," Kip replied, waving as Jesse pulled out into traffic.

Jesse went first to the courthouse and got a tag for the truck, then, making several detours to be sure he wasn't being followed, he drove to Hartsfield International Airport, parked the pickup in the short-term lot, went into the terminal and bought a round-trip ticket for Miami, with a two-hour wait before the return flight.

On the flight down, he went into the men's room, opened the lining of his suit and removed a key that was sewn in place, then he had lunch and slept like a baby. In Miami he took a cab to the bank and told the driver to wait. He signed in at the safety deposit desk and an attendant took him into the vault; using his own key and Jesse's, the man unlocked a large box. Jesse took the box into a private booth and opened it.

He removed a small satchel containing forty thousand dollars that he had stolen from a bust the week before he was arrested, then he returned the empty box to the attendant and turned in his key. He had a snack and a beer at the airport, then flew back to Atlanta.

It was too late to do anything else that day, so he checked into a hotel near the airport, had dinner and watched TV in his room. Television was wonderful, he thought.

Next morning, he was at an office supply store when it opened. He bought a small safe, the kind meant to fit between a building's studs; then he found an army surplus store, where he bought a sleeping bag and some work clothes. He sold his suit to the man behind the counter for twenty bucks, then he rode around Southwest Atlanta until he found a small, independent car repair shop.

A mechanic slid out from under a car. "What can I do for you?"

"How much to rent some space, your welding equipment and some tools for half an hour?"

"I don't know, man; there's liability problems, you know?"

"I know how to use it; how's a hundred bucks?"

The man smiled.

Jesse began by drilling a quarter-inch hole in the back of the little safe; he then wired into a spare fuse, then ran it to the cellular telephone charger inside the safe. He put the truck on the shop's hoist, found a space in the frame and welded the safe in place. When he was sure the mechanic wasn't looking, he counted out a thousand dollars, stuffed it in his pocket, then put his own forty thousand and the fourteen thousand he had left of the government's money into the safe, along with the cellular telephone, which would be constantly on charge when the engine was running. He loaded the pistol and put that and the spare ammunition inside, then locked the safe and let the vehicle down. He memorized the combination, then threw away the paperwork.

"That's it," he said to the mechanic, handing over the money. Then he got into the truck and drove west on the interstate. When he had crossed the Alabama line, he stopped and called the 800 number, tapped in the extension and got a recording. "I'm on my way," he said. "Calling from eastern Alabama; I'll check in again tomorrow."

HEAT

●

*   *   *

He drove west, marveling at the light and the open spaces. Occasionally, he left the interstate and drove through small towns, grinning at their filling stations and fast-food joints. He'd thought he'd never again have a fast-food hamburger, and he wolfed them down joyously.

He reveled in driving the pickup, in charge, master of his own fate, sort of. No guard sat beside him; no wall barred his way; no citizen wanted to beat him to death. He was a free man again.

He stopped in Mississippi for the night, sleeping in the camper box, and called in again the following morning. He drove on, astonished at what a big country it was, trying to forget the oppression of a six-by-eight cell. He stopped feeling panic at the sight of a police car, setting the cruise control at sixty-five, enjoying the slow ride. He spent one night in Amarillo, and he kept waking up, thinking about Mexico, a day's drive to the south. He lay there, pondering total escape. He had fifty-four thousand dollars and a used pickup truck, but that wouldn't get him far. He didn't want to be a bum in Mexico; he wanted to be a free man, able to go wherever the hell he wanted to go, and he had a chance of pulling it off in Idaho. He went back to sleep.

He spent a night in Santa Fe and another in Denver, alternating between motels and the camper. He stopped in Jackson Hole, Wyoming, and allowed himself half a day to look around Grand Teton National Park. It was early autumn and the changing leaves were magnificent.

The following day at sunset he reached the city limits of St. Clair, Idaho, and checked into the town's only motel. He gorged himself once more on pizza and television and slept soundly. The next morning was clear and frosty as he left the motel.

Fun was over; it was time to go to work.

●

CHAPTER

8

Jesse walked down the main street in the early morning light and took note of St. Clair. Low clouds hung over the town and the dim light made it seem earlier than it was. There was only a single block of Main Street—a couple of dozen stores, two filling stations, newspaper office, doctor's office, veterinarian. The buildings were mostly red brick, with tin awnings out front—looked as if they'd been built around the turn of the century. The place was like a lot of small Georgia towns Jesse had seen. One difference, though: outside the police station, a modern building, there were five squad cars parked. As he walked past, four uniformed men came out of the building, got into the cars and drove off. Must be the early shift, Jesse thought. He also thought that five squad cars were a lot for a town this size.

He stopped and peered through the window of something called Nora's Café. A woman was busy behind the counter, and she was alone in the place. He tried the front door; it was locked, but when the woman saw him she came and let him in.

"Morning," she said.

"Did I get here too early?" Jesse asked.

"Seven on the dot," she replied, looking at her watch. "Coffee?"

"Thanks, yes."

"Take your pick," she said, waving at a row of booths along the wall.

A boy walked in with a stack of newspapers and put them on the counter. Jesse picked one up, left some change on the counter and sat down in a booth.

The woman came over with his coffee. "New in town?"

"Brand new; just passing through, really."

"I'm Nora; I run the joint."

"I'm Jesse. How you doing?"

"I'm okay. You're not from around here, are you? Not with that accent."

"Naw, I'm a hillbilly, from Georgia."

"They got hills in Georgia?"

"They got mountains; not like the ones around here, though."

"What do you feel like for breakfast, Jesse?"

"Two scrambled, bacon. . . I don't guess you've got grits?"

Nora laughed aloud. "You're a long way from home, Jesse; we got hash browns."

"That'll do."

"Toast? English muffin?"

"English muffin."

"Juice?"

"Orange."

"Good choice; I squeeze it myself." She left him with his newspaper.

Jesse read through the paper carefully; it was as good an introduction to the town as anything. There was a problem with the sewage treatment plant, and it looked like property taxes might go up; a main-street merchant had died at sixty-eight; the high school football team had won its first game; and St. Clair Wood Products had gotten a big order for plywood and chipboard from a company building a new ski resort near Park City, Utah. An unsigned editorial blasted a gun control bill now in the state legislature; letters to the editor dealt with the need for new playground equipment at the grammar school, a complaint about drunk drivers in the county and a yard sale at the First Church on Saturday.

Jesse sipped his coffee and watched half a dozen customers wander in and take booths or stools at the counter. The sound of bacon sizzling was pleasant to the ear, and nobody put any money in the jukebox across the room, for which he was thankful. He was not fond of rock and roll or country music.

Nora came with his breakfast, and he forced himself to eat slowly. He had lost a lot of weight in prison, and he thought he'd better watch his eating, or he'd gain it all back. He'd finished his breakfast and had accepted a second cup of coffee when a man in a policeman's uniform entered the café and took a stool at the counter. He and Nora exchanged pleasantries, and she poured him a cup of coffee. There was another, quieter exchange between the two that Jesse caught in his peripheral vision, then the cop walked over to Jesse's booth, carrying his coffee.

"Morning," he said to Jesse.

Jesse looked up. "Good morning to you," he replied.

"Mind if I join you?"

"Take a pew," Jesse said.

The cop eased into the booth opposite Jesse and set down his coffee. He stuck a hand across the table. "I'm Pat Casey," he said. "I'm the law around these parts."

The name registered from his briefing; this was

●
40

one of Jack Gene Coldwater's top two men, one of the ones he was going to nail. "Jesse Barron," Jesse replied, shaking the man's hand.

"Don't recall seeing you before," Casey said.

"Naw, I just rolled in last night," Jesse replied. "Probably move on tomorrow, the next day. Thought I'd take a rest from the road; I've been driving for a week."

"Where you headed?"

Jesse leaned back in the booth and sighed. "I was thinking about Oregon. Hear that's nice country."

"It is; I've been there."

"Pretty nice around here, too."

"We like it. I can't place your accent."

"Georgia, north Georgia. Town called Toccoa, up in the mountains. Hillbilly country."

"I thought that was Tennessee and Kentucky."

"Us hillbillies are all over."

Casey grinned. "You're a long way from home, boy."

Jesse let himself look a little sad. "Boy, I guess I am."

"What caused you to up and leave Georgia?"

Jesse shrugged. "Hard times, I guess. I had a little business went under."

"What kind of business?"

"Construction. Remodeling and additions mostly. Folks weren't spending their money like they used to; I guess it's the recession."

"Got any family back there?"

"Not anymore," Jesse said, gazing into the middle distance. "Oh, I got a granddaddy, but he's in a home. He doesn't know anybody anymore, not even me."

"How'd you travel in here, Jesse?"

"I got a pickup over at the motel."

"You got any means of support, Jesse?"

Jesse looked up from his eggs. "Well, I haven't done any work for a few weeks, but I put a little by."

"How little?"

"I guess I could get by two or three months, if I stretched it. You're not looking to get me for vagrancy, are you?"

Casey grinned. "Not at the moment. I wouldn't want you to become a drain on the public purse, though."

Jesse changed his tone just a little. "Listen, Pat, I've never been a drain on nobody in my life; I worked since I was twelve, and I haven't given it up yet."

"You got some ID, Jesse?"

Jesse produced a wallet and tossed it onto the table between them. "I guess you're the welcoming committee in St. Clair, huh?"

Casey went through the wallet carefully, looking at the driver's license, credit card and bits of paper. Jesse had put that package together very carefully.

"Looks like your license expires five years from last week," Casey said.

"I just renewed it."

Casey nodded. "You ever been in jail, Jesse?"

"Not to speak of."

"Now, what does that mean?"

"I had a little conversation with the sheriff when I was eighteen or nineteen. We haven't spoken much since."

Casey nodded. "Well, I guess I can't hold your youth against you." He peered closely at Jesse's face. "Looks like you've been roughed up a little."

"Car wreck," Jesse said. "I spent a few days in the hospital."

"Were you drunk?"

"Nope; the other guy was though, the nigger."

"That's not a politically correct word these days," Casey said.

"Well, I'm sorry if I offended you," Jesse said, reaching into his pocket for some money. He left five dollars on the table and got up.

"Rushing off?"

"I sort of get the idea that I'm not too welcome around here. I guess I'll have a look at Oregon."

"Aw, sit down, Jesse; I'm just doing my job. C'mon, sit down."

Jesse sat down.

"Let me buy you a cup of coffee."

"Thanks, I've already had two."

Casey nodded at the newspaper on the table. "You read the *Standard*?"

"Yep."

"You see any reports of crime in there? Juvenile delinquency? Drug busts?"

"Nope."

"That'll give you an idea of the sort of town we got here. Our last drug bust was nearly four years ago."

"Sounds like a real safe place," Jesse said.

"Exactly," Casey said, "and I mean to keep it that way. That's why I'm so inquisitive; I like to know who's in town and what they're doing here."

"That's reasonable, I guess," Jesse said, sounding mollified.

"Take your time in St. Clair; have a look around; there are worse places to settle."

"Any work around here?"

"Most of the work's down at Wood Products. The place is humming right now; you might find something there."

"Thanks, maybe I'll take a look at it."

"You do that. If you decide to stay a while, come see me down at the station. I'll see if I can't help you settle in."

"Thanks, Pat, I appreciate it."

Casey got up and stuck out his hand again. "Well, I got to do my rounds. Good talking to you."

Jesse shook the man's hand again. "See you around."

Casey picked up Jesse's plate, cup and glass. "I'll take these over for Nora; save her a trip."

Jesse nodded. "Thanks." He took a deep breath and let it out. That went pretty well, he thought. He watched as the policeman walked to the lunch counter and set down the dishes. Casey turned and left, and Jesse saw that his orange juice glass wasn't on the counter with the plate and the cup.

"Well, Pat," Jesse muttered to himself, "you sneaky bastard, you."

CHAPTER

9

Pat Casey strolled into the police station, walked over to the desk where a young, uniformed man sat and gingerly handed him the orange juice glass. "Pull the prints on this and run 'em, Rick," he said. "Nora's are on there, too, but it's the other ones I want."

"Right, Chief," Rick replied. He took the glass, one finger at the top and one at the bottom, and went into a back room.

Casey went into his office, sat down at his desk and picked up the phone. He looked up the area code for Georgia, dialed information and asked for the number of the sheriff's office in Toccoa, Georgia. He wrote down the number, then dialed it.

"Hello, this is Chief of Police Pat Casey in St. Clair, Idaho. I'd like to speak to the sheriff."

"Yes, sir, I'll connect you."

There was a click. "This is Tom Calley, Chief Casey. Was that Idaho you said?"

"Yessir. I just want a little information, if you can help me."

"Do my best."

"You know a fellow named Jesse Barron?"

"Sure do. Where'd *you* run across him?"

"Right here in St. Clair. He's down the street at the café drinking coffee."

"Well, I'm glad to hear it. Tell you the truth, I thought Jesse was dead."

Casey's grip tightened on the phone. "Oh? Why's that?"

"He didn't tell you what happened to him?"

"Said something about a car wreck."

"That's right. A bad one."

"Would you tell me about it?"

"Well, Jesse and his wife and three little girls were coming home from a movie out at the shopping center, and a drunk, a colored fellow, ran head on into their car. Jesse—"

"Can you hang on a minute, Sheriff?" Casey interrupted. One of his officers had just entered the station, and Casey waved him into his office. He punched the hold button. "Jim, you see if our man is out of the way, and if he is, go down to the motel and turn over his room and his truck—and do it *neat*, you hear?"

"Yessir, Chief."

Casey punched another button on the phone. "Sorry, Sheriff, you were saying?"

"I was about to tell you that Sally and the girls were killed in the wreck, and Jesse was busted up pretty good. When he was able to get out of the hospital, he went out to the cemetery and looked at the graves, then he went downtown and got on a bus to Atlanta, and that was the last anybody saw of him around here. Tell you the truth, I thought he'd gone out and put a bullet in his head. I'm glad he's all right, though; I always liked him."

"Can you describe him for me?" Casey asked.

"Sure, I guess he's six-one or six-two, about two

hundred pounds, brown hair, going gray and receding, blue eyes. He had some injuries around his head and face; I'm not sure just what he'd look like after those heal."

"That's our man," Casey said.

"Has he broken the law up there?"

"No, sir; I just wanted to be sure he's who he says he is. How long you known him?"

"Most of his life, I guess; his family moved here from Young Harris when he was in grammar school."

"Was he ever in any kind of trouble?"

"Nothing serious. The summer after he got out of high school I had to pull him and a couple of other young fellows in."

"What was the charge?"

"Well, a colored family moved into a house down the road, and a lot of folks around here didn't take kindly to it. The boys broke a few windows, that sort of thing. Justice of the Peace gave 'em three days and expunged the record, because of their youth. I never had any more trouble with Jesse."

"When would that have been?"

"Oh, early seventies, I guess; around there."

"What sort of a fellow is Jesse?"

"Solid, hardworking. Wasn't his fault his construction business went under; just wasn't enough work around here. I'd have made Jesse a deputy, if I'd had an opening. He's on the quiet side, but he's real smart."

"Do you think you might be able to get hold of a photograph of Jesse for me?"

"I might be able to. Chamber of Commerce might have one."

Casey gave the sheriff his fax number. "I'd appreciate it if you'd fax it to me, if you can find one."

"Glad to; I'll send somebody down there right now."

"Sheriff, I appreciate your help."

"You see Jesse again, you tell him I said we miss him around here."

"I'll do that." Casey hung up and swung around to the computer terminal next to his desk and began typing. Early seventies; the closest newspaper with a computerized database was probably Atlanta. He found a listing for the *Atlanta Journal-Constitution* and dialed the number. Shortly he was connected and called up the index. A few more keystrokes and he had a list of stories containing the name Barron between 1970 and '75. He got the right one on the second try: TOCCOA YOUTHS ARRESTED IN RACIAL ATTACK. It was brief and as the sheriff had described the incident. Jesse Barron was one of the boys named.

Rick stuck his head in the door. "Chief, I've got the record on screen two."

Casey cleared the screen and typed more keystrokes; the record came up. The photograph wasn't great, but it was nearly two decades old. Jesse Adam Barron had no known criminal record. He had been fingerprinted when he had tried to enlist in the marines; rejected because of a knee injury resulting from high school football.

He typed more keystrokes, and the printer at his side disgorged the record and the photograph. Casey looked at the picture more closely. He was younger, skinnier, had more hair, hadn't been in a car crash. Casey thought he'd have had a hard time putting together the face he had just met at Nora's with the face in the photograph if he hadn't known the man, but it was a match. The prints matched; that was the important thing. Casey sat back and waited for Jim to return from the motel.

"I did it like you said, Chief," the officer said, easing into a chair opposite Casey.

"What did you find?"

"A couple of old suitcases, some clothes, the usual toiletries, some books, mostly old novels, and what looked like a family picture."

"Tell me about the picture."

"Just a snapshot in a frame; a woman and three children, girls."

"Any ID documents?"

"Nossir, I guess he must have 'em on him."

"Any weapons?"

"Nossir."

"What about the truck?"

"Some tapes and a bill of sale in the glove compartment. He bought the pickup in Atlanta ten days ago."

Casey sat back and thought about this. The man seemed what he said he was, but two things bothered him: his driver's license was new, and so was the truck, both acquired about the same time. Still, Barron had said he had the license renewed, and the sheriff had said that he had left Toccoa on a bus. It made sense that in a wreck that had killed three people, Barron's car would have been totaled. "Hang on a minute," Casey said.

He turned back to the computer and spent a minute and a half getting connected to the Georgia Motor Vehicles Bureau in Atlanta. In another moment, he had the driver's license he had just seen up on his screen. He printed that out, then moved down a couple of screens to the historical record. It showed that Barron's old license would have expired before the month was out. He went into vehicle registration and found that two pickup trucks were currently registered to Barron, the one at the motel and another, larger truck, the kind with a back seat. That would have been the one in the wreck, he thought. Nobody had canceled the registration yet. He printed out the record.

"Jim, anything strike you as odd about this man's stuff? Anything at all?"

Jim shook his head. "Looked real ordinary to me, Chief. Except—"

"Except what?"

"Well, it's a little thing, but the tapes in his glove compartment—"

"What about them?"

"They were classical stuff. You know, symphonies, and like that?"

Casey nodded. "You'd think a guy in a pickup would be listening to country music, wouldn't you?"

"Yessir, I guess I would."

"Well," Casey said, "it takes all kinds, I guess."

"I guess."

"Thanks, Jim, that'll be all for now."

The officer left, and Casey sat and thought about what he had on Jesse Barron. He had been expecting another undercover man from the ATF for weeks and, after what had happened to the last two, he expected one with a good cover. Still, Barron's background seemed too good to be just cover. It was the sheriff who had made the difference. He'd gotten the information, one cop to another, and that made it right.

Casey heard the fax machine ring in the outer office. He got up and walked to the machine and waited. A moment later it disgorged a sheet of paper. Casey picked it up and looked at the photograph. He was four or five years younger, dressed in a business suit, hair neatly cropped and combed; the hairline hadn't yet started to recede. He looked a lot less beat up than the man Casey had just met, but he was the same man, no doubt about it. The picture was clipped from some sort of business directory. Underneath it, set in type, were a few lines of copy:

Jesse A. Barron, president, Barron Construction,

specialists in additions, renovations and remodeling. Mr. Barron takes pride in finishing jobs on time and on budget. Free Estimates. Member of the Chamber since 1981.

Casey walked back to his desk, picked up the phone and dialed a number.

"Yes?"

"Hi, it's Pat. I don't think he's who we're expecting."

"What makes you so sure?"

"He checks out to a tee—background, paperwork, everything." Casey told him about Barron's history.

"Wouldn't you expect him to check out?"

"Yeah, but it's more than that. First of all, I talked to a local sheriff in Georgia who's known him since he was a boy. It was all good, and get this—as a kid he got arrested for trying to run some niggers out of his neighborhood. I checked the back newspaper editions and found a confirming story."

"How do you know this guy is the guy the sheriff is talking about?"

"He faxed me a photograph. It's the same man."

"I don't know. . . "

"One more thing: I've known a lot of cops, and I can usually spot 'em a mile away. This guy is less like a cop than anybody I ever knew. If I'd had to guess I'd have said he was an ex-con, but I guess that's because the injuries make him so rough looking. St. Clair didn't seem to be his destination, either; said he was on his way to Oregon."

"Well, if he decides to stay don't hassle him; make it easy for him, but keep tabs on everything he does."

"Of course. If he's real, he sounds like he might be our kind of guy."

"We'll see." He hung up.

* * *

In Toccoa, Georgia, Sheriff Tom Calley dialed an 800 number.

"This is Fuller."

"Mr. Fuller, this is Tom Calley, in Toccoa, Georgia."

"Yes, Sheriff?"

"The call came, like you said it would."

"Everything go okay?"

"Seemed like it. He asked for a picture, so I faxed the thing you fixed up."

"That's good, Sheriff; thanks for your help."

"Not at all."

"And you'll let me know if the real Barron turns up?"

"Yessir, I will."

"And I'd like to hear about it if anybody else calls about Barron—anybody at all."

"Sure thing."

Jesse closed the door to his motel room and looked around. His things were, if anything, more neatly arranged than when he had left. So far, so good.

CHAPTER

10

Jesse strolled down Main Street, taking stock of the town. The place was still overcast, but the light was becoming brighter; the clouds would burn off soon.

His first impression of Main Street was of something out of the twenties or thirties, and for a while, he couldn't figure out why. Certainly, it was very clean and neat, with every storefront looking freshly painted, but that wasn't it. Finally, it struck him. Although it was daylight, he saw that there were no electric signs, just the old-fashioned, hand-lettered kind. It was as though the business district was constructed and maintained to some very strict, but out-of-date design code.

He stopped in front of a small shop. The windows were soaped over, and above, on the facade, there were holes in the brickwork where a sign had been removed. He had noticed it because it was the only vacant storefront on the street, and at a time when most small town businesses were struggling to stay open, competing with the new malls. Some lettering on the glass front door caught his eye: "J. Goldman, Jeweler and Watchmaker," it read.

Jesse continued his walk, stopping in the drugstore for a Boise newspaper. To his surprise, there was a soda fountain taking up one wall of the store. He hadn't seen one since high school. A wave of nostalgia washed over him, a memory of sharing a strawberry soda with a teenaged girl—two straws. And even in those days the soda fountain had been mostly an anachronism.

"Good morning," the druggist said as he rang up Jesse's quarter.

"Good morning," Jesse replied.

"New in town?" The man stuck out his hand. "I'm Norm Parsons."

Jesse shook the man's hand. "Jesse Barron. I'm so new I might not even be here tomorrow."

"Sorry to hear it," the druggist said. "We need new blood all the time. Fine place to live, raise a family, St. Clair."

"I can believe it," Jesse said, waving goodbye with his newspaper. He took a right at the corner and walked through a residential neighborhood. The houses were mostly Victorian or that most American of houses in the middle third of the twentieth century, bungalows. A new house was going up on the corner, and that, too, was an old-fashioned bungalow.

"Time warp," Jesse said aloud. Each house was neatly painted, and its front lawn was closely clipped. He couldn't spot a weed in a flower bed, not anywhere. He stopped on the corner and looked up and down Elm Street. "Jesus Christ," he said aloud to himself. "Isn't this where Andy Hardy used to live?"

Back on Main Street Jesse was waiting to cross at what was apparently the town's only traffic light when a patrol car pulled up next to him, and Pat Casey got out. "How's it going, Jesse?"

"Not bad. This is a real pretty town you've got here."

"Glad you think so. Thinking of sticking around?"

"I don't know," Jesse replied, looking up and down the street. "You sure this isn't a movie set?"

Casey laughed. "We like it that way. You stick around, and you'll get to like it, too."

"I sure like the soda fountain down at the drugstore," Jesse said. "I haven't seen one since I was a kid."

"Yeah, and Norm whips up a mean milk shake or banana split."

"Mmmmm," Jesse moaned.

"I spoke to your sheriff back in Toccoa, Georgia," Casey said.

Jesse let his eyebrows rise. "You're a thorough man, Pat."

"I am that."

"How is old Tom?" Jesse asked.

"He seemed well. Had a good opinion of you."

"He sort of spanked me once, a long time ago. We got along pretty good after that."

"That's what he said. You interested in some work?"

"Might be."

"You make up your mind, you drive out the road there about a mile, and you'll come to St. Clair Wood Products, our local industry. Ask for Herman Muller; tell him I sent you."

"Thanks, Pat, I'll keep it in mind."

Casey took a small notebook from his shirt pocket, scribbled something on a page and tore it out. "The motel gets expensive after a while. If you want a nice room and home cooking, try this lady, and—"

"Tell her you sent me?" Jesse laughed.

"Just part of the service," Casey said, then got back into his car and drove away.

Jesse read the notebook page. "Mrs. Weatherby, 11 Elm Street," it said. The street where Andy Hardy used to live.

* * *

Jesse pulled the pickup into a large parking lot, got out and surveyed St. Clair Wood Products. A long, low building sat fifty yards from the highway, and the noise of machinery could be heard from inside. Jesse found an entrance that said "Offices" and went in.

"Can I help you?" a middle-aged woman behind a desk asked.

"I wonder if I could see Mr. Herman Muller?" Jesse asked. "It's about a job. Chief Casey sent me."

She looked at him a moment without reacting, then said, "Have a seat; I'll see if Mr. Muller's available."

Jesse sat down and watched as she walked into an adjoining, glass-enclosed office and spoke to an elderly man who was sitting at a large, rolltop desk. He nodded and said something to her, then she returned.

She took a sheet of paper from her desk and handed it to Jesse with a pen. "Fill this out, please, then Mr. Muller will see you."

Jesse filled out the application, taking time to describe his new job background, then he was shown into Herman Muller's office.

Muller stood up to greet him, a lean, tan seventy-year-old, Jesse figured. Muller shook his hand and waved him to a sturdy oak chair. He took the application and read it slowly before he spoke. "Nice to meet you, Jesse," he said when he had finished.

"Thank you, sir," Jesse replied. "It's nice to meet you. Pat Casey said there might be some work going here."

"Might be," Muller replied. "I see you've been in the construction business."

"That's right," Jesse said. "Had my own business until the recession came along."

"We've been lucky around here; in fact, we just got a nice new contract for chipboard."

"I read about it in the local paper," Jesse said.

"Were you good at running a business?" Muller asked.

"I think I was," Jesse said. "I never could seem to get together enough capital to bid on the big jobs, but I had a lot of happy customers on the little ones."

"How many people worked for you?"

"I only had three, full time, but if we got a nice job I'd have a dozen or so at work, plus the subcontractors."

"How'd you get along with them?"

"Nobody ever quit me, except for more money than I could pay."

Muller glanced down at Jesse's hands. "Looks like you've done some hard work before."

Jesse looked at his own hands and saw what Muller meant. They were gnarled and scarred, and Muller didn't know that they'd gotten that way from beating up other men. "I guess I've done my share," he said. "I started working for my daddy when I was twelve, and I never stopped. In fact, right now is the only time I've ever been out of a job."

"You got any family?"

"I lost my family in a car wreck," Jesse said, avoiding Muller's eyes.

"I'm sorry to hear it," Muller said. "I'm a widower myself, and I lost my only grandson not long ago." He rubbed a hand quickly over his eyes. "Let me tell you how we work around here. Everybody starts at the bottom. I've got a force of five hundred and two people, and everybody started at the bottom. I've never hired a manager or a foreman; I've always promoted from within. I'll offer you the worst job I've got around here, feeding the chipper; pays seven dollars an hour. You give me a day's work for a day's pay, and I'll give you something better to do before long. How's that sound?"

"It sounds all right to me," Jesse said, managing a smile.

"Good. Let me take you down to the floor and I'll introduce you to Harley Waters; he'll be your foreman." Muller rose and started for the door, then stopped. Two men had just come into his outer office, men wearing suits; one of them was carrying a briefcase. "Uh, oh, looks like I'll have to talk to these gentlemen," he said. He opened the door. "Agnes, this is Jesse Barron, he's going to work on the chipper. Will you call Harley and ask him to come up here and get Jesse?"

"Yes, sir, Mr. Muller," Agnes said. She turned to Jesse. "Have a seat; Harley'll be here in a minute." She picked up a phone and tapped in a four-digit number.

Herman Muller waved the two men into his office, followed them in and shut the door.

Jesse noticed he didn't shake their hands. He watched as the two men sat down, and one of them opened his briefcase. He removed a thick sheaf of paper and handed it to Muller, who took it and began reading. The second man offered Muller a pen, which the old man ignored. Muller opened a desk drawer, dropped the papers into it and turned back to the men.

"I'll think about it," Jesse thought he said.

The two men sat, staring at Muller, saying nothing. One of them said something briefly, then they got up and left Muller's office.

"Good morning to you, Mr. Ruger," Agnes said as they passed her desk.

"Morning," Ruger replied, and then they were gone.

A man in a hard hat walked into the office from the direction of the factory.

"This is Jesse Barron, Harley," Agnes said. "Jesse, this is Harley Waters."

Jesse shook the man's hand.

"Follow me," Waters said. "I'll show you around."

"That would be fine," Jesse replied.

"When can you start?"

"How about tomorrow?"

"That's good; I can use you."

Ruger, Jesse thought. That's Coldwater's other right-hand man, and Herman Muller didn't seem too pleased to see him.

The machinery was noisy, and Jesse was given ear protectors, a kind of headset without electronics. Harley Waters started at the beginning of the chipboard production line and walked him through to the end, shouting comments over the noise, while Jesse nodded his understanding.

When they were finished, Waters walked him to the car park exit. "This is a good place to work," he said, "because Herman Muller is a good man to work for. He built this business from nothing, designed a lot of the equipment himself, picked every man who works here. He must have liked you, or he wouldn't have hired you, not even when he needs people bad, because of this new contract."

"I liked him, too," Jesse said.

"Good; I'll see you in the morning," Waters replied. "We work seven to five Monday through Thursday, and we take Friday off. It's a good deal."

"Sounds fine to me," Jesse said. "See you tomorrow."

He got into the pickup and drove back to town, wondering what this man, Ruger, was up to with Herman Muller. As he drove back into town, the sun broke through. On Main Street, Jesse stopped the truck, got out and looked up. Right behind the business district, a sheer mountain wall rose a good five hundred feet. It looked as if it might fall on the town.

Wow, Jesse said to himself. With the sky overcast, he had never known it was there.

CHAPTER

11

Jesse pulled up in front of the house and gave it a good look. A two-story Victorian with a beautiful lawn and flower beds, a wide front porch and gingerbread everywhere. It looked old but was in perfect condition. He got out of the pickup, walked up the front walk, climbed the steps to the porch and rang the doorbell. He reckoned on a long wait, while Mrs. Weatherby made it to the front door with her walker.

He had turned and was admiring the flowers when a low voice behind him said, "Good morning." He turned to find a much younger woman than he had expected. Mrs. Weatherby's nurse, no doubt.

"Good morning," he replied. "My name is Jesse Barron. May I speak with Mrs. Weatherby?"

She rewarded him with a quizzical smile. "I'm Mrs. Weatherby," she said, opening the screen door. "Please come in." She turned and walked toward the rear of the house, expecting him to follow.

Jesse followed. "Forgive me, I suppose I was expecting a nice little old lady—the widow Weatherby," he said to her back.

"I am the widow Weatherby," she said without turning, and there was amusement in her voice. She led him into a large kitchen and indicated a chair at the breakfast table. "I was just making some tea; would you like some?"

He sat down and looked at her again. She was nearly as tall as he, slim, in her mid-thirties, he guessed, with gray streaks in her light brown hair. She wore a simple cotton dress that emphasized her small waist and full breasts.

"Would you like some tea?" she repeated, and as if on cue, the kettle began to sing.

"Oh, yes, I'm sorry. My mind was wandering, I guess."

"Milk?"

"Just lemon, if you have it."

She poured the tea and set it before him with a wedge of lemon on the saucer. "Sugar's there on the table," she said as she poured herself a cup. She set down her tea and pulled up a chair.

Her nose was slim and straight, her large eyes wide apart and her mouth broad, revealing large teeth when she opened it. She sipped her tea tentatively and gazed at him in a direct manner.

"Pat Casey said you might have a room to rent," he said, trying not to seem unsettled.

"Jesse, you said?"

"That's right."

"You look like a pretty tough guy, Jesse."

"I was in an accident; I used to look a little more respectable."

"I'm sorry," she said, and a hint of a blush ran up her cheeks. "It's just that I'm particular about who comes into my house, even if Pat Casey did recommend him."

"That's understandable," Jesse said. "I don't blame you a bit."

"I have a little girl, you see; she's at school right now."

"How old?"

"Six. She's in first grade."

Jesse looked away, a move that was becoming more natural as he perfected his performance. "I had three girls, once," he said.

"Are you divorced?"

"Widowed. My wife and daughters were killed in the car wreck that made me look like this."

Her face fell. "Oh, I am sorry. I can only imagine what it must be like to lose a child, let alone three."

"Thank you; I'm living with it."

"Was the accident your fault?"

"No, thank God. I don't think I could have lived with that."

Slowly, methodically, she extracted his story from him, leaving nothing unexamined. Jesse gave her what she wanted, a little at a time.

"Thank you for telling me all this," she said finally.

"Not at all. But you've told me nothing about yourself." He smiled. "I'm particular whose house I live in."

She laughed. "All right, I'm a local girl, married in my late twenties, lost my husband in my early thirties, in an automobile accident."

"I'm sorry. That's your whole story?"

"Just about. I dote on my daughter, I help out at the local library, do some volunteer work."

"No regular job?"

"My husband provided for us."

"It's a lovely house," he said.

"Thank you. I have the time to work on it." She set down her tea cup. "Come, I'll show you the room." She got up and led the way down the hall and up the stairs. "Carey's room is straight ahead," she said, when they had reached the top of the stairs. "And—"

"What did you say?" The name was an arrow through his heart.

"It's my daughter's room; Carey's."

"How do you spell the name?"

She spelled it.

"I used to know a little girl named Carrie," he said, spelling it.

"Oh. Well, my room is to the right, and the spare room is to the left, here." She led the way into a large, sunny bedroom, comfortably furnished with a double bed, a chest of drawers and a comfortable chair. "The bath's over there."

"It's very nice," he said.

"I'd be happy to have you here, if you want it," she replied. "The rent is fifty dollars a week and another fifty with three meals a day. I cook well."

"I'm sure you do," Jesse replied. "I'll take the room and the meals. Is a month in advance all right?" He counted out eight fifty-dollar bills.

"Thank you, yes, and you should open a bank account, Mr. Barron. That's a lot of money to be carrying around."

"Good idea, and will you please call me Jesse, or Jess, if you like?"

"Sure. My name is Jenny." She held out her hand for the first time.

He took it and didn't want to let go. "I'm starting at the Wood Products plant tomorrow morning," he said.

"Then you'll want an early breakfast. That's all right, we rise early here. Go to bed early, too."

"That's fine by me."

"Cereal or eggs?"

"Eggs, please, scrambled?"

"I can manage that. I'll put lunch in a bag for you. When would you like to move in?"

"I'll go back to the motel and get my things and be back in half an hour."

"Fine."

"May I have a door key?"

She laughed. "Oh, we don't lock our doors in St. Clair," she said. "No burglar would dare operate in our town."

Jesse pointed the pickup toward the motel and reflected on his good fortune. A very handsome landlady, and a little girl in the house, to boot. He would have to be very careful not to sweep her into his arms when he saw her. The daughter, he meant, chuckling to himself.

On Main Street he passed the Bank of St. Clair, and, on impulse, pulled into a parking spot. He might as well start getting respectable, he thought. He got out of the truck and walked toward the building. He opened the front door, stepped in and immediately knew something was wrong. A young man was backing toward him and, across the marble floor, a guard stood, a riot shotgun held tensely at port arms. He'd never seen a bank guard with a shotgun before he thought, as the man continued to back toward him, apparently oblivious of his presence. Before Jesse could move, the man bumped into him.

The younger man spun around, his face full of surprise, and Jesse saw the pistol coming around. Instinctively, he grabbed the man's wrist, made the gun point toward the ceiling and twisted hard. The gun came away in his hand. At that moment, all hell seemed to break loose. Jesse saw the guard's shotgun swing toward the robber and, flinching, he turned his body away. The shotgun went off at exactly the moment that the front window of the bank caved in.

The robber flew toward Jesse, knocking him off his feet, then there was another shotgun blast. Jesse thought it was the third. He looked out onto the street and saw another young man, looking frightened, standing next to a pickup truck and yelling.

"Come on, Dan, get out of there!" he screamed.

Dan was lying on top of Jesse, and he wasn't going anywhere. The young man outside suddenly figured this out and leapt into the pickup. As he did, a police car suddenly appeared, skidding sideways into the truck, and another squad car rammed the pickup from behind. The driver started out the truck's door, but before both his feet had made the ground there were half a dozen gunshots, and the young man was lying on his face in the street.

Jesse pushed the robber's body off him and started to get up, but he was pushed back onto the floor by a large foot. The bank guard was standing over him, pumping the shotgun.

"Hold it, Frank!" somebody shouted from the street, and the guard stepped back, still pointing the weapon at Jesse.

"I don't think he's one of them," the voice said, and then Pat Casey was helping Jesse to his feet.

"Well hello, Pat," Jesse said. "I was just coming in to open an account. Does this happen every day in St. Clair?"

Casey laughed. "Put down the shotgun, Frank; this is a customer."

The bank was suddenly filled with policemen, and Jesse was herded off to one side. Eventually, somebody took his particulars, accepted his money and gave him a temporary checkbook. The man called Ruger watched from an office and talked with Casey, occasionally nodding at Jesse.

Jesse finished his business and left for the motel, to collect his things. On the way he reflected on the bungled robbery, and it occurred to him that at least one of the robbers, the one he'd taken the gun from, had been shot unnecessarily, after Jesse had the pistol.

The other one had been shot down very quickly, too, but Jesse hadn't seen that as clearly.

He remembered Jenny Weatherby's comment that no one would dare commit a burglary in St. Clair. Now he knew why. He bet himself that there were no prisoners in the city jail.

CHAPTER

12

Jesse packed his things, then checked out of the motel and drove up Main Street. He parked in front of police headquarters, went inside and asked for Pat Casey. Casey, who was sitting in a glass-enclosed cubicle, waved him into his office and into a chair.

"What can I do you for, Jess?"

"I just wanted to thank you, Pat. I arrived in this town less than twenty-four hours ago, a complete stranger, and now I have a job and a very nice place to live and you to thank for all of it."

"I'm glad to be of help. I'm grateful for your help, too. It seems you disarmed one of the bank robbers."

"It seemed like a good idea at the time."

Casey laughed. "It certainly was."

"I'm a little overwhelmed, I guess," Jesse said. "Since I got out of the hospital I've been sort of numb, just going through the motions, wandering across the country. Now, all of a sudden, I seem to have some sort of life again. I just want you to know I appreciate your help, and I hope I'll be able to find a way to repay you some day."

Casey shrugged. "Who knows? One of these days you might be able to do something for me. I'll let you know. In the meantime, just settle into St. Clair and be one of us."

Jesse stood up. "That, I'll do." He shook Casey's hand and left the station.

Jesse carried his bags up the front steps of Jenny Weatherby's house and was met at the door by a somber little girl with hair so blonde it was nearly white.

"Hello," Jesse said to her. "I'll bet you're Carey."

"How did you know?" the little girl asked.

"Oh, I know all about you. You're six years old and in the first grade."

She smiled shyly. "Mama told you."

"That's right, she did."

"Are you going to live with us?"

"I sure am, and I hope you and I are going to be good friends."

"That depends," Carey said. "Do you like niggers?"

Jesse was brought up short. "Why do you ask that?" he asked.

"Because at school they told us we're not supposed to be friends with nigger lovers."

Jesse set his bags down at the bottom of the stairs, struggling for a way to continue this conversation. "And where do you go to school?" he asked lamely.

"At the First Church school," Carey replied. "Everybody goes there."

"And do you like school?"

"Oh, yes," she said. "We get to learn lots of stuff."

"Well, I want to hear all about that," Jesse said, "just as soon as I take my things upstairs."

"Carey!" her mother called from the kitchen. "Who's that out there?"

She turned to him. "What's your name?"

"Jesse."

"It's Jesse, Mama," she called out. "I'm helping him take his stuff upstairs."

Jesse handed her his small bag and followed her up the stairs to his room.

"Do you like this room?" Carey asked. The phone rang downstairs.

"I like it very much," he said, sitting on the bed. "And I think I like you very much, too."

The little girl giggled and ran out of the room and down the stairs.

Jesse was stretched out on his bed, dozing, when there was a soft rap at the door.

"Come in."

Jenny opened the door. "Seems you're the local hero," she said.

"You've heard already?"

"It's a small town."

"I'm lucky I didn't get my head blown off."

"Luckier than you know," she said. "Supper's in half an hour; would you like something to drink before? I've got some gin and some bourbon and some beer."

"I'd love a bourbon on the rocks," Jesse said, swinging his feet over the edge of the bed and standing up. "But room and board can't include liquor. I'll buy my own."

She smiled. "Tonight you're my guest."

"Carey's gorgeous," Jesse said. "She comes by it naturally."

The little blush again. "Come on downstairs, and I'll fix your drink."

Jesse splashed some water on his face, brushed his teeth and went down to the kitchen. Jenny handed him a large drink. "What time does the evening news come on in Idaho?"

"You mean on TV?"

"Right."

"We don't have much TV," she said. "Not in St. Clair. Oh, they've got a satellite dish at Harry's Place, where the fellows go to watch football, and down at the motel, I guess, but TV is sort of frowned on around here."

"Oh," Jesse said, nonplussed. Never in his life had he been to a place that didn't have much TV. He sat down at the kitchen table and raised his drink. "Will you join me?"

"Sure," she said, and poured herself a bourbon and water. She peeked under a pot lid, then sat down and sipped her drink. "You think we're missing anything by not having TV?"

"Well, I guess you're missing the news and some movies and a few good programs," he replied. "But you're missing a hell of a lot of junk, too, and, on balance, I'd guess Carey might be better off without it."

"That's sort of what I thought," she said.

"When I was a kid we didn't have a TV for a long time," Jesse said, then stopped himself. He was about to start talking about Jesse Warden instead of Jesse Barron, and he couldn't have that.

"Strict father?"

"That's it."

"I had one of those, too. If he could see me now, sitting in my kitchen with a strange man who's just moved into my house, sipping whiskey with him, he'd roll over in his grave."

"You've always lived in St. Clair?"

She nodded. "Always."

"Have you traveled much? Seen any of the country?"

"I've been to Boise half a dozen times," she said, "and once I went to Seattle to visit my mother's sister. That's about it."

"Is your mother still alive?"

"No, she died before my father did, when I was fifteen."

"What did your father do?"

"He worked out at Wood Products, like everybody else."

"That's been here a long time, has it?"

"Sure has; all of my life and before. Herman Muller's daddy came here from Germany to farm, and when he died, Herman sold the farm and started that business. It's grown and grown. Soaked up just about all the farm boys around here." She talked while gazing out the window into the middle distance.

Jesse took in her fine profile and the gray in her hair, and he wanted her. "Girls as beautiful as you are don't usually stay in small towns," he said.

"Why, thank you sir," she said, raising her glass to him. "I haven't heard anything that nice for a long while." She sighed. "Once, when I was twenty-one or twenty-two, I was putting some gas in my car and a fellow in a Mercedes pulled into the filling station, got out and gave me his card. He was with Paramount Pictures, he said, and he wanted to put me in the movies."

"That doesn't surprise me in the least," Jesse said. "What did you say to him?"

"Shoot, I didn't say anything. I just paid for my gas and got out of there!"

Jesse laughed aloud, and it suddenly occurred to him that he had not laughed in at least two years. A rush of well-being came with the laugh.

"I think I've still got his card somewhere," she said, blushing.

Jesse laughed again.

"I like the way you talk," she said.

"You mean, my hillbilly accent?"

"Yes. There's nothing like it in St. Clair. Everything has a sort of sameness about it around here."

"Seems like a beautiful part of the country."

"I guess it is. You tend not to notice when it's all you've seen all your life. What's it like where you come from?"

"We've got mountains, too, but smaller ones, with lots of pine trees."

"How about the town?"

"Not very different from this one, but not so neat. I think most American small towns are alike."

She started to say something, but stopped.

They ate in the dining room—roast beef, Idaho potatoes and fresh green beans. Jesse and Jenny both had another drink with their dinner. Afterward, she put Carey to bed, and then they went into the living room, where Jesse was surprised to find a piano, and even more surprised to hear her play it well. She played a Chopin etude without referring to the music and something else she said was Mendelssohn that he had never heard before.

"Where did you learn to play so well?" he asked.

"My mother was the piano teacher," she said. "It would have looked bad for her if I hadn't learned to play. I always enjoyed it, and I still don't let a day go by without playing."

His mother had taught piano, too, but he couldn't mention that.

She fixed them another bourbon, then switched on the record player and sat down in a chair facing his. Symphonic strains filled the room.

"Beethoven's Sixth," Jesse said. "The Pastoral Symphony."

"It's my favorite," she said.

"I have it on tape in my truck; listened to it all the way across the country. It seemed to fit the landscape."

"I can't think of a landscape it wouldn't fit," she

said, then laughed. "Even if I've never seen much landscape."

"One of these days," Jesse said, and he found himself meaning it.

She finished off her drink. "One of these days."

She seemed to mean it, too, or was that his imagination. Jesse finished his drink, and they walked upstairs, pausing on the landing.

"It was a wonderful dinner," he said. "A fine welcome to St. Clair."

Again she started to speak, then stopped.

"What?"

"I'm glad you enjoyed it," she said. "Good night, Jesse."

"Good night, Jenny."

Jesse lay in bed and tried to sleep, but couldn't. He replayed every part of the evening in his head—the bourbon, the beef, the little girl and, most of all, Jenny. It had been like having a date, and he had given up hope that he would ever again have an evening like that. His breathing was shallow, and his heartbeat rapid. In his whole life, so far, he had slept with only one woman: Beth. Certainly, he was no seducer, but an hour before, on the landing, he had thought for a moment she might say something that would allow him to take her in his arms. A presumptuous, foolish thought. An arrogant thought. This was not a perfect world, he knew that.

There was a tiny creak, and the door to his room opened. He lifted his head from the pillow and looked, but the darkness was too thick, he could see nothing. He could hear, though, and feel.

A rustle of fabric and the covers were pulled back, and she was in bed beside him, in his arms. They kissed eagerly, then struggled from their night clothes.

There was no foreplay, just the immediate, ecstatic joining of two hungry human beings, taking each other quickly and, astonishing to him, because he was so quick, finishing together, muffling their cries so as not to wake Carey.

They lay together, panting. Jesse turned to her. "Jenny, I—"

"I guess you think I'm pretty bold," she said, interrupting.

"Bolder than I am, anyway," he said, laughing.

"I got the impression that if I'd waited for you to make the first move it might have been months."

He laughed again. "You read me well."

"I don't know what made me do it," she said. "I guess I was lonely and thought that you were, too. I may be brazen, but it seemed like the right thing to do. You won't hold it against me, will you?"

He lay back and hugged her to him. "I'll just hold *you* against me."

"Mmmm," she moaned. "I like it here."

"I like it here, too." He had been in St. Clair for little more than twenty-four hours. What a difference a day made!

13

When Jesse woke there was a gray light in the room, and she was gone. For a moment he was sure he had dreamed too well, but her scent was still in the sheets, arousing him again. He heard her bedroom door open and close and her steps on the stairs; it was five-thirty A.M. by his bedside clock.

Jesse rose, showered, shaved, dressed in work clothes and went downstairs, not knowing what to expect from her. All seemed normal; Carey was eating her cereal while reading a schoolbook, and Jenny was at the stove, her back to him.

"Good morning," he said.

"Good morning, Jesse," Carey said. "Mama's fixing your breakfast."

Jenny did not speak, but turned and looked at him, and there was uncertainty in her face.

"Good morning, Jenny," he said with the warmest smile he could muster.

She blushed, then smiled. "Good morning, Jesse. You're timing's good; your eggs will be ready in ten seconds."

A glass of freshly squeezed orange juice awaited him, and he sat down and drank it. The eggs were perfectly cooked, and the sausage was wonderful. "The sausage must be local," he said.

She nodded, eating her own eggs. "I get it from one of our few remaining farmers."

He finished his eggs, then glanced at his watch. "I think I should be a little early on my first day," he said. "Can I drop Carey at school?"

Jenny shook her head. "She's not due there until eight, and it's close enough for her to walk."

"That's nice. See you later, then, Carey."

"Goodbye, Jesse, have a nice day," the little girl said.

He winked at Jenny, then left the table and started for the front door, grabbing his jacket from the coatrack in the hall.

"Jesse," Jenny said. She had come out of the kitchen and into the hall.

Jesse looked to be sure Carey was still in the kitchen. He smiled.

"Don't say anything," she said, raising a hand. "Not yet." Then she smiled broadly at him. "I just wanted you to know that I'm not feeling the least guilty this morning."

He laughed. "Neither am I."

"Go safely."

In the truck he shoved the Pastoral tape into the player and hummed along with it. The morning was spectacular—chilly, crisp, with sparkling sunshine. He thought his heart would leap from his chest.

The Wood Products factory was quiet when he arrived, but the employees' door was open, and Harley Waters was there before him.

"Morning, Jesse."

"Morning, Harley."

"Come on, I'll show you the drill."

Jesse followed him to the back of the building and watched as Harley hit a button and the truck entrance clattered noisily open. They climbed a few steps to a wooden platform. Harley pointed. "It's real simple," he said. "The trucks back in there, through the doors, and dump their loads. Further down there, they're unloading cordwood, but here, at your station, it's the remnants, and everything has to be fed into the hopper, there, by hand." He handed Jesse a hardhat, some ear protectors and a pair of heavy gloves. "Don't fall behind. Herman doesn't like it when the trucks have to wait." He took off his hardhat and scratched his head. "I think you're smart enough to see that there's nothing but your good sense to keep you from falling into that hopper yourself, Jesse, and if you do fall in, this machinery will make chipboard out of you."

"I got you," Jesse said, glancing at his watch. Ten minutes to go. "Have I got time to use the john?"

"If you hurry." Harley walked away, and Jesse headed for the men's room. He was back in time to see the first truck backing in.

The truck dumped a load of odd-sized pieces of wood, branches and trimmings, a real mess, Jesse thought. The machinery was turned on, and he began to grab stuff and throw it into the hopper.

At nine-fifteen, a bell rang, and the machinery stopped. Jesse thought he would faint with relief. His face, arms and body were covered in scratches from the logs and branches he had manhandled into the hopper. He walked stiffly to the men's room to pee and to throw some water on his face. Harley Waters came in and assigned him a locker, and he drank some coffee from the thermos Jenny had prepared for him.

"How you like it so far, boy?" Harley laughed.

"It's just swell," Jesse replied.

When the bell rang again at five o'clock, Jesse could hardly walk to his truck. His body ached from one end to the other, and the only thing that kept him going was the knowledge that when he got home, Jenny and Carey would be waiting for him. He turned out to be half right.

When he walked through the front door, Carey appeared from the living room. "Mom's upstairs getting dressed," she said.

"I see," Jesse replied. "Well, I think I'll have a bath and change clothes. He trudged up the stairs to his room and peeled off his work clothes while the water ran in the tub. When it was full he climbed stiffly into it and sank under the water with a groan. He had, he reckoned, just done the hardest day's work of his life. Herman Muller hadn't been kidding when he said it was the worst job in the plant.

Jesse was wakened slowly by the cooling water. He climbed out of the tub, feeling half-human again, got dressed and started downstairs, glancing at his watch. He had been in the tub for more than an hour. The doorbell rang.

There was a man at the door, wearing a suit and looking as though he didn't often wear it. Jesse walked to the door and opened it. "Evening, can I help you?"

The man stared at him. "I'm expected," he said. "Who are you?"

Jesse opened the door and offered his hand. "I'm Jesse Barron; I'm boarding here."

"Fred Patrick," the man said shortly, shaking Jesse's hand.

HEAT
•

Carey appeared from the kitchen. "Oh, hello, Mr. Patrick," she said, "Mama will be down in a minute."

As if on cue, Jenny came out of her room and down the stairs. "Hello, Fred," she said to the man, pecking him on the cheek. "Oh, Hello, Jesse."

"Hi," he replied.

"Fred and I are going to a dinner out at the Legion Hall," she explained."

Jesse's heart fell. He had been looking forward to seeing her. "I see. I'll be happy to take care of Carey."

"That won't be necessary," Jenny replied. "She's staying with a friend for the night."

"For the night?" Jesse said dully.

"Yes, I won't be back until late. I left you a plate in the oven."

"Thanks," he managed to say. "You folks have a nice evening."

"Let's go, Fred," Jenny said.

Jesse watched them to the door. As they went out, Fred Patrick shot a suspicious glance at Jesse.

Jesse didn't blame him a bit. He went into the kitchen, retrieved the warm plate from the oven and sat down disconsolately to eat it.

It wasn't the evening he'd had in mind.

14

Jesse washed his dishes, dried them and put them away. The food had revived his exhausted body and made him able to think again, but he didn't want to think. He was experiencing some sort of strange emotion, and he didn't like it.

He slipped on his coat and walked out the back door toward the garage; there his pickup truck rested beside Jenny's sedan. He wriggled under the truck, worked the combination on the safe and took out the cellular telephone, stuffing the pistol and the money back inside the steel box. He got into the truck and, resisting the temptation to start the engine for warmth, switched on the phone and waited for signal strength. He glanced at his watch; it would be nearly ten o'clock in Washington, so there was no point in calling the 800 number. He dredged up Kip Fuller's home number from his memory and dialed it.

There was the expected ringing, then a click and a squawk from the handset, followed by a series of beeps, then Kip's voice.

"This is Fuller."

"It's Jesse. How openly can I talk on this thing?"

"It's an encrypted unit; my phones, both at the office and at home can read it, so we're very secure. How's it going, Jess?"

"Better than I could possibly have hoped," Jesse said. He gave a detailed account of the past two days.

"Doesn't it bother you a little that it's going so well?"

"I don't know," Jesse said. "I mean, they could hardly be expecting me."

"They're expecting *somebody*," Kip said. "After all, they've already had two agents up there and dealt with them both. They can't think the government is going to just give up."

"Well, sure, I've got to be careful for a while, but I get the impression they need people, that they're recruiting. I think I'm just their kind of guy."

"I hope so. I didn't expect you to see Casey and Ruger the first day. Any sign of Jack Gene Coldwater?"

"No, and no word of him, either."

"For Christ's sake, don't ever mention his name to anybody; wait for them to mention it to you."

"Don't worry."

"How are you feeling, Jesse, I mean, really feeling?" Kip sounded concerned.

"A hell of a lot better than I was a couple of weeks ago," Jesse replied. "I'm still a little numb in some ways, but I'm getting used to the idea of being a free man."

"Don't get too used to it," Kip said. "Remember, there's somebody who'd love to see you back inside, if he could get what he wants from you first."

"I'll remember."

"I've had word from the lady at the adoption agency. She says that the adoptive parents have your letter, and they'll think about what to do. It'll be a long time, of course."

"I understand. I just want her to know that her mother and I didn't deliberately abandon her."

Kip was quiet for a moment. "That phone uses more juice than an ordinary cellular phone; you've only got about four minutes talk time between charges."

"I'd better sign off, then."

"Keep me posted; if I don't hear from you at least twice a week, I'll get worried."

"Okay, take care."

"You too." Kip hung up.

Jesse returned the phone to the safe under the truck, plugged it into the charger and locked up. Back outside, he discovered he didn't want to go back into the empty house. He wandered in the direction of Main Street, only a couple of blocks away.

The shops were closed now, their windows mostly dark. Only one lighted sign remained on the street: Harry's. Jesse ambled into the place and stopped inside the front door.

The smell of stale beer and tobacco smoke reached his nostrils, and the sound of pool balls clicking together came from the rear of the long room. Country music was playing on the jukebox. He'd never liked country music. Fifteen or twenty customers, all men, were scattered about the place, some of them watching a sports program on a silent television set above the bar. It was the sort of place he'd avoided all his life.

Jesse walked to the bar and took a stool a little away from anybody else. A man wearing an apron approached.

"Get you something?" he asked.

"A draft," Jesse said.

The man pulled the beer and set it in front of Jesse. "Passing through?"

"I guess not. I went to work out at Wood Products this morning."

The man stuck out his hand. "I'm Harry Donner; this is my place."

Jesse took the hand. "Jesse Barron." Harry seemed friendly enough.

"Where you bunking?"

"I'm boarding over at Mrs. Weatherby's."

"Nice lady."

"Seems to be." Jesse sipped his beer. "How long you been in business, Harry?"

"Nineteen years," Harry replied. "Before that I tended bar in Boise. I come up here and took a job doing the same thing, and a couple years later the boss died, and I bought the joint from his widow. Yours isn't a local accent; where you from?"

"North Georgia, up in the mountains. I was wandering West, headed more or less toward Seattle, when I happened on St. Clair."

"You coulda done worse. How'd you end up at Wood Products?"

"I ran into Pat Casey, and he recommended it."

"Herman Muller's a good man; he'll treat you right."

Jesse laughed. "Well, he just about killed me today."

Harry smiled. "They put you on the hopper?"

"That's right."

"They do that to everybody; stick it out, and Herman'll find you something better."

"I'll do it, if I live."

Another customer sat down at the bar, and Harry moved to serve him, leaving Jesse alone.

This is what he had never wanted, he thought, sitting in a saloon somewhere crying into his beer. It was just the sort of place his father would have figured him to end up in, he knew, and the thought made the evening even more painful.

Suddenly, he identified the emotion he had been dodging all evening: it was jealousy.

Jesse had known Beth all his life, and since high school he'd never had anything to do with any other woman. She'd been his from the ninth grade on, and he'd never given a moment's thought to her running off with somebody else. Now Beth was gone, another woman had crawled into his bed and made him happy, and she was out this evening with another man.

What the hell, he thought, he had only just entered her life; she might have had that date for a long time. Why should she break it just for him? Still, that was what he would have wanted her to do.

This jealousy was powerful stuff, he realized, made up of equal parts of anger, pain and depression. He finished his beer and trudged back toward Jenny's house.

She wasn't home when he got there, and he turned in quickly. Exhausted, he didn't hear her when she came home.

CHAPTER

15

Jesse barely made it to work on time. He'd over-slept, then had to make his own breakfast. Jenny still hadn't surfaced by the time he left for work.

He faced the first of the day's many truckloads of scrap lumber and branches, and occasionally he got a tree limb so big he had to trim it with a brancher, a hooked steel cutting implement fixed to a long handle. He looked upon that work as a welcome break from the monotony of feeding the hopper.

He got through the morning, then at lunchtime dis-covered that he had nothing to eat; he'd forgotten to fix himself a sandwich. He sat down on a bench in the locker room, too tired and numb to do anything about it.

Harley Waters came in and sat down beside him. "Aren't you eating anything, Jesse?"

Jesse shook his head. "Forgot to bring something. In a minute, when I get up the strength, I'll ride into town and pick up a burger."

Harley handed him a thick, carefully wrapped sandwich. "Take this; my wife always makes me too much."

"You sure? I can pick up something in town."

"I'm sure; I still have to deal with a piece of pie."

Jesse got a cold drink from the machine and sat back down next to Harley.

"Where you from, Jesse?"

Jesse told his story yet again. It came so naturally now that he hardly remembered his real background. "How about you?"

"Been here all my life," Harley replied. "My grandad worked for Herman Muller's old man, on his farm. That was a long time ago."

"You've known Herman a long time, then?"

"Oh, sure; I went to work for him right out of high school."

"Has the business changed much since then?"

"It's gotten bigger, I guess; Herman's built it up practically with his own hands. Once in a while he gets an offer from one of the big companies, like Georgia Pacific, but he's hung onto it. Tell you the truth, after that boy died, I thought he'd sell out."

"His boy?"

"James, his name was; his grandson, really. Car accident."

"That's bad."

"It was a mess, I'll tell you. Nobody's ever figured out who killed him."

Jesse looked up from his sandwich. "Somebody killed him? An accident, you mean?"

"Well, Pat Casey said it was an accident, but I didn't like the look of it. He ran off the road coming down the mountain."

"The one that sort of hangs over Main Street?"

"That's the one. Kill Hill, they call it; Herman's boy wasn't the only one to run off that road. Real steep."

"This happen recently?" Careful, don't ask too many questions, he told himself.

"Four, five months ago. Herman was real broke up about it. I thought he'd sell."

"He's had a lot of offers, huh?"

"Three or four. Latest one was . . . " Harley looked up to see another workman walk in. "Well," he said, standing up. "I'll see you."

"Thanks for the sandwich," Jesse said. He watched as the other man sat down on a bench across the room. He was a big one, six-four, maybe six-five, heavy-set.

"You're the new fella," the man said.

"That's right. Name's Jesse Barron."

"Good for you."

What the hell did that mean? Jesse wondered. He munched on his sandwich and sipped his drink.

"How you like it on the hopper?"

"'Bout the most fun I ever had," Jesse replied.

"First time I ever heard anybody say that."

"It was kind of a joke," Jesse said.

"I guess I don't have much of a sense of humor," the man said.

Jesse knew this man, in a way; there had been one in every schoolyard in every town his father had preached in. Big guy, bad attitude, didn't like newcomers, especially preachers' boys. "I didn't get your name," Jesse said.

"Phil Partain," the man said, lighting a cigarette. "Cigarette smoke bother you?"

"It's your lungs," Jesse said.

"That's lucky for you," Partain said, blowing a cloud in Jesse's direction, "'cause I'm not putting it out. So if you're one of them antismoking types, I guess you'll just have to put up with it."

Jesse was one of those antismoking types, he guessed, and he had learned in every one of a dozen schoolyards how to put a stop to this. He got up, walked over to where Partain sat, plucked the cigarette from his fingers, dropped it on the floor and stepped on it.

Partain looked astonished for about a second, then anger flashed across his face and he started to stand up.

Jesse, who was standing no more than a foot from Partain, reached out, put a hand on his shoulder and sat him back down. "Listen to me, Phil," he said before the man could try again to get up. "Let's you and me concentrate on safety in the workplace. Neither one of us wants to get fired for fighting in the locker room; I know I don't, and that's just what Mr. Muller would do to both of us, don't you reckon?"

"Fuck Muller," Partain said, starting to rise again.

Jesse pushed him back down onto the bench. "Let me give you some good advice, Phil," he said quietly. "Never pick a fight with a stranger. You never know what you're getting into."

"That's advice you might take yourself," Partain said, looking up at him.

"Oh, I don't want you to get the wrong idea," Jesse replied, smiling. "I'm not picking a fight, I'm nipping one in the bud. In fact, I'm going to make a real effort to get along with you, just as long as you don't blow cigarette smoke at me, and I hope you'll make an effort to get along with me. Life's going to be a whole lot sweeter that way."

"Oh, yeah? Sweeter for who?" Partain asked.

"Why for both of us, Phil," Jesse said in the friendliest tone he could muster. "We're both all grown up now, and when grown men get into fights, somebody gets hurt, likely as not, and I don't want it to be me. I mean, you're a big fella."

"You noticed that, did you?"

"Couldn't miss it," Jesse laughed, slapping Partain solidly on the shoulder. He looked at his watch. "Well, I'd better get back to work." He turned and strolled out of the locker room, back toward the waiting hopper. Phil Partain remained seated on the bench.

Jesse took a deep breath and thought about his pulse. Back in the schoolyard, his heart would have been hammering after an encounter like that, but now it beat right along, just the way it was supposed to. In the yard at Atlanta Federal Prison he had learned to fight without being angry and to avoid fights when he was angry, and the experience was serving him well. He hadn't felt the need to prove anything to Phil Partain; he'd done all his proving back in Atlanta.

He faced the hopper once more.

CHAPTER

16

As Jesse walked up the front steps of the house he was struck by a scent from his past, an aroma of small-town Georgia, of the inadequate kitchens of parsonages in the mountains, of his mother making do and doing wonderfully. Somebody was frying chicken.

As he opened the door Carey ran out of the kitchen toward him. "Mama says you get your bath right now," the little girl said. "Supper's in half an hour."

Jesse trudged up the stairs, trying to deal with the emotions that the smell of fried chicken were causing to well up in him. He shaved, then soaked in the tub for fifteen minutes, then got dressed and went downstairs. The table was set, and Jenny's back was to him; she was dishing something up from the stove.

"Hey there," she said, turning toward him. "That's perfect timing; have a seat."

Jesse held a chair for Carey, who beamed up at him as she sat down, then he took a seat. Jenny set a platter of chicken before him, next to a bowl of green beans and another of corn, plus a plate of biscuits.

"You being a Southerner, I thought I'd whip up something Southern," she said, placing an open bottle of beer and a glass on the table, then opening one for herself.

"I started smelling the chicken about halfway home," Jesse said, spearing himself some white meat. "I can't tell you how long it's been since I had some." He wasn't lying; the last time was before Beth had gotten sick. Two years? Three? They hadn't served fried chicken in prison.

"I'm glad you like it," she said, watching him tear into the food.

"The beans and corn are what my mother used to make. The biscuits, too."

"I'm a good guesser, then."

"You certainly are."

The three of them consumed their dinner, and when they had finished, Jenny produced a hot peach cobbler from the oven, and Jesse thought he had died and gone to heaven. It was different from wishing he had.

"About last night," Jenny said when they were comfortable in the living room. Carey was doing the dishes.

"You don't owe me any explanations," Jesse said, and he hoped she didn't believe him.

"Fred and I have been out a few times. There's nothing there—not for me, anyway; he's just okay, no more. We met some other people at the Legion Hall for a dance, and I had a lot to drink, mostly because I wasn't where I wanted to be, which was with you."

Jesse flushed, and it felt wonderful.

"I was hungover, I guess, and I overslept. I'm sorry I wasn't up to get your breakfast."

"It's okay," he said, patting her knee.

"I told Fred Patrick last night that I wasn't available anymore," she said. "Maybe you think that's rushing things, but it was the way I felt. Still do."

"I'm glad you told him that," Jesse said, and I'm glad you feel that way.

She reached over and kissed him lightly. "Carey'll be in bed in half an hour," she said. "I'll come to you."

As he climbed the stairs to his room Jesse was overcome with the feeling that he was now Jesse Barron, not Warden; that he had become the man he pretended to be. Reality was no longer the Atlanta pen and Kip Fuller and Dan Barker. Reality was St. Clair Wood Products and Jenny Weatherby and her little girl and fried chicken on the table. By the time he had crawled into bed the past was receding from him at the speed of light, and when Jenny opened his door and climbed into bed with him and pressed her naked body against his, he sloughed off the broken man called Jesse Warden like a dirty shirt.

CHAPTER

17

Pat Casey got out of his car and walked toward the church, nervous at the prospect of the meeting. He had known Jack Gene Coldwater for more than twenty years, and he could not remember a relaxed moment in his presence. There was something in the man that kept Casey on edge, but also something that made him want to please his leader.

Kurt Ruger was waiting in the anteroom and stood as Casey entered. They walked together to the office door and knocked.

"Come," a deep voice replied.

The two men entered the room and took seats opposite the man who sat at the desk. Casey saw Coldwater only once a month, unless there was some special reason, and this was the regular monthly meeting.

Coldwater was bent over the desk, reading a document, and the sunlight through the window fell on his white hair, which was long and tied at the nape of the neck. The effect was nearly that of a halo, and Casey wondered if the man had planned it that way.

"Good morning, gentlemen," Jack Gene Coldwater said in his rumbling voice.

"Morning, Jack Gene," Casey said in unison with Ruger. They were the only ones who were allowed to call him that, in memory of their early days together in Vietnam.

"Let's hear from finance first," Coldwater said, nodding at Ruger. "Kurt?"

"You've seen the monthly financial statement," Ruger said, indicating the document on Coldwater's desk. "We're in pretty good shape, if a little cash poor."

"Did you talk to Schooner?"

Ruger nodded. "He poor-mouthed me; said the stock was down, and there's a threat of an antitrust suit from the Justice Department over the acquisition of Security Software."

"I told him to expect that," Coldwater said. "It's winnable."

"I tried to buck him up, but he's shaky. I think maybe you should consider talking to him."

Coldwater swiveled in his chair and gazed out at the mountains, offering Ruger and Casey his Indian profile. "Perhaps it's time we had Schooner up here for a little retreat; get his mind concentrated."

"Excellent idea, Jack Gene," Ruger said. "Shall I call him?"

"I'll call him myself," Coldwater said. "What else do you have for me?"

"Collections are coming in well, except for Herman Muller, of course."

"Of course. He turned down our latest offer?"

"He did."

"How much do you think he'll take?"

"Jack Gene, it's my feeling about Muller that he just won't sell. He doesn't need the money—I mean, the man's an elderly, childless widower who lives like a monk; the business keeps him alive, and he knows it."

"Maybe it's time just to remove Muller from the scene," Coldwater said. "He's beginning to annoy me."

"I'm not sure that's wise," Ruger said. "He's childless, but he has relatives out of state. We don't know who would inherit, and we could just be opening a big can of worms."

Coldwater nodded, then turned back to face his two subordinates. "Let's hear from security. Pat?"

Casey sat up a little straighter. "All's well, Chief."

"That's it? 'All's well'?"

"Everything is running as smoothly as we could want. There's no threat from any quarter. It's what we've planned for all these years."

"What about the new boy? I hear he did well during the bank robbery."

"That's true, although Frank damn near shot him. Barron's settled down at the hopper, working his ass off. Settled in at home, too, from all appearances."

"Good. He could still be a cop or a fed, though."

"Possible, of course, but, in my judgment, very unlikely."

"I've always trusted your judgment, Pat," Coldwater said. "You're a hard man to fool; you've proved it over the years."

"Thanks, Chief."

"But we're entering a critical time."

"I know that, Jack Gene, and that's why I've been so careful with him. I've checked him every which way, and he adds up."

"If the feds were putting in a new man, they'd have an airtight background for him, wouldn't they?"

"It's not just his background, though that certainly checks out. It's the kind of man he is. I've known one hell of a lot of cops, and, believe me, he doesn't fit the mold. I've nudged him a little, and—"

"Nudged him? How?"

"I let Phil Partain push him, just to see how he'd react."

"And how did he react?"

"He didn't take the bait, but he didn't back down, either. I think Partain's a little scared of him."

"Partain's a bully; he's scared of anybody who stands up to him," Coldwater said.

"That's true," Casey agreed, "and it would take a pretty sharp guy to figure that out right off the bat. Partain's got a real mean streak; Barron could have walked into a buzz saw, but he didn't. Partain was impressed; so was I, when I heard about it."

Coldwater gazed off into the middle distance. "Doesn't fight, but doesn't back down; I like it. That's how I chose you, Pat; did you know that?"

Casey blinked. "No, I didn't."

"The first time I laid eyes on you was some godawful bar in Saigon. There was a drunk marine raising hell, and he tried to take you on. I liked the way you handled him; you didn't fight him, but you didn't back down."

"I remember that," Casey said. "It was quite a while before we met."

"I marked you down on the spot," Coldwater said. "Later on, I got you transferred." He winked at Ruger. "I picked Kurt, here, for different reasons."

"Partain says Barron's foreman likes him, that he'll recommend to Muller to move him to the line, when a vacancy comes. Partain doesn't like that, figures he's in line first."

"Tell you what," Coldwater said. "Let Barron stew on the hopper for a couple of weeks more, then make a vacancy."

"One of our people?" Casey asked.

"Certainly not," Coldwater replied. "One of Muller's."

"Consider it done."

"I know you'll do it subtly, Pat; you usually do."

"I will."

"Don't come between Barron and Muller; let them build a relationship, then we'll see how he reacts when we bring Muller down."

Ruger sat up straight. "We going to bring Muller down?"

"Somehow. I don't see any other way, do you?"

Ruger shook his head. "No, but it's going to be tricky; we certainly can't let it get around that we had anything to do with it. He's awfully popular, and there are still questions around town about the grandson."

"I'm aware of the affection in which most of the town holds Muller. I'm not about to do anything precipitous."

"You never do, Chief," Ruger said. "I'll look forward to seeing how you handle it."

"I'll handle it simply," Coldwater said. "Simple is always best."

"I'll get Barron promoted," Casey said.

"Good," Coldwater replied. "And when Phil Partain finds out about it, don't get in his way. I want to know what will happen when the two butt heads."

"Partain will kill him, if he gets the chance."

Coldwater shrugged. "If Phil Partain can kill him, then Barron's not for us, is he?"

CHAPTER

18

Jesse had been at St. Clair Wood Products for nearly a month when Harley Waters approached him just as the workday began. Another man was with him.

"Hey, Jesse, Herman wants to see you in the office. This guy's going to spell you."

"Okay, Harley," Jesse replied. He dusted off the shavings that clung to his clothes and walked upstairs to Herman Muller's office. The secretary showed him in.

Muller stood up and shook his hand. "Morning, Jesse."

"Morning, Mr. Muller."

"My folks all call me Herman," Muller said. "Have a seat."

Jesse took a chair, wondering what was going on.

Muller leaned back in his chair. "Jesse, I'm real proud of the way you've worked on the hopper; so is Harley. I'm promoting you."

"Well, thanks, Mr. . . . ah, Herman."

"No thanks due; you've earned it. I'm putting you further up the production line, on the pressing equipment. The pay's nine dollars an hour, and when you've learned the equipment, I'll raise it to ten. I don't think it'll take you long to get the hang of it, but remember, that machinery has to be run right, and right every time. The quality of every sheet of chipboard that comes out of this plant depends on this job being done right. You understand me?"

"Yessir, I sure do. I promise you, I'll do a good job."

Muller stood up. "That's good enough for me, Jesse. Harley's down showing your replacement the ropes; when he's done, he'll take you up the line and get you started."

Jesse shook the man's hand and went back to the plant floor. His replacement was stoking the hopper with a truckload of scrap timber, under the watchful eye of Harley Waters. Poor bastard, Jesse thought.

Harley waved him to follow, and Jesse bade a sweet goodbye to the hopper. He followed Harley through a door into another room of the plant, and the noise subsided a bit. Harley led him up a ladder to a glass booth ten feet above the production line. He slapped a worker on the back. "Take a break, Bob." Harley took over operation of the machinery. "Okay, Jesse, I'm going to run a few sheets, and you follow me as I work the controls.

Jesse became aware that somebody was watching him from below. He looked down and saw Phil Partain dumping a bin of wood chips onto a conveyer belt that led to the press. Partain was spending more time watching him than doing his work.

Jesse watched Harley Waters operate the machinery for a while, then took over himself, operating under Harley's sharp eye. It was pleasant to be doing something that took some skill and coordination; he hadn't liked being a laborer. By the time the noon whistle blew, chipboard was emerging smoothly from the press, under Jesse's operation.

"Go get your lunch," Harley said. "I'll stay on with you the rest of the day, and then I think you'll have it down pat. I've got a new job for the man you replaced."

Jesse went back to the locker room, retrieved his lunch and walked out back of the plant. It was a clear, chilly autumn day and the aspens were a bright gold on the mountains behind the factory. Jesse sat down under a tree, ate his sandwiches and drank his soft drink. After that, he rested his head against the tree and dozed.

He was awakened suddenly as someone sharply kicked the soles of his shoes. He opened his eyes and looked up to find Phil Partain standing over him.

"Get on your feet, Barron," Partain said.

"What do you want, Phil?" Jesse asked laconically.

"I want to kick your ass," Partain replied, then kicked Jesse's feet again.

Jesse guessed it was time. He got slowly to his feet. "Phil, I gave you some real good advice the last time we talked. Remember that?"

"You keep your fucking advice to yourself, you bastard," Partain said, circling Jesse to his right. "I was in line to operate that machine, but I guess you've been sucking Harley's cock real regular."

"Phil, Phil," Jesse said wearily, "I'm going to have to ask you to shut your mouth."

"Shit," Partain said, "you're going to be sucking *my* cock in just a minute." He feinted with his right, then came around with a left hook. Jesse stepped back, and the punch grazed his cheek. He stepped into Partain and planted a short left in the man's considerable gut.

Partain grunted, but he kept coming. That gut had been pretty solid, Jesse thought. He ducked under Partain's right and landed a stiff punch in the ribs. Partain still kept coming, and now he had a knife in his right hand.

I wonder, Jesse thought, how Phil feels about the sight of his own blood? As Partain swung the knife, Jesse stepped inside the swing and struck the man's wrist hard with the edge of his hand, then he knocked back Partain's head with a pair of left jabs, and the bigger man's nose started to bleed.

Partain wiped his face with his sleeve and looked at it. "You goddamned son of a bitch!" he roared.

Jesse kept his guard up. The sight of his own blood apparently made Partain steaming mad. Jesse dodged as the man rushed him and landed a hard right to a kidney as he passed. Partain went down on one knee with a cry of pain, and Jesse punched him in the side of the neck. Partain hit the ground, rolled over and got to his feet again.

Jesse began to use everything he had learned in the yard at Atlanta, kicking a shin, punching under the heart and landing teeth-rattling punches to the jaw. Partain landed a few shots, mostly on Jesse's arms and shoulders. He seemed unaccustomed to fighting somebody who knew how to fight back.

Jesse wore the big man down, hurting him, but leaving him on his feet until he seemed ready to go down. Finally, he doubled Partain over with a left to the solar plexus, then straightened him up with an uppercut. Partain's knees buckled, and he went backward like a felled tree.

There were some shouts, and Jesse looked up to find that a small crowd of workers had gathered. The whistle blew, and Jesse walked back to the plant, leaving Partain where he lay. Nobody, he noticed, went to the man's aid.

Partain didn't come back to work after lunch, and the following morning, he was replaced by a new man. Jesse heard later that Herman Muller had fired Phil Partain.

CHAPTER

19

Jesse sat on the hood of his truck, which was parked in deep woods outside St. Clair, and talked to Kip Fuller on the scrambled cellular phone.

"I'm moving up in the world," Jesse said. "Making nine bucks an hour, now, and I expect to get raised to ten any day." He told Kip about the promotion.

"Glad to hear it, Jess."

"Not everybody is as happy as you are about my advancement," Jesse replied. "Fellow called Partain took exception."

"And what did you do about it?" Kip asked, sounding worried.

"I hit him until he got over it," Jesse replied.

"Listen, Jess, I know you're good at that sort of thing, but it can only draw attention to you. I hope you stayed away from anything they taught us at Quantico."

"I did that; I wasn't anxious to look like a federal cop in a fight."

"Good."

"I think it was a setup."

"Oh, shit."

"It's natural that they'd be very wary. I think they wanted to see how I'd react."

"So you reacted by beating the shit out of the guy?"

"Not at first; I let him push me some, first. From the reaction of my coworkers at the plant, I gather he wasn't the most popular guy around."

"So you won a few admirers?"

"Maybe."

"Has there been any reaction from the opposition since this happened?"

"Not so far; it's been a couple of weeks, so I wonder if they're going to react at all."

"I hope you're not going to make a habit of this, Jess."

"Depends on whether they make a habit of it."

"You getting any ideas about where Coldwater is getting his money?"

"I gather the church has a piece of a few businesses around town. He's apparently tried to hustle Herman Muller into selling out, but so far, Herman is standing pat. I hope he goes on doing that; it's hard not to root for the guy."

"No evidence of big money behind Coldwater, though?"

"Nope. It's hard to see how any big money could get generated around here. It's not a big place, and Muller's business has got to be the important earner in town. So far, I can't see that Coldwater is spending any big money, either."

"Let's not make that judgment, yet," Kip said. "You haven't really had a chance to look around, have you?"

"I've deliberately not done any looking around, just traveling where my life here leads me. Snooping could get me burnt."

"I'm glad you see it that way; I don't want you burnt."

"That's sweet of you, Kip; I know Dan feels that way, too."

Kip laughed. "You always did have a sense of humor, Jess."

"Well, I'd better get back to town. I'm supposed to be running an errand for Jenny, and I shouldn't be gone too long."

"No need to call me too often, until something happens," Kip said. "Next week will do."

"Right, see you then." Jesse broke the connection and crawled under the truck to put the phone away. As he closed the safe, he heard another vehicle approaching down the dirt track. He crawled out from under the truck in time to see a police car pull to a stop and Pat Casey get out.

"Hey, Pat," he said, brushing off his clothes.

"Howdy, Jesse." The chief of police watched him warily. "What are you doing out here?"

"I turned down this road to take a leak, to tell you the truth, and what with the bumps, I thought my muffler was loose. I went under there to have a look at it."

"You should have taken it down to the filling station and put it on the rack."

"Not while I'm making nine bucks an hour, I won't," Jesse replied.

Casey grinned. "Guess not. How's it going out at Wood Products?"

"Pretty good; I got promoted. I'm running a press, now."

"That means Herman likes you, I guess."

"I guess."

"I hear you and Phil Partain had a little rumble."

"A little one."

"I'm impressed you came out of it with your ears on your head," Casey said. "Partain's messed up more than one fellow around here."

"Partain's a schoolyard bully, that's all."

"I guess that's true, but he can be dangerous, especially if you've made a fool of him, like you have. I'd watch my back."

"I'll keep it in mind."

"I wouldn't take it hard if you killed the son of a bitch," Casey said.

"I'm not out to kill anybody, but I'm not going to let him kill me," Jesse said.

"That's a reasonable attitude," Casey said.

"Well, I've got to go to the drugstore for my landlady," Jesse said, digging for his keys.

"You do that; never keep a woman waiting."

Jesse got the truck started, turned it around and headed back toward the highway. He glanced in his rearview mirror and saw Casey starting to look around the clearing where he'd been parked. He was going to have to find a better place to use the telephone.

Jesse stood at the magazine rack in the drugstore and waited for Jenny's prescription to be filled. He flipped through a home improvement magazine, taking care not to be seen reading the *New Yorker* or *Esquire*. He had been there only a moment, when a tall, thin man wearing glasses and a full beard walked into the store and past him. Jesse tensed, but tried not to show it. He knew that man, but he couldn't remember from where, and he hoped to hell the man didn't recognize him. Who was he? Jesse racked his brain.

"Jesse, your prescription is ready," the druggist called out.

"Thanks, Mike," Jesse called back, returning the magazine to the rack and keeping his back to the visitor. Then, as he was about to turn toward the counter, a computer magazine caught his eye; the cover photograph was of the same man who had just entered the store. Melvin Schooner, Jesse realized. Head of one of the fastest-growing software companies in the world. Jesse had read about him half a dozen times in the business section of various newspapers. Schooner departed the prescription counter as Jesse approached, and Jesse got another good look at him. No doubt about who he was.

"There you go, Jesse," Mike said. "I put it on Jenny's account."

"Thanks, Mike. Say, that fellow who just left looks familiar."

"Sure, that's Mel Schooner, the computer guy; hometown boy, he is."

"Oh, yeah, I've seen him on TV, or somewhere."

"Mel's done real well, but he still has time to come home and see his mother," Mike said. "Real nice fellow; belongs to the church here. Been real generous with local contributions."

"That's nice. Take care, Mike."

Jesse went back to his truck with a new thought in mind. Just which contributions had Schooner been so generous with? He got into the cab, and peeked into the bag at Jenny's prescription. Was she ill? He smiled. Nope. Birth control pills. He was glad to know she was taking those.

He drove back toward the house, wondering about Melvin Schooner and his software company. The papers said he was fast gaining on Bill Gates at Microsoft. The guy wasn't forty yet, and he was supposedly a multibillionaire. He wondered if Schooner was acquainted with Jack Gene Coldwater.

As he drove toward home, it began to snow, and Jesse, who had spent nearly all of his life in the South, felt excited, like a schoolboy. The snow was one more indication of how far from Atlanta Federal Penitentiary he had come.

CHAPTER

20

Almost as soon as Jesse had begun to operate the press, he was made foreman of his section. He was startled, and then, looking around, he realized that Herman Muller was no fool; he could look at a crew and know who the best man was. And Herman, Harley Waters explained, wasn't one to stand on any such ceremony as seniority. He was suddenly making fifteen dollars an hour, and it amused him that it seemed to be big money.

Then, the week before Thanksgiving, Jesse got the shock of his life. Herman Muller summoned him to his office, sat him in a chair and regarded him solemnly.

"Jesse," Herman said, "I'm not getting any younger."

"I hadn't noticed, Herman," Jesse replied.

"Oh, I'm not getting all that much older, either, I guess, but yesterday my doctor put me on some medicine for arthritis, and it kind of shook me up. I mean, in all my life I never took any medicine for something that wasn't likely to go away pretty fast."

"Arthritis isn't all that much of a problem these days, is it?"

Muller shrugged. "I guess not; it was just the notion of having a chronic ailment that got me thinking."

"I wouldn't worry about it, Herman; you'll bury most of us."

"I expect to," Herman said, allowing himself a small smile, "but I guess it wouldn't hurt for me to have some help upstairs, here."

Jesse didn't reply, since he had no idea what Muller was talking about.

"I told you when you came here, not so very long ago, that it's my policy to promote from within."

"That's right, you did, and I guess I've benefitted from that policy."

"Well, this morning I sat down and I went through my list of foremen. There's six of you fellows, and you've all got different qualities to recommend you. None of you has a lot of education, but some of you are smarter than others, and I think you're the smartest of the lot."

"Why thank you, Herman."

"I was looking back over your employment application and remembering our first conversation, and it appears that you're the only one of my foremen who's ever run a business."

"I am?"

"Yessir, and even though you went bust, I don't think it was your fault; it was the times, is my guess."

"That's what I'd like to think myself," Jesse said.

"Anyway, you've had some experience running a business, keeping costs down and volume up; you've handled men, I can tell from the way you do your present job."

"I guess I have."

"Well, I've decided that I need a . . . well, a kind of assistant manager, I guess; somebody who can learn the business from my perspective and who can keep the place going if I'm out with the flu for a few days."

"I see," Jesse replied.

"You're my man, Jesse; I've looked 'em all over, and even though you're the newest foreman, you're the best, and the job's yours, if you want it."

"Herman, I sure do want it, I'll tell you that," Jesse said, not without feeling.

"You'd have to wear a white shirt and a tie every day, like me," Muller said.

"I guess I can handle that."

"You'd have to learn the computer bookkeeping system."

"I can handle that, too, even though my wife took care of that part of my old business."

"You'll have to learn to buy materials, and I mean *negotiate*. You'll have to hire and fire—with my consent, of course—and you'll have to order machine parts and keep an eye on the salespeople. I've only got three, and they're all in the West. One of these days I'll have a shot at some Eastern markets, I guess."

"I'll give it my best, Herman," Jesse said.

"All right, you can start by picking out a foreman from your crew. Watch him for as long as you think necessary, and when you think he's ready, you put on that white shirt and tie and come on up here."

Jesse stood up and stuck out his hand. "I really appreciate your confidence, Herman. I won't let you down."

Muller shook his hand. "I don't believe you will, Jesse."

Jesse turned to go.

"Oh, I guess we'd better talk money," Muller said. "How's seven-fifty a week, to start?"

"That's fine with me, Herman."

"Do a good job, and you'll get more."

"Thank you, sir."

"Go on, get back to work. Your crew will be messing up, without you there."

Jesse stopped on Main Street and bought a suit and some shirts before going home to Jenny. When he told her the news of his promotion she threw her arms around him and kissed him on the neck.

"Good Lord! You're setting records at Wood Products! Assistant manager!"

Jesse hugged her and savored the moment. He pushed away his past and tried to believe that he was just an honest working stiff who'd gotten a promotion.

"Why don't I take you and Carey out to dinner? We'll celebrate."

"We'd love to! You wait, and I'll change my clothes and get Carey dressed up. We'll go to the Steak Shack, is that all right?"

"Fine with me," he laughed. "I love a good steak."

He watched her run up the stairs like a happy schoolgirl, and he felt happy himself.

CHAPTER

21

Kurt Ruger picked up Melvin Schooner at the motel and drove him toward the mountain. Schooner, he thought, looked nervous, but that was understandable. Everybody was a little nervous around Jack Gene Coldwater.

"Why does he want to see me?" Schooner asked, dabbing at his forehead with a shirtsleeve.

"I think he just wants to say hello, Mel. He knew you were home visiting your mother, of course."

"It's about the money, isn't it?"

"Don't worry about it, Mel. Jack Gene's not mad at you." He turned at the church and started up the mountain.

"He just doesn't understand the cash flow," Schooner said. "We've spent the past two years updating our word processing product and that cost us a bundle. You can't imagine how much cash is soaked up by three or four hundred programmers sitting there, day after day, writing code."

"Jack Gene will understand," Ruger replied soothingly. "If there's anything he understands, it's cash flow."

"Yeah," Schooner said disconsolately.

The road steepened, and they climbed past houses tucked back into the trees, houses occupied by the elite of the church. Near the top of the mountain Ruger turned into a driveway, then stopped in front of a small television camera and waited until he was recognized and the wrought-iron gates were electronically opened.

"We're going to his house?" Schooner asked, sounding almost alarmed.

"Yes. He wanted to see you here."

"I've never been to his house. Jesus Christ."

"Just about," Ruger replied.

Jack Gene Coldwater received them in the garden, which was English in style, planted with many flowers and perennials. This time of year, Ruger noted, the place was still green, even though the flowers were not in bloom and patches of snow appeared here and there on the grass. Two of Coldwater's wives were gardening, working away, crouched or kneeling, doing their master's work.

"Have a seat here," Ruger said, indicating a stone bench. The two men sat on the cold granite and pulled their coats closer around them. They had only a moment to wait before Jack Gene himself appeared from around a corner of the garden path, striding toward them, his breath coming in clouds of mist. Ruger and Schooner stood to meet him. He shook both their hands and sat down on one end of the bench, placing Schooner between Ruger and himself.

"Mel, how are you?" Coldwater asked.

"I'm just fine, sir," Schooner said, like a schoolboy called into the principal's office.

"I'm glad to hear it. How's the work coming on the new release of the WordPlay software?"

"We're just finishing up the beta testing; I'm planning to release the first of the year."

"Good, good. I know what a drain on resources such a huge project can be."

"Yes, sir, it certainly has been a drain."

"What sort of acceptance of the new version do you anticipate?"

"Well, the feedback from the beta testing has just been phenomenal. My marketing people think we will ship two million copies the first forty-five days; most of them upgrades, of course."

"Sounds as though I should buy some more Schooner stock," Coldwater said, rewarding Schooner with a broad smile.

"Oh, God," Schooner moaned, "let's not get into any insider-trading problems with the SEC. I'm already worried about the antitrust division of the Justice Department; they're breathing down our necks on the acquisition."

"Don't worry, Mel, I'll be discreet; I'll buy through third parties, and I'll spread the buys around—some in Texas, some in New York, some in California."

"I'd appreciate that, sir," Schooner said, sounding relieved.

Coldwater gazed off into the distance. The view was spectacular from so high up, and he seemed to drink it in for a full minute of silence. Then he spoke. "Mel, I'm concerned about your spiritual state."

Schooner looked alarmed. "Oh, sir, I'm certainly working to keep straight."

"I know you are, Mel; you always have." He turned and looked at Schooner. "It's what I've come to expect from you," he said slowly.

Perspiration appeared on Schooner's forehead. "Thank you, sir," he said.

"But I want to see a manifestation of your spiritual state," Coldwater said, keeping his eyes on Schooner's.

"I want more than words; God wants material evidence of your continuing commitment to the church." He paused. "So do I."

"Sir, right now ten million dollars is difficult," Schooner said, his voice trembling.

"Ten million?" Coldwater asked, his eyes widening slightly. "Is that what Kurt has asked you for?"

"Yes, sir; that was the figure he mentioned."

"I think, say, five million dollars would satisfactorily demonstrate your faith," Coldwater said.

Schooner seemed almost to swoon with relief. "Oh, I can manage that, sir. I'll have it in the church account by Monday."

"In my own account," Coldwater said. "The Cayman Islands account."

"Whatever you say, sir."

"You said you'd ship two million copies of the new WordPlay the first forty-five days?"

"That's what we anticipate, sir."

"Good. You can send the other five million the middle of February, to the church account."

Schooner gulped. "I should be able to do that by then, sir."

"You won't disappoint me?" Coldwater asked, placing a fatherly hand on the younger man's shoulder.

"Oh, no sir," Schooner blurted. "Of course not."

Coldwater clapped Schooner sharply on the back. "Good man! Your church can always depend on you!"

"Thank you, sir," Schooner said, managing a smile.

"You have a very fine soul," Coldwater said, his gaze boring into Schooner. "Go with God." He stood up and walked back up the garden path.

Schooner and Ruger stood as he left.

"Mel, would you mind waiting in the car for a moment?" Ruger asked.

"Sure," Schooner replied, and turned back toward the house.

Ruger walked up the path and rounded a curve. Coldwater was standing beside an iron deer, gazing out over the view.

"Jack Gene?"

Coldwater turned and looked at Ruger.

"There's something I thought you'd want to know."

"What is it?"

"Herman Muller has made Jesse Barron the assistant manager at Wood Products."

"*What?*"

"I know, it's entirely unexpected."

"Barron hasn't been there eight weeks yet, has he?"

"Just about that."

"Herman has never let anybody help him manage that place."

"It occurred to me that it might be some sort of defensive move."

"That's possible, I suppose. We haven't entirely coopted Barron, yet. Maybe Herman thinks of him as an ally against us."

"I think that must be it."

Coldwater turned and looked out over the mountains again. "Still, eight weeks on the job, starting on the hopper like everybody else. That's *very* impressive."

"I suppose it is," Ruger replied.

"Kurt, I think it's about time I met Jesse Barron."

"I'll see to it, Jack Gene."

"Let's keep it subtle; I just want to get the feel of him."

"Consider it done."

Coldwater's attention seemed to drift back to the landscape. "Thank you, Kurt."

Ruger backed away, then went to join Schooner.

CHAPTER

22

Jesse stood by the truck and looked at the First Church of St. Clair. It was medium-sized, as churches go, prosperous looking, a Greek facade topped by a soaring steeple. The building sat on a broad lawn, now covered by snow, at the base of the mountain that loomed over the town. It was a respectable-looking church, Jesse thought.

Jenny took Carey to church faithfully, every Sunday morning, but she had never asked Jesse to come. Then, that morning, she had snuggled up to him in bed, pressed her naked breasts against his back and said, "There's a communal Thanksgiving dinner at the church today. Carey and I would like you to come."

"I'd like that," he had responded, relieved that she had finally given him an excuse to see the congregation up close.

Jenny led him into the auditorium, and Jesse was stopped in his tracks at the sight of the place. It was not very different from the more prosperous churches where his father had preached, with one exception: at the rear of the church, looming over the choir loft, was a large stained-glass window depicting Jesus Christ, who was holding in his hand, not a dove, but a pair of lightning bolts. Jesse's attention was drawn to the face; something about it was odd. As Jesse followed Jenny down a side aisle, the face seemed to change slightly, until another face was revealed. It recalled the optician's billboard in *The Great Gatsby*; the eyes seemed to follow him as the face changed.

He followed Jenny down a flight of stairs, and they emerged into a large basement room with a table that stretched nearly the length of the church. There was a great bustle as women set the table and streamed from the kitchen with platters of food, while others stood to one side of the room with their children. Carey ran over to a small group and greeted two other little girls.

On the other side of the table, standing in threes and fours, the men waited, chatting idly and watching the progress of food from the kitchen.

Jenny tugged at his sleeve. "Why don't you go over there and introduce yourself to some of the men?" she asked. Then, without waiting for a reply, she followed Carey to the clutch of women.

Feeling abandoned, Jesse walked around the long table and approached the men. He was relieved to see somebody he knew.

"Hey there, Jesse," Pat Casey said, extending his hand. "Let me introduce you to some fellows. This is Luther Williams, that's Paul Carter, and over there is Hank Twomy."

Jesse shook their hands and sensed a reserve among the men. They had stopped talking as he approached.

"I'm glad to see you here," Casey said. "We should have gotten you to church a long time ago."

"Thanks, Pat; I'm glad to be here."

"Congratulations on your promotion. You're moving right up at Wood Products."

"Thanks," Jesse said quietly.

"Herman Muller must think highly of you."

Jesse shrugged. "I'm glad to make a little more money. I appreciate you sending me down there. I don't know where I'd be if you hadn't been nice enough to do that."

"Glad to be of help, and I'm glad to see you settling into our town so well. It's starting to seem like you've always been here."

"It seems like that to me, too," Jesse replied, truthfully. "If you'd have told me three months ago that I'd be where I am now, I'd have thought you were crazy." That was the truth, too. In fact, he had expected to be dead by this time.

There was the sound of movement in the crowd and Jesse turned to see Jenny beckoning to him from the table. He went forward with the other men and took a seat opposite her and Carey, all the men on his side and all the women and children on the other. Then, as if at some secret signal, the room fell suddenly quiet, and Jesse followed Jenny's gaze to the head of the table. There stood a tall man dressed in white trousers and a white silk shirt, open at the throat. His skin was bronzed and his long hair was entirely white, and Jesse thought he looked like nothing less than an apparition. His face was just recognizable as that of the young man in uniform that Jesse had seen in the photograph at his briefing in Atlanta; moreover it was recognizable as the face that had alternated with the face of Jesus in the stained-glass window upstairs.

The sound of a door slamming caused Jesse to look toward Coldwater's right. There, staggering drunk and making his way toward the minister, was Phil Partain. The two men seated nearest Coldwater, one of them Kurt Ruger, jumped up and intercepted Partain, steered him from the room. The minister seemed not to notice.

HEAT

•

Jack Gene Coldwater raised his hands wide and his voice was like the rumble of thunder. "We thank our God for this day; for the lives we lead together; for the love we share; and, most of all, for the purity of the consecrated blood that flows in our veins."

Jesse suddenly realized that his was the only face turned toward the speaker. Every other head was bowed, yet he was unable to wrest his gaze from Coldwater.

"We thank our God for the new world that awaits us, just beyond our sight; for his choosing of us from all the people of the earth, to do his final will; for the lightning from heaven that awaits our enemies. We thank our God for this food, this plenty afforded to those who follow his new word. Amen."

"Amen!" the group said in chorus, startling Jesse.

He leaned across the table toward Jenny. "Who is that?" he asked.

"That's our pastor, Jack Gene Coldwater," she replied, then began to eat. She didn't seem anxious to continue about Coldwater, so Jesse began to eat, too.

Pat Casey spoke up from beside him. "He is a very remarkable man, Jesse. You will get to know that."

The dinner was over, and people were making their goodbyes as the dishes were taken away. Jesse stood with Jenny and Carey, ready to leave, but Jenny seemed to be waiting for something. Shortly, Pat Casey tapped Jesse on the shoulder from behind.

He turned to see the police chief standing with Jack Gene Coldwater, who was gazing expectantly at Jesse.

"Jack Gene, I want to introduce you to Jesse Barron, a new member of our community. Jesse, this is Jack Gene Coldwater, our pastor."

Jesse's hand was enveloped in Coldwater's, which was large and surprisingly soft.

"Jesse," Coldwater said, "I want to welcome you to our church. This is the first of many visits, I hope." He did not let go of Jesse's hand.

Jesse stood, fixed in Coldwater's gaze, suddenly seized with the feeling that the man could see inside him, see who he really was and why he was there. "Thank you, pastor," he managed to say. "It was a very fine dinner."

"Those who dine at my table never want for anything," Coldwater replied. "Anything," he repeated.

Jesse didn't know how to respond to that, so he said nothing.

Coldwater continued to clasp Jesse's hand. "Come and see me Monday, after work," he said. He gave Jesse's hand a final shake, then turned and walked away without acknowledging Jenny or Carey.

"Come around to the station when you get off," Casey said. "I'll take you up there to see him."

"All right," Jesse replied. There didn't seem to be anything else to say.

"Let's go home," Jenny said, taking his arm.

On the drive home she said nothing.

"You're very quiet," he said. "For you, I mean."

She smiled up at him. "I'm just full," she said. "Eating that much always makes me sleepy."

"I'd better get you home to bed," he said.

"I guess you'd better," she said, then winked at him.

Jesse drove home, looking forward to bed, looking forward to the weekend off and looking forward to his appointed meeting with Jack Gene Coldwater.

CHAPTER

23

The four men arrived separately in Seattle: two at Seattle-Tacoma International airport on different flights from different destinations. The third arrived by Greyhound bus a little after nine in the evening, and inside an hour had stolen an anonymous van and changed its license plates with those of a Toyota Corolla parked nearby. He then picked up the two men at Seattle-Tacoma airport.

After midnight, the fourth man landed a light airplane, a fixed-gear Cessna 182, at Tacoma Narrows, a small, general-aviation airport on one of the many islands in the area. He taxied to a remote end of the tie-down area and cut the engine. Immediately, the van pulled up to the airplane, and its contents were quickly transferred to the vehicle. Two of the men refilled the airplane's fuel tanks from jerry cans stowed in the luggage compartment. Not a word was spoken. The men got into the van and drove toward Seattle.

The four men were named, for the occasion, Black, Gray, Brown and White. Black, who had piloted the Cessna, held a flashlight to a map of the city and gave monosyllabic instructions to Brown, who drove, while Gray and White quietly slipped into boiler suits in the back of the van. It was nearly 2 A.M. when the van arrived at its destination.

"Around the block at twenty-five miles an hour," Black said. As they turned the first corner, a police car passed them going in the opposite direction.

Brown stiffened at the wheel, but Black put a hand on his arm. "It's all right; in fact it's good. Better now than in half an hour." He began climbing into a boiler suit. "Stop there and change," he said, pointing to the curb. When Brown had donned his suit, he drove back toward their destination.

Black pointed to the parking lot of a printing company across the street, and Brown pulled into a parking place. Two small canvas duffles were handed forward from the rear of the van, and the occupants got out. Wordlessly, the four men crossed the street and walked at a moderate pace down the sidewalk along a high hedge, each carrying an identical canvas bag. Black was counting paces under his breath.

He raised a hand, and his companions stopped. Gray and White plunged their arms into the hedge and parted it, while Black and Brown stepped through; then Gray and White followed them. The hedge closed behind them.

Quickly now, Black led them to the rear door of the building. Each man unzipped his canvas bag and removed a pistol with a silencer affixed. Black produced a key, unlocked the door, and the four men stepped inside, then their leader went to a security keypad just inside the door and tapped in a four-digit code. A soft beep sounded. Black turned to his companions and shone his flashlight on his wristwatch. He held up three fingers, for three minutes. His companions nodded, and on a hand signal from Black they spread out into the building.

Black found room number one, sat cross-legged on the floor under the central table and laid his pistol on the floor beside him. He took a small packet from his canvas bag and taped it to the table pedestal, making sure to leave a six-inch length of aerial wire exposed. He went back into the hallway and to the rear door, where he was joined by his three companions. He took another packet from his bag and taped it to the rear door. Glancing at his wristwatch, he tapped a number into a keypad on the unit, then looked at the others and nodded.

Black opened the rear door. To his astonishment he was staring down the barrel of a .38 caliber pistol.

"Freeze! All of you!" The uniformed man cried.

Black did not hesitate; he swung his canvas bag at the man's weapon and felt a round blow past his head. He fired one shot into the middle of the man's face, then stepped over his body and waved the others to follow.

"Jesus Christ," White said.

"Shut up," Black barked. "Nothing has changed." He looked carefully through the parted hedge, up and down the street. It was deserted, but he saw a light come on in a house across the street. "Don't run, walk," Black growled at the others. They made their way toward the van, and Black heard a door open and voices. "Walk!" he said again.

They reached the van and got in. Brown started the engine, and Black put a hand on his shoulder. "Twenty-five miles an hour, no more," he said. He switched on his flashlight and started to give instructions again. From the distance came the sound of a police siren.

"Jesus Christ!" Brown shouted, then floored the accelerator.

"Slow down!" Black yelled. "Twenty-five; no more!"

"People came out of that house," Brown said. "They had to get a look at the van."

At that moment a huge explosion erupted behind them, and the interior of the van was lit with a fiery light. The two men in the rear of the van cheered.

"Shut up," Black said to them. "We can't return the van to where you stole it," he said to Brown. "We go to Plan B. Right at the next intersection; we'll stay off the big streets and go through neighborhoods to the Plan B rendezvous. We've got a local contact waiting there for us, just in case. Now left at the corner. And slow down!" He turned and looked over his shoulder at the two men in back. "Listen to me carefully. If a cop car gets on our tail, we won't run. Brown will slow down; you kick open the back doors and pour everything into their windshield."

"We've already killed one cop," Brown said.

"That was a security guard, and anyway, we've already bought the death penalty if they get us, so another cop or two won't matter."

Brown set his jaw and drove.

"Two rights, now." In a moment they were approaching a school. "Turn in here; drive around back." As they came around the corner of the building the van's headlights picked up a Lincoln Town Car parked near a dumpster. "That's our ride," Black said. "Make sure everything is out of the van. Everybody still wearing gloves?"

Affirmative noises came from all three men.

Black got out and rapped on the driver's window of the Lincoln, and as it came down he found himself looking into the face of a plump, pretty blonde woman. "Hit your trunk release," he said. He turned to his companions. "I want all three of you in the trunk."

"What?" Brown asked, incredulous.

"They're looking for four men in a van, not a woman and a man in a Lincoln. Don't worry, it's a big trunk."

The three men got out of their boiler suits and arranged themselves in the trunk; Black tossed his suit into the trunk along with his bag, tucked his pistol into his waistband and closed the lid. He got into the passenger seat and fastened his seat belt. "All right, let's go," he said. "I'll give you directions."

The woman turned toward him. "Did everything go all right?"

"Shut up and look straight ahead," Black said. "Have you forgotten your instructions?"

The woman snapped her head around. "I'm sorry."

"Let's move it, then! Don't turn your lights on yet; drive to the corner of the building and stop."

The woman obeyed, sitting quietly while he looked up and down the street.

"All right, turn right out of the parking lot; twenty-five miles an hour, no more."

The woman followed his instructions. "I thought you weren't coming," she said. "I was about to leave."

"I'm not going to tell you again to shut up," Black said. "If you speak again, I'll throw you out of the car. Do you have your story straight if we're stopped? Nod your head."

She nodded.

He finally seemed to have gotten through to her. He began to concentrate on giving her directions.

Half an hour later they crossed a bridge to the island and immediately turned left at a sign for the airport. "Stop here," he said. He opened the glove compartment and pressed the trunk release button, then got out of the car. His three companions were extricating themselves from their cramped positions and stretching their limbs. One of them took their equipment from the trunk.

"Hey, we made it!" White said, seeing the airport sign. "Good going, Chief Casey!"

Casey opened his mouth to yell at the man; then

he saw the woman. She had gotten out of the car and was standing at the rear bumper, looking at them. "Partain," he said, "you are one stupid son of a bitch." He pulled the pistol from his belt and raked the woman across the head with the silencer. She went down with no more than a sigh.

"What did you do that for?" Gray asked.

"I did it because she was stupid enough to see all of our faces, and because Partain, here, stupid as he is, told her my name! Now get that bitch into the front seat of the car."

"What are we going to do with her?" Partain asked.

"What do you think?" Casey said. "Get behind the wheel. You two guys wait here." He got into the backseat. "Drive back down to the bridge and stop just before you get to it."

Partain did as he was told. Casey got out and pulled the limp woman into the driver's position. He turned the steering wheel to the right, put on the emergency brake and put the transmission in drive. He moved the woman's right leg until her foot rested on the accelerator, pressing lightly on the petal. The car revved slightly and strained against the parking brake. He turned to Partain. "Come here."

Partain walked over. "Yeah?"

"Release the parking brake," Casey said.

Partain scratched his head, stepped forward and, after a moment's hesitation, pulled the control that released the brake. The car jerked forward and began to move toward the side of the road.

As it passed, Casey slammed the driver's door. The car left the road, gaining speed, and started down the slope of the bridge approach, knocking down small pine trees as it went. At the bottom of the incline the car went over a small cliff and flew through the air toward the narrows. There was a loud splash and white foam spread across the black water.

HEAT

Casey stood and watched as the waters quieted. Then the Lincoln popped to the surface, or nearly so. The roof could be seen as the car drifted away from the bridge with the current.

"It's not going to sink!" Partain cried.

"It's going to sink," Casey said. "If not here, then down a little ways. The farther from the bridge, the better." As he watched, bubbles spilled from the cabin, and the car slowly sank from sight. "There," he said. "They won't find her for a while."

The two men trudged back up the hill and joined their two companions. It was a few minutes' walk to the airport. They skirted the building where the night attendant was and boarded the Cessna, tossing their bags into the luggage compartment with the empty jerry cans. Casey worked his way through the checklist deliberately; he could not allow himself to rush. The engine started quickly, and Casey taxied onto the runway, turning upwind. He pushed the throttle all the way forward; the airplane started its roll, and in a moment, they were airborne.

As they climbed away from the field the lights of Seattle appeared in the distance. Near the center of the city, Casey could see a large fire burning.

"Wow, look at that," Partain said from the backseat. "We must have ignited a gas main."

Casey stayed under a thousand feet until they were clear of the Seattle Terminal Control Area, then he began his climb and pointed the Cessna east, toward Idaho. All that remained for him to do on arrival was to remove the taped-on, fake registration number from the side of the airplane and reapply the original numbers.

That, and beat the shit out of Partain, he mused.

24

J esse left work on Monday afternoon and drove into town. He parked his truck, picked up a Boise paper at the drugstore and walked down to the police station. A young officer was manning the reception desk.

"Hi, I'm Jesse Barron," he said to the officer. "Chief Casey is expecting me; will you tell him I'm here?"

Pat Casey gave him a wave from his glass-enclosed office, took his hat from a hook and walked into the reception area. "How you doing, Jesse?" he asked shaking his guest's hand. "Ready for your meeting?"

"Sure," Jesse said. He followed Casey outside and into a patrol car. Casey backed out and drove toward the church.

"You know, Pat, that's a real impressive station you've got there. Not what you'd expect to see in a small town."

"You're right about that, pal; we've got all the latest computer stuff, and we can plug into any of half a dozen law enforcement networks with a few keystrokes. My squad cars have got computer equipment, too. You know, Jesse, I ran a check on you the day you hit town."

Jesse tried to look surprised. "No kidding? You're a careful man, Pat."

"I try to be."

"And what did you find out?"

"That you're not a liar. You know, I thought about offering you a job on the force, but you moved up so fast at Wood Products that I couldn't afford you now."

"You think I'd make a cop?" Jesse asked.

"I think so. You're a smart guy, and you've got guts; you showed that when you took on a guy the size of Phil Partain."

Jesse shrugged and unfolded his newspaper.

"What's in the news?"

"Looks like somebody took out another abortion clinic," Jesse replied, scanning the story. "That's the fourth one in a month, and it's okay with me." He could feel Casey's gaze on him.

"You against abortion?"

"Murdering babies? Damn straight, I am. I had three girls, you know, and the second two were big surprises. I wouldn't have stopped either one of them for anything."

"I'm with you, pal," Casey said, swinging past the church and starting up the mountain.

"We're not going to the church?"

"The pastor wants to see you in his home. That's a rare honor, believe me."

"I'm flattered." Jesse glanced down at the bottom of the newspaper's front page. SEATTLE ANTI-ABORTION ACTIVIST DEAD IN PUGET SOUND PLUNGE, it read.

"What's that piece?" Casey asked.

Jesse read aloud: "'The body of Martha Terrell Peary, a prominent member of Seattle's pro-life movement, was found in her car near the Tacoma Narrows bridge yesterday, the victim of an apparent accident. Raymond Peary, her husband, said his wife often took late-night drives and that she must have lost control of her car. Mrs. Peary had taken a leading part in many demonstrations against family planning clinics in the Northwest over the past four years, and it seemed ironic to her friends that she should have died on the night of the firebombing of the Parsons Street Clinic, in Seattle, by unknown perpetrators.' That's it."

"Well," said Casey, "win some, lose some."

Jack Gene Coldwater's house was situated at the end of a long drive, very near the top of the mountain. It was a solid-looking stone structure, with elaborate plantings along the drive and in the turnaround at the front door. Jesse thought it looked like something out of an architectural magazine. This impression was reinforced when they were let inside by a pretty young woman and shown to the pastor's study.

Coldwater sat in a leather armchair, his striking profile toward the door, apparently lost in a book. The room was paneled in walnut and lined with bookcases. Books were everywhere, on a sofa, on a coffee table, on the floor and on the limestone mantelpiece. A cheerful log fire burned in the grate.

"Pastor," the woman said softly, "your guests are here."

Coldwater looked up and smiled. "Jesse, how are you?"

"Fine, sir."

"Miss Betty," Casey said to the young woman, "do you think you could find me something to nibble on in the kitchen?"

"Of course, Chief," she replied, and led the way. Casey closed the door behind them.

"Come and sit down," Coldwater said, indicating a matching chair facing his own.

Jesse sat down.

"I believe the sun is over the yardarm," Coldwater said, looking out the window at the winter twilight. "May I offer you something to warm you up?"

"Thank you sir, maybe a bourbon."

Coldwater went to a drinks trolley and poured them both a stiff drink, handed Jesse his, sat down and raised his glass. "To a better day."

Jesse raised his glass and drank. It was excellent.

Coldwater took a small sip, then set his glass down on a side table. "What do you know about us here, Jesse?"

"About the town?" He set his drink down.

"About the church; about me."

"Not very much, I guess. The Thanksgiving dinner was my first visit to the church."

"No gossip around town?"

"I've been spending most of my time at home, when I'm not working."

Coldwater nodded. "At Jenny Weatherby's. A fine young woman, Jenny; fellow could do a lot worse. Nice little girl, too."

"I've grown fond of them both."

"Good. A man needs the affection of a woman."

They sat silently for a moment, and Jesse elected not to speak first. After all he had been summoned here.

"I want to tell you something of the background of this place," Coldwater said. "I came here some twenty years ago, fresh out of the army and the Vietnam war. I came with a couple of thousand dollars in back pay and two friends, Pat Casey and Kurt Ruger. Pat, you know; have you met Kurt?"

"No, sir."

"A financial wizard. One of the best minds for

money in the country. On Kurt's advice, we pooled our funds and made a down payment on land that includes this mountain. We built a log church on the site where the First Church now rests, lived in it, worshiped in it, conducted our lives in that building for years. We worked hard, marshaled our resources and attracted others to our way of life. We multiplied and prospered." He stopped and looked at Jesse. "Are you a religious man, Jesse?"

"My father"—he stopped himself; he had nearly said that his father was a minister—"kind of rammed it down my throat, I guess. I didn't feel close to the church at home, but I. . . I guess I sort of carved out my own religion from all of what was thrown at me as a boy. I believe in God, I really do."

"Do you believe that some people are chosen *personally* by God?"

"Yes, sir, I believe that. I've never known what he wanted me to do, though."

"Jesse, I believe God has brought you here, to us. Do you believe that God can do that?"

"I believe God can do *anything*," Jesse said, nodding vigorously.

"Good man. Do you believe that God speaks directly to some people?"

"I'm sure he must," Jesse said. He looked into the fire for effect. "Sometimes I wish he'd speak to me."

"Do you believe God chooses some groups of people over others?"

"Well, the Israelites were the chosen people of the Bible, weren't they?"

"Yes, until they renounced and murdered his son," Coldwater replied softly. "God has never forgiven them for that; they are, each of them, cursed. God has a new chosen people now." He leaned forward and bored his gaze into Jesse's eyes. "They are here, in this community, and God has chosen *me* to lead them to him."

Jesse let his eyes widen slightly and his jaw drop.

"Do you believe that is possible?" Coldwater asked.

"Yes, sir, I do."

"Do you think I am insane, Jesse?"

"No, sir; you seem very sane to me."

"People to whom God speaks are often thought to be insane. Some of them are, I suppose, but I assure you, I am not."

Coldwater suddenly sat up straight and pressed his back against his chair. "Jesse," he said, and his voice seemed to waver, "Jesse, sometimes God gives me to know about people, and he is speaking to me of you at this moment."

Jesse leaned forward. "About *me?*"

"You have had a great tragedy in your life," Coldwater intoned, closing his eyes. "You have lost those dearest to you in the most violent way."

"Yes," Jesse said, "it's true."

"There are three little girls and a lovely woman; they are with God."

"Yes," Jesse said again, allowing his voice to waver. I'll match you con for con, he thought.

"They are happy, but they are worried about you," Coldwater said. "They want you to have a new life."

"Can you see them?" Jesse asked.

"God can see them. God has chosen this moment to heal your wound, to make you whole again."

"Oh, God," Jesse moaned. He was actually enjoying this. The guy was some salesman, and this was some pitch.

Coldwater opened his eyes and looked at Jesse, then closed them again and his brow furrowed. "There is someone else," he said.

"Sir?"

"Another little girl, younger than the three."

A chill ran through Jesse. What was going on here?

"She was torn from you, but she has not forgotten her love for you."

Tears sprang involuntarily to Jesse's eyes. "*Sir?*"

"She is far from here, but with kind strangers."

"Who?" Jesse demanded. "Who is she with?"

"A young couple in a sunny place."

Miami, Jesse thought, she's still in Miami. What the hell is going on here?

Coldwater opened his eyes again, then reached out, took Jesse's hand and pulled him to his knees. "Will you pray with me?"

"Oh, yes, sir!"

Coldwater pressed a palm onto the top of Jesse's head. "God, Jesse and I have heard you. He is with us now, his wound healed. Give him the strength to go forward with us!" Coldwater released Jesse and sank back into his chair. The spell seemed broken.

Jesse struggled to his feet and sat down. He grabbed his drink, took a large swig and tried to slow his breathing.

"I'm sorry if I frightened you, Jesse," Coldwater said. "I have these . . . visitations from time to time, when I am told things. Did it all make sense to you?"

"Yes, sir; I had a wife and three little girls, and they were killed in a car accident."

"What about the fourth child?"

"I don't know about that, sir; it didn't make any sense to me, unless it was really one of my girls."

"Yes, that must have been it." Coldwater stood. "Our time is up for today. Will you come and see me again?"

"I'd like that, sir," Jesse said, rising.

Coldwater took Jesse's arm and steered him toward the door. "Jesse, God has work for you to do here with us. Will you join us? Will you do His will?"

"Yes, sir; I want to be with you," Jesse said earnestly. "You just tell me what to do."

"I'll have something for you soon," Coldwater said. Then he pulled Jesse to him and embraced him in a bear hug.

Jesse had the breath crushed from him. He put his arms around Coldwater, feeling small. The muscles in the man's back were as hard as nails.

Coldwater held him at arm's length. "Goodbye, my good friend. I will see you again soon."

"Goodbye, Pastor," Jesse said, and allowed himself to be shown out of the study.

Pat Casey was waiting for him and led him to the squad car, saying nothing.

Jesse sat in the passenger seat of the car, staring out the windshield. What had happened back there? Had Coldwater, in the middle of that *spiel,* somehow tapped into his soul for that moment? Carrie still remembered him, Coldwater had said. He hoped to God the man was right. Casey silently delivered him to his truck, then said goodnight. Jesse drove home slowly, thinking of Carrie. She was never far from his mind.

CHAPTER

25

He's made you," Kip Fuller said.

"I don't think so," Jesse replied. He was in the woods behind the Wood Products plant, on his lunch hour. "I've thought about it, and I don't think so."

"He couldn't just pull something like that out of a hat, for Christ's sake. How could he possibly know about your daughter? I'm pulling you out of there."

"No, no, Kip; listen to me. It's just possible that he could have broken the Jesse Barron cover; I don't know how, but since I'm not Barron, it's possible. What's not possible is that he could figure out who I really am. There's just no way he could do that."

"You have a point," Kip admitted.

"No, I think it was something real, just for a minute there. He used what Casey had told him about Barron, and then he just . . . I don't know, he read some part of me."

"Now, that's *really* scary."

"There are people who can do that, you know,

and I suspect that Coldwater is a very intuitive guy. That's the mark of any good con man, knowing how to read his mark."

"But you think you're in now?"

"I think so. I've had a formal invitation from the man himself, and I've accepted. Let's see what happens next."

"I want to know about it if Coldwater comes up with any more stuff about your past life, do you hear me?"

"I hear you, Kip."

"I mean, sometimes it helps to have another valuation of what's going on, not to just trust your own perceptions."

"I have a feeling I told you that when you were a rookie."

Kip laughed. "You probably did."

"I've got to get back to work; I'll call you when I can."

"Don't keep me waiting," Kip said.

Jesse cut the connection, folded the phone and put it into the false bottom he had made in his lunch box. He would transfer it later to the safe under the truck for charging.

Back in his office he found Herman Muller waiting for him.

"I was looking for you, Jesse," the old man said.

"Sorry, Herman; I walked back up in the woods a ways to have my lunch."

"Jesse, I'm going to ask you to do one of those things that I don't want to do anymore."

"What's that?"

"I want you to go to New York for me next week. I've bid on a good-sized job—chipboard and plywood for a new hotel that's building next year, and the architects want to see somebody from Wood Products up close. It's the sort of job that could lead to others, but to tell you the truth, I just hate New York City. I swear, I think it's hell on earth, and it just scares me to death."

Jesse did not share Herman's feelings about the city. "I'd be glad to go, Herman," he said, trying not to sound too happy about it.

"You're sure you don't mind?"

"Not at all. What do I have to do?"

"They want to know about our plant and our production facilities—capacity, quality, reliability. I'd send one of my salesmen, but to tell you the truth, they're more comfortable talking to lumberyards than architects, and I think you'd handle yourself better."

"Well, thank you, Herman; that's high praise."

"I want you to take some pictures of our plant and equipment and write up a little history of the company and some of the jobs we've handled, like the ski resort in Park City. Do whatever you think will make up a good presentation."

"I'll get right on it, Herman."

Muller nodded and went back to his own office. Jesse leaned back in his chair and took a deep breath. New York! He hadn't been there in years. He'd take Jenny, and they'd have a good dinner or two, maybe see a show. The phone rang.

"Jesse Barron."

"Jesse, it's Pat Casey."

"Hi, Pat."

"Listen, can you stop by the station for about an hour on your way home tonight?"

"Sure, what's up?"

"I'll tell you when you get here."

"Sure. I'll see you a little after six." He hung up the phone. Maybe he was about to be let inside at last. He picked up the phone and called Jenny.

"How'd you like a weekend in New York?" he asked gleefully.

There was a shocked silence for a moment. "I don't know," she replied.

"What do you mean, you don't know? Herman's sending me on business. We'd have a terrific time."

"Can we talk about it when you get home?"

"Sure we can. Oh, I've got to make a stop on the way. I should be there around seven or seven-thirty."

"I'll make dinner for seven-thirty, then."

"Perfect; maybe I'll pick up a bottle of wine on the way."

"Sounds good."

"Bye."

"Bye."

He was disappointed in her reaction to the possibility of a New York trip; he'd thought she'd be dying to go, to get out of this little town for a change.

Jesse stopped at the liquor store and chose an extra-good bottle of California Cabernet, then he drove over to the police station.

The place was quiet, with only one officer on duty. Pat Casey met him in reception. "Hey, Jesse. Come on back here with me." Casey led him down a corridor to the rear of the station. He opened a door with a four-digit combination, and showed Jesse inside.

Jesse was careful to memorize the combination. You never knew. But something he saw in the room nearly made him forget the numbers. Sitting on a table in the center of the room was something he had not seen for a long time, and the sight of it made his blood run cold.

"Have a seat, Jesse," Casey said. He motioned to a chair next to the table, then pulled up a chair for himself. "Something we have to get out of the way, just a formality."

"Yeah?" Jesse asked, trying not to sound nervous.

"Yeah. Jack Gene wants you to take a polygraph test."

"A what?"

"A lie detector test."

CHAPTER

26

J esse sat and stared at the machine. He remembered a conversation he'd had with an FBI polygraph operator whom his unit in Miami had
borrowed from time to time. "You can't beat the
machine," the man had said. "Not if the operator's
good. An experienced man will pick up the lies every
time. There's only one way you can beat it, and that's
by believing your own lies."

"Excuse me a minute," Casey said, "I've got to get
another roll of paper for this thing."

What did the machine measure? Respiration and
pulse and something to do with skin reactions: sweat?
It was cool enough in the room, but he slipped off his
jacket and hung it on the back of his chair. How could
he handle the respiration and pulse changes? Yoga. He
didn't know much about it, but his wife, Beth, had
bought a book on the subject once, and she had read to
him about a breathing exercise that he had tried. He
could hear Casey in conversation with someone out in
the hallway.

Jesse got as comfortable as he could and began the

relaxation exercise he'd learned. He took slow, deep breaths, counting to ten as he did so, and released them to the same count. After ten of those, he began holding his breath for a count of ten before releasing. Casey continued to talk outside.

I've got to believe myself, he thought. Don't think about what will happen if I fail this test; think about Jesse Barron, *be* Jesse Barron. Nobody else exists in this body; the other guy is dead. He started as Casey reentered the room.

"Sorry, didn't mean to scare you," Casey said.

Jesse breathed less deeply, but kept the rhythm. He relaxed his toes, his arches, his calves and thighs, then his stomach muscles, arms, neck and shoulders. While the chief connected him to the apparatus he thought of his new life, of Jenny, of his coming trip to New York. He breathed and let his mind wander over his existence. He thought of Jenny in bed with him, of Carey laughing at his jokes, of dinner by candlelight with Jenny in New York.

"Okay," Casey said, "I'm going to start asking you questions, and all you have to do is answer them truthfully by saying yes or no. Got that?"

Jesse nodded.

"Say yes."

"Yes."

"Is your name Jesse?"

"Yes." Easy first question.

"Are you fifty-five years old?"

"No."

"Do you live in St. Clair, Idaho?"

"Yes."

"Are you six feet five inches tall?"

"No." He began to pick up a kind of rhythm in the questioning.

"Have you ever been convicted of a crime?"

Jesse felt his pulse lurch. "Yes."

"Do you know how to drive a car?"

"Yes." He slowed his breathing, tried to calm down.

"Are you a police officer?"

"No." God's truth.

"Do you work at St. Clair Wood Products?"

"Yes." Jenny was nuzzling his ear.

"Did anyone send you to St. Clair?"

"No."

"Do you know Jack Gene Coldwater?"

"Yes."

"Do you drive a Cadillac?"

"No."

"Had you ever heard of Jack Gene Coldwater before coming to St. Clair?"

"No."

"Are you a Christian?"

"Yes." Sort of.

"Do you believe everything you read in the Bible?"

"No."

"Do you live in the home of Jennifer Weatherby?"

"Yes."

"Do you sleep with Jennifer Weatherby?"

He hesitated.

"Answer all questions immediately. Do you sleep with Jennifer Weatherby?"

"Yes." He felt Jenny's body next to his.

"Do you like your work?"

"Yes." Breathe slowly.

"Have you ever lied to me?"

"No."

"Were you born in North Georgia?"

"Yes."

"Did you grow up in North Georgia?"

"Yes."

"Have you ever been married?"

"Yes."

"Do you like spaghetti and meatballs?"

"No." Another lie. Maybe a few lies to inconsequential questions would help scramble the results.

"Have you ever had any children?"

"Yes."

"Do you go to church regularly?"

"No."

"Is your wife living?"

"No."

"Have you ever fired a gun?"

"Yes."

"Have you ever had any weapons training?"

"Yes."

"Are your children living?"

Jesse managed something like a wince. "No."

"Did you love your wife?"

"Yes."

"Do you prefer the company of white people to the company of blacks?"

Be Jesse Barron! "Yes."

"Do you believe white people are superior to other races?"

"Yes."

"Have you ever had sex with a black woman?"

"No."

"Do you like your steak cooked rare?"

"No."

"Have you ever had sex with a man?"

"No."

"Have you ever been in prison?"

"Yes."

"Do you like apple pie?"

"Yes."

"Have you ever been addicted to alcohol or drugs?"

"No."

"Are you an escaped convict?"

"No."

"Do you believe you could kill in defense of your own life?"

"Yes."

"Do you like ice cream?"

"Yes."

"Have you ever killed another person?"

"No."

"Have you ever stolen anything?"

"Yes."

"Do you sometimes drive too fast?"

"Yes."

"Are you opposed to abortion?"

"Yes."

"Do you believe in God?"

"Yes."

"Are you a police officer working undercover?"

"No."

"Do you like sports?"

"Yes." This was a lie.

"Are you employed by a federal law enforcement agency?"

"No." He breathed the word.

"Have you told any lies during this examination?"

"No."

"Are you wearing socks?"

"Yes."

"Is your true name Jesse Barron?"

"Yes."

"Is your shirt red?"

"No."

"Before St. Clair, did you live in Toccoa, Georgia?"

"Yes."

"Okay, that's it," Casey said. He switched off the machine.

Jesse had tried to keep count; he had lied nine or

ten times, he thought. "How'd I do?" he asked. If he got the wrong answer, his plan was to grab the pistol Pat was wearing, walk him out of the police station, then make a run for it.

"You lied three times," Casey said.

Jesse tried not to look relieved.

"No, I didn't."

"You never stole anything," Casey said, looking at the tape.

"I stole five dollars when I was treasurer of the agriculture club in high school."

"You said yes to being a Christian."

"Well, if I could have, I'd have said I was sort of a Christian."

"The other one is funny. I got a reaction when you said no to being an escaped convict."

Jesse couldn't help but laugh.

"You said yes to having been in prison."

"Well, in jail, once, in Toccoa, when I was a kid."

"Oh. But you're not an escaped convict?"

"Nope."

"Actually, Jesse, you did better than most. What I was looking for was a pattern of lies, and that didn't show up."

Jesse could feel the sweat under his arms. "I swear, I didn't tell you a single lie."

"Well, if I were a more expert operator, I might not have called the three I did. Mostly, Jesse, I wanted to know if you are a cop."

Jesse tried looking amazed. "Why on earth would you think I'm a cop?"

Casey slapped him on the back. "Never mind, it's not important. You better get on home for dinner."

"Okay, see you later."

"Goodnight, Jesse."

Jesse walked out of the station into the cool night air, breathing deeply. He got into his truck and started for home, nearly limp with relief. Then he had a disturbing thought: what if Pat Casey were a better polygraph operator than he'd let on?

When Jesse had left the station, Casey called Jack Gene Coldwater.

"How'd it go?" Coldwater asked.

"There were two anomalies that might be important," Casey replied. "First, I got a reaction when I asked if he were an escaped convict, but judging from his other answers, I think that was a fluke. No ex-con would have a sheriff in his hometown vouching for him."

"And the other?"

"I think maybe he once killed somebody."

"Natural enough to lie about that," Coldwater said. "Is he who he says he is?"

"The polygraph says yes. Oh, and he admitted to sleeping with Jenny."

Coldwater laughed. "Well, at least we know he's not queer."

CHAPTER

27

Jesse stood at the kitchen counter opening the wine while Jenny put dinner on the table. He poured a little wine into a glass and tasted it.

"Where'd you learn to do that?" she asked.

"Oh, I've been to a good restaurant or two, you know."

"You have? Where?"

"Atlanta, mostly, and, of course, New York."

Her eyes widened. "You've been to New York?"

"I've been around."

"Why in the world would you have gone to New York?"

Jesse thought fast. "I went to a builder's show at the Coliseum, once. Spent nearly a week up there."

"What's it like?"

"Why don't you find out for yourself?"

She put her arms around his waist and hugged him. "I'd love to."

"You mean it?"

"I do."

"Shall we take Carey?"

"No, not if it means missing school."

"It would, I'm afraid." He wasn't afraid at all; he looked forward to having her all to himself in the big city.

"The school frowns on kids missing a day for *any* reason."

"Can she stay with a friend?"

"I'm sure she can. Come on, let's eat." She called Carey to dinner and sat down. She had cooked steaks, his favorite.

Jesse tore into his dinner.

"Can I have some wine?" Carey asked.

Jenny looked shocked. "Certainly not, young lady. Not until you're twenty-one!"

"Aw..."

"Carey, would you like to stay with Harriet Twomy for a few days next week? I'll call her mother."

"Sure, but why?"

"Jesse and I are going to New York City for a short vacation."

"Why can't I go?" the child wailed.

"You know very well you can't miss school."

"And who gave you permission to go?" Carey demanded.

Jenny reddened. "I don't need anyone's permission."

"You'll get in trouble," Carey said.

"That's enough, young lady; eat your dinner."

Jesse drove to Coeur d'Alene the following morning and bought a 35mm camera. As his purchase was being wrapped he spotted a Polaroid instant camera, and he bought that, too. On the way back to St. Clair he pulled over at a rest stop and retrieved his cellular phone from his lunchbox.

"This is Fuller."

"It's Jesse."

"How's it going, buddy?"

"More and more interesting. Pat Casey gave me a polygraph examination last night."

"Oh, holy shit!"

"Looks like I passed."

"How could you beat a polygraph?"

"A combination of a little yoga breathing, and, I suspect, Casey is either a green operator or a piss-poor one."

"Are you sure you're in the clear?"

"I'm still alive. The acid test will come next week, when I go to New York."

"New York? What are you talking about?"

"My employer is sending me to make a pitch to an architectural firm. If Coldwater lets me get out of town, then I figure he trusts me."

"How long will you be there?"

"Going Thursday, coming back Monday."

"Where are you staying?"

"I haven't figured that out yet."

"You're staying at the Roosevelt, at Madison and Forty-seventh Street."

"Why?"

"I think it would be good for you and I to meet and have a talk."

"Okay, sure."

"Call the hotel direct and make the reservation. I'll take care of the rest."

"How will I contact you?"

"I'll contact you."

Jesse put the phone away and drove back to St. Clair. He had one errand to run for Jenny; he parked in front of the courthouse and went to the county registrar's office.

"Can I help you?" a woman asked.

"Yes, Mrs. Jenny Weatherby would like a copy of her daughter's birth certificate," he said. "It's for school; apparently the principal's office says her records are incomplete. Her name is Carey Weatherby."

"It'll just be a minute," the woman said.

He watched as she went to a long row of filing cabinets and looked for the certificate. She plucked it from the file, went to a copying machine and made the copy, then returned the original to the file cabinet. Then she took a rubber stamp from a desk drawer, stamped the certificate and signed it. "There you are," she said, handing him the paper. "All certified. That'll be two dollars."

He paid her and left. As he was folding the certificate he glanced at it and saw something that mystified him. In the block for the mother's name, Jenny's name appeared, but in the block for the father's name there was only a blank space. He put the certificate in his pocket and thought no more about it. He did, however, think about what he had just seen in the courthouse, and he remembered it.

CHAPTER

28

Jesse spent an entire day photographing the Wood Products plant, machinery and employees for his presentation and working on the text, and when the factory closed for the day he stayed on, explaining to Herman Muller that he wanted shots of the machinery bays with no people in them.

When he was sure that he was alone in the factory, he walked down to the machine shop and turned on the lights. He went to the storeroom and found a package of replacement hacksaw blades and moved to a small electric grinder. He took a pair of heavy shears, cut a blade into several smaller pieces, then donned safety glasses, switched on the grinder and began work on the thin ribbons of steel. First, he ground off the sawteeth, then he began grinding each strip of metal into a particular shape. An hour later he had what he wanted. He closed up and went home.

After dinner, Jesse produced his new Polaroid camera and insisted on photographing both Jenny and

Carey repeatedly, then asked Jenny to photograph him. He wanted the pictures for his wallet, he told them.

Some time after 2 A.M. Jesse woke and gingerly got out of bed. Jenny always slept deeply, and she never stirred. He dressed in his dark dress trousers and a dark blue shirt; downstairs he slipped into a coat and went to the garage. There was a bit of a slope, and he allowed the truck to coast down to the street before starting it. He drove into town and parked the truck in an alley near the courthouse, then walked the rest of the way.

He skirted the square stone building until he saw what he was looking for—a door on the side of the building that housed the county registrar's office. After looking carefully around the street to be sure it was still deserted, he went to the door and took out his wallet. He knelt and, using a small flashlight, examined the lock. It was an ordinary Yale deadbolt and, from the strips of steel he had machined earlier in the day, he selected two picks. He was rusty, but he still had the door open in under two minutes. He closed it softly behind him and found himself in a narrow rear hallway. He listened carefully. The building was made of stone and marble and any sound would echo through the halls. Hearing nothing, he slipped off his shoes and padded around the building, making sure there was no night watchman.

When he was sure he was alone in the building, he went to the registrar's office and began work on the lock. This one was unfamiliar and very frustrating. He tried three sets of picks before he got the hang of it. Finally, the door swung open, and he had the place to himself. His eyes had become accustomed to the darkness, and he could see quite well without resorting to the flashlight. There, on the opposite wall, was a lucky break. He walked across the large room and examined the steel cabinet closely; the lock was nothing more than a common desk lock, and he had it open in seconds. Arrayed before him on hooks, clearly labeled, were the keys to every filing cabinet, desk and cupboard in the office.

He started with the filing cabinets. Switching on his little flashlight, he opened drawers until he had found both Jenny's and Carey's birth certificates. He took them to the desk of the clerk who had helped him the day before, then worked on the desk lock. Soon he had the certification stamp she had used on the copy of Carey's certificate.

Now he needed something else, and rifling the clerk's desk didn't produce it. He began a systematic search and finally found what he was looking for in a bank of pigeonholes that held office stationery. He went back to the desk and switched on the electric typewriter that sat on a wing.

He needed names, names that were new, but close enough to their real ones. He rolled the first form into the machine and, under the space for a name, typed Jeffrey Warren. He invented names for parents close to those of his own, chose a birth date a year later and shortly he had a brand new birth certificate.

Then, working from the original forms, he created new certificates for Jenny and Carey. He carefully forged the necessary signatures of the doctor and recording clerk, then went to the copying machine and made two copies of each certificate. He then applied the certification stamp and forged the illegible signature of the clerk. All that remained was to file the new certificates in the proper place in the filing drawers, and it was as if these three brand new people had always existed.

He was about to leave, when he had another thought. He located the files for marriage certificates, found the proper form, made copies and filed the new certificate in the proper place. No one would ever suspect.

He put everything back in its place, locked the key cabinet, the desk and the door and he was about to leave the building when he had an inspiration. Directly across the hall was a door painted with the legend, "Idaho State Police, Licensing Division."

He got the door open and entered the room. There were benches lined up for the waiting public and there, on the high desktop separating the public from the workers, was the machine, the one that photographed, laminated and recorded driver's licenses.

He sat on the stool behind the machine and tried to figure it out. There weren't a lot of controls, but none of them made sense. This was too good an opportunity to pass up, though, and he began a search. Shortly he had found the instructions for the machine, nicely printed on a single sheet of paper and laminated. After that, it was simple. He typed out the license application, stood himself before the machine, took his own picture, flinching at the flash, then waited while the thing hummed and worked and produced a laminated Idaho driver's license in the name of Jeffrey Warren. He put everything back in its place, and, as a final touch, added his completed application to a stack waiting to be entered into the state's computer network. Tomorrow some clerk would do his job, and Jeffrey Warren would exist with the state, as well as with the county.

He had just let himself out and locked the door behind him, when there was the loud bang of a door closing.

Jesse grabbed his shoes and ran soundlessly down the hallway. At the end he stopped and saw the beam of a flashlight from around the corner. He took refuge behind the nearest door—the ladies' room, as luck had it. He ran the length of the room and ducked into the last stall, stood on the toilet seat, crouched and waited, breathing deeply to get his pulse and respiration down. He could hear the footsteps of the searcher, hear each door as it opened and closed. When the ladies' room door opened, Jesse stopped breathing.

"All right, you son of a bitch," a male voice said. "You come out of here right now, because if I have to look in those stalls I'm going to shoot whatever I see."

Jesse squatted on the toilet seat, put his hands on the walls to either side and got ready to spring. He'd have to overpower the guy and hope he didn't get shot while doing it.

"Last chance," the man said, and took a step, his shoe leather ringing on the marble floor.

Then the floor under Jesse was illuminated as a strong flashlight searched for feet in the stalls.

"Shit," the man said. There were more steps, and the door closed behind him.

Jesse tried to make himself comfortable; he was not going to move until his muscles forced him to, and he figured he could last a while. He waited and listened as the cop radioed in; the voice was faint from the hall, but he could make out the words.

"It's Prentice," the cop said. "Call somebody who has the keys to the courthouse and get him over here. I found a side door unlocked."

There was a rasp and an unintelligible squawk as the reply came.

"I thought I saw a flash of light from inside the building, so I investigated," the cop said back. "But everything seems okay, except the open door. I'll stick around until somebody comes and locks it. Ten-four."

His footsteps echoed down the hallway, and Jesse heard the side door open and close. Painfully, he straightened up, then sat down on the toilet seat to wait. Half an hour passed before somebody showed up with the keys and locked the door. Jesse waited another fifteen minutes before letting himself out of the building and heading for the truck.

The first light of dawn was in the sky before he crept back into bed with Jenny.

CHAPTER

29

As Jesse was loading Jenny's car for the trip to the Spokane airport, Kurt Ruger drove up and got out, carrying a briefcase.

"You're up early, Kurt," Jesse said. It was not daylight yet.

"Jack Gene sent me, Jesse," Ruger said. "He'd appreciate it if you'd do him a favor while you're in New York."

Jesse wasn't sure how Coldwater could know that he was going to New York, but he smiled. "Sure, glad to."

Ruger handed him the briefcase. "He'd like you to deliver this to an address in midtown Manhattan at eleven o'clock tomorrow morning." He handed Jesse a card with the address typed on it. 666 Fifth Avenue, suite 7019, and a name, Mr. Enzberg.

"I can do that; my appointment isn't until tomorrow afternoon."

"Jesse, the contents are very important; you're not to let the case out of your sight, not even to put it in the overhead luggage rack on the airplane. Keep your hands on it at all times. When you arrive in New York tonight, put it in the hotel safe and get a receipt."

"All right, I'll do as you say."

Ruger nodded, got into his car and drove away. Jesse looked at the briefcase. It was black aluminum, the sort of thing that might usually hold cameras, and there were two combination locks, one for each clasp. He hefted the case; heavy, something solid inside.

The airplane set down at La Guardia in a light rain, and by the time it had taxied to the ramp Jesse was practically having to hold Jenny in her seat.

"I'm sorry," she said, trying to be patient, "but I've never been this excited before."

"La Guardia is the least exciting part of this trip, believe me," Jesse said, laughing.

They got their luggage and a cab, and as they approached the Midtown Tunnel, the lights of the skyscrapers swam out of the fog.

"I've never seen anything so beautiful," Jenny sighed.

"Not even the mountains of Idaho?"

"I never want to go back. I want to live in one of those buildings."

They were at the hotel by six and, as they approached registration, Jesse saw Kip Fuller. He was behind the front desk, pretending to use a computer.

"My name is Barron; I have a reservation," he said to Kip.

"Yes, Mr. Barron; just a moment." Kip tapped a few computer keys. "Here we are; a room with a view. How did you wish to pay?"

Jesse handed him his credit card, and Kip produced two room keys. "Bellman!" he snapped, and a uniformed man appeared at Jesse's elbow. "Please take Mr. and Mrs. Barron up to their room." He handed the keys to the man.

"Oh, by the way," Jesse said, "I'd like to put this case in your safe." He waited for the receipt.

As they made their way to the elevator Jenny tugged at Jesse's sleeve. "They must know you here, the way they're treating you," she said.

Jesse laughed all the way up.

The room was large and sported views of both the Chrysler and Empire State buildings. Jesse tipped the bellman generously and began unpacking, while Jenny inspected everything in the room and read all the information in the hotel's information packet.

"You can have dinner in your room!" she exclaimed.

"We're not going to do that," he said. "I'm taking you someplace fancy."

"Where, where?"

"A place called Café des Artistes." He had booked the table a week before. The phone rang, and Jesse picked it up.

"Out your door and to the left," Kip said. "First door; it'll be ajar." He hung up.

"I'll be right down," Jesse said into the dead telephone.

"Where are you going?"

"They didn't get a proper imprint of my credit card, so I have to go back to the front desk for a minute. Why don't you get into a tub? Dinner's at eight."

Jenny began removing clothes from her luggage.

Jesse left the room and went next door. He pushed open the door and closed it behind him. Kip Fuller stood up, smiling, and offered Jesse his hand.

"Jesus, it's good to see you," he exclaimed, clapping Jesse on the back.

Jesse smiled back. "You too, Kip."

Kip turned and indicated another man. "This is Ted Manners, from our office. Ted, this is Jesse Barron."

Jesse noted that Kip had used his cover name.

"Ted, will you excuse us?" Kip said.

Manners nodded and left the room.

"I wanted him to get a good look at you," Kip said. "He's going to be following you while you're here."

"Following me?"

"Or maybe I should say, following the man who's following you."

Jesse blinked. "Somebody followed me here?"

"About thirty-five, five-nine, a hundred and sixty pounds, dark hair, gray suit and a gray felt hat. He was on your flight."

"I guess they're not taking any chances," Jesse said.

"What's in the briefcase you checked downstairs?"

"I don't know, but I suspect that's why I'm being followed. I guess they want to see if I'll do as I'm told."

"It was pretty heavy," Kip said. "Felt like a lot of money, to me."

"Why would they send me to New York with a lot of money?"

"Where are you supposed to take it?"

Jesse produced the card, and Kip made a note of the address. "We'll check it out. Listen, I want you to make time for a serious debriefing while you're here. When's good?"

Jesse shook his head. "Not if I'm being followed. I'm not taking any chances on getting busted, not at this stage of the game. Anyway, you know everything that's happened so far."

"I didn't know about the woman," Kip said. "She's lovely."

"My landlady. Well, that's how it started out, anyway. Things developed."

"I see. What will you be doing while you're here?"

"I've got an appointment at an architect's office at Fifty- Seventh and Fifth tomorrow at two. There's a chance I could have to see them again on Monday. I'm to drop off the briefcase at eleven tomorrow morning."

Kip nodded. "What will you do with the rest of your time?"

"Show Jenny the town, I guess, maybe do some Christmas shopping."

"Your tail will probably drop off after you've delivered the briefcase. If that happens, I'll pull Manners off, too."

"Thanks, I'd appreciate that. I don't want to spend the weekend looking over my shoulder."

"We'll have a look at the briefcase overnight."

"Be very careful, Kip; I don't want any marks or scratches on the thing. It might even be alarmed or have a dye bomb inside."

"We'll X-ray it; don't worry, I'll handle it with kid gloves."

Jesse glanced at his watch. "I've got to get back; anything else?"

Kip shook his head. "Nothing. If you need to reach me, there'll always be somebody in this room. Just ask the operator to ring extension two-zero-four-six."

Jesse looked at Kip narrowly. "Is my room bugged?"

"Behind the mirror over the chest of drawers."

"Is there a two-way mirror?"

"Nope. We'll respect your privacy."

"Thanks." He started for the door.

"Let me take a look first." Kip opened the door and looked up and down the hall. "Okay, go."

Jesse slipped out of the room and let himself in next door. He could hear the bath water running.

"Jesse?" she called.

"It's me."

"I'm going to smell great tonight," she said. "There's wonderful bath oil here."

"You always smell great. We have to leave here in an hour."

"I'll be ready."

Jesse stretched out on the bed and looked at the ceiling. With two men following him it was going to be a lot harder to accomplish what he had planned for New York City.

They had barely sat down at the restaurant when Jenny looked around and said, "There are naked ladies on the wall here."

"I know. They were done by a famous illustrator of the thirties named Howard Chandler Christy."

"How do you know that? How do you know this place come to that?"

"On my trip to the convention, a supplier brought me here and told me all about it. Do the naked ladies make you uncomfortable?"

She looked around the room. "They have different faces, but they all seem to have the same body."

"He must have had a favorite model," Jesse said, laughing.

"They don't make me uncomfortable, exactly," she said. "They make me want to see you naked."

"Order some dinner," he said, "and I'll see what I can do."

They swept back into the hotel room, full of good food and wine, stripping off clothes as they went.

"Just a minute," she said, "I've got to go to the bathroom."

Jesse made sure she was gone before he lifted the corner of the mirror, located the hidden microphone and held it to his lips. "Fuck you, Kip," he said, "and the horse you rode in on."

He found a pair of nail scissors, snipped off the microphone and dropped it behind the chest of drawers.

Jenny came running to him.

CHAPTER

30

Jesse left the hotel at eight o'clock the following morning, the briefcase in his hand, and walked uptown on Madison Avenue. Jenny had still been in the tub when he'd left, and she had a morning of sightseeing planned. The street was full of other men and women, most carrying briefcases, hurrying to their jobs, and he felt anonymous among them, until he caught sight of his tail in a shop window.

He had to be somewhere at nine; that gave him an hour to lose both his followers. He walked up to Fifty-Seventh and Madison, cut over to Fifth Avenue and headed for the park. He walked as far as the zoo, then exited the park and headed down Fifth at a leisurely pace, doing a lot of window shopping and making a point of not looking at his watch, taking in the available clocks on the street and in the shops to keep his schedule.

He made Rockefeller Center by a quarter to nine, and he stood for a moment and looked down into the ice rink. Then, still playing the tourist, he walked into 30 Rockefeller Plaza and found the nonstop elevator to the roof. On reaching the top he immediately got onto a down elevator. Back in the lobby he walked quickly to Fifth Avenue and north a block, skirting behind the statue of Atlas and into the building. A quick glance at the directory gave him the floor for the United States State Department. He walked up and down the lobby twice to make sure he had shaken his tail before taking the elevator.

His timing was good; the doors were just being unlocked and a line of a dozen people was being let in. He waited a few minutes for a vacant window, set the briefcase between his legs and pulled a thick envelope from his inside pocket. "I'd like to apply for passports for my family and myself," he said, removing the documents and handing them to the woman behind the counter. "We're flying to London tomorrow, and I understand a one-day service is available here."

"That's correct," the woman said, looking through the papers. "Let's see, you have three birth certificates and a marriage certificate?"

"That's right," he replied. "Here are the photographs of my wife and daughter. Are they all right? We took them ourselves."

"They meet the specifications," she said, handing him a set of forms. "Please fill out these applications; you can sign for your wife and daughter."

Jesse sat down on a bench and quickly filled out the forms, inventing what information he didn't have. He returned to the window.

"These seem to be complete," she said. "There's a fifty-five dollar charge for each passport, plus twenty-five dollars each for the one-day service, a total of two hundred and forty dollars."

Jesse paid her in cash.

"And I'll need to see some form of identification," the woman said.

He produced his brand new Idaho license in the name of Jeffrey Warren.

"Thank you, Mr. Warren; you can pick up your passports after three o'clock."

Jesse thanked the woman and left. They would certainly check with the county seat on the authenticity of the birth certificates, but that would not be a problem, since the originals were in the county registrar's files.

He had been in the office about half an hour. He went back downstairs and resumed his stroll downtown. At Forty-Eighth Street he spotted a very worried young man in a gray suit and hat and looked away before he was seen. A pity, he thought; he would have liked to see the expression on the man's face.

He walked downtown to Forty-Second Street, crossed to the east side of Fifth and strolled back uptown. He reached Sak's Fifth Avenue at Forty-Ninth Street exactly at ten o'clock, and he spent the next forty-five minutes Christmas shopping. He found a beautiful negligee for Jenny and a very pretty winter coat for Carey that he hoped was the right size, and he bought some neckties for himself. He took the neckties with him and had the gifts sent to St. Clair.

At quarter to ten he started up Fifth Avenue again toward number 666. He reached the seventieth floor one minute before the appointed time and quickly found the suite. There was only a number on the door, and although the reception room was luxuriously appointed, there was no company name visible.

"May I help you?" the woman behind the reception desk said.

"My name is Jesse Barron. May I see Mr. Enzberg, please? I believe he's expecting me."

"Just one moment, please." She picked up a phone, tapped in a number, spoke briefly in German and hung up. "He will be right with you," she said to Jesse.

Shortly a beautifully dressed man in his forties appeared. "Mr. Barron? Will you come with me, please?"

Jesse followed the man to a small, clinically furnished office, where he was asked to wait. "May I have the case, please?"

Jesse handed it over.

"I will return shortly," Enzberg said. He left the room. Ten minutes later, he returned and handed the briefcase to Jesse. "A receipt is inside," he said.

"Thank you, Mr. Enzberg," Jesse said, and left. He was followed into the elevator by the young man in the gray suit.

"I'm from Pat Casey," he said.

"Oh?"

"You may give me the briefcase now."

"I wasn't given any such instruction," Jesse said.

"You have your instructions now."

The elevator reached the ground floor. "Come with me," Jesse said to the man. He walked to a bank of public telephones and telephoned Pat Casey. "Hi, Pat," he said. "I've made the delivery Kurt Ruger asked me to, and now there's a guy who says he's from you and wants the briefcase."

"It's okay, Jesse," Casey said. "Give it to him, and thanks for your help. Have a good time in New York."

Jesse handed over the briefcase. "There you are," he said, "and have a nice day."

The man took the case and left the building.

Jesse walked slowly back down Fifth Avenue, thinking. He'd had occasion in Miami to see large sums of cash displayed from time to time—once an even ten million dollars in hundred dollar bills. He thought about the bulk that had represented and he figured that the briefcase had held two million. He got a cab back to the Roosevelt, picked up his presentation materials from his room, put on one of his new neckties then knocked on the door of the next room. Kip opened the door.

"Everything go smoothly?"

"No problem."

"Manners lost you for half an hour; where were you?"

"Doing some sightseeing. Couldn't he keep up?"

"No, and neither could your other tail."

"Their problem, not mine."

"We X-rayed the briefcase last night, but no joy. The technician reckoned it was lined in lead foil. However, the office you delivered it to is the New York branch of a small, very private Swiss bank."

"I reckon it was two million," Jesse said, explaining his reasoning. "My tail approached me in the elevator and asked for the case. Enzberg said there was a receipt inside."

"Very interesting," Kip said. "We now know Coldwater is not short of a few bucks, not if he's sending millions outside the country."

"I've got a theory about the source," Jesse said. "Mind you, it's only a guess."

"Tell me."

"St. Clair is the hometown of one Melvin Schooner; ring a bell?"

"The software billionaire?"

"One and the same. I spotted him in the local drugstore."

"What makes you think he's funding Coldwater?"

"Like I said, I'm only guessing, but one of the richest men in the country has a St. Clair connection."

"You could have something there," Kip said.

"Now don't put the IRS on him or anything; let's not muddy the waters."

"Right. Do what you can to develop your theory."

"If I've learned anything on this assignment, it's not to develop anything, but to let them do the developing. So far, they can't say that I've so much as asked an untoward question, and I'm going to keep it that way."

"Do it your way."

Jesse looked at his watch. "I've got a lunch date with Jenny at the skating rink at Rockefeller Center, and my business appointment is at two. I'd better get going."

"Okay, looks like we're all finished here. I'll pack up and go; you and your lady have a good weekend. And you take care of yourself, Jess."

They shook hands, and Jesse left. He walked to Rockefeller Center and found Jenny gazing up at the huge Christmas tree.

"Isn't it the most spectacular thing you've ever seen?" she asked.

"It certainly is. You hungry?"

"Starved."

They found a table at the skating rink restaurant, and Jesse heard the story of her morning. He kept his appointment at two, and left with assurances that orders for chipboard and plywood would be placed almost immediately.

Back at Rockefeller Center, he made sure he wasn't still being followed, then went back to the State Department office. He walked back down Fifth Avenue toward his hotel, the new passports in his pocket, regretting that he couldn't have taken the two million dollars and Jenny on the next plane to South America. At least, now, he had an out that included the two people in the world who were most important to him.

As that thought came to him he stopped dead in his tracks. A woman and a little girl were just turning into a shop. He watched them through the window for a moment and convinced himself that the child was not his own Carrie; she was too tall and her hair was too long. The woman looked oddly familiar, though. He walked back to the hotel, remembering that there was a third person, somewhere, who was terribly important to him, and that his chances of ever seeing her again were just about nil.

CHAPTER

31

Pat Casey sat in Kurt Ruger's office at the bank and watched the young man on the sofa. He had trained the man himself, and he felt proud.

"The two subjects made the plane on schedule," the young man, whose name was Ken Willis, said. "At La Guardia they got their luggage and took a cab to the Hotel Roosevelt and checked in. Barron put the briefcase in the hotel safe, just as you said he would. He and the woman stayed in their room until dinnertime, then left the hotel and went to a restaurant on West Sixty-Seventh Street. They were back at the hotel and in their room by eleven o'clock."

"Tell me about the next day," Ruger said.

"Barron was earlier than I'd expected," Willis said, glancing at a notebook. "He picked up the briefcase at the front desk at eight o'clock and walked uptown. He seemed to be on a sort of sightseeing trip."

"What sort of a sightseeing trip?" Casey asked.

"He walked uptown to Central Park and through the zoo, then he started down Fifth Avenue. At Rockefeller Center he watched the skaters for a couple of minutes, then he went into the NBC building and took the elevator to the roof."

"Good place for a meet," Ruger said. "Did he speak to anybody?"

"No, sir."

"Did he bump into anybody, even look at anybody?"

"No, sir; he seemed preoccupied with sightseeing."

"Then what?"

"He did some more walking; went into Sak's and bought some things, apparently for the woman and a little girl, also some neckties. Then he walked up Fifth to number 666 and arrived at the office exactly on time. I waited in the hallway, and when he came out I asked him for the briefcase. He insisted on calling the chief before he'd give it to me."

"From the time Barron picked up the briefcase at eight o'clock until he turned it over to you, was he ever out of your sight? Even for a few seconds?"

"No, sir," Willis lied solemnly.

"Did you follow him anymore after that?"

"No, sir; I went straight to the airport, as I was instructed to do."

Casey spoke up. "I only wanted to be sure he delivered the case; I saw no point in any further surveillance. If he'd done something untoward, we'd have heard about it."

Ruger nodded. "Let me have the briefcase," he said to Willis.

The young man placed the aluminum case on the desk.

Ruger worked the two combination locks, opened the case and removed two sheets of papers. "The receipt is in order," he said, then he examined the other sheet. "Enzberg says that Barron behaved correctly and expressed no curiosity about the transaction." He looked at Casey. "Pat, do you have any other questions for Ken?"

"Nope," Casey replied.

"That'll be all, Ken," Ruger said. "You did a good job."

"Thank you, sir," Willis said, and left the office.

"Are you pleased, Pat?" Ruger asked.

"I certainly am," Casey replied. "He did as he was asked to do, and I'm particularly pleased that he wouldn't give Willis the briefcase until he'd called me."

"Yes, I agree that was kind of a bonus. Shows he's both a thinker and that he's of a cautious nature."

"I think Jesse Barron is quality material," Casey said.

"What is Jack Gene's take on him?"

"You know Jack Gene; he relies more on intuition than judgment."

"And what did his intuition tell him?"

"That Jesse is covering up something."

Ruger chuckled. "Who isn't? Did you pick up anything like that on the polygraph?"

"Not really."

"What does that mean?"

"Well, I got the impression that he lied about a couple of things there was no need to lie about. He could have been planting a lie or two to cover a real lie."

Ruger frowned. "If he actually did that, then we have something to worry about."

"I know. Nobody of Jesse's background—his stated background—is going to know anything about defeating a polygraph."

"Pat, if you were Jesse and you were a fed, how would you have played the New York delivery?"

"I'd have tried to find out what was in the briefcase," Casey replied. "But there's no indication that he tried, and there's no indication that he even contacted anybody before he delivered the case."

"But if you were a cop trying to gain our confidence, might you just do as you were told?"

Casey shook his head. "Maybe, but I think the briefcase would be too much of a temptation."

Ruger took a magnifying glass from a desk drawer and began examining the case closely. Casey joined him, switching on the desk lamp. "You see any sign of attempted entry?"

"Nope, not a thing."

"Could they have X-rayed it?"

"The lead foil lining would have obscured the contents, and the combination has to be reset after the case has been opened twice. If they'd cracked it, you wouldn't have been able to open it with the same combination."

"What do you think our recommendation to Jack Gene should be?"

"Well, Jesse has had as much or more scrutiny as anybody else who's joined us, and he's passed with flying colors so far. Still, as long as Jack Gene has doubts, I don't think we want to go the whole hog."

"I agree. What should we do then?"

"I've already done it." He explained his action to Ruger. "All we have to do is wait."

CHAPTER

32

Jesse had been back from New York a week when Pat Casey called and invited him to do some shooting on a Saturday morning. Jesse wasn't sure what Casey meant by shooting, but he accepted.

Casey picked him up mid-morning and drove toward the mountain. They passed the church and started to climb and, near the top of the mountain, shortly after passing Coldwater's house, they turned right onto a dirt road. They emerged from the trees into a clearing that had, apparently, been scraped into the side of the mountain by a bulldozer. To Jesse's left, some one hundred feet away, was the exposed side of the mountain, with many pockmarks and a rail system for transporting targets to and fro. They got out of the squad car, and Casey went to the trunk.

"You done much shooting in your time?" Casey asked.

"A good bit."

"What with?"

"I've owned a twelve-gauge shotgun for birds and a thirty-ought-six for deer."

"Handguns?"

"Somebody gave me a World War Two–vintage forty-five automatic once. I could never hit anything with it."

Casey was rummaging in the trunk. "A formidable weapon at close range, but a pig otherwise. The newer stuff is a lot easier to handle. Give me a hand, will you? Grab that ammunition box." Casey walked away from the car with a cased rifle under his arm and a canvas hold-all in the other hand.

Jesse picked up the ammunition box, and it was a lot heavier than he'd expected. As he closed the trunk lid a Mercedes sedan drove into the clearing, and Jack Gene Coldwater got out.

"Good morning, Pastor," Jesse said.

"Good morning, Jesse; glad you could join us."

"I didn't know you'd be here."

"Shooting is a hobby of mine." Coldwater took a large bag that looked as though it might hold skis from the backseat of his car.

Casey removed an assault rifle from his gun case. "Come over here, Jesse, and try this."

Jesse accepted the weapon and looked it over as if he'd never seen one.

"It's an AR-fifteen that's been converted to an M-sixteen," Casey said. "Only takes a few legally obtained parts and it becomes fully automatic." He showed Jesse how to operate the weapon, then attached a paper target to a metal rack and pulled a rope until the target was against the bank a hundred feet away. "Try a few rounds."

Jesse brought the rifle up and fired carelessly in the direction of the target. He was expert in this, but he certainly didn't want to appear so. Holes appeared in the top right-hand quadrant of the target.

"You're pulling the trigger," Casey said. "Do it more slowly and squeeze."

Jesse fired more rounds and brought them closer to the center of the target.

"Looking good," Casey said.

Coldwater stepped up to the firing line, shoved a clip into his own rifle and emptied it quickly. The bull's-eye became one large hole.

"That's very fine shooting," Jesse said.

"My country taught me well," Coldwater replied. "A little practice, and you'll do well, too."

"Try the prone position," Casey said, spreading a blanket. He helped Jesse arrange his body into the proper position.

Jesse fired more carefully prone, then moved into a sitting position, then into a kneeling position. With each clip his accuracy improved.

"I believe you're a natural, Jesse," Coldwater said. "Draw a finer bead; you're still a little high."

Jesse followed instructions, and his target no longer had a center.

"Let's try a handgun," Casey said, removing a pistol from his hold-all. "This is a Heckler and Koch nine-millimeter automatic." He instructed Jesse on loading and firing, then stepped back.

Jesse turned his shoulder toward the target and fired a round. It went high and wide of the target. "Not so good," he said. "I haven't had much experience with handguns."

"Turn your body square to the target," Casey said, "and support your shooting hand with your left. Again, squeeze off your rounds."

Jesse obeyed, and his shots began to hit the target, although erratically. He concentrated on seeming to concentrate, but he didn't allow himself to improve much.

Coldwater stepped up. "Watch me," he said. He assumed a firing position and emptied a clip into his target. Again, the bull's-eye disappeared.

"You look a lot more relaxed than I do," Jesse said.

"That's right. You were much too tense."

Jesse rolled his head around and shook his arms to loosen up. "Keep both eyes open this time," Coldwater said. "Don't draw a bead, just point where your eyes fall on the target."

Jesse squeezed off a round and clipped a corner of the bull's-eye.

"Much better. Now use up the clip, but do it slowly, one at a time."

Jesse kept firing, and put everything near, but not in, the bull's-eye.

"A little off, but a nice grouping," Casey said, taking Jesse's pistol and reloading it.

"If your target had been a man, he'd be very dead," Coldwater said. He shoved a new clip into the pistol and handed it to Jesse.

"That's what you're going to be, Jack Gene," a strange voice said. "Very dead."

Jesse was already in the firing position, and he swiveled his head to the left to see what was going on. Phil Partain, his face very red, stood ten yards beyond Coldwater, a heavy revolver in his hand. It was pointed at the pastor's middle.

"I've had enough," Partain said. "You won't give me any responsibility; you give me shit work to do, and there's no respect for me in this crowd." He thumbed the hammer back.

Jesse realized he was the only other person with a firearm. Without moving his feet, he turned his upper body toward Partain and put a round into the man's right shoulder. Partain's weapon fired wild, but he held onto it; he spun around and fell face-down, the pistol still in his hand. He began struggling to get up.

Coldwater reached out and took Jesse's pistol. He walked the few paces to where Partain lay and stepped on his gun hand. "Well, Phil, you've made a big mistake, haven't you?"

"Please, Jack Gene," Partain squealed, "don't hurt me. I'll do good, I'll do right by you. I'll do whatever you want."

"I want you to die, Phil," Coldwater said, then fired one round into the back of the man's head. Partain convulsed, then lay still.

"Jesus," Jesse said. He had shot to wound, but Coldwater had simply executed the man.

"That was a nice shot, Jesse," Coldwater said calmly, turning away from Partain's corpse. "Where were you aiming?"

"At his bellybutton, I think," Jesse replied. "I hardly thought about it, I just fired."

"You were high and to the left, but of course, you weren't in position, and you didn't have much time. I thank you." He clapped Jesse on the back.

"Is he dead?" Jesse asked.

Casey walked over to the body and looked at it. "You bet he is." He bent over, picked up Partain's pistol and wiped the dirt from it. "It's just as well; Phil was at the end of his usefulness."

"Well, I guess we don't have to call the cops," Jesse said.

Coldwater laughed aloud. "I guess not. Pat, get rid of that," he said, nodding at Partain's body.

"Toss me that blanket, Jesse," Casey said.

Jesse picked up the blanket he'd been firing from and took it to Casey.

"Open the trunk, there, will you?"

Jesse opened the trunk, then watched as Casey rolled Partain's body into the blanket.

"Give me a hand?"

He helped Casey lift the corpse into the trunk of Casey's car.

Casey closed the lid and turned to Jesse. "No need to mention this to anybody," he said.

"Just forget it happened," Coldwater chimed in.

"You've removed a nuisance from our midst, not to mention saving our lives, and I'm grateful to you, Jesse."

Jesse couldn't think of anything to say.

"Well, I think that's enough shooting for one morning," Coldwater said, stretching and yawning. "You fellows want some lunch?"

"Sure, Jack Gene," Casey said. "You hungry, Jesse?"

"I'm not sure," Jesse replied.

He and Casey got into Casey's car and followed Coldwater up the mountain to his house.

It was as if they had been expected; the kitchen table was set, and food prepared. Jesse sat down with the two men and had some soup, while they talked of hunting, but he could not forget that Phil Partain's dead body was outside, in the trunk of Pat Casey's car. It came home to Jesse, as never before, that if he made a mistake with these people he would be dead very quickly.

On the way home he could not get over the feeling that the incident had been orchestrated to test him and that he had passed.

CHAPTER

33

Jesse had been regularly attending Sunday morning services at the First Church, and Jack Gene Coldwater's sermons had become more and more apocalyptic. He noticed, too, that outsiders never heard these sermons, because guards, in the person of ushers, were posted at the doors and around the building. On one occasion he had seen a man using electronic debugging equipment around the pulpit before a service.

Coldwater's references were, increasingly, indicating a siege mentality, along with a strong suspicion of any stranger in town. Nobody that Jesse knew of had come to live in the town from outside since his own arrival. The plant had not employed any new people, though he was quite certain that Coldwater had had nothing to do with that—Herman Muller was far too independent to let anyone dictate any policy to him.

On the Sunday before Christmas Coldwater seemed very disturbed during his sermon, and he made repeated references to "last days" and quoted extensively from Revelations. His audience was more than rapt; they were, literally, on the edge of their seats, and Jesse tried to exhibit the same concentration.

When the service ended, Pat Casey approached him. "Jesse, Jack Gene would like you to have Sunday lunch with him." He turned to Jenny. "You and the girl go on home; I'll bring Jesse later."

Jesse turned to see if that was all right with Jenny, but she had already headed toward her car, Carey in tow. "Sure, Pat, I'd be honored," he said. He followed Casey around the corner of the building and found Coldwater waiting for them in his Mercedes.

Lunch was roast beef, Yorkshire pudding, fresh vegetables and apple pie, accompanied by a bottle of California red wine that Jesse reckoned was expensive, called Opus One. He enjoyed the food, but only the most perfunctory conversation took place, with Coldwater rambling on about the weather and Casey trying, unsuccessfully, to start a conversation about college football.

When they had finished lunch, Coldwater stood. "Jesse, you're one of us, now, and it's time you knew some things. Come with me." The three men got back into the Mercedes, and Coldwater drove to the top of the mountain.

It was the first time Jesse had been there, and he was surprised at what he saw. They passed through solid-looking gates and a maze of concrete forms that required a car to make three ninety-degree turns before entering what turned out to be a sort of compound at the mountaintop. There were a number of small buildings scattered about four or five acres of quite flat land, and several pieces of heavy construction equipment were scattered about. One very large stone building had an official air about it, like a government building. Coldwater parked in front of this building and motioned for Jesse to follow him.

Jesse got out of the car and took in the facade. It was built of rectangular slabs of cut stone and had high, narrow windows along its front and sides.

Coldwater spoke up. "What you see here is the last refuge of my people and me," he said solemnly. "The world is against us, we know that; our activities are commissioned by God himself, but the government of this country is opposed to our beliefs. Government money, raised from exorbitant taxes, is spent on abortions for our African-American and Hispanic friends." His descriptions of these groups were sarcastic. "They send agents to spy on us, to try and learn the source of our funds and our various activities. We have dealt with these people before, and, no doubt, we will again. Of course, we mean to survive, but should we have to fight we will make a stand like no one has ever seen in this country." He turned to Jesse. "You were in the construction business, weren't you?"

"Yes, sir," Jesse replied.

"Then I think you will find this structure interesting. Come inside." Coldwater led the way to the front doors and let them inside with a large key, then went to a switchbox and flipped several switches.

Jesse found himself in an entrance hall, oddly narrow and ending only a few feet away in a concrete wall. As his eyes became accustomed to the light, he put a hand on the wall next to him. It was made of long blocks of concrete, and he suddenly understood that what he had thought was an exterior of cut stone was really the ends of these blocks. He was stunned. This meant that the walls of this building consisted of an eight-foot thickness of reinforced concrete.

"Jesus Christ," he murmured.

"Indeed," Coldwater said. "I see you have grasped something of the construction already."

"I've never seen anything like it," Jesse said truthfully.

"Neither has anybody else," Coldwater replied, smiling. "Not the Maginot Line, not the Germans' defenses in Normandy, not even Hitler's bunker itself was constructed as heavily as this. There are a number of government installations, I am given to believe, that have been constructed to withstand a direct hit by a large nuclear device. Only those structures are stronger than this, but then the government would never use a nuclear bomb in a populated area of this country."

"I certainly hope not," Jesse said.

"You may count on that. Come, let me show you more." Coldwater led the way to the end of the entrance hall, then turned left. They were faced with a heavy steel door. Coldwater tapped a code into a keypad, and the door slid noisily aside. Ahead of them lay a long hallway with doors on either side. Coldwater began opening them.

On the left were rooms containing heavy weapons, not all of which Jesse recognized. There were certainly antitank weapons and some sort of recoilless rifles, and they were aimed out the narrow windows he had seen from outside.

"First line of defense," Coldwater said, leading him down the hall. They turned a corner to the right and he opened more doors, revealing huge amounts of ammunition and explosives. They descended a flight of stairs and came to what appeared to be an enormous dormitory. Rows of bunk beds disappeared into the distance; crates of food and bottled water were stacked in piles among the bunks. Coldwater showed him three large and well-equipped kitchens and two infirmaries, each of which looked like the emergency room of a large hospital. Here and there among the bunks were television sets and speakers were everywhere.

"I can communicate with any part of the structure instantly from my quarters," Coldwater said. "Come, I'll show you." He led the way downstairs to yet another floor and toward the rear of the building. Double doors opened into an extensive suite of rooms, filled with computers, fax machines, telephones and every manner of office equipment. Finally, Coldwater showed him to another set of steel doors, behind which lay another suite. "I can live and work here for years, if necessary," he said, waving an arm around a large living room lined with books and showing Jesse an apartment with every comfort.

"It's breathtaking," Jesse said.

"Questions?" Coldwater asked.

"How is it ventilated?"

"There are three discrete ventilation systems, each of which is more than enough to put fresh, filtered air anywhere in the structure."

"Electric power?"

"Again, three systems: first, we have hydroelectric power from a small plant down the mountain, which has its own extensive defenses; second, we have two twenty-five-thousand gallon tanks of gasoline stored far underground to operate generators; third, we have an extensive solar collector system that can supply eighty percent of our needs all by itself. It is inconceivable that even a very large force could deprive us of electricity."

"I am astounded," Jesse said, and he truly was. "What did this cost?"

"If we had built it in the conventional way, perhaps twenty-five million dollars," Coldwater said. "But by doing it with our own people over a period of years, we've done it for half that. Not including armaments, of course."

"Where on earth did the money—"

"Don't ask," Casey said, speaking for the first time.

Coldwater glanced at his wristwatch. "It's later than I thought; let's get Jesse home to his family."

Jesse followed Coldwater as he retraced his steps. He counted his paces as he went, trying to get some idea of the size of the place; he memorized everything about it he could. As the front doors opened, he blinked in the sunlight, glad to be above ground again.

Coldwater pointed at the other, much smaller buildings on the mountaintop. "Those contain other defensive systems to deal with aircraft or an invading force."

Jesse pointed in the direction of the town. "Can you see the town from here?"

"Yes, have a look."

Jesse walked a hundred yards and found himself looking over a precipice at the bottom of which lay Main Street. He also noted defensive positions dug into the rock near where he stood. He returned to Coldwater and Casey. "This is absolutely fantastic," he said with enthusiasm.

"I thought you might think so," Coldwater said.

"An army couldn't take it," Jesse gushed.

"You are quite right."

Coldwater drove them down the hill and toward the town. "I've shown you this, Jesse, because there is no faster way to impress upon you the seriousness of our purpose here."

"You've certainly done that, sir," Jesse replied, although Coldwater had said nothing of his purpose.

CHAPTER

34

Jesse thought for several days about what he had seen before making any attempt to report it. In his mind he wandered through Coldwater's redoubt, making new discoveries each time; he sat at his desk and used a calculator to translate his pacing into area; he tried to figure out what the hell it all meant, and he could not fathom it.

On Christmas Eve he and Jenny stayed up late arranging Carey's gifts for the following morning, and, long after Jenny had fallen into an exhausted sleep, he crept from the bed, went to the garage and retrieved his scrambled telephone.

"Jesus Christ, what time is it?" Kip asked blearily.

"It's very late, but it's very important, too," Jesse replied.

"Wait a minute while I go to another phone."

Jesse waited on hold until Kip was away from his no-doubt sleeping wife.

Kip picked up another extension. "All right, what's so important?" he demanded.

"I hardly know where to begin," Jesse said. "The whole thing is so unbelievable."

"What's unbelievable?" Kip was awake, now.

"Last Sunday, I think I was finally fully accepted by Coldwater," he said.

"That's certainly good news, but couldn't it wait until after the holidays?"

"I wanted you to have the holidays to think about what I'm going to tell you, Kip, because you're going to have to figure out a way to make Barker and the attorney general believe you—or rather, me."

"It sounds as though you've finally figured out what Coldwater is up to."

"No, I haven't. But I think I can safely say that, whatever it is, he expects to fail at it."

"You're not making any sense, Jesse."

"I know, and I'm sorry; but what I saw on Sunday doesn't make any sense unless Coldwater expects to go out in a blaze of glory."

"What did you see on Sunday?"

"He invited me to lunch with Casey, and when we had finished, he drove me to the top of the mountain that rises above the town."

"Did he show you all the earth and offer it to you on a platter?"

"No, I think what he offered me was the opportunity to die with him."

"Go on."

"Coldwater and his people have, over a period of years, I'm not sure how many, constructed a series of defensive positions on the sides and top of the mountain that probably isn't like anything else on earth."

"What sort of defensive positions?"

"A long list of various types of heavy weapon, well dug in and placed strategically to repel any invader—antitank weapons, probably anti-aircraft weapons—more hardware than exists anywhere in this country outside a military base."

"What else?"

"He's constructed what I can only describe as a cross between the White House Situation Room and Hitler's Berlin bunker."

"How big?"

"At a conservative estimate, something in excess of sixty thousand square feet."

"*What?*"

"And that's only the beginning of it. The exterior walls are a good eight feet of reinforced concrete."

"*Eight feet?* What's he expecting?"

"Armageddon, apparently. Let me go on. The place is on three levels, only one of which is above ground, and the thickness of the floors seems equal to the outside walls. There are weapon emplacements on the top, or ground, level on all four sides, and he has amassed an extraordinary amount of munitions to support them. There are living quarters for, I don't know, in excess of a thousand people, maybe a lot more—kitchens, infirmaries, entertainment facilities, and food and medical supplies stacked to the ceilings. On the lower level, Coldwater has a suite of offices, completely equipped, and an apartment for himself. It looks as though he could take his people inside and remain for years, and I'm not exaggerating."

"What sort of force do you think would be required to take it?" Kip asked, still sounding skeptical.

"Kip, I'm no military genius, but my guess is it couldn't be taken—at least, not without wildly unacceptable losses on the part of the attacking force."

"Jesse, there can't be any such thing as a civilian installation that can't be taken by a military force."

"It isn't a civilian installation, Kip; it's an unbelievably fortified military defensive position. It sits on top of a mountain that has about a twelve hundred foot sheer wall on the south side and very steep sides on the other three. Mountain goats might be able to make it to the top, but infantry couldn't and neither could tanks. There's only one road to the top, and that must be heavily defended. They could simply blow the road and bar all access to the top of the mountain."

"What about aircraft—helicopters with assault troops?"

"Any slow-flying aircraft would be shot to pieces before it could even land, and even if it could land, its troops would be cut up the minute they were on the ground. There's simply no cover. You could bomb the site with high explosives, but you'd probably destroy the town in the process; you'd certainly have to evacuate thousands of people. Coldwater says only a nuclear weapon would have any effect, and he's right when he says the government would never use it. I swear, you could spend a year attacking the place at a cost of thousands of casualties, and you might not even make a dent."

"He's got to have some sort of outside support," Kip said. "He couldn't exist inside a mountain without it. What about power, water and air?"

"He's got it all, and in triplicate."

"Jesse, this just doesn't make any sense."

"I know it doesn't, but it's real, I promise you that. And I'll tell you this, I don't think Coldwater would have built it if he didn't intend to use it."

There was a long silence from Kip's end of the line. "I don't know what to say," he said finally.

"Neither do I, except you'd better report this as soon as you can, and you'd better see that all knowledge of it is absolutely secure. If Coldwater had the slightest notion that the government knew about it, he'd go in there right now and zip it up behind him. And God only knows what he'd do before he went inside."

"When can you call again?"

"When do you want me to call?"

"I need to think about this before I spring it on my people. I'll do that on the first day of business of the New Year. Try to call me around that time—during office hours, if possible. They may want to pass instructions to you."

"All right, I'll try to do that."

"I'm certainly not going to sleep tonight," Kip said forlornly.

Jesse laughed. "Well, if I can't, why should you?"

"Oh, go to hell," Kip grumbled, then hung up.

Jesse put away the phone and went back to the house. As he let himself in the back door, Jenny came out of the kitchen.

"Where on earth have you been?" she demanded.

CHAPTER

35

Jesse gulped. "I went outside for a while," he said. "What are you doing up at this time of night?"

"I had to go to the bathroom, and you weren't in bed. I was frantic."

"There's no need to be upset," he said soothingly, taking her in his arms. "I just couldn't sleep, and I thought some fresh air might do me good."

She pushed away. "But what were you doing in the garage? I was at the kitchen window, and I saw you come out of there."

"I was looking for my spare key to the truck, and I thought it might be in the glove compartment."

"It's upstairs in that little tray where you keep change and things," she said.

"Oh. I don't know why that crossed my mind, it just did."

"Jesse, is something wrong? Is there something I should know about?"

He put a hand on her cheek. "No, of course not; everything's fine. I couldn't imagine things being any finer."

She stepped closer and looked up at him. "Jesse, do you love me?"

"Of course I do; haven't I told you often enough?" He put his arms around her again.

"Sure, after making love. But I want to know if you love me *all* the time."

He turned her face up. "*All* the time," he said. "At the dinner table, at the breakfast table, at work, in bed—everywhere, all the time."

She relaxed in his arms. "Oh, I'm so glad to hear that."

"I can't believe you doubted it," he said, rubbing her neck.

"Maybe it's going to be all right after all," she said, sighing.

"It's going to be all right. I'll make it all right."

"Do we have a future together?" she asked.

"I certainly hope so. That's what I'm counting on."

"Because, if we don't, I'll just make a trip to Spokane and take care of it there. I won't do it their way any more."

"Jenny, sweetheart, I don't have the faintest idea what you're talking about. What's this about Spokane?"

"Well, they've got a clinic there that hasn't been bombed yet."

He held her at arm's length and looked at her closely. "What do you—"

"I'm pregnant," she said. "I'm going to have your baby."

He pulled her to him again so that she wouldn't see his face. God in heaven, he thought, what have I gotten this girl into? "How long have you known?" he asked.

"I guessed a few days ago. This afternoon I used one of those home pregnancy tests."

"And it was positive?"

"It was positive. Jesse, is this all right? Do you want this baby?"

He tried to quell the panic inside him. What was he going to do? Here he was, undercover, his life in danger at every moment, Jack Gene Coldwater waiting for him in one direction, the federal government and its prison system waiting in the other. Was he going to get this girl killed or just banished from her community? "Yes," he heard himself saying, and he knew it was true. "Yes, I want this baby and you and Carey. I want to take care of you all forever. Let's get married tomorrow, Jenny, or as soon as it can be done in this state. Will you marry me?"

"Oh , yes, yes!" she cried, then began sobbing.

He stroked her hair, said soothing words, held her close and after a while she stopped crying. "I'm sorry I doubted you, Jesse; I should have known you would make it right; I should have trusted you."

"Trust me now and from here on," he said. "I promise I'll never let you down." It was a promise he knew he might not be able to keep, but he was god-damned well going to try.

"I will trust you," she said. "I'll never keep anything from you again."

"You should have told me when you first suspected," he said.

"That's not what I mean," she replied, and started to cry again.

The birth certificate, he thought. She wasn't married to Carey's father and the secret must have been eating at her. "Don't worry," he said. "And don't talk about it now. You're exhausted." He took her hand and led her toward the stairs. "Let's get some sleep."

Upstairs, she snuggled next to him, and he wiped away her tears. "Sleep," he said. "Tomorrow's Christmas Day, and we'll have a wonderful time with Carey. Don't think about anything else for now."

"All right," she said, moving closer.

I won't think about anything now, either, he thought. I'll sleep, and when I wake up I'll have an answer for us. He had a question of his own, too.

In the middle of the night he got out of bed, tip-toed across the room then crossed the hall and entered Jenny's bedroom. In her bathroom he silently opened the medicine chest and found what he was looking for. Only three of the birth-control pills had been removed since he had delivered the package, and that had been more than a month before.

Jesse replaced the pills in the medicine chest and padded back across the hall. He did not sleep again that Christmas Eve night; he was wide awake when Carey came to tug them from bed.

36

They went to a Christmas morning service at the church and watched a children's nativity pageant in which Carey took part. Coldwater's sermon was mercifully brief and free of his usual cant. When the service ended, Jesse and Jenny approached the pastor.

"Good morning, Jesse, Jenny," Coldwater boomed. "Merry Christmas to you."

"And to you, Pastor," Jesse said.

"I thought Carey looked very pretty as the Virgin Mary," Coldwater said.

"Thank you, Pastor," Jenny replied.

"Pastor," Jesse said, "Jenny and I have decided to be married, and we would be honored if you would perform the ceremony."

"Well, congratulations to you both," Coldwater said, beaming at them. "When would you like to hold the service?"

"We thought Sunday, just after the regular service. We'd like to keep it as small and quiet as possible," Jenny replied.

"I'll put it on my calendar. Will you have a honey-moon?"

"We hadn't gotten that far," Jesse said. "I'll have to talk to Herman Muller about getting some time off when he can spare me."

"Good, good. I'll see you on Sunday." Coldwater wheeled and walked out of the auditorium.

Jenny was unusually quiet on the way home and during Christmas dinner. It was not until Carey had gone out to show her friends her presents that Jesse spoke up.

"Jenny, what's the matter? And what were you talking about last night, about keeping things from me?"

She beckoned for him to follow her, then led him out of the house. He found an old broom and brushed the snow off a picnic table, then they sat down. It was cold and clear, and they wouldn't be comfortable for long.

"First of all," she began, "I want you to know that I wanted to get pregnant; I did it deliberately. Does that make you feel trapped?"

"No, it doesn't. I think that if you'd asked me I'd have wanted to wait for a while, but that doesn't matter now. I learned last night that you haven't been taking the birth-control pills, and I thought about it a lot, and I decided it was all right with me. I'm curious, though; why did you do it that way?"

"Because that's what Jack Gene wanted."

Jesse stopped breathing for a moment. "How's that again?"

"Pat Casey came to see me and said that Jack Gene wanted me to get pregnant. You're new in the community, and I think they wanted to test you, see how you'd react."

"And you were willing to do that for them?"

"No, not exactly; I love you, and I wanted a child; but I wasn't in a position to say no to them."

"I don't understand."

"When you went to the courthouse to get Carey's birth certificate, did you look at it?"

"Yes."

"So you saw that there was no father listed?"

"Yes, but it didn't matter to me."

"I sent you to get the certificate so you'd see that and ask me about it. I was surprised when you didn't."

"Like I said, it doesn't matter."

"Do you understand why there's no father listed?"

"I assume you weren't married."

"I was married, in a way."

"Then why wasn't the father's name on the certificate?"

"Because I can't be certain who the father was."

"I'm sorry, but this is very confusing. Why don't you just tell me the whole story?"

"All right," she said. "I'll tell you from the beginning. I was a little girl when Jack Gene Coldwater came to St. Clair, along with Pat Casey and Kurt Ruger. My parents became his followers, and they lived by his every word. When I was fifteen our house caught on fire. My bedroom was downstairs, and I managed to get out, but they didn't."

"I'm sorry, I never knew."

"I was alone in the world, and Jack Gene took me in." She paused and a tear ran down her cheek. "He married me."

Jesse gulped. "At fifteen?"

"Yes. It wasn't a real marriage in the usual sense. He performed a kind of ceremony, and I became one of them."

"One of who?"

"One of his wives."

"How many did he have?"

"I was one of five at the time. There've been more at times and less at others."

"And Jack Gene fathered Carey?"

"I think so, but I'm not sure."

Jesse was becoming very uncomfortable with this conversation, but if she was willing to talk about this, he was willing to listen. "Tell me why you're not sure."

"I didn't get pregnant at first. I tried not to. And after a while, Jack Gene began to get impatient. He wanted children, a lot of them, and he hadn't much use for those of us who couldn't give them to him. We were separated from the other women, those of us who couldn't get pregnant, or who had girls. Jack Gene wanted boys, you see."

Jesse was at a loss for words.

"So he put us aside—there were three other women—and sometimes, if he got bored with the wives who were living in his house, he would come to visit us. And he would bring Pat Casey and Kurt Ruger."

In spite of the cold Jesse began to sweat inside his coat.

"And it was during one of these . . . visits . . . that I got pregnant."

"All three of them?" Jesse asked quietly.

"All three," she said, and the tears flooded down her face.

He reached for her, but she pushed him away.

"I want to finish this," she said. "When Carey turned out to be a girl, they put me out of the inner circle, which was all right with me. I was nineteen; they put me in this house and gave me an allowance. I wanted to leave town, but Jack Gene wouldn't allow it. They made me send Carey to that awful school, and if I had tried to teach her different from what they did, she was trained to tell them. They would have taken her from me and . . . I don't know what would have happened to me. Sometimes people just disappear from this town. I had no money, no education, no skills. There were no relatives I could go to, nobody at all. The only place I existed was here, and it was at the whim of Jack Gene. He seemed to forget about me for a long time, but when you came to town I heard from Pat Casey."

"He told you to take me in?"

"Yes."

"He told you to get into my bed?"

"Yes."

Jesse laughed ruefully. "And I thought it was because I was so irresistible."

"I'm sorry; it's so difficult to tell you all this, but I felt I had to."

"Why?"

"Because I fell in love with you that first night, and I don't want us to go any farther on false pretenses. If, having heard all this, you want to forget about marriage, I'll understand."

He took her shoulders and turned her toward him. "I'm glad you told me all this," he said. "None of it matters, but I'm glad you had the courage to tell me."

"You don't mind about . . . my background?"

"I'd change it if I could, but I want you the way you are, no matter how you got to be you."

She snuggled her face into the hollow of his neck. "Oh, I love you so much, Jesse. Even more, now, I think." Then she jerked away from him. "We can't stay here after what I've told you," she said.

"I don't want to stay here, but I have to for a while. Can you stand it a little longer?"

"How much longer?"

"I'm not sure."

"I have to get Carey away from that school and these people. She's Jack Gene's child, I'm as sure of that as I can be, and he'll want to keep an eye on her. He'll use her as he used me; marry her off to one of his cronies, or just put her into a house of women, as he did with me. I'll kill him before I'll let that happen."

"I understand, and I want to take you away from here, but I can't just yet."

"Why not? What is there to keep us here?"

"Did Pat Casey ask you to pass on information about me?"

"Yes, he calls once or twice a week. I brought you out in the yard, because I thought he might have some way of listening to us in the house."

"What have you told him?"

"Whatever he wanted to know. I don't know anything about you that he would think derogatory. If I had, I wouldn't have told him."

"I'll take you away from here, Jenny, you and Carey, I promise; but I have to stay on for a while, and I can't tell you why. I don't want to put you in the position of knowing about me and having to lie to Casey."

"What I don't know, I can't tell him, is that it?"

"It's for your protection. I'd trust you with my life, but you and Carey are safer knowing only what you know now, that I love you, and I'll take care of you both."

"I guess that's good enough for me," she said.

"Good. You have to go on living your life as usual, for a while. You can't say anything at all to Carey. We have to let Coldwater do this ceremony; I'll give you a better one later. And one of these days I'll say to you, 'Let's get out of here,' and—"

"And I'll go with you the second you say it," she said, and put her arms around him.

Jesse's mind was elsewhere. He was having fantasies of castrating Jack Gene Coldwater.

CHAPTER

37

They were married on the Sunday after Christmas, in a brief, entirely conventional ceremony performed by Jack Gene Coldwater. Jesse had trouble with the occasion. Up until Christmas Day, he had not hated Jack Gene or Casey or Ruger; now he did, for what they had done to Jenny. His best chance of bringing revenge to all of them lay in calling in the feds, and he could not wait to talk to Kip Fuller again.

Eight days passed before the first business day of the new year, and they were difficult for Jesse. He was glad to be married to Jenny, but nervous about the possibility of the house being bugged. Coldwater's people stayed away from him, and for that he was grateful.

On Monday, the fourth, he took his telephone into the woods behind the plant and called Kip Fuller.

"Jesse, I've been waiting to hear from you."

"What kind of reaction did you get from Barker?"

"You're not going to like it."

"They don't believe me?"

"Something like that."

"Kip, my deal is that I get Coldwater on a felony indictment, and I'm out of here. Well, I've got him; it's a felony to buy or possess the kind of armament he's got stashed up on that mountain."

"That's Barker's point," Kip said. "He thinks you're making this up to get out."

"Well, I'm prepared to prove it; all he has to do is to bust Coldwater, Casey and Ruger, then search the place. What's the big deal?"

"It's too fantastic, that's all. You're going to have to get proof of your allegations."

"Jesus Christ! What are you, a judge of the federal court? Act on my information and you'll have your proof."

"The proof has to come first."

"What do you expect me to do? Walk in there with a camcorder and tape Coldwater posing with a lot of munitions?"

"Not exactly; you'll have to use something a little more subtle than a camcorder. I can take care of that."

"Kip, I don't know if I'll ever be allowed into that place again. It was a fluke that I saw it at all. How am I supposed to get back in?"

"That's up to you," Kip replied, and he didn't sound happy about it. "We've got to find a way to get a small camera to you."

"This is insane; I'll never be able to do it."

"What about some other way, some other felony?"

"I think they may be bombing abortion clinics, but I don't have a shred of evidence to back that up."

"Get them to take you along, then."

"They haven't asked me to do anything illegal, so far. Oh, I did shoot a guy, and Coldwater finished him off."

"Tell me about it."

"We were target shooting with M-sixteens and handguns, and a guy named Partain appeared out of nowhere and tried to waste Coldwater. I hit him in a shoulder, and Coldwater, cool as ice, took my pistol and put one into the back of his head. Casey was there; does murder count in our deal?"

"You got any other witnesses?"

"Just Coldwater, Casey and me."

"Then it's your word against theirs, and I'll be willing to bet it would be hard to prove this guy Partain ever even existed. Also, Ruger wasn't there, and we've got to have him, too. Come to think of it, he wasn't at the fort with Coldwater and Casey, was he?"

"That's right."

"Well, then, you've got to tie all three of them in a neat bundle, or your deal's no good."

"Ruger runs the local bank; I'd be willing to bet that a stiff audit would turn up all sorts of stuff. There's the money I took to the Swiss bank in New York, for instance."

"You want me to call in the bank examiners while you're there in the middle? That might make them suspicious, since you're the new boy."

"You have a point."

"Listen, the fort is your best chance. Can you find an excuse to go to Coeur d'Alene this week?"

"There's no office supply store in St. Clair, and we're low on some things at the plant. I might be able to manage it."

"What day?"

"Let's try for tomorrow."

"Okay, on the outskirts of town—you'll pass it on your right driving from St. Clair—is an old fashioned hamburger joint called Mack's. What time will you go?"

"I should be there by ten, if all goes well."

"Okay, from ten to eleven, there'll be a guy at the counter drinking coffee and reading a Seattle newspaper. He's six-four, two-fifty, and he'll be wearing a checkered shirt and a down vest and a New York Yankees baseball cap. You sit next to him, have a cup of coffee, and when he has a chance he'll pass you a package. There'll be a camera inside a Zippo cigarette lighter; it'll be loaded with thirty-six exposures of a special, low-light color film, and it will shoot in anything but total darkness, if you brace it against something to hold it still. There'll be typed directions inside; memorize them and burn them—the lighter works. The guy will leave first; you finish your coffee, then go on your way. When you get your shots, FedEx them to me, care of the Justice Department, and don't get caught doing it."

"Okay, but I can't guarantee that I can get back inside the fort."

"Then nail them on something else; make them take you on an abortion clinic raid."

"But if I participate, will my testimony be any good?"

"As long as you can make a case for duress, it will. Are you going to stick it out, Jess?"

"Do I have a choice?"

"Not that I see."

"Then I'll stick it out." He hung up.

Jess walked back to his office deep in thought. By the time he was at his desk he had made up his mind. He knocked on Herman Muller's door. "Herman, I've got some news; Jenny Weatherby and I got married a week ago Sunday."

"That's wonderful, Jesse; congratulations," Muller replied, bestowing a rare smile.

"I wondered if I could get a few days off for a honeymoon sometime soon."

Muller turned to his calendar. "Let's see; we're starting the New York plywood order this week. If things go smoothly, I should think you could take off the week after next."

"I haven't been here long, Herman; I'd be happy to take it without pay."

"Call it a wedding present," Muller said, and smiled again.

"Thank you, Herman; that's very generous. Oh, we're running low on a bunch of things in the office; I thought I'd run up to Coeur d'Alene in the morning."

"Sure, go ahead."

Jesse went back to his desk. He had the passports; he had, what, something over fifty thousand dollars in his safe under the truck. It wouldn't last long on the run, but it was better than nothing. San Francisco, that sounded good for a honeymoon, and it offered flights to half a dozen Far Eastern countries.

The more he thought about it, the more he knew his fifty thousand wasn't enough. He'd have to put his mind to finding more over the next couple of weeks.

CHAPTER

38

Jesse spent an hour at the office, making a list of needed supplies, then left for Coeur d'Alene. As soon as he left the plant's parking lot, he noticed the car behind him, and it stayed there all the way through town and up the road to the city. This must mean that the office was bugged. In the countryside it kept a car or two between them, but it was always there. Jesse was tempted to pass up the meet at the hamburger joint, but the camera offered at least one possible way out, and he couldn't pass it up. Mack's restaurant hove into view, and he pulled into the parking lot and got out.

There was a variety of vehicles parked out front, everything from a UPS van to a couple of eighteen-wheelers. Jesse wondered what his contact was driving. Inside the door he put some change into a machine and got a copy of *U.S.A. Today*, while looking over half a dozen men seated at the counter. None of them fit the description of his man. He glanced at his watch; ten past ten; his contact was late.

Jesse took a stool at the end of the counter, away from the other customers and with a pair of empty stools next to it. He ordered a cup of coffee and a doughnut and glanced into the mirror behind the counter. A young man, very like the one who had followed him in New York, came through the front door, looked around, then, spotting him, took a stool near the center of the counter and ordered coffee.

Jesse took his time over the coffee and the newspaper, but he couldn't be seen to tarry, and his contact didn't show. Finally, when he'd been there for twenty-five minutes, he paid his check and got up to leave. As he approached the door, a man fitting the description of his contact walked into the place and headed for the counter. Jesse prevented himself from even pausing and continued on out of the restaurant.

Cursing the man's tardiness for screwing up the meet, Jesse got into his truck and started the engine, then looked down and saw a package of Bicycle playing cards on the front seat beside him, and they didn't belong to him. He waited until he got to cruising speed before opening the package; inside was the Zippo lighter and a tightly folded sheet of instructions. He glanced in his mirror and saw that his tail was one car back, then he held the sheet against the steering wheel and read it carefully, alternating with watching the road. If he started a fire in the truck it might be noticed, so he wadded up the paper and slipped it into a pocket; he'd deal with that later.

At the huge office supply store he got a shopping cart and began to fill it from his list. Halfway through the store he caught sight of his tail, pushing a cart and pretending to shop. Then, as he was about to approach the checkout counter, he saw exactly what he needed. A pretty young woman was demonstrating, of all things, a shredder. He stopped and, keeping his back to his tail, removed the wad of paper from his pocket and opened it up. "Can you shred this for me?" he asked the woman.

"Just shred, or would you like to see our burn feature, too?" she asked.

"I'd just love to see the burn feature," Jesse replied, handing her the folded sheet of paper. He watched as she fed it into the machine, and he followed it with the playing card package. A puff of smoke rose from the bin as the paper was converted to ash. "That's very impressive," he said.

"Can I order a machine for your company?"

"I'll have to ask my boss," Jesse replied. He smiled at her and continued to the checkout desk. He noticed that his tail preceded him from the building and was waiting in his car.

Jesse loaded the supplies into the back of the pickup, got in and drove back toward St. Clair, occasionally glancing in the rearview mirror to be sure his tail was in position. He drove straight through the town and back to the plant and, as he was unloading the supplies, he saw the tail's car make a U-turn and head back toward the town. The young man would have nothing to report, Jesse thought, with some satisfaction. It was clear, though, that someone—Coldwater or Casey—didn't yet entirely trust him.

At supper, he broached the subject of San Francisco. "Herman says I can have the week after next off."

"That sounds wonderful," Jenny said, glancing worriedly at Carey. "I don't think Carey could miss school, though."

"Well, it is a honeymoon, after all; I thought maybe she could come just for the first weekend. We could fly from Spokane on Friday night, then send her back on Sunday afternoon. Do you think we could get someone to meet her at the airport?"

"Oh, please, mommy, I want to go to San Francisco," the little girl said.

"Well," Jenny said, reluctance in her voice, "Let's see what we can do. I'm not promising, though."

The little girl was practically jumping up and down with excitement.

"I'm sure we can work it out," Jesse said, reassuringly. Carey beamed at him.

After dinner, when Carey was absorbed in her homework, Jesse put down his newspaper. "Want to take a stroll around the neighborhood?" he asked Jenny. "It's a starry night."

"Sure," she replied. "I'll get our coats."

When they were away from the house and Jesse was reasonably sure they were not being watched, he spoke up. "I have some things to tell you," he said. "First of all, we're talking about a lot more than a honeymoon."

"I was hoping you'd say that," she said, slipping her hand into his.

"I don't want you to ask any questions about this, but I have three valid passports with yours, Carey's and my photograph in them. I also have enough money to get us out of the country."

She squeezed his hand. "I've never been out of the country," she said excitedly. "Where would we go?"

"Maybe Hong Kong, as a first stop. There are excellent airline connections from there to points all over the world. I want to give some more thought to where we might end up on a more permanent basis. Where would you like to live?"

"Anywhere you say is fine with me," she replied. "I mean that; Carey and I will go *anywhere* with you."

"Here's what we'll do, then; we'll drive to Spokane and leave the truck there, then fly to San Francisco. We'll check into a hotel, the three of us, and stay until Sunday. When time comes to take Carey to the airport for her flight back to Spokane, we'll simply get onto another flight. I'll have to check the schedules and see what our best bet is, and we'll have to go with only the clothes on our backs. We won't even check out of the hotel. Carey will have some things with her, of course, but that will be all we can take."

"There's nothing here that I can't live without," Jenny said. "Not one damned thing."

"My, my, I've never heard you use strong language, ma'am."

She laughed. "I guess I must feel pretty strongly about it."

"Something I have to know about," Jesse said, serious again. "Carey. Just how firm a grip does the church and school have on her?"

"I know this isn't a very good answer, but it's hard to say. You've heard her spout the racial stuff they're taught there, and as I've said before, they insist that she never miss a day's school, unless she's certifiably ill. The children are also taught to report any derogatory remarks their parents make about the church or Jack Gene; I think they use them as a sort of early warning system against parents who seem to be straying from the fold."

"Have there ever been consequences for those people?"

"As I said before, people have been known to disappear."

"Are there ever any questions asked about these disappearances?"

"People are afraid to ask questions. Sometimes there's a story that they've been expelled from church and are ashamed to show their faces in St. Clair; sometimes they're just gone."

Jesse nodded. "We're going to have to be very careful with Carey. It's important that she not have the slightest idea of what we're planning. Answer her questions about the San Francisco trip, but don't overdo it; tell her we'll visit Fisherman's Wharf and the Golden Gate Bridge and see all the other sights. We'll do that on her weekend with us. I don't want her to know that anything at all has changed until the last possible moment, when we're at the airport, and you're going to have to figure out what to tell her to be sure that she's not upset by the change in plans."

"I understand."

"Also, talk with her about things beyond the San Francisco trip, things at school or at church. Make the trip seem like just one event in the coming months. That way, if anybody questions her, she'll have the right answers."

"I think the best way to handle things at the airport is to tell her that Jack Gene is sending us on a trip, a secret trip, maybe, to do something or other for him or the church."

"Good. You'll have to build our name change into the story, too."

"What is our new name going to be?"

"Warren. I'm Jeffrey, you're Jillian, Carey is Katherine."

"I like the sound of them," Jenny said. "Jeff, Jilly, and Kathy, the all-American family."

"That's us," Jesse said. "Something else: I've got enough money to keep us for a while, if we're careful, but we could certainly use more."

"I rarely have more than a hundred dollars in the bank at any one time, after I've paid the bills," she replied.

"That's not what I was thinking of," Jesse said. "When you lived with Jack Gene, did you live in the house he's in now?"

"Yes. He'd just built it when I went to live there."

"Did he keep large amounts of money in the house or in the church?"

"There was a big safe in his study," Jenny said, holding out a hand at waist level. "This high, at least. I watched them install it, but I never saw what was in it. Jack Gene always seemed to have a lot of cash in his pockets, though, and it could have come from the safe."

"Where in the study was it?"

"Opposite the fireplace, behind a bookcase that swung out. Jesse, you're not thinking of trying to rob Jack Gene, are you?"

"I will, if I get the chance."

"This is what I think," she said. "I think that if we just disappear, he might not take the trouble to look for us much, especially if we've left the country. We won't be able to hurt him in any way, after all. But Jack Gene has a monumental temper, and in the past he's gotten maddest when somebody stole from him. If we take his money, he'll never stop looking for us."

"You're right," Jesse said. "We'll manage on the money we've got." But, he thought to himself, after what Jack Gene has shown me up on the mountain, he'll never stop looking for us, anyway, so what the hell?

CHAPTER

39

Jesse was leaving his office on Wednesday, two days before the beginning of his honeymoon, when Pat Casey pulled into the parking lot in his squad car.

"Hey, Jesse," Casey said.

"Evening, Pat."

"Jack Gene wants us up at his house for a meeting."

"When?"

"Right now."

"Let me go back inside and call Jenny; I don't want her to worry."

"Forget about that; get in."

Jesse got into the patrol car. "What's up?"

"You don't ever ask that when Jack Gene calls a meeting; you just go."

"Glad to," Jesse said mildly. He did not speak again on the trip.

They were greeted at the door by an attractive young woman, not the same one Jesse had seen on his last visit to the house, and shown to Coldwater's study. Coldwater and Kurt Ruger were already seated on a sofa before the fireplace, and Coldwater indicated that Jesse and Casey should sit opposite them.

"How's married life, Jesse?" Coldwater asked.

"Couldn't be better," Jesse replied, smiling.

"Good, good, glad to hear it. Jesse, it's time we had a talk about something that's been going on for some time, and it concerns you."

Jesse nodded. He didn't like the sound of this.

"You've been accepted into our midst, Jesse, but I've never really talked to you about what that means, have I?"

"Not specifically," Jesse replied.

"In order to keep the coherence of our group, I require a very high degree of loyalty from my congregation."

Jesse said nothing.

"Have I ever told you what loyalty means to me?" Coldwater asked.

"No, sir, not in so many words, but I've had the strong impression that you would not have told and shown me the things you have unless you felt I was capable of loyalty."

"You're quite right, Jesse; I always seem to be underestimating you. You've understood from the beginning without my spelling it out for you." Coldwater rewarded him with a large smile.

"Maybe you'd better spell it out," Kurt Ruger said suddenly. "That's the only way of being sure."

"Of course, Kurt," Coldwater said smoothly, but he seemed miffed by the interruption. "First of all, Jesse, I don't think I have made it clear to you the sort of rewards that are available to the people who are loyal to me."

"I've never asked for any reward," Jesse said.

Ruger interrupted again. "But you knew there was something in it for you, didn't you, Barron?"

Jesse turned and looked directly at Ruger. "Kurt,

when I came to this town only a few months ago, I was at rock bottom. I had lost my wife and children and my business, and I thought I might go crazy. Since I've been in St. Clair I've come to have good work, a wonderful wife and little girl and the friendship of the people of the First Church. My life has been transformed, and I just don't know what more reward than that I could ask for."

"Don't get sanctimonious with me, you—" Ruger began.

Coldwater cut him off. "That's enough, Kurt. You apparently don' t recognize gratitude when you see it."

"Jack Gene, I only meant that—"

"I said, that's enough."

Ruger stopped talking and looked at the floor.

Coldwater turned back to Jesse. "Jesse, you've proven to me that you want to be a part of what we have here, and I think you're ready to play a more important role in our community."

"Thank you, sir," Jesse replied.

"From today, you are going to be a part of, shall we say, management. There are three divisions of our group; Pat, here, is charged with protecting us from outsiders who might harm what we stand for. Kurt is the financial director of our organization; nominally, he is president of the Bank of St. Clair, but what he does is far more important than that. Kurt marshals our resources, invests in income-producing ventures and, through what you might call sub-managers, directs, in a broad sense, the operation of those ventures we own. I am the third and higher arm of the organization. In general, I administer our affairs, and I take a great interest in what both Pat and Kurt do in their daily work."

"I see," Jesse said.

"Good. Now, ever since the three of us came to St. Clair, an essential part of the financial structure of this community has eluded us, and the time has come when we can no longer tolerate that."

Jesse knew what he was getting at now, and he was both relieved that there was no new suspicion of him and worried about what was about to be said.

"The only business of any size in this town that we do not control is St. Clair Wood Products," Coldwater said. "We have made repeated offers to Herman Muller for the business, but he has always rejected them, and my patience is wearing thin."

Ruger spoke up again. "Did you know about this? Has Muller ever mentioned this to you?"

"Herman has never mentioned it, but on the day I went to work out there, you and another man were in his office, and I got the impression that you had made him some sort of offer that he hadn't accepted."

"Did you hear what was said?"

"No, I was sitting in the waiting area, and Herman's office is glassed in. It was pretty obvious what was happening."

"I see," Ruger said, then was quiet again.

Coldwater spoke up again. "Eventually, we will control Wood Products, and when we do, I want us to be able to operate it efficiently. Are you getting an overview of how the business is run?"

Jesse nodded. "Yes, sir. That's what Herman has said he wants me to do. Before he promoted me, he seemed to run every aspect of the business personally, and he still does; but he seems to feel that he needs some backup. I have to tell you, though, that I don't see how anybody could run that business more efficiently than Herman does. There isn't an ounce of fat in that company, and I'm sure its profit margins must be much higher than for most businesses of the same kind."

"Has he revealed any of the financial operations to you?" Ruger asked.

"No; he takes care of that himself. He signs every paycheck, every purchase order, makes every decision to do with money."

"So you have no real idea of the financial condition of the company?"

"I don't see how it could be anything but very healthy. Herman has never hesitated to order new equipment when we need it, and he pays every bill the day it comes in. You must have some idea of his financial condition, since you're the only bank in town."

"He doesn't bank with me, except for a small account; he banks in Coeur d'Alene."

"I didn't know that," Jesse admitted.

"Where does he keep the books?" Ruger demanded.

"He does it on computer. I've never seen a ledger in the office."

"Do you use the computer?"

"I do for word processing, that sort of thing. Once I wanted to see if a particular bill had been paid, but when I tried to access the check register I was barred. Herman apparently uses some sort of password to get into the bookkeeping software. And I've never seen any ledger printouts."

"You don't know the password?"

"No."

"Could you find out what it is?"

Jesse shrugged. "I don't know. Herman sits in a corner of his office, and the computer screen faces the corner."

"Jesse," Coldwater said, "I would be very grateful to you if you could learn what that password is."

Jesse thought fast. He was being asked to betray Herman Muller, and he didn't like that. On the other hand, if he resisted doing so, Coldwater would be unhappy with him, and he might lose much of the good will he had built up. "I'd be glad to try," he said.

Coldwater smiled broadly. "Thank you, Jesse.

Now, as I said before, I'm elevating you to a management level with us, and you will find there are many benefits at this level of trust. First of all, you will be put on a salary of ten thousand dollars a month."

Jesse had no trouble looking stunned.

"It will be paid to you by Kurt in cash each month, so there will be no need to mention it to the Internal Revenue Service."

"Why, that's wonderful, Pastor," Jesse managed to say.

"In addition, any medical treatment you or your family may require will be made available to you, free of charge, at our own clinic in town, and you will find there will be other benefits."

"I hardly know what to say, sir," Jesse said.

"Say nothing, but I will count on your help in acquiring Wood Products."

"I have a lot of respect for Herman Muller," Jesse said. "I hope that he will be treated fairly."

"More than fairly," Coldwater said, standing to indicate that the meeting was at an end. He stood for a moment, making small talk with Ruger and Casey.

Jesse now had an opportunity to look at the bookcase opposite the fireplace. He had not noticed it on his first visit, but the books in the lower part now seemed to be only spines. He wondered how to get at the safe. Something else caught his eye, too: at one end of the bookcase was a compartment that held a couple of dozen rolled-up blueprints. There were too many for just a house; they must be for some larger structure.

"Have you thought any more about a honeymoon, Jesse?" Coldwater asked suddenly.

Jesse started. "Yes, sir. We're going to San Francisco for a week starting Friday."

"Good, good. Where are you staying?"

"I don't really know; I thought we'd find a room when we got there."

Coldwater turned to Ruger. "Kurt, arrange a nice suite at the Ritz-Carlton for Jesse and Jenny, and have the bill sent to you. And be sure that Jesse gets his first month's salary before he leaves on Friday."

"That's extremely kind of you, sir," Jesse said. Certainly, he could use the ten thousand dollars.

"Don't mention it," Coldwater said. "A couple needs to get away alone when they've just been married. What will you do with the child?"

"She's going to spend the first weekend with us, but she'll fly back on Sunday, so that she'll be in school the next day. We didn't want her to miss school."

"Yes, yes, quite right," Coldwater said. "I'm surprised you'd want a child on your honeymoon."

"Carey and I get along very well, and we didn't want her to feel excluded," Jesse explained.

"I see. Well, thank you for coming today. I'll look forward to your reports on Herman Muller and his business."

He shook Jesse's hand, then Casey drove him back to the plant.

As Jesse got into his truck he made a note to have a serious conversation with Herman Muller before he left. After Friday, he wouldn't be around to help the old man, and he felt sorry about that.

CHAPTER

40

Jesse woke up feeling elated. It was his last day in St. Clair, and he couldn't wait to get out of the town with Jenny and Carey. Jenny was no less excited than he; he could see her restraining herself at breakfast, talking casually with Carey about the sights of San Francisco.

"When is your science project due?" Jesse asked Carey.

"In two weeks," the child replied.

"We'll be back in plenty of time for me to help you, then," Jesse said.

"We're not supposed to have any help," Carey said.

"Oops, sorry."

"Well, maybe you could help a little," she said, smiling.

"You work on it next week, and if you have any questions, make a list and I'll answer them when we come back."

"Okay, Jesse."

* * *

At lunchtime Jesse put on his coat and boots and took his periodic walk in the woods, the telephone hidden in the bottom of his lunchbox. He took a fork in the path that went along the mountainside; there was a steep drop off to a stream two hundred feet below, and he kept to the inside of the narrow path. The skies were low with heavy cloud; it looked like snow before the day was over. He ate his sandwich slowly, thinking about what was ahead. He knew a life on the run was not going to be easy for any of them. The telephone weighed heavily in his pocket; he had one more call to make to Kip Fuller, and the single purpose of that call was to buy time.

"This is Fuller."

"It's Jesse."

"Did you get the camera all right? Our man said he couldn't make a straight pass at the restaurant."

"I got it, but I haven't had an opportunity to use it."

"What else is happening?"

"I've been promoted to management."

"At the factory?"

"No, in Coldwater's organization. He likes me, but Ruger doesn't."

"What's the problem with Ruger?"

"I don't know. Certainly I'm too far down the pecking order to be any sort of threat to him. It may have something to do with the fact that Herman Muller trusts me, and he'll barely speak to Ruger. Coldwater wants Wood Products, and he's going to use me to get it."

"How?"

"Right now all he wants is information about the business. It's wholly owned by Muller, and he plays his cards very close to his chest. He even banks in Coeur d'Alene to avoid dealing with Ruger."

"What are you going to do?"

"Play along, for now. If I don't, Coldwater might

move a lot faster, and Muller could get hurt. It's possible that they took out the man's grandson a while back."

"Have you learned anything new about Coldwater's organization?"

"No, but I'm in a better position to do that, now. If I can get Wood Products for him, he'll think I hung the moon. The man likes me, that much I can tell."

"Do you like him?"

Jesse hesitated, thinking about what Coldwater had done to Jenny. "He's a likeable fellow; every con man is."

"I've got some news; Arlene had a baby boy yesterday; nine pounds, one ounce."

"Kip, congratulations; that's wonderful news! You've waited a long time."

"We're thrilled, of course. I had almost given up."

"Now that you know you can do it, you'll have to have some more kids."

"I think one more will do me. Listen, Jess, you've got to get back into that building somehow. My people here are really on my back about this."

"I was at Coldwater's the day before yesterday, and I noticed a lot of blueprints in his study. If you bust him, then you ought to make his house your first target, get in there and clean it out. Those plans would tell you a lot about the fortifications."

"Good idea, but I'm not going to get to bust anybody until you get me those photographs."

"Kip, I can't just ask to go back in there and have a look around. I've got to wait until Coldwater feels the need to take me back inside there, and you're just going to have to be patient. Unless, of course, you want to just pour in here and nail the lot of them right now."

"You know I can't do that, Jess."

"Kip, if this ends badly, I want you to remember that I did what I was ordered to do; that I got you everything you need to indict."

"Jesse, you know goddamned well that, if it were up to me, I'd be in there today with a dozen swat teams, the army, if necessary. But I answer to other people."

"You make sure Barker remembers what I said," Jesse said hotly.

"That I'll do."

"Listen, Kip, I'm not going to be able to call for a while. I'm under a lot of scrutiny right now, especially with Ruger's attitude being what it is. Every time I leave town there's somebody on my tail, and the house may be bugged, too."

"You've been leaving town?"

"Just to go to Coeur d'Alene on business."

"Jesse, if you go any farther afield, I want to know about it, you hear?"

"Sure, Kip. I'd better go now; I'm due back at the plant. You give my best to Arlene and the new baby."

"I'll do that, Jess. You call me as soon as you can."

Jesse broke the connection and put the phone back in his pocket. It had started to snow, and he turned to retrace his steps to the plant. As he did, he found himself looking down the barrel of an automatic pistol, maybe six feet away.

"Just hold it right there," the man said. "I heard all of that; I'll take the phone." It was the young man who had followed him to Coeur d'Alene on his last trip.

"What's going on?" Jesse asked.

"I said, I'll take the phone. Toss it over here."

"Why do you want my phone?" Jesse asked.

"If you don't throw it over here right now, I'm going to shoot you someplace painful. Nothing fatal, just painful. You have a lot of questions to answer, my friend."

"You want the phone, you can have it," Jesse said. "Just don't get careless with the gun. When I've had a chance to talk to Coldwater you're going to see this in a different light, and it would go a lot better for you if there weren't any holes in me."

"The phone," the man said.

Jesse pointed to his pocket. "It's in here."

"Take it out very slowly and toss it to me."

Jesse slowly removed the telephone from his pocket, and, holding it in two gloved fingers, tossed it high and to the right of the man. As he had hoped, the man's gun hand swung around in the direction of the phone. Jesse took two running steps and dived at that hand.

The two men hit the ground together, dangerously close to the outer edge of the path. If they went off together, Jesse thought, he hoped the other guy would be on the bottom. He doubled his grip on the man's wrist and twisted outward. The pistol fell into the snow. Jesse got the man's arm behind him and shoved his wrist up between his shoulder blades.

The man screamed.

"Shut up, or I'll break it off. What the hell are you doing following me with a gun?"

"You'd better let me go, if you know what's good for you."

Jesse twisted the wrist again. "I asked you a question, and if you want to live through this little meeting, you'd better start talking."

"Ruger sent me," the man grunted.

"Not Casey?" Jesse asked, surprised. Casey handled security.

"It was Ruger; I've been following you for a couple of weeks. Now do the right thing; let me go, and let's go see Ruger."

Jesse didn't have to think about that for very long. There was only one possible result of this meeting, and it wasn't seeing Ruger. He grabbed the pistol, then got to his feet still holding on to the man's wrist. "All right," he said, "we'll go see Ruger, but not with a gun in my back, agreed?"

"All right, agreed," the man said. "Just ease off on my arm, okay?"

"Which pocket do you keep the pistol in?"

"Shoulder holster, left side," the man said.

Jesse reached inside the man's coat, found the holster, wiped the snow off the gun and shoved it into the holster. He also found a leather tab and snapped it across the trigger guard. "All right, do I have your word you won't draw that again?"

"Yeah, yeah," the man said. "Now, *please let go of my arm.*"

"Sure," Jesse said. First he turned the man so that his back was to the steep slope, then he let go of the arm. Then Jesse hit him once, in the gut. He made himself watch as the man left the path and started down. There was one short scream that ended when his head struck a boulder, then the limp body ricocheted down the slope and free fell the last hundred feet to the stream below. The man ended up face down in the stream, wedged between two rocks.

Jesse sat down for a minute and tried to restore his breathing and his thinking to normal. The man was dead, that was sure; either the blow to the head had done it, or he would drown in the stream. He found it strange how easy it was to kill somebody when his own life was in danger. He looked around him; the snow, now falling heavily, was already obliterating signs of a scuffle. In ten minutes the whole area would be covered. Jesse waited the ten minutes before going back to the plant. He had two choices: say nothing and get on that plane tonight; it might be days before they found the man; or play innocent and try to carry it off.

He ran the last two hundred yards; he had to be out of breath when he reached his office and telephoned Pat Casey.

CHAPTER

41

P at Casey stood on the path and looked down into the ravine. "Who is he?" he asked.

"I don't know," Jesse replied. "I was sitting on a rock up there a few yards. I had just finished my lunch when I heard somebody shout, or maybe it was more of a scream."

"Did you see him go over?"

"No, in fact I almost didn't see him at all. I walked back down the path to about here and looked around, but it had begun to snow, and I didn't see anything at first. Then the red jacket caught my eye."

"Did you try to help him?"

"Are you kidding? How the hell was I going to get down there? I'm not a mountain goat." Jesse looked down the path and saw half a dozen people coming; two carried a stretcher, the others had rope and equipment.

"Okay, you guys," Casey called out, "he's right down there; go to it." He turned back to Jesse. "What were you doing up here, Jesse?"

"I come up here once or twice a week to eat my lunch."

"You were eating lunch outdoors in this snow?"

"It hadn't started when I got here; it had only just begun when I heard the sound."

"You're going on your honeymoon tonight, aren't you?"

"We're getting a nine o'clock plane from Spokane."

Casey nodded noncommittally. "Merv, don't you fall down there with him! Be careful!" he yelled at the rescue party, who were halfway down the incline. "Maybe you better wait a few days before you go, Jesse."

"I can't do that, Pat; we've got a big order for plywood, and we have to start on it the week after next. We'll be on it well into the spring, and I promised Jenny and Carey San Francisco." He looked down the path and saw Kurt Ruger walking toward them through the snow. In his suit, tie and overcoat he looked distinctly out of place.

"Hey, Kurt," Casey said.

"What's going on, Pat?" Ruger asked.

"We got a guy all the way down there in the creek; don't know who it is yet."

Ruger nodded, and he was looking straight at Jesse. "Did you throw him down there?"

"Don't be ridiculous," Jesse said. "I don't even know who the guy is; why would I want to throw him down there?"

Casey spoke up. "Jesse says he was having lunch up there a ways, and he heard the fellow holler. Could be he slipped right about here; the path's narrow, and it slopes that way."

"Barron did it," Ruger said.

Jesse squared toward Ruger. "Now you wait just a goddamned minute before you start accusing me of murdering people. Do you know who that guy is? Do you know something about this?"

Ruger looked down the incline to where a stretcher was being hauled up, but he said nothing.

"Now we'll get a look at him," Casey said, grabbing a rope and helping to haul the stretcher onto the path. He pulled back the blanket. "It's George Little," he said to Ruger. "He works for you; what was he doing up here?"

"See if he has his gun," Ruger said.

Casey pulled open the man's coat. "Right there in its holster; the safety tab is still on. Doesn't look like he was about to use it."

"Your pal Jesse killed him," Ruger said. "I suggest you lock him up while I tell Jack Gene about this."

"Lock me up?" Jesse said, outraged. "I don't even know the man. Just what the hell are you talking about?"

"Come with me, Kurt," Casey said, walking farther up the path. Ruger followed him, and they spent five minutes arguing and gesturing at each other. They came back to where Jesse stood. "You come on with me, Jesse; we're going to see Jack Gene." He glanced at Ruger, then back at Jesse. "Bring your truck; you can follow me up there."

Ruger glowered at Jesse.

Coldwater seated the three in his study and looked at them. "All right, what's happened?"

"George Little is dead," Ruger said. "Barron threw him off a mountain."

"I don't even know George Little," Jesse said.

Ruger started to speak, but Coldwater held up a hand. "One at a time; you first, Jesse."

"I went up on the mountain behind the plant to eat my lunch; I do that every so often; there's a nice view. I had just finished eating when I heard somebody yell or scream. I looked down the path, but there was nobody there. It had started to snow about that time, and it took me some time looking before I saw a man in the creek, about two hundred feet down the mountain. I ran back to the plant and called Pat and told him to bring some men, then I waited there for him to arrive."

"Pat?" Coldwater said.

"I've got no reason to contradict Jesse," Casey said. "George was wearing a gun, but it was still in his holster and strapped in. I think it's true that Jesse didn't know him."

Coldwater looked at Ruger. "All right, Kurt, let's have it all."

Ruger looked embarrassed. "I've had George following Jesse for a while."

"Why?"

"Because I don't trust him, and I don't think you should either. There's something wrong about him, and I want to know what it is."

"Jesse, did you know somebody was following you?"

"News to me; I didn't have a clue."

"Let's get it all in the open right now, Kurt. Tell me exactly what's bothering you about Jesse."

"He's gotten in too fast," Ruger said. "What is it, three or four months? We haven't had time to check him out thoroughly."

Casey spoke up. "Checking him out is my job, Kurt, and he has been *very* thoroughly checked."

"It's happened too fast, Pat," Ruger said. "You're getting sloppy."

"There was *nothing* sloppy in my investigation of Jesse," Casey said. "I think you know that, Jack Gene."

Coldwater turned to Ruger again. "All right, Kurt, tell me specifically what you know that Pat doesn't."

Ruger sat very still and didn't speak for a moment. "I don't have any hard evidence; it's just a suspicion."

"Have you confided this suspicion to Pat before now?"

"No, I haven't."

"Kurt, you know how we work here; if you had a problem with security on Jesse, you should have gone to Pat with it, or at least come to me."

"I didn't have anything definite," Kurt said. "Not until now."

"And what do you have now?" Coldwater asked.

"He killed George, that's what."

Jesse spoke up. "Pastor, this is ridiculous. I didn't know the man, had never laid eyes on him. Why would I kill him?"

"Because he caught you at something," Ruger said.

"Caught me at *what*?"

"I don't know, do I? What were you doing up that mountain?"

"Eating my lunch; I already told you that."

Coldwater spoke up again. "Jesse, please wait outside for a moment, would you?"

"Yes, sir," Jesse replied. He got up and went into the hall, closing the door behind him, and sat on a bench. He could hear nothing from inside the study. This could not have happened at a worse time, he thought; a few more hours and he would have been on his way. Why the hell hadn't he watched his back more carefully? The door to the study opened, and Casey waved him inside. Jesse resumed his seat and waited.

Coldwater looked at Ruger. "Kurt, I believe you have something to say to Jesse."

Ruger turned toward him. "Jesse, I'm sorry; my suspicions were unfounded, and I now believe the death of George Little to have been an accident."

"Thank you, Kurt," Jesse said. He turned to Coldwater. "I'm sorry I couldn't be more helpful in this, but I honestly had never seen the man before."

"I know that, Jesse," Coldwater said. "You go on to San Francisco; you deserve a good honeymoon. This matter is closed. " He rose, and the others stood with him.

Jesse eyed the bookcase that concealed the safe. If he'd just had more time, he thought, he might have gotten inside it.

Back at the plant he told his story to Herman Muller. "I'm sorry to have been away all afternoon, Herman, but—"

Muller held up a hand. "Of course, I understand, Jesse." He glanced at his watch. "If you're going to make your plane to San Francisco, you'd better get going. You and Jenny have yourselves a nice honeymoon."

Jesse couldn't leave yet. "Herman, you've been very kind to me, and I want you to know I'm grateful."

"Don't mention it; you're doing a fine job for me."

"Herman, I've gotten the impression that Kurt Ruger has been trying to buy the business from you. I know it's none of my affair, but I'm concerned about it."

"Don't you worry; I'm going to die running this business," Muller said.

"I hope you do, sir. I just think you ought to be real careful with Ruger. It would be better to sell than to get into a fight with him, I think."

Muller regarded him through half-lidded eyes. "Jesse, I believe you've been listening to rumors around here about my grandson."

"It's been mentioned," Jesse said. "I'm just worried that if Ruger wants the business bad enough, well—"

"The thought has crossed my mind," Muller said, "and I've taken precautions. Don't you worry about it. You go to San Francisco and have a wonderful time, then you come back here raring to go. We've got a big year ahead of us."

Jesse shook his hand and turned to go.

"And while you're there, you be sure to have dinner at Ernie's. I haven't been to San Francisco in years, but I remember that restaurant fondly."

"I'll do that, Herman," Jesse said, then left the office.

When he got home, Jenny and Carey were standing on the front porch, shivering, talking to another woman. He climbed the front stairs.

"Jesse, have you met Margery Twomy?" Jenny asked.

Jesse smiled and shook the woman's hand. "I've seen you at church, Margery. I believe Carey is staying with you while we're on our honeymoon."

"That's right," she replied. "I've just come to get Carey now."

"But she's coming to San Francisco with us for the weekend," Jesse said. "She'll be back Sunday night."

Jenny spoke up. "Jesse, I'm afraid that's not going to be possible. The school is having a special science workshop for Carey's class this weekend and next, and attendance is mandatory."

Jesse's heart was pounding against his ribs. "Well, surely a weekend away wouldn't hurt," he said.

"It's all right, Jesse," Carey said. "I have to stay and go to the workshop. Maybe we can go to San Francisco another time."

He looked down at the little girl. She didn't seem in the least upset about the sudden change in plans. "Whatever you say, honey."

When Margery Twomy had left with Carey, Jesse took Jenny inside and put his arms around her. "I'm sorry," he said, holding her away from him, pointing at the ceiling and tapping his ear. "I know you were looking forward to showing her San Francisco."

"It's all right," she said. "We'll have a family vacation next year and take her there." She laid her head against his shoulder and sobbed silently.

"Well," he said, "If we're going to make that plane, we'd better get our luggage in the car and get going."

All the way to Spokane, he kept glancing in the rearview mirror. Sometimes a car was there, sometimes it wasn't.

CHAPTER

42

Jesse spent half an hour going through the suite at the Ritz-Carlton, looking for bugs, and he didn't find a thing. Apparently, Jack Gene Coldwater's arm was not long enough to reach inside a San Francisco hotel suite. He came back into the sitting room, where Jenny was curled up on a sofa, watching CNN on television.

"It's clean," he said, and sat down next to her. "We can talk."

"You understand that I can't leave without Carey," she said quietly.

"Of course I do."

"I was so excited about going abroad, but I'm excited about being in San Francisco, too. Can we see *everything*?"

"We sure can." He picked up a phone, called the concierge and asked him to book a table at Ernie's for the following evening. "Herman Muller recommended it," he told Jenny.

"I never thought of Herman as a restaurant critic," she said, laughing. "What are you getting me into?"

"It's a famous restaurant, an old San Francisco

favorite." He found a room service menu, and they ordered a late dinner.

"Have you ever been to San Francisco before?" she asked.

"Once, for a conference six or seven years ago. Mostly, it consisted of getting drunk with a lot of other agents."

Her eyes widened. "You were some kind of agent?"

"I'm sorry, I shouldn't have said that. You'll be a lot safer if you don't know any more than you do."

"Jesse, we're married now," she said firmly, "and I'm entitled to know everything. I've certainly told you everything about me."

Jesse sighed and leaned back on the sofa. "All right, I guess it's time. You're not going to like some of this; I hope it doesn't make a difference to you."

"You just tell me."

"For a start, my name is Jesse, but not Barron; it's Warden."

"Like a prison warden?"

"Like that. I'm a minister's son."

"Uh, oh; you know what they say about the minister's boy."

"And they're not far wrong. Oh, I started out as the straightest arrow you ever saw; then I became a cop for the federal government, and being a cop has a way of getting you bent."

"How did you get bent?"

"I stole some money."

"A lot of money?"

"Yes, some tens of thousands of dollars."

"Why?"

He told her about Beth and her illness, and about Carrie.

"So the story about the wife and three daughters—"

"Was a cover; it was somebody else whose name I took. But Beth and Carrie were real, and they're gone."

"I'm so sorry, my darling," she said, running her fingers along his cheek, then kissing him. "That's more trouble than anybody should ever have in a lifetime. Where's Carrie now?"

"She was adopted when I went to prison, and I probably won't ever know where she is."

Jenny put her arms around him and held him close. "I know how I would feel if I were separated from Carey," she said, "so I know how you feel. Do you think there's any hope of ever finding her?"

"I'd like to think so, but I have to be realistic. That's why I was prepared to leave the country without her. Adoption agencies are a tough nut to crack, and I'm hardly in any position to try."

"Why not?"

"There's a lot more that I haven't told you. I went to prison."

"For stealing the money?"

"No, they never found out about that. It was drug money that we'd confiscated; I just swept it under the rug, and no record was ever made of it."

"Why did you go to prison?"

"I was convicted of killing my partner and stealing a great deal more money, but I was innocent on both charges."

"Then why were you convicted?"

"Because someone in my agency was determined that I would be. It was set up so that I would never have a chance, and, of course, I didn't. Somebody else wanted the money, and he was willing to kill my partner to get it."

"How long were you in prison?"

"Fourteen months."

"So short a time for such serious charges?"

"The man I used to work for and another agent, a friend, got me out, because they wanted something done."

"What did they want done?"

"Jack Gene Coldwater."

"They sent you to St. Clair alone to arrest Jack Gene?"

"To find out enough about him so that they could arrest him. I'm not a cop anymore, just a spy."

"Does Jack Gene suspect?"

"No, but Kurt Ruger does. Not that he knows anything, he just suspects I'm not quite right."

"Can he hurt you?"

"Not so far. There was a nasty incident earlier today, but Pat Casey and Jack Gene took my side."

"What happened that was so nasty?"

"Do you know a man named George Little?"

"Yes, and he's pretty nasty, too."

"I killed him this afternoon."

She stared at him. "He wasn't *that* nasty."

"He caught me making a telephone call to my contact in Washington. I was up on the mountain behind the plant, and I found an opportunity to push him into a deep ravine."

"My God," she said, putting a hand to her face. "There must have been some other way to handle the situation."

"There was another way: I could have gone up to Jack Gene's house at gunpoint with George Little, and I'd be dead by now."

She put her arms around him again. "In that case, I'm glad you did what you did. And if you have to do it again, you go ahead."

The doorbell rang, and Jesse let the waiter into the room. They had a quiet dinner by candlelight, not talking much.

As they were finishing the wine, Jenny said, "Everything has changed, hasn't it? Nothing will ever be the same."

"You're right," he replied.

HEAT

●

She raised her glass. "To nothing ever being the same again," she said.

They touched glasses and drank. In bed they didn't make love; instead, they lay in each other's arms until they fell asleep.

CHAPTER

43

On their first day in San Francisco they walked. Jesse wanted to know if he was still being followed, and walking was the best way. They walked from the Ritz-Carlton to Union Square, and Jenny went shopping.

She had never seen anything like it; there were Sak's Fifth Avenue, Macy's, Neiman Marcus and the Ralph Lauren shop, all within a few steps of each other. With his first ten thousand dollar payment from Coldwater in his pocket, Jesse made her shop. After all, he thought, they wouldn't be abandoning their luggage at the hotel to sneak out of the country.

Jesse watched constantly for a tail, checking reflections in shop windows, never looking behind him, and it wasn't long before he found his man. He didn't recognize this one; he was tough-looking, better than six feet, more than two hundred pounds, close to Jesse's own size. He was very good at his work, Jesse thought.

They had lunch in a pub, then shopped some more. Finally, when they were ready to drop, they took the cable car up Powell Street and walked a block or two to the hotel, lugging many packages and shopping bags.

At Ernie's that night they were treated as old friends, given a secluded table and served to within an inch of their lives.

"I've never seen such a beautiful room," Jenny gushed, waving at the mahogany paneling and the fresh flowers. "How much is this costing?"

"It's not costing us a dime," Jesse replied, smiling. "It's all on Jack Gene, one way or another. We can take some comfort in that."

The following morning, Jesse rented a car and they drove north, over the Golden Gate Bridge, through Marin County and up into the wine country. They followed the road up the Napa Valley and found an Italian restaurant, Tre Vigne, for lunch. It was an unusually warm day for the time of year, and they asked for a table in the garden, which they had to themselves.

They ordered pasta and a good bottle of Napa chardonnay and had a leisurely lunch. As they were finishing, there was a sudden scraping of chairs, and men in suits occupied the tables on either side of them. Then, another man in a suit pulled a chair up to their table and sat down.

"May I join you?" he asked, somewhat tardily.

"Hello, Kip," Jesse said.

"Hello, Jesse. And may I be introduced?"

"Jenny, this is Kip; Kip, this is Jenny."

"I'm very pleased to meet you, Jenny," Kip said. "I wonder if you would be kind enough to go to the ladies' room? Mr. Smith over there will guide you." He nodded toward a man at the next table.

"It's all right, go ahead," Jesse said.

Jenny got up and left.

"Well, Jesse," Kip said, "what brings you to this part of the country?"

"I'm on my honeymoon," Jesse replied.

"I thought I told you not to travel without . . . What did you say?"

"I said I'm on my honeymoon."

Kip's mouth fell open. "You got *married*?"

"That's what you do, right before a honeymoon."

"Are you completely crazy?"

"Kip, I thought you'd be pleased; it's excellent cover."

Kip stared at him a moment, then smiled. "You're right, it is excellent cover; I'm pleased. I mean, congratulations. I never thought you'd go this far, Jess."

"She was my landlady from the beginning. It didn't take us long to fall in love."

"You're a lucky man, Jess—so far."

"Why so far?"

"What happens if this all goes wrong? What are you going to do with a wife?"

"Having a wife is good motivation to keep things from going wrong, isn't it?"

Kip shook his head. "I'm flabbergasted, I have to admit it."

"Kip, stop being flabbergasted and tell me what you're doing here, intruding on my honeymoon."

"You were spotted on Friday night at the airport. Remember a guy named Hennessy, from the South Florida Task Force?"

"Vaguely."

"He called Dan Barker, and Barker called me. Barker was *not* happy. He thought you were planning to skip the country."

"You can put his mind at rest. We're here for the week, and we're going back next Sunday."

"How do I know that without keeping a tail on you?"

"Jenny has a daughter; she was supposed to come with us, but at the last minute she was required at a weekend school project."

"So Coldwater is keeping you on a short leash?"

"That's about it. He knows Jenny wouldn't go anywhere without her daughter."

"Jesse, if you're going to go bouncing off like this, maybe I'd better put somebody else in St. Clair to keep an eye on you."

"You got somebody you want immediately dead?" Jesse asked. "Or is it just that you want me immediately dead?"

"We're a little slicker than that."

"Kip, listen to me. You reached into the gutter and you picked just about the only guy in the world who could waltz into that town and do what I've done. Two guys had already vaporized, remember? You send somebody else in there now, you'll not only kill him, you'll kill me. I'm your only shot at wrapping up this crowd, and you'd better not fuck with me, do you understand?"

Kip nodded. "I understand, Jess; I was just pulling your chain a little. After all, Barker's been pulling mine."

"You tell Barker that if these people tumble to me and start asking me questions under, shall we say, duress, I'll give *him* to them. One dark night they'll snatch him off some Georgetown street corner and disembowel him. They're like that."

"I'll mention it."

"Tell me, when you decided to put a team on me, did it occur to you that Coldwater might have been in there ahead of you with his own team?"

"That's the first thing we checked for. Remember, we spotted your tail in New York."

"Another thing: I was on to the tail yesterday, practically as soon as we left the hotel. If I find somebody else behind me during my honeymoon, I'll drag him into an alley and break his arms, and I mean it."

Kip held out his hands. "Jesse, Jesse, there's no need to get riled. You did something you weren't supposed to, and you got caught. Don't repeat the experience."

Jesse nodded. "Now, since I have no information to impart to you that I didn't impart in our conversation on Friday, I'd like you and your merry band of flatfeet to be gone before my wife returns to the table."

Kip stood up and gestured to the others. "Sorry for the intrusion. I'll give Barker your message." He turned to go.

"Kip?"

Kip looked back. "Yeah?"

"How's the new baby doing?"

"Just great."

"I'm glad. Give him my best."

"Thanks." And he was gone.

Jenny came back to the table. "What was that all about?" she demanded.

"Kip is the guy who sprung me from the joint."

"Joint?"

"Prison."

"And he's who you're working for?"

"He's my contact."

"What did he want?"

"He wanted to be sure we weren't skipping the country. Seems a colleague of his recognized me at the airport the other night, and there was a general panic that I was about to bolt."

"What if we had been bolting?"

"It wouldn't have worked. I'm going to have to give bolting some additional thought."

CHAPTER

44

Jesse and Jenny arrived home late on Sunday evening, exhausted and happy from their time together and, especially, their time away from St. Clair. As they climbed the front steps with their bags Jesse was again feeling the strain of being someone else, and he was filled with dread to see an envelope pinned to the front door. He ripped it open and read the note.

> Meeting tomorrow morning at eight sharp at J.G.'s.
>
> Casey

Here we go again, he thought.

Jesse was normally at his desk by eight, and he had to call Herman Muller and beg an hour or two. When he arrived at Coldwater's house there were half a dozen cars and pickup trucks parked in the forecourt, and when he was let into Jack Gene's study there were as many men there. He took a few steps into the room and froze. Sitting in a chair beside the fireplace was perhaps the one person in the world he least wished to see at that moment. His presence meant that Jesse was, from this moment, effectively a dead man, that perhaps the only thing between him and death was torture.

Charley Bottoms rose from his chair at the sight of Jesse, and his gaze bored into him from across the room. He was dressed in neat sports clothes, a contrast to the jeans and leather he had worn in Atlanta Federal Prison. Long sleeves covered the prison tattoos, and he seemed, if anything, more massive than when Jesse had last seen him in the punishment cell at Atlanta.

"Good morning, Jesse," Coldwater boomed. "I want you to meet some colleagues."

Jesse's mind went nearly numb as he was introduced and shook hands with four strangers, and finally, he snapped back to reality as Charley Bottoms took his hand.

"And this is Charley Bottoms, who heads a clan of the Aryan Nation about a hundred miles north of here."

"Pleased to meet you, Jesse," Bottoms said, holding on to his hand for a moment.

"Good to see you, Charley," Jesse replied automatically.

"Let's all have a seat and talk for a minute, then we'll take a tour of the top of the mountain," Coldwater said. Everyone sat down, and Coldwater continued. "Most of us have met before in passing, at least, but it seemed to me that we have enough in common that we might do some good for each other. Yesterday afternoon, after your arrival, you saw the town, some of the local businesses and the Wood Products plant, which Jesse here takes a hand in running. We expect to be in control of that business in the near future, and that will consolidate our control of the town. In a few minutes I'm going to show you something that might surprise you, and I hope that what you have seen and will see here will give you some ideas about how to gather power in your own communities."

Coldwater droned on about how much everyone had in common, while Jesse fought the urge to throw up on the beautiful oriental rug at his feet. What was Bottoms waiting for? Did he want to get Jack Gene alone before he blew the whistle? Jesse looked around. There were only two ways out of the room: Casey sat between him and the door, and if he should throw himself through the windows he had at least a fifty-foot drop. He was sweating now, and he didn't want to call attention to himself by mopping his brow.

"Is it warm in here, Jesse?" Coldwater said suddenly. He got up, opened a window and sat down again.

"Thank you, sir," Jesse said, taking a deep breath.

Coldwater talked about cooperation and togetherness for another ten minutes, then he rose. "We'll have to take more than one car, it seems; you two can ride with me, Pat, you take Bob, there, and Jesse, Charley can ride with you." Coldwater retrieved a roll of blueprints from the bookcase, then the men filed out of the house and went to their respective cars. Coldwater drove off, leading the way.

Bottoms got into Jesse's truck and slammed the door. He pointed at the dashboard and mouthed, "Is it bugged?"

"No," Jesse replied. "I've been over it."

"Well," Bottoms said, "I guess I gave you a jolt, huh? I mean, I think I scared the shit out of you."

Jesse glanced across at the big man. "That's a fair statement, I guess."

"I wanted to warn you earlier, but you were out of town until last night, I hear."

Jesse nearly drove off the road. "You knew I was here?"

Bottoms laughed. "Haven't you figured it out yet?"

"Charley, what the fuck is going on?"

"Well, a couple of days after Barker sprung you, he sprung me. I'm supposed to keep an eye on you, make sure you're not so unhappy you'd fly the coop, or so happy you'd change sides."

"I should have known Barker would have a backup in place. It's like him to be that cautious."

"Backup is not far wrong. The deal was, I'd come up to Idaho, where a couple of old acquaintances had established the Nation up north, and get in good with them. Then, if they popped you, I'd be in place to step in. And, of course, I would burn the whole bunch in return for a free pardon."

"Let me get this straight," Jesse said. "You were willing to turn in your biker buddies to save your own ass?"

"Damn straight," Bottoms said. "I never met anybody on a bike, or on foot, come to that, whose ass was as valuable to me as my own. I never even liked most of 'em. Fuck 'em, is what I say, if it gets me a fresh start."

"You been dealing with Kip Fuller?"

"Right."

"I told the son of a bitch not to send anybody else in here. Is he *trying* to get me burned?"

"I doubt it. I think Barker insisted."

Suddenly, Jesse was delighted to see Charley Bottoms. "Well, I'll tell you, Charley, you aren't going to believe what you're going to see, but I want you to remember every fucking detail of it and report everything to Kip and Barker. They wouldn't take my word for it."

"Sure thing, pal. You know, I always wondered

what would have happened if you and me had gone toe to toe in the yard. Didn't you?"

"Never crossed my mind."

"Well, you got out just in time, buddy; I'd have smeared you across the pavement real good."

"You know, Charley, it might have been interesting. Up until the time we met in solitary, I had just been trying to stay alive. But I think that after our chat, I would have started killing people, and you would have been first in line."

Bottoms grinned. "I like you, Jesse; I always did. You always handled yourself real good in the yard; took out some guys I'd have thought would have stomped you into the ground. I'd have hated to kill you, but I'd have done it the minute you set foot out of that cell. I'm glad our present circumstances don't require me to do that."

"That's sweet of you, Charley," Jesse replied.

"I never saw anybody I couldn't take in about a minute," Bottoms mused, "except maybe Coldwater."

"Coldwater scares you, does he?"

"You heard the stories about him in Nam?"

"Nope."

"Shit, he'd go out in the jungle and hunt Slopes with nothing but a knife; they say he killed more people in silent combat than anybody in any service, including the marines and the CIA. And now he turns up in Idaho with all that hair, talking like a preacher. I bet if you looked at him cross-eyed he'd tear your throat out with his hands without even blinking."

"You might keep that in mind, seeing that you're doing what you're doing here," Jesse said. He drove through the gates, then pulled up on the mountain top and parked the truck.

Bottoms stepped down and looked around him. "What we got here, summer camp?"

"Stick around, Charley," Jesse said. "Your eyes are about to be opened."

They stood around a conference table in Coldwater's underground office, following him as he took them through the blueprints of the installation. Jesse, as he had been doing for the past hour, snapped photographs with his Zippo lighter/camera whenever he had the opportunity. He took the opportunity to look closely around Coldwater's quarters, too, and he saw something he'd seen before: a bookcase that held spines only, and, unlike the one that hid the safe back at Coldwater's house, the false front was narrower and went nearly all the way to the ceiling.

"Jack Gene," somebody interrupted, "I don't see why you've stored gasoline instead of diesel in your underground tanks. Twenty-five thousand gallons of gas could make this place awful hot."

"That's an easy one," Jack Gene replied. "First of all, the gasoline is in super-hardened tanks, no closer than fifty feet to the surface; second, in the last ditch, gasoline can make a powerful weapon, even if only in Molotov cocktails. And we've got flamethrowers we can use, if we have to."

"I see your point," the man said.

"Well, that's all, gentlemen," Coldwater said, rolling up the plans. "Let's go back to the house for some brunch. He handed the rolled-up blueprints to Jesse. "Hang on to those for me." Then he led the way from his underground redoubt.

Back in the truck, Jesse dropped the blueprints behind the seat as he got in.

"Shit!" Bottoms breathed. "You ever seen anything like that?"

"No, and neither has anybody else. When are you talking to Kip again?"

"Soon as I get out of St. Clair."

"Tell him what you saw, will you? In the greatest possible detail?"

"You better believe it," Bottoms said.

Jesse drove back down the mountain toward Coldwater's house, feeling optimistic again. Maybe Bottoms's testimony would put some spine into Barker and get him moving. And Jesse now had one more opportunity to convince Washington.

45

Jesse went back to the office and spent the morning with Herman Muller, going over the production schedule on the New York plywood order. At lunchtime the plant emptied, and Muller, as usual, went into town for a hot lunch.

Jesse got Coldwater's blueprints from his truck and spread them out on his desk. He adjusted his gooseneck desk lamp for the best light and, one by one, photographed the pages with the Zippo camera. When he was done he went into Muller's private bathroom, got his telephone from his lunchbox and called Kip.

"What's up, buddy?" Kip asked

"Two things: first, Charley Bottoms showed up this morning and nearly caused me to clutch my chest and turn blue."

"Sorry about that; if you'd called in I could have warned you."

"Second, I've photographed a good chunk of Coldwater's fortifications and all of the blueprints."

"Holy shit! You really came through for me, Jesse!"

"You bet I did, buddy; now, how am I going to get the camera to you?"

"Got a pencil? I'll give you an address, and you can Federal Express it. Here we go, send it to John Withers, Nashua Building Supply, 1010 Parkway, College Park, Maryland." He added the zip code and phone number. "It's a drop I've set up. Can you get the camera off today?"

Jesse glanced through his glass wall toward the reception desk and the out box. "Yes, they haven't picked up yet today."

"Great, I'll look forward to your shots."

"Charley is my backup on this, Kip. Now you have all the evidence you need, right?"

"If all goes well, we'll be in there inside a week. I'll need a few days to plan and assemble a force."

"All right. The next time I talk to you, I want to hear that you're on your way."

"Over and out."

Jesse broke the connection, then went to the reception desk, found a FedEx form and envelope and addressed it as instructed. He inserted the envelope into a pile of a dozen waiting for pickup, then took the plans back to his truck. He spent the rest of his lunch hour eating a sandwich and leafing through the blueprints, and what he saw confirmed his suspicions about the bookcase in Coldwater's underground suite. When he got back to his desk, the phone was ringing.

"It's Jack Gene," a deep voice said. "What happened to that roll of blueprints I asked you to carry?"

"Oh, I'm sorry, Pastor; they're in my truck; I forgot all about them. I'll run them by your house after work."

"Run them by my house now," Jack Gene said and hung up.

Jesse scribbled a note to Herman, then left the plant. He drove up to Coldwater's house, noting that the visiting cars had left, and rang the bell. Yet another beautiful young woman, this one pregnant, showed him to Coldwater's study. The room was empty.

"The pastor is on the phone in the kitchen," she said to Jesse. "He'll be with you in a few minutes." She left, closing the door behind her.

Jesse glanced at the telephone on the coffee table; a single red light glowed; Coldwater was on line one. Quickly he set the blueprints aside and went to the bookcase. He was surprised that the hinged false front yielded to only a slight tug; not even locked. Behind it sat a large red safe, a reproduction of a nineteenth-century model. Jesse had seen it offered in mail order catalogs. He knelt and put an ear to the safe, first glancing at the phone to be sure the red light was still on, then he slowly twirled the combination knob, listening to the tumblers. The mechanics of this safe had not changed for a hundred years, and Jesse believed he could open it in a couple of minutes.

He had once had a short course in safecracking from a snitch of his in Miami, an old-time thief who had turned to drug running for easier and bigger money, and he could open, he reckoned, about half of the safes he'd ever met. His snitch would have thought this one to be a piece of cake. Jesse looked at the telephone, and the light was out.

Quickly, he closed the cabinet and leaned on it, and one second later, Coldwater entered the room.

"There you are, Jesse," he said. "Take a seat; would you like some coffee?"

"Thank you, sir, yes," Jesse replied. He handed over the blueprints. "I'm sorry I took these with me; I just forgot they were in the truck."

"Don't worry about it," Coldwater said, lifting the telephone and pressing the intercom button, "I just don't want them out of the house. Bring us coffee for two," he said into the phone.

The two men settled into chairs before the fireplace, and Coldwater gazed sleepily at him. "What did you think of Charley Bottoms?" he asked.

"Big fellow," Jesse replied. "I wouldn't want him mad at me."

"Quite right," Coldwater said, smiling. "Did you think he was bright?"

"I didn't have much of a chance to form an impression," Jesse said. "Is he important to you?"

"He could be; any of those men here this morning could be, in the right circumstances. They and their followers have a lot of combat experience among them."

"Are you anticipating combat?"

"I've learned to anticipate every eventuality," Coldwater replied. "I'm always ready for anything." The coffee arrived, and Coldwater poured for them.

"This is a beautiful house," Jesse said, looking around. "Did you build it?"

"I did, and I designed it, too. Tell me, have you spotted the safe yet?"

"I beg your pardon?" Jesse said. His heart was beating faster now. Maybe Coldwater did have some sort of weird sixth sense.

"There's a safe somewhere in this room. Can you find it?"

Jesse looked around. "Behind a picture?"

"Nothing as obvious as that. Come on, you're a builder; where would you hide it?"

"May I look around?"

"Go right ahead."

Jesse walked slowly around the room, pretending to search, and he saw something he hadn't noticed before; there was another false bookcase that matched the one in Coldwater's underground study. He kept moving, then stopped in front of the bookcase that hid the safe. He fingered a book spine, determined it to be fake, then ran his fingers along the shelf. It opened easily.

"Well done," Coldwater said. "Do you know you're the first person to find it in under a minute? Pat Casey, as good as he is, took nearly ten."

"I guess Pat has never built a bookcase," Jesse said, sitting down again and picking up his coffee.

"You know anything about finance, Jesse?" Coldwater asked out of the blue.

"Just that part of it that pertains to running a small business. I've never been in the stock market or had any investment more complicated than a CD."

"Pity," Coldwater said. He seemed suddenly discouraged. "I've begun to think that Kurt Ruger, as talented as he is, as long as he's been with me, might no longer be the right man for his job."

"He certainly seems very competent," Jesse said.

"Yes, but suspicious to the point of paranoia. That's a good trait, up to a point, but Kurt went past the point a long time ago, and he's beginning to make a nuisance of himself. You saw the way he behaved over George Little's death."

"Well, yes; I did find that surprising. Flabbergasting might be a better word."

"Yes, flabbergasting. Pat Casey was furious with him." He looked up. "Jesse, is there anything you want?"

"How do you mean?"

"Anything. Anything that you don't already have, I mean."

"Not at the moment. I'm very content with my lot."

"If there's anything you ever want, you come to me," Coldwater said. "Doesn't matter how difficult it might be. You just come to me, and it's yours."

"Why, thank you, Pastor," Jesse said. "I'm very grateful."

"Well, you'd better get back to work," he said. "Anything to report on Wood Products?"

"Well, no sir; I haven't spent a great deal of time there since we talked about it."

"Of course not; you let me know when you have something."

They shook hands, and Jesse left. Driving back to the plant, he reflected on how he might get his hands on that safe. When the feds launched their raid, he had to get to that safe before anybody else.

CHAPTER

46

Jesse waited until the end of the week before he called Kip. It was hard to wait, and he had grown very tense. He was having a hard time sleeping, and when he did his dreams were confusing and disturbing. He was always back in New York, walking down Fifth Avenue, window shopping, and what he saw had an awful effect on him. He would wake up, shaking and bathed in sweat, and not be able to remember what he had dreamed. His appetite diminished and he didn't feel well. Herman Muller had commented on how pale he looked.

On Friday at lunchtime, when the office was empty, he called Washington. He no longer felt comfortable doing this on the mountain, so he did it from his desk, from where he could see anyone who came up the office stairs.

"This is Fuller."

"Kip, it's Jesse."

"Hi." He didn't sound happy about the call.

"What's going on? What was the reaction to the photographs?"

"Well, the shots weren't what we hoped they'd be; all we could see was hallways and boxes; hard to tell what was in the boxes."

"I did what you asked with the equipment you gave me."

"I know, Jesse, and it's not your fault."

"Haven't you heard from Charley Bottoms?"

"Yeah, but Barker—"

"Barker what?"

"Barker is getting paranoid about this, I think. He seems to believe that you and Charley are somehow colluding to make an ass of him."

"What about the shots of the blueprints?"

"The shots are a little washed out. The camera was loaded with a special, low-light film, and you lit the plans too brightly when you photographed them."

"All I used was a desk lamp."

"It was too much; you'd have been better off just using ambient light."

"Listen to me, Kip: our deal was that I would get evidence to indict Coldwater and his partners. I've done that; I've provided you with both testimony and documentary evidence, and Charley's testimony confirms it. Now I'm at the end of my tether, and you're going to have to move your ass if you want my testimony in court."

Kip ignored this. "Let me ask you, since you know the territory, how many men are we going to need, and how should we come in?"

Jesse thought for a minute. "First of all, the best cops in the world are not going to be enough; you're going to need soldiers, and I don't mean the Idaho National Guard. I would get the attorney general to go to the president and request crack troops, trained in urban tactics, street fighting."

"That's not going to be easy," Kip replied.

"You're going to have to do a lot of things

simultaneously; you're going to have to put troop-carrying choppers on top of that mountain, establish a perimeter and hold it, to keep Coldwater and his people from getting into that underground system. Unless you can do that right off, a siege situation will develop and you'll look like idiots.

"Simultaneously, you're going to have to take Coldwater, Casey and Ruger; otherwise they'll rally their followers, and you'll have a pitched battle on your hands. Cut off the head of the snake, and the rest will be easier.

"Third, you're going to have to seal off the town to prevent anyone from getting in. Coldwater now has alliances with other groups, like the one that Charley Bottoms is in, and they might well come to his aid. Also, you can't let any of Coldwater's people get out. The nasty part of this is that, even if you capture the mountain and arrest Coldwater and his principal aides, you're going to have to round up the rest of the church congregation from wherever they are, and they may fight on an individual basis."

"How many people are we talking about?"

"Judging from what I've seen at the church, I'd estimate somewhere between five hundred and a thousand men, and three or four times that many women and children. They seem to have a lot of kids."

"Will the women fight?"

"My guess—and it's only a guess—is that Coldwater doesn't invest enough confidence in women to train them, and that you'll have to deal mostly with men and boys. I'd count on being opposed by teenagers with assault rifles, if I were you."

"What you're saying, essentially, is that, no matter how we do this, it's going to be a mess."

"I think you have a choice between a mess and a godawful, mind-boggling tragedy that could shake this country to its roots, that could make the attorney gen-

eral, the president and the military look like bumbling
idiots who can't be trusted to keep order. I think that if
you screw this up you have the chance of having the
biggest pitched battle in this country since the Civil
War."

Kip was silent for a long moment. "We're going to
need armor, aren't we?" he asked finally.

"You're going to need it, but how the hell will you
get it here without alerting Coldwater? If you fill up
the roads of northern Idaho with tanks and armored
personnel carriers, it'll be on radio and television a
long time before they can get here, and Coldwater is
going to be ready. Your best bet is choppers, a lot of
them, and enough men to mop up the town on a
house-to-house basis."

"Is there an airport?"

"Yes. I've seen a sign pointing to it, but I've never
been out there."

"You better take a look at it and get back to me."

"That's a good idea; I'll do it."

"How many troops are we talking about?"

"What was it they called Field Marshal
Montgomery in World War Two? Something like
Martini Monty, because he wouldn't attack unless he
had a six-to-one advantage. I think you'll need that, if
you fail to cut off the head of the serpent first."

"So we're talking five, six thousand men with full
field gear, assault weapons, flak jackets, the works."

"I think you better bring in heavy weapons, too, in
case Coldwater makes it to his fortress. You'll want to
be at least as well armed as he is."

"Nothing like this has ever happened in the history
of this country," Kip said, sounding disconsolate. "At
least, not since the Civil War, as you pointed out.
American troops carrying out a full-scale assault on an
American town? It's insane."

"Maybe so, but comparatively speaking, it's even

more insane to do nothing, not to mention negligent. Something else, Kip, and I hate to bring this up: you'd better be ready for casualties. This could be bloody, so you'd better have both the medics and the PR people on alert to handle the dead and wounded and to break it to the public."

"Barker wants to round up a thousand federal agents from the FBI, from the U.S. marshals, from Alcohol, Firearms and Tobacco and the Treasury Department and send them in there on the ground, in APCs, with bullhorns, telling everybody to surrender."

"You tell Barker for me that, if he does that, he's going to lose half of them, and the other half will have to run, if they're not surrounded. *Then* he'll have to bring in the military to pull it out of the fire, and he'll have to destroy this town to win."

"I don't know if he's going to buy your recommendation."

"Then, Kip, you have to go over his head; you have to go outside the Justice Department, if necessary, straight to the White House."

"If I do that, they'll hang me out to dry, my career will be over, and I'll have a wife and two kids that I can't support."

"If you don't do it, Kip, the press will hang the whole thing on you and Barker. After all, you're the official contact with Bottoms and me. When this is over, and the president appoints a commission to investigate why such a huge tragedy occurred, you'll not only be hung out to dry, you might end up in prison, and where will your family be then?" Jesse was trying hard to scare Kip to death; he had the feeling that if he didn't, nothing was going to happen. He played his last card. "You tell Barker I'm going to give him fourteen days to act, and in force. If he doesn't, I'm getting out, and if I'm arrested by your people I'll see the whole business on the front page of the *New York*

Times and the *Washington Post*. I'll write a book about it; I'll sell it for a TV movie; and I'll never *ever* shut up. Do I make myself clear?"

"Jesse, don't even think about doing that."

"I've already thought about it, Kip, and as God is my witness, I'll do it. Your only other choice is to get me a presidential pardon *now*, and let me and my family get out of here. That'll shut me up."

"Call me Monday."

Jesse had a desperate thought. "Wait a minute, Kip."

"Yeah?"

"I want to come to Washington and make a presentation to your people, the military and somebody from the White House."

"That's crazy, Jess; an escaped convict standing up in front of that kind of meeting? What kind of credibility would you have?"

"The credibility of an eyewitness who knows what he's talking about."

"How would you get out of town without Coldwater knowing about it?"

"This drop of yours that I sent the camera to—is that a real building supply company?"

"Yes, and a big one, out in College Park."

"Do this: call St. Clair Wood Products, ask them for their fax number, then fax Herman Muller a request for a presentation by a salesman. Say that you're looking for a major new source of plywood and chipboard, and you'd heard good things about his company. Tell him your need is urgent, and you want to see somebody right away; he'll send me. Coldwater will know about it, but it won't worry him, because I did the same thing in New York."

"I'll do what I can, Jess, but I can't promise. Barker will have to approve this, and I think it's unlikely. If Muller gets the fax, then you'll know you're on. I won't contact you again, just go directly to Nashua Building Supply, 1010 Parkway, in College Park, and ask for John Withers; he'll take it from there."

"Just remember that I might be followed."

"I'll plan for that."

"Something else, Kip; call somebody at the National Security Agency and get some satellite shots of the St. Clair area; they'll help me make my case, and they'll help you when you go in."

"I'll see about that."

"Thanks, Kip."

"Thank me when I make it work." Kip hung up.

CHAPTER

47

O n Sunday afternoon after lunch, Jenny was helping Carey with some homework. "I think I'll
take a drive," Jesse said to her. "Will you join
me?"

"We've got work to do here," Jenny said. "You go
ahead."

Jesse got into the truck, drove to the center of
town and set the odometer of his truck at zero. He
drove east, past Wood Products for another mile, and
turned right at the sign for St. Clair County Airport.
He noted that the road was paved and broad, and after
a couple of minutes he came to the airfield. An asphalt
strip stretched out in both directions; there were some
small T-hangars and one large hangar with an office
shed attached and a fuel truck parked alongside. The
doors to the large hangar were open, and Jesse saw
someone working under the cowling of a Cessna single-
engine airplane. He drove toward the hangar, and, as
he approached, he saw that the man was Pat Casey.

Jesse got out of the truck. "Hey, Pat."

"Hey there, Jesse, what brings you out this way?"

"Just went for a Sunday drive, and I saw the sign. First time I've been out here."

"I'm out here every chance I get," Casey said. "Nothing I love better than flying."

"Pretty nice setup," Jesse said, pointing toward the runway. "What is it, about thirty-five hundred feet?"

"Forty-five hundred. You can get a corporate jet in here, no problem. You ever done any flying?"

"Yeah, I had about thirty hours in a Cessna 172 back in my hometown. That was seven, eight years ago. I soloed and did the required cross-country stuff, but never got my license." This was true, but it had been in Miami.

"I'm just finishing up on a little light maintenance here, cleaning the plugs. Want to do a little aerial sightseeing?"

"Sure, love to."

"Give me five minutes."

Jesse moved his truck so that Casey could get his airplane out of the hangar, and, when the police chief had finished his work, helped him roll the Cessna out onto the apron.

"Want to fly left seat?" Casey asked.

Jesse grinned. "That depends on if you can land it from the right seat, should you have to."

"I can. Hop in the left side, there."

Jesse got in, adjusted his seat and fastened his seatbelt; Casey climbed in beside him, cleared a double handful of charts and books off the copilot's seat, dumped them on the backseat and handed Jesse a headset. "Nice panel," Jesse said. "A lot better than the old 172 I learned in."

"Yeah, I got rid of the original avionics and put in a whole new panel last year. All King stuff, except for the GPS—that's from Trimble."

"That's Global Positioning System?" Jesse knew more about it than he let on.

"Right. It's satellite based and accurate to within about a hundred feet, I think. Wonderful navaid. All you have to do is enter the three-letter identifier of any airport, press this button twice, then set the course into the course deviation indicator right in front of you. Switch on the autopilot, and it'll fly you straight there." Casey produced a laminated sheet of paper. "I've already done a preflight inspection, so I'll read you the cockpit checklist; it'll all come back to you."

Jesse was surprised that it did come back. Soon they were taxiing to the end of the runway.

"This is a 182, which is larger and heavier on the controls than your 172 trainer, but not all that different. I'll work the radios for you." Casey announced their intention to take off on the local frequency. "Okay, let's go; set the trim in the green and put in fifteen degrees of flaps, that's the first notch; throttle all the way in."

Jesse slowly shoved in the throttle, and the airplane began to move down the runway. There was no wind, and the takeoff was uneventful. Jesse got the flaps up.

"Climb to four thousand feet," Casey said. "The airport elevation is three thousand, so that'll put us a thousand feet above ground level."

Jesse did as he was told, then leveled off at four thousand feet.

"Okay, reduce power to, let's see, about twenty-three inches of manifold pressure and twenty-three hundred rpm. Good, now I'll lean the engine, and we're in business. Turn left to two-seven-zero, and hold your altitude."

Jesse made the turn without losing any altitude.

"Want to see St. Clair from above?"

"Sure."

"See the church steeple there? Head for that."

Jesse picked out the steeple rising above the trees, then saw the mountaintop just behind it. He headed for the church, then continued straight on toward the mountain.

"Look, there's Jack Gene's place," Casey said. "Head over there."

Jesse turned the airplane slightly, and soon the snowy swath of Coldwater's garden hove into view.

"There's Jack Gene in the garden," Casey said, smiling. "Let's do a low pass over his house. Drop down a couple hundred feet, and when you get over the house, make a thirty-degree turn to three-six-zero."

Jesse pushed forward slightly on the yoke and the airplane began a descent and picked up airspeed. He could see the figure in the garden now; he was sitting on a bench and seemed to be holding a book.

"Here we go, start your turn," Casey said.

Jesse looked at the attitude indicator and picked out the thirty-degree mark, then rolled the airplane to the right.

"You're losing altitude," Casey warned.

Jesse hauled back on the yoke and the airplane began to climb again.

"Now roll out level for a minute and then turn left to two-seven-zero."

Jesse leveled the wings momentarily, then turned left. As he rolled out again on the westerly heading, he looked to his left and saw that he was level with the mountaintop and only about three hundred yards away from it. Then he saw something else: around fifty feet down from the mountaintop there was an opening in the brush, and, set into the mountainside, a large round opening with a grate over it.

"Let's circumnavigate the mountain, now," Casey said. "Just fly right around it, and we'll head back to the airport."

Jesse continued around the mountain, and he saw two more of the grates. Somebody came running out of one of the small buildings on top and trained binoculars on the airplane.

Casey took the copilot's yoke and wagged the

wings. "They know my airplane," he said. "Anybody else would get a stinger up his ass, flying this close to the mountain."

Jesse continued around the mountain and, on the town side, which was sheer cliffs, he saw two more grates.

"Now fly a heading of zero-niner-zero until you see the field. That'll put you on a downwind for runway two-seven."

The field appeared after a couple of minutes, and Jesse, following Casey's instructions, entered a right downwind for the runway, descending slowly, while Casey announced their intentions over the radio. Jesse turned base, then turned onto the final approach.

"You're a little high," Casey said. "Reduce power a good bit. That's right, now she'll fly you right down to the threshold."

Jesse pulled back on the throttle, and the airplane settled toward the end of the runway.

"Start your flare, now, and reduce power even more. You want an airspeed of seventy knots over the numbers. Here we go, flare some more, now."

Jesse hauled back on the yoke, the stall horn went off, and the airplane struck the runway solidly. "Sorry about that, Pat."

"That was just a nice firm landing," Casey said, laughing. "You just fell about the last five feet."

Jesse taxied back to the hangar, and Casey showed him the shutdown procedure.

"Pat, that was a real treat; thank you."

"You did real good, Jesse; you must have had a pretty good instructor."

"Fellow by the name of Floyd; a real old-timer with about ten thousand hours."

"Those guys are the best. I've got my instructor's ticket; you want to start working on your license again? Cost you eighty bucks an hour for the aircraft and fuel; I'm free."

"That's a terrific offer, Pat; I'd really like that."

"Next Sunday, same time?"

"You bet."

"I'll get you the instruction book and a new logbook."

"Can I borrow your pilot's operating handbook until next week? I'd like to read up on the operating speeds and all that."

"Good idea." Casey reached into the cockpit and handed him a thick notebook.

"Thanks, see you next Sunday," Jesse said.

"Hey, Jimmy!" Casey called to a man near the fuel truck. "Top her off, will you? Just the right tank."

Jesse got back into his truck and drove off. He checked the speedometer for distance, then drove home. He'd learned a lot more than he'd expected to on a Sunday afternoon.

That night, Jesse had the dream again. He was walking down Fifth Avenue in New York, and he saw the little girl he had taken for his own Carrie. He had decided it wasn't Carrie, and this was where the dream had stopped. Only this time it continued. It was if they were all in slow motion. The woman bent over and pointed to something in the shop, as Jesse watched through the window, and she seemed terribly familiar. Then she straightened up, and Jesse could see for the first time that, even under the overcoat, the woman was pregnant. He jerked awake, this time with the scene fixed in his mind. Then he remembered something Kip had said, about how he would take care of his family if he lost his job.

Jesse sat very still, hardly daring to breathe, lest the dream should leave him. Machinery in his mind turned, like the tumblers in a safe, and the combination clicked.

Doors swung open. He fell back on the pillow, exhausted from his insight.

CHAPTER

48

The fax arrived on Tuesday morning. Jesse saw it spat from the machine, and he resisted walking over there. The secretary took the document from the machine, glanced at it and took it into Herman Muller's office.

Muller read the letter, then read it again, then picked up the phone and dialed a number. He spoke for some minutes, nodding a lot, then hung up and walked into Jesse's office.

"Jesse, I've had a fax from a company in Maryland that's looking for a new supplier. I called the fellow— Withers, his name is—and it looks like he's hot to trot. You think you could fly east the next day or two and make the same presentation to him you made to the folks in New York?"

"I'd be glad to, Herman."

Muller handed him the fax. "Here's the letter; you work it out with Withers about when you'll meet." He went back to his office.

Jesse went out to the receptionist. "Agnes, could you check on a flight schedule for me tomorrow from Spokane to Washington D.C. National Airport?"

"Sure, Jesse. You're becoming the real jet-setter, aren't you?"

"That's right; I'm meeting Elizabeth Taylor there."

When Jesse had the schedule on his desk he picked up the phone, called Nashua Building Supply and asked for John Withers.

"Mr. Withers, this is Jesse Barron at St. Clair Wood Products. My boss, Herman Muller, said you'd like to get together and talk about plywood and chipboard."

"That's right, Mr. Barron," Withers said, "and we're kind of in a hurry. When do you think you could get to College Park?"

"You're right near Washington, aren't you?"

"Yep. Just north of there. I could meet you at National Airport."

"Tell you what; I'm looking at a schedule that would get me into Washington early tomorrow evening. How about we meet at your office the following morning."

"Ten o'clock sharp?"

"That's fine with me. Your address is on your letterhead."

"Right, any map of the area will show you where we are. We're not far from the University of Maryland."

"If I get lost I'll call you."

"See you Thursday morning," Withers said.

Jesse stayed late at the office, working at the computer. He wrote a document of some twenty pages, then printed out half a dozen copies. He put each copy into a Federal Express envelope, made some phone calls to information in New York, Washington, Los Angeles, Atlanta, Miami and Seattle, then filled out the FedEx forms and inserted one into the plastic holder of each envelope. He put them into his briefcase, locked up the office and went home.

At dawn the next morning they were driving toward Spokane.

"We can talk," Jesse said. "I've been over this truck with a fine-toothed comb and it's not bugged."

"Why am I driving you to the airport?" Jenny asked.

"If anybody asks, your car doesn't have four-wheel drive, and you wanted the pickup to use if it snows. It's supposed to snow."

"Okay, I understand. What are all these envelopes on the front seat between us?"

"They're Federal Express packages. I'm going to call you when I get to my hotel, and again before I leave the hotel the next morning. I'll just ask how you're doing and if you and Carey are okay; innocuous stuff like that. Don't talk about anything important. After that, if I fail to call you every twelve hours, or if I say the words, 'I love you very dearly,' on the phone, I want you to go straight to the Federal Express substation in town and hand them these packages. They're already addressed and the cost will be billed to Wood Products' account."

"Why do you want me to do this?"

Jesse told her, at length, what he was planning.

She didn't say anything for a long time, then she sighed. "Are you sure there's no other way to do it?"

"I can't think of another one."

"All right, that's good enough for me. I'll get Carey ready. This is what I'll tell her." She spelled out a story.

"I like that; it should do the job."

"When will we leave St. Clair?"

"As soon as I possibly can after I get back. A lot depends on what happens while I'm gone."

"What if this doesn't work? What if it all goes wrong and you can't come back?"

"If that happens, if you don't hear from me during any twelve-hour period, I want you to drive the truck into your garage, and crawl underneath it. There's a safe welded to the chassis; it'll be covered with mud and ice, so you'll have to clean it off before you can open it." He told her the combination and asked her to repeat it to him. "Good, now don't forget it; repeat it to yourself a lot.

"Inside the safe are several things: there are passports for you and Carey; there is a little over fifty thousand dollars in cash; and there is a pistol. I want you to take Carey, and, in the dead of night, take some clothes, get into the truck and drive to Seattle. Find a downtown parking garage and leave the truck there, then find a travel agent. There are nonstop flights from Seattle to Tokyo; make two reservations and pay for them in cash. Then go to a bank; buy ten thousand dollars in traveler's checks, keep a couple of thousand in cash, then buy a cashier's check with the remainder of the money. Go to the airport, get on the plane and fly to Tokyo. When you arrive there, don't leave the airport; buy two tickets on the next flight to Hong Kong, then make room reservations at the Peninsular Hotel for seven nights. When you get to Hong Kong, check in, get some sleep and do some sightseeing. If I am still free, I'll meet you in Hong Kong within the week or I'll call you with other instructions. If you haven't heard from me in a week, fly to Sydney, Australia, and check into the Harbour Hotel.

"An old friend of mine tends bar in the hotel; his name is Arthur Simpson, but everybody calls him Bluey. Call or see him once a week; I'll be in touch with him. If he tells you I'm in prison, then it's time to forget about me, because I'll be there a long time. Bluey will help you get work papers and find a job and a place to live. Start a new life."

"Without you?"

"If I'm free, I'll be with you eventually; if I'm not, I won't be, and either way, Bluey will hear about it. Your passports are real, so you don't have to worry about that; you can renew them at the embassy when they expire. After a year or two, it should be safe to come back to this country, if that's what you want. I'd feel better if you stayed in Australia."

"What's the gun in the safe for?"

"That's to use on anybody who tries to keep you from leaving St. Clair. If Pat Casey or any of his people follows you and tries to take you back, shoot him where he stands. I take it you know how to fire a pistol?"

"Everybody in St. Clair knows how; we learned as children."

"If you can get out of town, even if you have to kill somebody doing it, I don't think they'll send out a police alert for you; you have too much of a story to tell, and if you are arrested, don't hesitate to tell it. The money will buy you a lawyer, and you won't be convicted for shooting somebody who tried to make a prisoner of you. And remember, throw the gun into the nearest trash can before you go into the airport."

Jesse pulled up at the airport curbside check-in. He switched off the engine and turned to her. "Jenny, you're a strong person; I know you can do this, all of it."

"I can if you want me to," she said.

"It's the best I can do for you." He took her in his arms and held her for a moment, telling her that he loved her, then he got out of the truck. "I hope I'll be back," he said, then he turned and walked into the terminal.

CHAPTER

49

Jesse arrived at Washington National at seven in the evening. In the gift shop he bought a book of large-scale maps of Washington and its suburbs, then rented a car and drove into the city. He checked into the Watergate Hotel, then phoned Jenny.

"Hi, I made it safely."

"Glad to hear it; everything all right?"

"Everything's fine; my appointment's at ten in the morning. If we finish by noon or so, I can make a three o'clock airplane home. I'll call you and let you know what plane I'm on."

"I'll meet you in Spokane."

"Did it snow?"

"Yes, and it's still snowing; we've had eight or nine inches, and they say we'll have a foot."

"I'm glad you kept the pickup, then. Well, I'd better get a bite to eat and some sleep; I'll talk to you tomorrow."

"I love you."

"You, too; say goodnight to Carey for me."

He hung up, then ordered dinner from room service. While he waited for it to arrive, he picked up a Washington phone directory, but could not find what he wanted. He had more luck with the information operator.

He studied his maps for a few minutes, then went downstairs and asked for his car. He forced himself to drive slowly, normally, not to get excited. He drove into northwest Washington and found Argyle Terrace, driving slowly until he spotted the house number. He drove to the end of the block, turned around, drove back down the street and parked a couple of houses away. His view was good. He could see the whole front of the house and one side, and it appeared that the kitchen was on the back corner. The lights were on there, and he could see a woman moving about, probably cleaning up after dinner.

When he had seen enough, he drove back to the Watergate and tried to watch a movie on television, but he couldn't concentrate. He switched it off and lay in the bed, planning the next day to the nth degree, rehearsing his actions. It was past two when he finally fell asleep.

He found Nashua Building Supply with no difficulty, across the road from the university, as Withers had said. It did not seem that he had been followed. He parked in front and went into the huge, hangarlike building. He was shown to an office constructed in the rear of the building and was greeted by John Withers, who shook his hand and closed the office door behind him.

"This way," Withers said, leading him to another door, which opened to the outside at the rear of the building.

A plain sedan was waiting, with only a driver inside. Jesse recognized him as the man who had followed him in San Francisco.

"We've only got a two-minute drive," the man said. "Kip has arranged for a room at the university. Get your head down."

Jesse was led into a red brick building and down a hallway to a room where another man in a suit stood guard. The man rapped on the door, and Kip Fuller stepped out into the hallway.

"Come over here a minute," Kip said, drawing Jesse away from the other two men. "There are some things I have to say to you before we go into that room."

"Shoot," Jesse replied.

"First of all, the people in there are Barker; an assistant attorney general with responsibility for oversight of Justice Department law enforcement agencies, reporting directly to the AG; an army brigadier general who oversees all unconventional warfare units for the Pentagon; and a bird colonel, who is a military adviser to the National Security Council, and who has the ear of the president. Does that sound like who you wanted?"

"It certainly does."

"Now listen; I have not reported your threat of 'move in two weeks or exposure' to Barker, and it's extremely important that you make no threats while you are in that room. These people are here to listen to you make your case, and they're your best chance of getting this done the way you want it done."

"I understand."

"Okay, follow me. By the way, I won't be making any introductions; they'll think you don't know who they are."

"Right." Jesse followed Kip into the room. The seats were arranged on steeply pitched tiers, and each desk had its own lamp. The shades were drawn and the room was lit by those lamps and by floodlights that illuminated the blackboard area, where satellite photographs of St. Clair and the surrounding area were mounted. The photographs that Jesse had himself taken were there, too, and he guessed that they had been computer enhanced. He followed Kip to the lectern.

"Gentlemen," Kip said, halting their conversation, "I'd like to introduce Jesse Warden. Jesse, why don't you begin at the beginning; explain who you are and how you came to be in St. Clair."

"Good morning, gentlemen," Jesse said, taking a deep breath and trying to calm a sudden attack of stage fright. "My name, as Mr. Fuller has said, is Jesse Warden. I was formerly an agent of the Drug Enforcement Agency, attached to the South Florida Task Force and specializing in undercover work. My commander at that time was Mr. Barker, and Mr. Fuller was my colleague in the office.

"Just over two years ago, I was arrested and charged with the theft of half a million dollars from the office evidence locker and the murder of my partner, whose body was found in the trunk of my car, along with the money."

There was the slightest stirring among his audience.

"I was innocent of both charges, but I was convicted of the murder of a federal official and theft of government property; I was given a life sentence and incarcerated in the Atlanta Federal Penitentiary. After serving fourteen months there I was released in the custody of Mr. Barker and Mr. Fuller and offered a presidential pardon, if I would assist in the conviction of the head of a religious cult and his two chief aides, who were rumored to be amassing large numbers of weapons and other materiel in a small town in the Idaho panhandle."

Barker was glowering at him; apparently, he had not expected any mention of the pardon.

Jesse took the group step by step through his infiltration of the First Church of the Aryan Universe, and finally, through a complete description of what he had seen in Coldwater's underground fortifications. His audience maintained a dead silence until he had finished, and the silence continued for another half a minute thereafter.

Finally, the man who Jesse assumed to be the assistant AG spoke. "Mr. Warden, have you determined what Coldwater's intentions are?"

"No, sir, I haven't, and I have the feeling that I won't know until it's too late to do anything about it. All I can tell you is that he's planning something that might make things so hot for him and his followers that he would have to retreat underground."

"Do you think Coldwater is insane?"

"I have no qualifications in that sphere; I can only give you my personal impression of the man. There are times when I think he's nutty as a fruitcake, but he is always very self-possessed and seems to always know exactly what he is doing. I think he certainly has very pronounced megalomaniacal tendencies, but I'm not sure whether that qualifies as insanity."

"Do you think he is fully capable of using this . . . facility he has built?"

"I have the very strong impression that he is determined to do so. Whether it will be in a day or a year, I cannot tell you."

The man who Jesse thought was the brigadier general spoke up. "For a start, why can't a detachment of federal officers in plain clothes simply drive up to Coldwater's house and arrest him?"

Jesse suppressed a wild laugh. "Sir, that would be about as easy as driving through the White House gates and arresting the president of the United States. The very first thing that must be done is to take the mountaintop and the reinforced facilities there, so that

Coldwater cannot bring his people inside and button it down tight."

"I'd be interested in hearing how you think that could be done," the general said. "I mean, after seeing these satshots of the place, I'd really like your suggestions."

"I'm not a military man, sir, but if it were up to me I'd go at it in three ways: first, I'd infiltrate a large armed contingent at night three or four miles north of the mountain and have them approach it on foot and scale the sides; second, I'd send a large truck or two, filled with troops and disguised in some way, right up the road to the top and try ramming the gates; third, I'd send helicopters, armed with armor-penetrating weapons to attack the smaller structures on top, and follow immediately with many troop-carrying choppers. There are, of course, drawbacks to each of these methods."

"And what are the drawbacks?" the general asked.

"First, it would not surprise me to learn that Coldwater has placed some sort of sensors in the woods to the north to pick up anyone on foot, and I know that there are machine-gun emplacements on all sides for the purposes of repelling infantry; second, I think the chances of trucks getting up the road undetected and breaking open the gates are no better than fifty-fifty; and third, I had a look at the top of the mountain in a light airplane last Sunday, and I was told that there were stinger missiles in place that would take out any approaching aircraft. You're likely to lose some choppers."

Jesse turned back to the satellite photographs. "I think, also, that in any first strike, you should take the police station, here, which is the security center; the telephone company, here; and I think you should cut the high voltage power line that brings in the town's electricity from the north, or get the power company to. That would do a lot to cut or, at least, confuse their communications with Coldwater and his with his people."

"You know," the general said, "if this were a proper war, I would just bombard that place with heavy artillery until there was nothing left standing, then walk in."

"I think you can see that that is impossible in this situation," Jesse said.

"Yes, I can see that," the general said wearily.

Jesse spoke up again, pointing to the photographs. "Coldwater lives here, Casey here and Ruger here. If you can knock out power, security and telephones simultaneously with capturing Coldwater, Casey and Ruger, your battle would be over, except for the mopping up. That, of course, could be nasty."

"It's all going to be nasty," the general said quietly.

There were other questions for nearly an hour, then the meeting broke up. The general approached the lectern and stuck out his hand. "You're a brave man," he said. "I'm glad I'm not in your shoes." He turned to Barker. "Dan, we'll get back to you first thing in the morning with some kind of rough plan."

Barker nodded and shook the general's hand. "Look forward to hearing from you."

The three visitors left, and Barker motioned for Jesse to take a seat. "I've got some questions for you, Jesse."

"All right," Jesse said. "Let's make it quick; I've got a three o'clock flight from Dulles Airport to make."

"When did you first meet Charley Bottoms?" Barker asked.

Jesse saw where this was going. "I saw him around the yard on those rare occasions when I wasn't in solitary," he said. "I never spoke to him until the day Kip came to get me out. He came to my punishment cell and said he wanted me to join up with the

Aryan Nation crowd in the joint, said they'd protect me from the other cons. He offered to beat me to death if I turned him down."

"And when did you next see him?" Barker asked.

"Last week, when he turned up at a meeting at Coldwater's house. We drove up to the top of the mountain together, and he told me you'd sprung him right after me. That's the sum total of our contact."

Kip spoke up. "I've spoken with Bottoms about this, and he confirms everything Jesse has said." He turned toward Jesse. "I know this wasn't part of our deal, but do you think you could take out Coldwater prior to our going in?"

"The chances of my getting at him and staying alive would be slim," Jesse said. "And you're right, that's not part of my deal. What I want to know, Kip, Dan, is are you going to stick by our deal?"

Barker glowered at him again. "You'll get the pardon when we've cleaned out this nest of maniacs, and not before. And I'll expect you to do whatever you're told to do when we go in."

Before Jesse could speak, Kip held out a warning hand. "Not now, Jess; we'll talk about it later."

Jesse shook Kip's hand, then, ignoring Barker, went back to his car and drove south. But he didn't head for Dulles Airport, or, for that matter, for National.

CHAPTER

50

Jesse drove slowly down Argyle Terrace, then back again, casing the house. In daylight he could see a fenced backyard behind the place, and as he watched, a woman passed through the kitchen and out the back door.

He quickly parked the car and walked to the front door. Glancing up and down the street, he pretended to ring the doorbell, then turned the knob; the door was unlocked. He walked into a large entrance hall and looked around; somewhere a television set was on. He turned left and walked through the dining room and into the kitchen. A coffee pot sat on a warmer, and he poured himself a cup and sat down at the kitchen table. He could hear voices from out back. A soap opera was on television; he hated the music that played constantly during the programs. It was good coffee.

After a few minutes, he heard a foot scrape on the back steps, and she walked into the kitchen.

"Hello, Arlene," he said.

She froze, staring at him, saying nothing.

"It's Jesse Warden," he said. "I'm sorry I don't look quite the same as I did in my Miami days."

Her shoulders relaxed, but her face remained wary. "Why are you here?" she asked, glancing at the wall phone.

"We'll call Kip in a few minutes," he said soothingly. "Now pour yourself a cup of coffee and have a seat. Let's talk."

She ignored the coffee but sat down at the table.

"It's been a while," he said. "What, two and a half, three years?"

"About that," she managed to whisper. "Why are you here, Jesse?"

"I want to see her. I want you to call her in from the backyard, tell her there's a friend here. After we've visited for a few minutes, we'll call Kip, then I'll leave."

She didn't move.

"You've nothing to fear from me, Arlene; I'm not here to hurt you. Call her from the door, please; don't go out into the yard."

Reluctantly, she rose and opened the back door. "Carrie, please come inside; you have a visitor."

"An old friend," Jesse said.

"It's an old friend, Carrie."

Jesse was suddenly filled with panic. She wouldn't know him, would scream at the sight of his battered face.

The little girl came into the kitchen, her cheeks red with the cold, her eyes bright. "Who is it, Aunt Arlene?" she asked. Then she saw Jesse.

"Hello, Rabbit," he said. Only he had ever called her that.

She blinked, staring at him. "Are you my daddy?" she asked, finally.

"I sure am," Jesse said. "And I'm so very glad to see you."

She came closer to him, gazing into his face. "You look different," she said.

"I know; I had an accident, but I'm fine now."

Suddenly, she rushed at him, threw her arms around him, laughing. "Oh, Daddy!" she cried. "Aunt Arlene and Uncle Kip told me you had gone to heaven."

"They were wrong," he whispered into her ear. "I'm right here with you, my Rabbit." He held her back and looked at her. "You've grown so; you're a big girl, now."

"I'm going to be six next month," she said.

"I know, sweetheart, and I'm going to get you a wonderful present. Six is a very important birthday; you'll be going to school in the fall."

"Where's Mommy?" she asked. "They said she was in heaven, too."

"She is in heaven, sweetheart, but she looks down on you, and she knows what a wonderful little girl you are." He was having trouble maintaining his composure; his throat was tightening up.

"I have a new little cousin," Carrie said. "He's in the backyard in the stroller. Would you like to see him?"

"I would in just a minute, Rabbit. Why don't you go and make sure he's all right, and Aunt Arlene and I will be out in a few minutes."

She gave him a big kiss on the cheek. "Don't be long," she said, then ran out the back door.

"Jesse, I want you to understand," Arlene said. "We never set out to steal Carrie from you; we thought you would spend the rest of your life in prison. We couldn't bear the thought of Carrie being put up for adoption; Kip and I both thought it was better that you didn't know where she was."

"I believe you, Arlene," Jesse said. "But you understand, things are different now."

"Are they so very different, Jesse? Kip hasn't told

me in any detail what you're doing, but it was my distinct impression that your life is constantly in danger. Do you think you're ready to make a home for Carrie?"

"Arlene, my life was constantly in danger when I was working undercover in Miami, and yes, I think I'm ready to make a home for Carrie. I've remarried, and she'll have a sister."

"I don't know how to argue with you," she said. "Carrie has missed you so much. She still talks about you all the time."

"Thanks for telling me that," Jesse replied. "Now, I don't have much time, and I'd better call Kip." He went to the wall phone and dialed the office number.

"She would never call us Mommy and Daddy," Arlene said quietly, and a tear ran down her cheek.

"This is Fuller," Kip said.

"Kip, it's Jesse."

"Did you miss your plane?"

"I'm afraid so; I had another stop to make."

"Another stop?"

"I'm at your house."

Kip made a sort of strangling noise before he could speak. "Jesse, if you lay a hand on any of them, I swear I'll have you back in jail today."

"Kip, Kip; there's no need for that. Everything is going to be all right."

"What do you want, Jesse?"

"It's very simple; I want my little girl."

"Jesse, you can't; we've adopted her, and it's all perfectly legal."

"Kip, take a couple of deep breaths, and listen to me."

"Let me speak to Arlene."

Jesse looked at the phone and saw a speaker button; he pressed it. "Arlene is right here," he said.

Arlene stepped closer to the phone. "I'm here, Kip; we're all right. He's seen Carrie; she knew him."

"I'm sorry he's put you through this, honey," Kip said.

Jesse spoke up. "I'm going to try to make this as easy for everybody as I can, Kip. I'm going to explain this to you and Arlene, so please listen."

"I'm listening," Kip said.

"And Kip, it would be a very grave error, bad for everybody, if you called the police."

"I haven't called anybody, Jesse; tell me what you want."

"This is how it's going to be: Carrie and I are going to leave the house in just a minute. Everything is going to be calm and orderly, and there won't be any fuss."

"Jesse, you can't do this," Kip said. "You'll put her in very serious danger."

"No, I won't do that, believe me, Kip; she'll be very safe with me and her new mother."

"Oh, God," Kip moaned.

"Arlene is taking this better than you are; now settle down and listen to me."

"I'm listening."

"First of all, I'm very grateful to both of you for taking such good care of Carrie. Arlene has explained your reasons for not telling me, and I accept them. Because I'm grateful, I'm going to try and forget that you knew Barker framed me—"

"Jesse, I couldn't prove it."

"Kip, listen to me. Barker was the only one who could have done it; you knew that, and Barker knows you know; that's why he's letting you run this show. I know you felt badly about it, and that's why you got me out of prison."

"I had no evidence, Jesse. If I had, I'd have nailed him."

"I believe you, Kip."

Arlene spoke up. "I'm going upstairs and pack some things for Carrie." She left the room.

"Daddy!" Carrie called from the backyard. "Come and see the baby!"

Jesse cracked the door. "I'll be there in just a minute, Rabbit!" He picked up the telephone receiver. "Kip, listen very carefully, because this is the last time you and I are going to discuss Carrie. She's coming with me, now, and you're going to think up something to tell the neighbors—the adoption went wrong, something like that."

"Jesse, you can't go on the run with Carrie," Kip moaned.

"I'm not going on the run," Jesse said. "I'm going back to St. Clair with Carrie, and now I'm going to explain to you why you aren't going to do the slightest thing to stop me or get her back."

"I'm listening."

"You remember the threat I made to Barker?"

"Yes."

"I'm withdrawing that; I'm going back to St. Clair and help you nail Coldwater, even though that exceeds our agreement. But if you make the slightest difficulty for me with regard to Carrie, I'll blow the whole thing sky high. I've already made arrangements to do that, unless I periodically make certain phone calls. If, for any reason, I'm unable to make those calls, half the newspapers in the country will receive a certain information packet containing irrefutable proof of what you're up to. If you make a move on me, Coldwater will immediately know everything, and you know what that means."

"I know," Kip said weakly.

"Even if you take Coldwater cleanly and shut down his operation, you still won't want the papers to know about me, Kip. You'd never be able to explain to the press why you had a convicted murderer released from prison, unless you exonerated me, and Barker can't let you do that, because he knows he'd go down. Do you understand me?"

"I understand."

"There's more than your career at stake, here, Kip; there's your life. If you make a move on me or Carrie, I'll find you, and I'll kill you, and you know I can do it."

"I know, Jesse."

"You still have a chance to be a hero in the department, Kip; arrange for Justice to forget about me, and I'll help you be a hero."

"I'll do as you say, Jesse."

"When this is over, my family and I are going to disappear."

"I'll get you in the witness protection program," Kip said.

"I don't want that; I'll make my own life, but you and the federal government are going to have to forget I ever existed."

"I'll see to it," Kip said.

"I want my fingerprint and criminal records destroyed."

"I'll do it."

"I don't want any problems from Barker."

"I can handle Barker."

"If he gives you a hard time about me, tell him I'll kill him, too. He understands that sort of threat."

"Barker won't be a problem; I won't let him."

Arlene came back into the room carrying a small suitcase and a teddy bear.

"Goodbye, Kip; I'll call you from St. Clair."

"Goodbye, Jess; don't let anything happen to Carrie."

"She'll be fine, I promise you."

Arlene set Carrie's things on the kitchen table. "She won't go anywhere without the bear," she said.

Jesse nodded. He'd given her the bear when she was no more than an infant. He stepped out the kitchen door and walked to where Carrie was waiting with the baby.

"Isn't he beautiful?" Carrie said.

Jesse knelt next to the stroller. "He certainly is," he said. "And do you know something? You've got more than a new cousin; you've got a new sister."

Carrie's eyes widened. "I have? Where is she?"

"You're coming home with me, and I'll tell you all about her on the way," Jesse said, scooping up his daughter in his arms.

In the kitchen he gave her the teddy bear, picked up her suitcase and turned to Arlene Fuller. "Thank you," he said, then he walked out of the house with his daughter.

CHAPTER

51

Jesse sweated National airport, even though he had told Kip he was leaving from Dulles. He turned in his rent-a-car and, with Carrie in tow, went to the airline counter and bought her a one-way ticket to Spokane, all the while sweeping the area with his eyes. The ticket bought, he went to a phone and called Jenny.

"Hi, everything's fine; I'm making the plane all right."

"Good, I'll meet you in Spokane."

"How's Carey?"

"She's just fine, and she's looking forward to ... seeing you. No problems at all?"

"Not a one; I think I sold some major plywood this morning."

"See you tonight."

Jesse had a few minutes before the flight, so he made a tour of the airport shops with Carrie, checking each window for the reflection of a tail. By the time they reached their gate, Jesse's heart was pounding. The boarding call asked for people with small children first, so he was able to sit on the plane and scan the face of each person who passed them. Any one of half a dozen businessmen fit the type he was looking for, but none of them showed the slightest interest in a man and a little girl.

Carrie was asleep before the airplane left the ground, and as soon as the seatbelt sign went off, Jesse ordered a double bourbon. He needed it. He stroked the little head on a pillow in his lap and tried not to think of the future. For the next few days he must live entirely in the present and not be distracted by dreams of yet another new life.

Halfway home, Carrie woke up. She stared into her father's eyes. "Where have you been?" she asked. "If you weren't in heaven, why didn't you come get me?"

"Rabbit, believe me, I came the first minute I could. When Uncle Kip and Aunt Arlene took you to Washington, they didn't tell me, so I had to look for you for a real long time."

"Oh," she said.

"Were they nice to you?"

"Oh, yes; they gave me lots of toys and things, but I wouldn't call Aunt Arlene mommy, and she didn't like that."

"You did the right thing, sweetheart," he said. "Now I have some wonderful news for you."

"Oh, tell me, tell me!"

"You remember I told you I had found you a sister?"

"Yes, where is she?"

"We're going to a town called St. Clair, and she's waiting for you there. It'll be real late when we get home, and she'll be asleep, but you'll meet her in the morning."

"Is her mommy in heaven, too?"

"No, her mommy is meeting us at the airport, and I think you're going to love her a lot. She's going to be your new mommy."

Carrie's eyes widened. "I didn't know you could have two mommies."

"When your first mommy goes to heaven, then your daddy can find you a new mommy."

"And you found me a new one?"

"I sure did, and she's wonderful."

"What's her name?"

"Her name is Jenny."

"Do I have to call her mommy?"

"Not unless you want to. It would make her very happy if you did, though."

"Did you and Jenny get married?"

"Yes, we did."

"Well, I guess she's my new mommy, then, isn't she?"

"Yes, she is."

"And I won't live with Aunt Arlene and Uncle Kip anymore?"

"No, you'll live with your new family."

"Will I ever see Aunt Arlene and Uncle Kip again?"

"Maybe, but not for a long, long time."

"Will it make them sad?"

"Yes, they'll miss you a lot, but they have the new baby to love."

"That's true," Carrie said, nodding gravely. "They won't be all by themselves." Soon she was asleep again.

Jesse carried the little girl, still sleeping, off the airplane, and Jenny was at the gate to meet them.

"I'll introduce you to your new daughter," he said, "if she ever wakes up."

"Plenty of time for that," Jenny said. "What have you told her?"

"I've told her about you and Carey."

"What are we going to do about the names? They sound just alike."

"I haven't a clue."

When they had left the airport and were driving toward St. Clair Jesse asked, "What did you tell Carey about us?"

"I've told her that you had a daughter by your first marriage. She immediately asked if all your daughters weren't killed in the car wreck, but I told her one of them wasn't in the car with you, and she had been living with friends in another town until you were ready to bring her to St. Clair."

"Do you think she'll tell anyone at school?"

"I've told her it's a big secret for the time being, and when she asked me why, I told her that was a secret, too. She seemed to accept that."

"Do you think she'll turn us in at school?"

"The school has warped some of Carey's attitudes, and we're going to have to work to help her get over that. But she and I have a bond that the school hasn't been able to penetrate, and if she tells me she'll keep the secret, then she will. You can depend on that."

Jesse hoped she was right.

They arrived at home in St. Clair after two in the morning, and Jesse carried the luggage into the house first, making sure they were not being watched.

They tucked Carrie into bed, and then Jesse spent another two hours going over the whole house, looking for bugs. It was after four when he finally went to bed.

"Did you find anything?" Jenny asked.

"There were two: one in the living room and one in the kitchen. I've disabled the one in the kitchen, so be sure and keep Carrie out of the living room when I'm away from the house."

Jenny snuggled up close. "She's a beautiful child. I'm going to love her, I know it."

"And she's going to love you," Jesse said.

52

Jesse arrived at the office the following morning to find a fax from Nashua Building Supply waiting, placing a large order for plywood. It was good cover, and he was grateful to Kip for that. He waited until everyone had left for lunch before calling Kip.

"How's Carrie?" Kip asked immediately, and there was pain in his voice.

"She's very well. She slept through most of the flight and all of the ride from the airport. She met her new mother and sister this morning, and she seemed very happy with them. But I don't want to talk about Carrie again."

Kip was suddenly all business. "All right. What's up?"

"You remember how you got the Zippo camera to me?"

"Yes."

"Can the same man deliver another package to me?"

"Sure; what do you want?"

"A list of things; got a pencil?"

"Shoot."

"I want a pound of plastic explosive and half a dozen detonators and timers, and an explosives mat about four feet square."

"What are you going to do with all that?"

"You're just going to have to trust me, Kip."

"All right, what else?"

"A couple of hand grenades; something incendiary. I also want a light machine gun and half a dozen clips of ammunition. And I want some night goggles, the lightest you can find."

"When do you need it?"

"Tomorrow night."

"I think I can do that. Where do you want it delivered?"

"On the road going east from St. Clair, just beyond the Wood Products plant, there's a bridge over a creek. Have him use duct tape to fix the package in the supports under the bridge. Tell him to make sure it can't be seen, except from underneath. Tell him after he makes the delivery to fix a twelve-inch strip of duct tape to the northwest end of the bridge, so that it can be easily seen from the road, as a signal that the goods are there."

"I'll get right on it. You sure you don't want to tell me what's going on?"

"I'm sure; do you have a date for your entry into St. Clair yet?"

"The army delivered a preliminary plan this morning, and we're still going over it. My best guess would be that the earliest possible time would be seven days; the latest, ten days."

"I'm going to try to make it easier for them," Jesse said.

"I'll tell them."

"I'll try to call you every day from now until you go in," Jesse said. "It's critically important that I know exactly what the plan is and when it begins. I can't be of any help to you unless I know that."

"I'll see that you're fully briefed. Do you think you could make a meet with somebody to go over the details?"

Jesse thought for a minute. "I doubt it; it could be too dangerous at this stage of the game. I'll think about it, though, and let you know."

"As you wish; I just want you to know everything we know."

"Thanks, but we'll probably have to do it on the phone." He said goodbye and broke the connection, and not a moment too soon. An instant after he had concealed the phone in his lunchbox, Pat Casey appeared in the reception room, carrying a red zippered briefcase.

Jesse left his office and greeted the police chief.

"Hear you've been out of town," Casey said.

"Just overnight; we had a call from a big building supply company in Maryland who'd heard about us, so I went out there and made my pitch. Come on in the office." He led Casey inside, closed the door and handed him the fax from Nashua. "Here's the result."

"Hey, good going," Casey said. "Jack Gene will be pleased to hear it. You making any progress on getting into Muller's computer ledgers?"

"Not yet, but I've hardly been in the office since we discussed it. I think the best way is for me just to ask Muller if I can see the books."

"Is there no other way?"

"His computer password is in his head; I don't know how else to get it."

"Use your own judgment, then; all he can say is no."

"The other way is to try to figure out what the password is, but that's a real long shot."

"I agree. I'll leave it in your hands," Casey replied.

He held up the red briefcase. "Oh, here's why I dropped by; it's your flight training materials."

Jesse accepted the case, opened it and shook out its contents on his desk. There were a large red-covered instruction book, a logbook, a book of sample test questions and a manual flight computer. He had seen them all when he had taken his first lessons years before.

"I'd like you to read the first four chapters before our lesson on Sunday," Casey said. "Since you've already been through most of the course once, we should be able to move fast."

"Okay, I'll start on it tonight."

"By the way, you remember the group Jack Gene had visiting last week?"

"That fellow Bottoms and the others?"

"Right; he's having them back next Wednesday for another meeting, plus a few others representing other groups in the Northwest. He'd like you to be there."

"What time?"

"There's a dinner at seven that evening, followed by an important business meeting. Jack Gene's going to be making a big pitch to sell them some weapons. We've got good sources, and we can make an outstanding profit."

"I'll be there."

Casey got up. "I'll see you Sunday afternoon at two."

"I'll be there, too."

When Casey had gone, Jesse looked at his watch. In ten minutes, people would be back from lunch. He got out the phone and called Kip again.

"You forget something?" Kip asked.

"No, I just heard something. You're going to have to go in next Wednesday night."

"Jesus, Jesse, today's Friday."

"You said you might be able to do it in seven days; that gives you six."

"Why Wednesday night?"

"Because there are going to be a bunch of people here from other white supremacist groups to hear a weapons sales pitch from Coldwater. I'll be a witness to the meeting, so you can bag them all for arms dealing. Casey and Ruger will no doubt be there, too."

"Well, that's a terrific idea; I'll bring it up with the planning group and push them to make it."

"You do that; I've got to hang up before somebody comes in. Oh, and you can give your man until Sunday night to deliver my package."

"The extra time will help. See you."

Jesse put the phone away. He had a lot to do before next Wednesday.

CHAPTER

53

Saturday was Jesse's first whole day with Carrie in more than two years, and he relished every moment of it. The two little girls took to each other immediately, and both reacted soberly when the rules of Carrie's stay—that she remain inside and out of the living room at all times and that Carey tell no one of her presence—were explained to them. Jesse spent nearly every minute of the day with the two girls, and after supper, when it was time for bed, he tucked them both into their beds in Carey's room.

He kissed Jenny, then sat down in an easy chair in the living room and began to study. Before he went to bed at 2 A.M. he had read not just the four chapters that Casey had assigned, but the entire flight manual.

Jesse arrived at St. Clair Airport half an hour early for his flying lesson. He nodded to the fuel attendant, then took a stroll around the big hangar, peering through the windows of small airplanes. Pat Casey's Cessna 182 was parked in the premier position in the hangar; no aircraft had to be moved in order to get the Cessna out onto the apron. He noted that two huge sliding doors secured the hangar, and he paid particular attention to a combination padlock hanging open on its hasp. Whoever had set the combination into the lock had done it the easy way; 1234 opened the lock.

Next, Jesse strolled into the little flight office and looked around. A large map of the United States hung on one wall, and Jesse spent several minutes locating St. Clair and measuring distances to various other airports. He looked, too, at a rack of air charts on a counter, picked up one and noted which charts covered which areas of the country. Finally, he found an airport directory and flipped through it, making mental notes. Then he saw Casey's patrol car coming and stepped out of the building to meet the chief of police.

"How you doing, Jesse?" Casey asked.

"Fine, and looking forward to my lesson."

"Great, but first we do ground school."

"Of course."

Casey sat down on an old sofa in the flight office and motioned Jesse to join him. He then took his pupil methodically through the first four chapters of the flight manual, asking and answering questions as he went. When he was satisfied that Jesse was familiar with the material, he got up and headed for the hangar.

"Let's do a preflight inspection," Casey said. He opened the airplane door with a key, got out a fuel tester, then led Jesse around the airplane, following a checklist. When he was satisfied that the airplane was flightworthy and the two men had pushed the airplane out onto the apron, he handed Jesse the key. "Okay, hop into the left seat, and let's get going."

Soon they were in the air. Casey instructed Jesse to head a few miles south of town, then climb to six thousand feet. "We're going to be performing some maneuvers, and we want plenty of altitude," he explained.

While Jesse flew, he took in the landscape surrounding the airport. The principal obstruction was the
mountain that rose above the town, and that was to the
west of the airport, plus the low mountains to the north.
Anyone taking off from St. Clair could fly in a southerly
direction and easily avoid obstacles while climbing.

Casey had him perform shallow and steep turns,
then do some stalls. Jesse found his old experience
coming back to him, and he performed well. On one
occasion, Casey reached forward and pulled the red
mixture knob all the way out. The engine died.

"Okay, what are you going to do?" Casey asked.

"Find a place to land the damned thing, I guess,"
Jesse replied.

"First, establish eighty-eight knots of airspeed—
that's your best gliding range. Good, now where you
going to put it?"

Jesse looked around, then pointed. "There's a
straight stretch of road."

"Yeah, and it's also got a straight stretch of telephone poles right alongside it. Telephone wires are a
no-no."

The airplane had lost a thousand feet of altitude
when Jesse spotted a green pasture. "How about over
here?"

"Head for it, and we'll take a look," Casey said.

Jesse pointed the airplane at the field, and, keeping his airspeed steady, allowed the machine to
descend. He had lined up for the field and was down
to six hundred feet of altitude when he saw the cattle.

Casey pushed in the mixture control and the
engine leapt to life. "Better get out of here," he said.
"Both you and the cows are hamburger. You're dead."
He laughed. "Got to watch out for everything in an
emergency landing. Let's go home; you're tired, or you
wouldn't have made that mistake. Know where the
airport is?"

"Afraid not," Jesse said. "All this maneuvering has confused me."

"Put the identifier into the GPS," Casey said, pointing at the instrument. "That'll give you a heading."

Following Casey's instructions, Jesse dialed in the correct identifier, pressed a button twice, and a heading popped onto the little screen. "There it is; we're six and a half miles out, and the heading is three-three-zero."

"Exactly right. Now engage the autopilot. First, put the arrow on the instrument in front of you on three-three-zero, then press the alt and nav buttons, then the on button."

Jesse did as he was told, and he felt the autopilot take charge of the airplane.

"Now the autopilot will maintain our present altitude, and it will navigate us directly to the airport."

"How do you find out an airport's identifier?" Jesse asked.

Casey reached between the seats and held up a little book. "This has all the information about every airport in the West. Or, you can simply enter the name of the city into the GPS, and it will give you the identifier. Simple, huh?"

"Dead simple." Jesse saw the field ahead. "Pat, what's the range of this airplane?"

"About six hundred and fifty miles at maximum cruise in a no-wind situation. Of course, you almost never get a no-wind situation. Generally, the winds are westerly—higher at high altitudes and lower at lower ones, but you can get an anomaly in the weather and get the opposite. The airspeed indicator gives you your speed through the air, once you've set in your altitude and the temperature, and the GPS gives you your actual speed over the ground. It also give you your ETA at your current ground speed. Over there on your left is the fuel flow computer, which gives you the hours and minutes of flight time available on the fuel you have remaining; it's accurate to within a gallon. You compare the flight time remaining on the fuel flow computer to the ETA on the GPS. Allow yourself an hour's fuel for safety, and you know at any moment if you have enough fuel to reach the airport. "

"And what sort of cruise speed do you get?"

"Standard is about a hundred and forty knots, but I've got a lot of speed equipment—fancy wheel skirts, aileron gap seals, etcetera, so I get closer to one fifty-five."

Jesse nodded and flew over the field to get a look at the windsock. He selected a runway and turned downwind. Soon, they were pushing the airplane back into the hangar.

"Top her off," Casey called to the fuel attendant. Then he shook Jesse's hand. "You did good. We'll have you a private license in a couple of months."

"Thanks for your time, Pat. Next Sunday?"

"For sure." Casey got into his car and drove away.

Jesse went into the flight office and bought some charts and an airport directory.

As soon as the girls were in bed, he went to work. He spread out the charts on the dining room table and began measuring distances to various destinations.

CHAPTER

54

Jesse pored over the charts until midnight, then he began reading the pilot's operating handbook for the Cessna 182. He concentrated on the airplane's systems, then memorized the operating speeds for takeoff and landing and for the stall speeds. He read up on the avionics, aircraft icing and emergency procedures. By two o'clock his eyes were burning. He put down the book and got into his coat.

He drove once around the town, as if he were simply an insomniac out for a wee-hours drive. All was quiet. He parked in an alley, as he had done before, and walked to the courthouse. The locks were easier this time, and inside half an hour he had entered the county clerk's office and forged a birth certificate for Carrie.

As he walked back toward the truck the waxing moon came from behind the clouds and lit the streets as if it were daylight. Jesse crossed the street to stay in the shadows and, at that moment, he saw the police car.

It was driving slowly up the street toward him,

swinging its spotlight back and forth from one side of the street to the other, checking the storefronts. Jesse flattened himself against a building, feeling terribly exposed; if he ducked into a doorway, he would be illuminated when the light hit the front door of the shop. He stood, frozen, waiting to be seen, trying to make up a story to explain his presence on the street in the middle of the night.

The spotlight hit the front of a shop across the street, then swung to the other side. As it moved, it caught Jesse full in the face, momentarily blinding him. It paused on the shop's front door next to him, then moved on down the street. After a few seconds, the police car turned right and disappeared around the corner. Jesse couldn't move for a moment. He had been fully visible to the driver, but he apparently hadn't been seen. He sprinted for his truck.

He gave the police car another minute to move on, then he started the truck and headed east from town. He passed Wood Products and came to the bridge over the creek. A foot-long length of duct tape was stuck to the railing on the opposite side of the road. He pulled the truck off the road and into the woods, then walked back to the side of the road. He looked in both directions, then sprinted across the road and down the embankment, snatching the strip of duct tape from the railing as he went.

His flashlight found the bundle, taped securely in a corner of the bridge supports. He used his pocket knife to cut it free, then stripped off the remaining bits of tape and stuck them in his pocket. Back at road level, he knelt behind the bridge railing and waited for an eighteen-wheeler to roar past, then ran for his truck.

Back at home, he took the bundle into the kitchen and ripped away the plastic covering with his knife. Inside he found a canvas backpack, and inside that were all the items he had requested, plus one more.

There was a typewritten note taped to it: "You *must* wear this wire to the meeting," it read. "The tape will be crucial to our court case." He ripped up the note and flushed it down the garbage disposal. The recorder was small, he'd give them that. If he wore it in some clever place, a body search might even miss it.

He put the materials back into the backpack, took it out to the garage and concealed it under a stack of firewood. Then he got under the truck, opened the safe and stashed Carrie's birth certificate with the passports.

As he climbed the stairs to bed, he thought carefully about his plan. He had nearly everything he wanted now; the remainder of his needs he would find at Wood Products.

On Monday morning, Jesse rapped on Herman Muller's office door, and Muller waved him in.

"Morning, Jesse."

"Morning, Herman; have you got a minute?"

"Sure I have. Sit you down."

Jesse sat. "Herman, I think I've got a pretty good grip on how the plant runs now, and I seem to have a little time on my hands. I just wondered if you could use a hand at the bookkeeping."

Muller regarded him for a moment, then smiled. "Jesse, you put your finger on the thing I hate doing most around here. My wife kept the books until she died; fortunately, she got the computer system up and running before she passed, and she taught me to run it. I guess it's time I taught you."

"I'll be glad to learn," Jesse said.

"Pull your chair around here and look over my shoulder," Muller said, switching on the computer. "You start from the main menu and press B for books, then it will ask you for your password. The password is Tommy."

Jesse spent most of the morning following Muller through the program; it really was very straightforward. When everybody left for lunch, Jesse went to the computer, entered the password and asked the program to print out a balance sheet for the previous year. It took less than a minute to do so.

He put the statement into his pocket, found his coat and went down to the parking lot, then he drove into town and parked in front of the bank.

"I'd like to see Kurt Ruger," he told the secretary. Then he looked up to see Ruger waving him into his office.

"What can I do for you, Jesse?" Ruger asked, and his tone was cool. "You want to borrow some money?"

"Thanks, Kurt, but I'm here to do something for you." He produced the balance sheet, unfolded it and handed it over.

Ruger read the document, then smiled, the first time Jesse had ever seen him do so. "Well, I'll be damned," he said. "The old goat is doing even better than we thought!"

"This year ought to be a lot better," Jesse said. "I've developed two new plywood outlets in the East, and I think those will lead to more."

"Yeah, Casey told me about the order from Maryland. That and the New York order, on top of the usual business, ought to keep the plant humming for the better part of the year."

"That it will," Jesse said.

"How'd you do it? How'd you get the computer password?"

"I just asked. I offered to help with the bookkeeping, and Herman jumped at it; said he hated doing it himself."

Ruger stood up and offered his hand. "Jesse, I've underestimated you, and I've been suspicious of you over nothing. I want to apologize."

Jesse shook the man's hand. "Don't mention it," he said. "Is there anything else you want from Herman's books?"

"If you could get me a temporary balance sheet for this year so far, that would help," Ruger said.

"I can do that; I'll drop it by tonight on the way home."

Ruger smiled again. "We'll own that business before the month is out," he said.

Jesse left the bank and went back to his truck. Before the month is out, he mused, you'll be in the joint. Or in hell.

CHAPTER

55

At lunchtime on Tuesday, Jesse made what he was sure would be his last call to Kip Fuller.

"Kip, it's Jesse. What's happening?"

"Jess, we need another day."

Jesse felt anger replace the dread. "Well, you can't have it."

"Listen to me, Jess; we're going to do it the way you wanted; the army is sending in a battalion of Rangers, the best they've got. But they need a little more time to get things in place."

"Well, they can't have it. They're just going to have to get their asses in gear and get it done very early on Thursday morning." He looked at his watch. "That's thirty-odd hours, and they'd better not be late."

"Let me tell you the plan; it's very close to what you suggested."

"Okay, tell me."

"The Rangers are being transported in a fleet of trucks—everything from a UPS van to eighteen-wheelers."

"That's good, I like that."

•

"At one A.M. on Friday morning they're going to simultaneously hit the police station and the telephone exchange. Ten minutes later, a specially reinforced truck carrying a heavy load of ballast is going to crash the gate at the top of the mountain; follow-up vehicles will discharge a company of Rangers, and at the same time, electric power will be cut to the whole town. This is very close to what you wanted."

"It is, and it sounds right."

"The Rangers will then take the weapons emplacements outside the main fortification, and when they've secured the ground-to-air missiles, the choppers will come in and put another two companies on the mountaintop.

"Right behind the troops at the main gate will be three heavy-duty swat teams of specially trained U.S. marshals; they'll hit the homes of Coldwater, Casey and Ruger at the very moment that the truck crashes the gates.

"Headquarters will be in another specially equipped eighteen-wheeler; when they get word that the big three are in custody and that the Rangers are on the mountaintop, they'll send in four C-130 aircraft, each of which will hold an armored personnel carrier and a complement of troops. Your airport at St. Clair has a forty-five hundred foot strip, and there's a thousand-foot grass overrun, winter-hard, at one end of the runway. That's enough for the C-130s. At the same time, other troops will arrive in unmarked cars and begin a door-to-door sweep of the whole town. We've arranged the biggest federal search warrant in history; it's good for the whole county. We reckon that by dawn the town will be ours, and we're counting on minimum casualties."

"Kip, I think your plan is good. But it has to happen Thursday morning."

"Jess—"

•

"Kip, shut up and listen to me. Tell them to hit at three A.M., not one. These people are likely to still be awake at one. I've got a shot at keeping Coldwater and his people out of the fortifications; if it hasn't happened by three A.M. it won't happen, and they'll have to take their chances on a security leak that could give Coldwater some warning. You better pray I make it."

"I don't understand—what's the big deal about another day?"

"The deal is, I can't last another twenty-four hours. I've hardly slept at all since Sunday, and I'm starting to come unglued."

"Come on, Jess, you're tougher than that."

"Kip, I don't have anything left, and that's the truth. I've planned for tomorrow night, and tomorrow night it is. Can this phone reach you at that time?"

"Yes, I can use call-forwarding to route your call to the headquarters truck."

"Is there any way for you to find my position by backtracking the telephone?"

"No, we can only tell what cellular service area you're in, and all of the area in the Idaho panhandle is in the same service area. We'll have to depend on position reports from you."

"I understand. Remember, now, hit the police and telephone buildings at three A.M., and not a minute before. I'm going to have a shot at paving the way for you, but I can't promise anything, so don't expect it." He hung up before Kip could reply.

He hadn't lied about his condition; he was a wreck, and he was going to have to get some sleep tonight, or he'd never make it.

56

Wednesday. Jesse suffered through the day, stopping work now and then to do his yoga breathing exercises, the only thing that seemed to help him relax. At the end of the day, he pretended to still be working while he waited impatiently for everyone to leave. When he was finally alone in the plant he went downstairs to the machine shop, found a canvas tool bag and started to select equipment. He wasn't sure what he'd need, but he chose a six-pound sledge, a couple of cold chisels, wire cutters, pliers, some screwdrivers, a thick roll of duct tape and a pair of short bolt cutters. Finally, he unplugged a heavy-duty, half-inch, battery-operated drill from its charger and dropped that into the bag, along with a spare battery. The bag wouldn't hold any more, so what he had would have to be enough.

He drove home, forcing himself to obey the speed limit, and parked the truck in the garage, then he dug out his bag of equipment from Kip and tucked it behind the seat of the truck, along with the tool bag. He crawled under the truck, opened the safe and extracted the contents. He put the pistol and spare clips into the canvas backpack and took the money, the passports and the miniature tape recorder into the house. Jenny was feeding the girls an early supper, as planned.

"Hey, everybody," he said, trying to sound jovial. He sat at the table and drank a glass of milk while they finished their dinner, and, when the girls had been tucked into bed, protesting, he took Jenny back downstairs to the kitchen.

"All right," he said, "time for final plans." He went to the sink, took a plastic tool box from underneath it and emptied out the tools, then he removed the money from its brown paper bag and packed it into the tool box. "That's a little over fifty thousand dollars," he said. "Pack some sandwiches around it."

"What's going to happen tonight?" she asked.

"I'm going to a dinner meeting at Jack Gene's house, and I'm going to record the proceedings; what I get there should be enough to put everybody present away for a long time."

"Do you want us to wait here?"

"No. I want you to pack one bag for each of us, and put them into the trunk of your car, along with the toolbox and some blankets, and at two A.M. I want you to take the girls and drive out to the St. Clair airport."

"Are we going to fly out of here?"

"Just listen. Be sure and have some story ready, in case you're stopped by a patrol car. There's a big hangar next to the flight office, and it has a combination lock; the combination is 1234. I want you to unlock the hanger and, just inside the door, along with several other airplanes, you'll find a Cessna—that's an airplane with high wings, the kind you can walk under—and the number on the side of it is N123TF. Got that?"

"N123TF," she repeated, "and the combination for the lock is 1234. That's all very simple."

"The airplane will be unlocked; there's a rear door to the luggage compartment on the left-hand side, and I want you to put all the luggage and the toolbox in there, then I want you to put the two girls in the back seat of the airplane with a couple of blankets. Then you drive your car into the woods, where it can't be seen from the airport, go back to the hangar, close the doors from the inside, get into the airplane and wait for me."

"Jesse, can you fly an airplane?"

"Sort of. Now listen; if I'm not there by three-fifteen, I want you to put everybody back into the car, drive back to the main road, turn east and then, as soon as you can, head south toward Salt Lake City. There, do what you were to do in Seattle the last time we planned this: get most of the money converted to traveler's checks and a cashier's check; make a reservation for Tokyo, this time through Los Angeles. Here are your passports and Carrie's birth certificate; you can talk her through with that.

"After Tokyo, it's the Peninsular Hotel in Hong Kong for a week, then to Sydney and the Harbour Hotel, ask for Bluey at the bar."

"I remember all that."

"I'll join you if I can. If I can't, take care of yourself and the girls; make them happy."

She reached across the table and squeezed his hand.

"I'll most likely make it to the airport, but if not, look for me in Hong Kong."

While Jenny was upstairs packing, Jesse took off his shirt and dropped his pants. It wasn't the first time he'd worn a wire. Using the special tape provided with the wire, he taped the recorder to the inside of his left thigh, high up, next to his testicles. In his experience, most men didn't like groping other men's crotches,

●
314

even in a search. He plugged in the microphone wire, then ran it between his legs and up between his buttocks to his waist, anchoring the wire there with tape. He then ran it up his back, taping as far as he could reach, then again at his shoulder. He ran it down his left arm, applying patches of tape as he went, then he attached the microphone to the wire and taped it securely to the inside of his wrist, a couple of inches above his watchband. A switch on the tiny microphone would allow him to start the recorder; after that, it would record whenever it picked up someone's voice.

He got dressed again, swung his left arm around and walked around the kitchen to be sure he had free movement. The microphone wire was very thin, and he didn't want to put any strain on it. He went upstairs, got his dark brown sheepskin coat, a pair of hiking boots and some thick socks, then came back down to the kitchen. Jenny joined him there.

"You're sure you understand everything?" he asked.

She nodded.

Jesse looked at his watch; quarter to seven; time to go. He took Jenny in his arms, hugged her, kissed her; he tried to keep it light; didn't want it to seem like goodbye, although God knew it might very well be.

"I love you," he said.

"I love you," she replied.

He got into his coat, tucked the sheepskin jacket and the boots under his arm and left the house.

CHAPTER

57

Jesse arrived precisely on time and was shown into Coldwater's study by one of Jack Gene's young women.

"The pastor will be with you shortly," she said. "Please make yourself at home."

As soon as she was gone, Jesse went to the false bookcase at the end of the room and tugged at it. The facade gave way to reveal a door, securely locked, and it was made of steel. Jesse rapped on it sharply with a knuckle; at least a quarter-inch thick, and there was an echo from behind it. He closed the bookcase and quickly found a chair.

Coldwater entered the room, followed by Pat Casey and Kurt Ruger, and at that moment the doorbell rang. "Ah, here they are," Coldwater said. "Good evening, Jesse."

"Good evening, Pastor," Jesse replied, rising. He nervously checked his necktie.

A moment later a group of men were shown into the room, led by Charley Bottoms, who winked at Jesse.

Don't *do* that, Jesse said to himself. He counted eight men as he was introduced; some, like Bottoms, had been in the last visiting group, but two were new. Jesse recognized one of them as the Reverend John Packard, a Seattle minister who specialized in racial and anti-Semitic epithets; he had often been on the news.

The young woman who had admitted them entered the room, opened a concealed wet bar and began offering drinks. Jesse accepted a bourbon, but he drank little of it.

"Gentlemen," Coldwater said to the room at large, "I hope you'll forgive the inconvenience, but in the interests of security, it will be necessary for each of you to be, ah, looked at more closely. Not you, Reverend, of course."

There was grumbling, but each man submitted to an expert search by Pat Casey and Kurt Ruger.

"Pastor," the reverend said, "I hope you won't take offense, but your crowd will have to be looked at, too."

"No offense taken," Coldwater replied. "Go right ahead."

"Charley, will you do the honors?" the reverend said.

"Sure thing, Preacher," Bottoms said. "You fellows mind unbuttoning your shirts?" He quickly patted down Casey and Ruger, then turned to Jesse. "You're next, pal."

Jesse's back was to the fire, but he still held his breath while Bottoms ran his hands over his body. If Charley wasn't on the feds' team, he would find out about it now. Charley found the wire running up his back. He turned to Packard. "They're clean, Reverend."

Jesse started breathing again.

"What did you fellows fly down in?" Coldwater asked the Reverend Packard.

"I got a King Air," the reverend replied. "I fly it myself; we made it in no time flat."

"I fly a rather old Commanche, myself," Coldwater said. "You like our little airport?"

"Real nice," Packard replied.

Charley Bottoms took a large swig of whiskey and announced, "I came in a Chevrolet. You guys are doing awful good for yourselves."

The Reverend Packard laughed heartily at this.

Jesse thought about the King Air out at the airport—a twin-engined turboprop. It flew a lot faster than the Cessna he was planning on leaving in, but he knew nothing about flying twins, and he wasn't going to start learning tonight.

The conversation grew louder as the alcohol circulated, and then they were called into dinner. Jesse aimed at a seat near the middle of the table, on Coldwater's right. There were twelve of them at the long table, and he wanted to be able to record as many of them as possible. From the middle of the table, he thought, the recorder might manage it.

Dinner was served, and Coldwater waxed eloquent about the wines, while Jesse ate and drank little.

"Jesse," Coldwater said suddenly, "you're not drinking my wine; what's the matter?"

Jesse placed a hand on his belly. "Some kind of bug, I think; my stomach's a little unsettled."

"Can we get you something for it?" Coldwater asked solicitously.

"Thank you, no; I think I'll be fine, if I take it easy."

"Sure you wouldn't like to go and lie down for a few minutes?"

This was a tempting possibility, but Jesse had to record the conversation in this room.

"Really, I'll be fine," he said.

"As you wish," Coldwater said. "Let me know if you take a turn for the worse."

"Thank you, sir; I'll do that."

Dessert and coffee were served, and a large decanter of brandy was placed on the table. Kurt Ruger, who was sitting near the opposite end of the table from Coldwater, got up and left the room.

Coldwater poured himself a brandy and passed the decanter. Jesse took none. Ruger came back into the room, but, instead of sitting down again, he leaned against the wall at that end of the table, his hands behind him.

When everyone had been served brandy, Coldwater tapped on the edge of his glass with a knife; the crowd grew quiet. "Before we proceed with our presentation," he said, "there is a little security matter we must deal with." The room was deadly quiet now.

Jesse pretended to scratch his forearm, while switching on the recorder. Wait a minute, he thought; did he say security?

Coldwater continued. "It seems a member of our party has not been entirely candid with us. When he was a prisoner in the Atlanta Federal Penitentiary, he seems to have been led astray."

Jesse's breath grew short. He was a long way from the door, and he didn't like the way Kurt Ruger was standing, with his hands behind him. In order to get out of the room, he'd have to go through Ruger at one end or Coldwater at the other. He stared down at the table. A trickle of fear ran through his bowels.

"Tell us, my friend," Coldwater said, staring down the table, "Just what did you do to get put into prison?"

Jesse swallowed hard and tried to take a deep breath. He would have to keep this as close to the truth as possible. He opened his mouth to speak.

"I was in for armed robbery and second degree murder," a voice said.

Jesse looked up. Charley Bottoms had spoken; Charley was sitting at the foot of the table.

"And what was your sentence?" Coldwater asked.

Jesse discovered that he had been holding his breath. He let it out in a rush. Across the table, Pat Casey glanced sharply at him, but Coldwater didn't seem to notice.

"I got twenty-five to life," Charley said. He was beginning to look ill at ease.

"Which means you would ordinarily serve, let's see, twelve and a half years?" Coldwater asked.

Charley said nothing.

"And how long did you serve, Mr. Bottoms?"

"Three years and two months."

"Three years and two months," Coldwater repeated. "Your behavior inside must have been *awfully* good."

Charley shrugged. "I got lucky, I guess."

"I guess you did, Mr. Bottoms. Out in three years and two months. What luck!"

Jesse placed his hands on the dining table, the more to get the microphone out in front of him.

"I'm going to ask you just once, Mr. Bottoms," Coldwater said. "Who got you out, and why?"

Charley continued to play dumb, which turned out to be a big mistake. He shrugged. "The parole board."

Coldwater looked up at Ruger. "Kurt, please escort Mr. Bottoms downstairs and put the question to him a little more firmly."

Ruger pushed himself off the wall and put an automatic pistol to the back of Charley's head. "Easy, now, Bottoms; let's not put your brains on the table."

"Jesse," Coldwater said.

Jesse's head jerked around toward Coldwater. "Yes, sir?"

"Give Kurt a hand." He reached inside his jacket, produced a 9mm automatic and handed it to Jesse.

Jesse took the gun. The evening was not going at

all the way he had planned. He stood up and followed Charley and Ruger out of the dining room. They entered the kitchen; two young women were washing dishes at a double sink; they looked up then quickly down again.

"Jesse, open the cellar door," Ruger said.

Jesse looked around and spotted the door; he opened it and stood back.

"Right down the stairs," Ruger said to Bottoms. "Come on down, Jesse." He switched on a light.

Jesse followed the two men down the stairs. As they walked down, Jesse considered his position, and he didn't like it at all.

"Right over there," Ruger said, shoving Charley.

Jesse saw a heavy wooden chair, and it was bolted to the floor.

"There's some cord attached to the back of the chair; tie his hands behind him."

Jesse followed Ruger's instructions, but he didn't tie Charley's hands too tightly.

Ruger tucked his pistol into his belt, picked up a length of pipe from the floor, then squared off before Charley Bottoms. "I know you're not going to answer my questions right away," he said, "so why don't we just skip that part." He struck Bottoms across the face with the pipe.

The sound was like a football being kicked, Jesse thought.

Ruger turned away for a moment, as if to take a deep breath. Charley Bottoms turned toward Jesse, his face bloody, and silently mouthed, "Shoot me."

Jesse looked away. If he helped Charley he'd give himself away, and they'd both be shot. Charley had just told him, in effect, that he expected to be killed and that Jesse should save himself.

CHAPTER

58

Ruger had been at it for half an hour, and Charley Bottoms was no longer recognizable. He was alive, though, and occasionally, he spat out some blood.

Jesse stood, the gun dangling at his side, and tried not to watch. Ruger drew the pipe back again, and as he did, the door at the top of the stairs opened, and Ruger and Jesse both turned to look. Coldwater's feet appeared on the stairs, and at that moment, Charley's right hand shot out. He grabbed the pistol from Ruger's belt and fired two rounds into his tormentor's head. Then, without hesitating, he flipped the gun around, got his thumb on the trigger and stuck the barrel into his mouth.

Jesse's shot went off simultaneously with Charley's. Charley lurched backwards and sideways, leaving blood and brains on the wall behind him. Without thinking, Jesse fired a second shot into the body.

Just as Jesse's knees buckled, Coldwater reached out and took the pistol from him, and he sagged into Pat Casey's arms.

HEAT

●

* * *

Jesse sat on the sofa in Coldwater's study, his face in his hands.

"Feeling better?" Coldwater asked.

"I should have been faster," Jesse said.

"I saw it all; you couldn't have done better," Coldwater replied. "He might have gotten me."

Pat Casey handed Jesse a damp face cloth. "Here," he said, "maybe this will help."

"Poor Jesse," Coldwater said. "And you weren't feeling well to begin with. Why don't you stretch out on the sofa for a while? I have a business negotiation to complete." He turned to Casey. "Pat, see that the mess downstairs gets cleaned up."

"Right," Casey replied, then left the room.

"Are you really better?" Coldwater asked, concern in his voice.

"Thank you, sir," Jesse muttered. "I'll be all right in a minute."

Coldwater clapped a hand on his shoulder. "You stay here; I'll check on you later." He left the room, closing the door behind him.

Jesse gave them fifteen seconds by his watch before he moved, then he got up, went to the bookcase and moved back the facade, exposing the safe. He put an ear to it and starting moving the tumblers. He couldn't hear well enough, so he went to the bar, got an empty glass, pressed it against the steel, put his ear to the glass and tried again. Better. He glanced at his watch.

Forty minutes later, the safe door opened; it had been harder than he had thought it would be. The bottom of the safe was full of papers, he didn't much care what, and the top shelf was lined with dozens of neatly banded stacks of hundred-dollar bills.

Jesse looked around the room, and his eyes fell on

●

323

a large, wicker wastebasket with a plastic liner. Jesse ripped out the liner, emptied the trash back into the basket and began raking the money into the bag. He hesitated for a moment, then he packed the papers at the bottom of the safe into the bag, as well. He closed the safe door, twirled the knob and shut the bookcase facade, then he took the corners of the plastic bag and tied them into a secure knot.

There were voices from the front hall. Jesse looked around for a hiding place for the bag and didn't see one. He ran to the windows, pushed one up and stuck the bag outside. He swung it a couple of times, then let go, tossing it in the direction of the road. The door behind him opened.

"Feeling better?" Coldwater boomed.

"Yes, thank you, sir; I was just letting in some fresh air. How did your meeting go?"

"A great success, I'd say." Coldwater poured himself a brandy from the bar and one for Jesse, as well. "This ought to make you feel a little better, and close that window, will you? It's freezing in here."

Jesse closed the window and accepted the brandy. He took a good-sized swig, then sat down.

"Jesse," Coldwater said, "I'd like you to take on some of Kurt's duties."

Jesse looked at him, surprised. The man had just seen his old friend and partner murdered. He moved his glass to his left hand, and scratched his arm with his right, made sure the recorder was going.

"That's very flattering, sir. I'm afraid I don't know much about finance."

"You're a highly intelligent and quick-witted man, though, and that's my need at the moment, now that Kurt is gone. Pity about Kurt; good fellow." He didn't sound grief-stricken.

"Yes, sir."

"Your first assignment is to take Wood Products

away from Herman Muller; do it any way you can; Kurt showed me that balance sheet you got him, and let me tell you, that company is a plum."

"I think I can handle that," Jesse replied.

"As soon as you do, you're going to become president of the bank," Coldwater said. "No need to know anything about banking; I know more than enough about that. But I need my own man in there."

"Thank you, sir," Jesse said, trying to sound brighter. Then he thought, what the hell, last chance to find out. "Pastor—"

"Call me Jack Gene; you've earned the right."

"Thank you. Jack Gene, I don't really have any grasp of what's going on here. I mean, what's the bunker for?"

Coldwater laughed aloud. "I suppose you must have thought I was mad," he said. "Well, I'm not. It's a very fine weapons store, isn't it?"

"It's all about weapons, then?"

Coldwater grinned. "You really are very bright, Jesse. If I was going to deal in weapons on any sort of scale, I had to have a secure storage site, didn't I?"

"But why all this religion business? Why found a church?"

"Think about it, Jesse; nobody can build something as big as what's inside the mountain without one hell of a lot of people knowing about it. With the church, I got to control the people who knew about it; the people who, in fact, built it, saving me millions of dollars in the process. Of course, I've enjoyed taking over and running this little town; that was fun. But it was all to protect the weapons business."

"And controlling the town meant that nobody asked questions about all the trucks that were bringing in and taking out the stuff?"

"Exactly. And there were a *lot* of trucks. We deal worldwide, you know—not just to people like those

•
325

yokels who just left. Mind you, I've equipped just about every bunch of nutters in the western half of the United States of America, and some in the East, too. The profits have been mindboggling. I have bank accounts in every safe haven in the world—Zurich, the Caymans, Singapore—so does Pat; so does Kurt, for that matter. After I've moved some of the money, I'll see that you get the numbers to his accounts. It wouldn't be fair to give you everything Kurt had earned, would it? I'll take half, give Pat a quarter, and you can have the rest. That number will approach ten million dollars."

Jesse blinked. "Thank you, sir. I must say, I'm a little surprised that Kurt would let you have the numbers to his bank accounts."

"Why not? I opened them for him and put the money into them. Casey's, too."

"So, if something happened to Pat—"

Coldwater smiled broadly. "Now you don't think I'd let anything happen to Pat? Couldn't get along without him."

Jesse thought, You're fucking well getting along without Ruger all right, aren't you?

"You're going to become as indispensable as Pat, Jesse, don't you worry. Listen, if you don't want to go abroad when this is over, I'll give you Muller's business. If you feel you *must* work, you can stay in St. Clair and play with that."

"When is it going to be over?" Jesse asked.

"Well, it's winding down already, isn't it? I mean, Charley Bottoms is the third federal agent we've had in here in the past year and a half. *Somebody* must suspect *something*." He chuckled.

"Doesn't that worry you?" Jesse asked.

"Not in the least; the feds are very slow to catch on to anything, and I control the local law completely. No, I've got another year, at the very least, before I move on to greener pastures."

"Well, it all sounds very exciting," Jesse said.

"More exciting that you can imagine," Coldwater replied, then his eyes lit up. "Maybe I should show you just how exciting." He pointed toward the bookcase. "Remember my safe? There's a million and a half dollars, cash, in there. It's yours." He made to get up.

Jesse threw up a hand. "Please, Jack Gene, *please*. You don't have to do that. I trust you completely."

Coldwater paused, half out of his chair. "You're sure?"

"Absolutely," Jesse said.

Coldwater grinned. "I trust you, too, Jesse; you were different from the beginning. You knew what was in your interests, but you didn't buy the religion, ever, did you?"

"I can't say that I did."

"The sheep," Coldwater said contemptuously of his congregation. "It has always astonished me the number of seemingly normal human beings who will follow, even lay down their lives for, any man who shows them some leadership. Did I tell you about the abortion clinics?"

"No."

"We've razed a good number of clinics in the Northwest, for no other reason than to get the congregation excited about something, and, not to mention, to incriminate a fair number of them."

"Why abortion clinics?"

"Oh, they're very fashionable among the faithful, you know, and they're also wonderfully easy pickings. They attract big headlines, too, and lots of TV time. The faithful like to know that their good works are not going unnoticed."

Coldwater put down his glass and massaged his temples. "Well, I'm a little tired; such a big evening. I think I'll turn in." He got to his feet.

Jesse rose with him. "I could use a good night's sleep, myself," he said.

Coldwater put an arm around Jesse and walked him to the front hall, then helped him into his coat. "Tell you what, why don't you come to lunch tomorrow? We'll break bread, drink a fine bottle of wine and talk about the future."

"I'd like that, Jack Gene," Jesse said, shaking the man's hand.

Coldwater suddenly embraced Jesse. "We're going a long way together," he said. Then he stood in the door and watched Jesse walk toward his truck.

"Not as far as you think," Jesse muttered to himself.

CHAPTER

59

Jesse drove slowly down the long driveway, and, at the road, he stopped. He switched off the head-lights, reached into the backpack behind the seat and extracted the night goggles. He slipped them on, then, instead of heading down toward town, he turned right and drove slowly up the mountain a few yards. He had no trouble seeing the road.

Coldwater's house was nearly at the top of the mountain; only one thing lay in the fifty yards between the house and the gates. When he was nearly at the top, he turned right, down the dirt road, and a minute later stopped at the firing range. He got out and looked up. A hundred feet above the earthen bank that received the bullets, he saw what he wanted. The full moon came out from behind the clouds for a moment, and in the bright light the goggles were almost too much.

He changed his shoes and got into his warm jacket, then retrieved the backpack and the tool bag from the truck and checked his equipment. He stuck the pistol into his belt and the spare clips into his pocket, then slipped on the backpack, slung the tool bag over one shoulder and the machine gun, an Uzi, over the other and started climbing the mountain.

It was tough going with only one free hand and so much gear, but he made it in twenty minutes. He sat down beside the ventilator grate and rested for a few minutes. He checked his watch; just after midnight; he had plenty of time, he hoped.

He stood up and, through the night goggles, examined the grating. It was much like a storm sewer grating, just as thick, but round and about three feet across. There was a noise from above him, and Jesse flattened himself against the mountainside, swiveling his head up and around. On the cliff twenty feet above him stood a man holding an assault rifle. He struck a match, lit a cigarette and tossed the match down the steep incline. It landed at Jesse's feet.

Jesse stood, frozen, until the man moved on. He waited another half minute, then looked at the grate again. It was secured by two large bolts, and the heads were not slotted. He considered using a chisel on them, but that would be noisy; same with the electric drill. Finally, he went into the backpack and came out with the plastic explosive. He got out his pocket knife and cut a large chunk from the main piece; he carefully divided it, then shaped and packed it around the four bolts. It took another few minutes to wire all four charges to one timer, then he took the explosives mat out of the back-pack and spread it over the grating. He taped it in place with some duct tape, and then he was ready.

But there was the matter of the guard above. Jesse put down the Uzi and very carefully, foot by foot, scaled the steep incline. He got a toehold just below the top, then stuck his head up and looked around. There were two of them, it seemed, and they were standing next to a shed nearly a hundred yards away, leaning on their weapons and smoking. Jesse thanked heaven for the night goggles. He turned around and slid the twenty feet down to the ledge where he had been working; he took hold of the timer and set it for thirty seconds, then quickly worked his way along the ledge away from the grating. He stopped, turned his head away and held his breath.

There was a muffled *whump*, and the explosives mat flew off and down the mountain. Quickly, he made his way back to the grating; it was hanging by one bolt. He tossed all his equipment into the pipe, climbed in and pulled the grating back into place. He sat that way, holding the grating, for half a minute before he heard the voices.

"What the fuck was that?" one man said.

"I didn't hear anything."

"You were farting, that's why."

"Maybe that's what you heard."

"Naw, I heard a kind of, I don't know, a—"

"It was probably an eighteen-wheeler backfiring down on the road."

"No, it was more like a—"

"Well, everything seems to be all right, doesn't it?"

"Yeah, I guess so."

"You can log the noise, if you want to, but I'm not going to say I heard it."

"Well, fuck you, then."

The voices faded away.

Jesse waited for them to go, then gently let the grating hang on the one bolt again. He turned and, pushing his equipment ahead of him, started down the tunnel on his hands and knees.

There was so little ambient light in the pipe that not even the goggles were of much use, so he pulled them down around his neck and switched on a small flashlight. Holding the light in his mouth, he moved on down the tunnel until he came to another obstacle.

This one was nothing more that a piece of chain-link fencing that had been cut to size and welded to the steel pipe; he wouldn't need explosives for this. He got out the bolt cutters and snipped his way through.

He was well inside the mountain now, and his next obstacle was a fan that nearly filled the tunnel. Suddenly, it came on, and there was a roar as air began to rush down the pipe. He got out his wire cutters, found the power cord and cut it. The fan slowly came to a halt. It took him half an hour to get the blade off and dismantle enough of the frame to get through. There was one last ventilator grate, but this one was of thin aluminum, and he was able to kick it out. He peered out into a long hallway; he was a good eight feet above the floor; about every fourth ceiling light was on.

He lowered his equipment to the floor, then jumped down, squatted and listened. It seemed unlikely that anyone was inside this place late at night, but he wanted to be sure.

Hearing nothing, he thought about his position and decided he must be in the north hallway on the first, highest, level. Then he remembered what was up the hall toward the main entrance. Leaving his tools where they lay he trotted up the hallway, turned a corner and opened a door. A small room was stacked to the ceiling with crates marked "ammunition: recoilless rifle." He tried a couple more doors, checking labels until he found a single crate, marked "C-4 Plastique." Perfect. The box held at least twenty pounds of the stuff. He got it open and took out two brick-sized blocks, wired a detonator to it and looked at his watch; one-twenty. He set the timer for one hour and forty minutes; it would go off at exactly 3:00 A.M. He took the crate and went back to where his tools lay, then he sat down and remembered what he could of the layout from his previous visits and from the plans.

By two-thirty, he had set more Plastique in half a dozen ammunition caches all over the complex. That would have been enough to keep anyone from using the facility any time soon, but it didn't satisfy him. There was one more job to do. He picked up his gear and ran down to the generator room on the second level.

The door was locked, and he had no time to pick the lock. He got out the drill and went straight through the cylinder. Inside the room were two enormous generators; his guess was that one of them was enough to light the facility; the other was a backup. Above them, built into the mountain were two hardened twenty-five-thousand-gallon gasoline storage tanks. Thank God they were on the north side of the mountain, away from the town, he thought. His Plastique might not punch through the tanks, but there was another, simpler and more effective way to deal with it. He set his equipment on a workbench, got out the bolt cutters and stepped behind the machinery; using his flashlight, he located the two armored fuel lines; the bolt cutters made quick work of both of them. He turned two taps, and gasoline began to pour onto the floor, he guessed at the rate of about twenty gallons a minute from each line.

He picked up his gear and got out of there. He was soaked up to the knees with gasoline.

Early on, he had decided not to go out the way he came in. The tunnel was too close to the gasoline tanks, and if he made some miscalculation, and the place went up while he was still in the tunnel, he would be fired from it like the human cannonball at the circus—that, or the mountain would simply collapse on top of him. There was a better way out, he was sure of it.

He charged down the steps to the lower level and ran toward the rear of the structure, toward Jack Gene Coldwater's offices. He realized that the hallways were all slightly inclined, and he could hear gasoline pouring down the steps behind him. He checked his watch; two forty-seven; thirteen minutes left. He didn't like the number.

He ran through the suite of offices outside Coldwater's and came to a stout set of doors, locked. He hadn't counted on this, and he didn't want to take the time to drill. He put on the night goggles for protection, aimed the Uzi at the lock and emptied a clip into it. The wood was splintered, but nothing had budged. He inserted another clip and tried again. Still holding. The final clip did it; the lock fell from its casing, and the doors swung open.

Jesse went straight to the false bookcase and moved it back; he found a steel door identical to the one in Coldwater's study. He heard a trickling noise and looked down; gasoline was streaming into the room. Too late to use the Plastique; not the Uzi, either, even if he had had the ammunition. The lock was brass, though; it shouldn't make sparks.

He got out the drill and started on the cylinder. It was tougher, though, than the lock to the generator room, and the drill began to falter. He looked at his watch. Six minutes to go. He dug in the tool bag for the spare battery for the drill, found it, ejected the old one and snapped in the new one. The drill came to life again. Half a minute later, the cylinder gave. He put down the drill and rammed the door with his shoulder. Apart from bruising his shoulder, nothing happened.

Jesse picked up the sledge and went to work on the door. Finally, it gave. Two minutes to go. He placed the remainder of his Plastique on the floor, put the two incendiary grenades next to it and set the timer, then he grabbed his flashlight, the drill and the sledge and ran through the doorway, pulling the steel door shut behind him. The tunnel sloped downward steadily, and there were no steps, so he could run quickly. He stopped thinking about the time, he just went as fast as he could. He had covered what seemed like about a hundred yards when the tunnel suddenly turned ninety degrees to the left and came to an end. The steel door was in front of him.

Forgetting about the noise, forgetting about everything, he dropped the sledge and, holding the flashlight in his mouth, put the drill to the lock and leaned on it. The bit skidded off the lock and hit the steel door with a clang. He started over. This time the bit seated, and he was boring away the brass. He put all his weight and strength against the drill, desperate to get through, and, a moment later, the drill and the cylinder came out the other side.

He picked up the sledge and began wildly banging at the lock. He hit it six times, then eight; on the tenth blow the door gave, pushing the false bookcase before it. He stepped through and found himself in Jack Gene Coldwater's study.

"*I made it!!!*" he screamed at the ceiling.

"You made what?" Coldwater's voice answered.

Jesse opened his eyes and found Coldwater and Pat Casey staring at him; both were holding guns.

"Well, Jesse, I wondered what all the racket was," Coldwater said. He motioned Jesse to move away from the tunnel door. "That escape route was meant for me; I never expected anyone else to use it. Tell me, what are you escaping from?"

Jesse stared at the man, mute. The pistol was still in his belt, but he could never fire it in time.

"I think it's time you told me who you really are," Coldwater said. He sounded very disappointed.

Jesse found his voice. "I'm the heat, Jack Gene, and you're burnt."

Coldwater raised his pistol and pointed it at Jesse's head. "Then you'll have to join your colleague, Mr. Bottoms," he said. He thumbed the hammer back.

Then, from somewhere deep inside the mountain, came a deep rumble, and the floor underneath them shook.

Casey was the first to speak. "What the fuck was that?" he asked.

Coldwater looked at Jesse questioningly, and, as he opened his mouth to speak, there was a loud roar, and the room shook like a baby's rattle. Beams crashed to the floor, and dust filled the air.

All three men were thrown to the floor, but Jesse was the first to his feet. He did the only thing he could do—never mind that they were fifty feet above the ground—he ran hard toward the windows at the end of the room and dove headlong through the glass.

CHAPTER

60

Jesse thought as he fell. Fifty feet. He couldn't survive that in one piece. Then he hit the tree. It rose a good thirty feet out of the ground, leafless, in its winter mode. Jesse, upside down, grabbed at branches, trying desperately to slow his fall. He tumbled, hit larger branches, held on to smaller ones, and suddenly, he was on his back in three feet of accumulated snow, wondering what had happened to him. A gunshot cleared his mind of fog. He rolled over and, clawing at the snow, got to his feet and ran toward the road, pulling the night goggles on as he floundered forward.

There were more gunshots and the soft "plop" that came when one struck the snow, but they obviously couldn't see him; they were just hoping for a strike. Jesse's mind was on something else, anyway; somewhere around here was a plastic bag with a million and a half dollars in it, and he was going to find it if he had to go through a gunfight to do it.

His pistol, amazingly enough, was still in his belt, and he drew it, just in case, to give himself the extra half-second. He stopped and looked around, and there it was, stuck into the snow like a bottle of champagne in a wine bucket. He snatched up the plastic bag and headed for the road. Then he stopped. He heard the front door of the house open and footsteps on the plowed driveway. Coldwater and Casey were in pursuit on foot.

They would think he was headed down the mountain, so he climbed a retaining wall of snow-covered boulders, ran across the drive and headed up the mountain, struggling through the snow. It was only twenty or thirty yards, he knew, even if it seemed like a thousand.

He made the clearing, and the truck was still there; he was afraid the mountain might have fallen on it. Then the vehicle became easy to see, because the sky was filled with light. He hit the snow, flat on his face and waited for the shock wave. When it came, it rocked the truck so much that he feared it would turn over. That explosion had been the gas tanks, he was sure, but they were on the north side of the mountain, thank God.

He got to his feet, got into the truck, turned it around and headed for the road. When he got there he turned off the engine and coasted down the mountain. Lesser explosions were going off, now, but they were increasingly behind him. Then, ahead, he saw a man in the road. It was Coldwater, and he was in a marksman's crouch, aiming a pistol at the driver's side of the truck.

Jesse ducked just as the windshield went white. He was driving from memory, now, trying to stay in the road. He heard Coldwater shout an obscenity as the truck passed him, then Jesse shoved the truck into gear and gave the engine a rolling start. No need to be quiet now.

He stuck his head up for one second and punched

frantically at the windshield, breaking out a hole that let him see, and just in time to make a sharp curve. As he did so, a round through the rear window sprayed him with broken glass. Jesse floored the accelerator and concentrated on his driving. At least two more shots struck the cab of the truck, and then he seemed to be in the clear. He passed the church and turned right, and as he did, he was greeted with an improbable sight. Two vehicles passed him going the other way, one a milk truck, the other an eighteen-wheel Mayflower moving van. He had already done their job for them, and he was glad he hadn't met them on the mountain road.

He came to an intersection and turned left, missing a Federal Express truck by inches. There was a soldier at the wheel. Checking the rearview mirror, he saw lots of headlights in the town behind him.

Two minutes later he turned onto the airport road. His hands were nearly frozen to the wheel since there wasn't much windshield to keep out the frigid night air. The moon came out, and he could see the outline of the big hangar ahead of him, with the Reverend Packard's King Air parked next to it. He had to get out of this airport before C-130s starting landing on it.

He screeched to a halt next to the hangar, grabbed the plastic bag, got out of the truck and kicked open the flimsy door of the flight office. He vaulted over the counter and played his flashlight on a board festooned with airplane keys, looking for the right one. He found it, then ran out of the office and toward the hangar. He shoved open first one big door, then the other, then the idea of a possible pursuit occurred to him. He pulled the pistol from his belt, and, taking careful aim, shot out the nosewheel tire of the King Air.

"Jesse?" Jenny's voice called.

"I'm here, sweetheart! Stay in the airplane!"

He ran around to the pilot's door, tossed the

plastic bag into the airplane and leapt in, slamming the door behind him.

"What's that?" Jenny asked.

"A new life," he replied. "I'll explain later."

He stuck the key into the ignition and groped between the seats for the checklist. Oh, the hell with it, he could remember enough to start it. He shoved the mixture and propeller control forward, flipped on the master switch, and began priming the carburetor. As he did, he looked up and saw, a mile away, a car's headlights; they were coming toward them at a high rate of speed.

Jesse turned the ignition key and prayed that the engine wasn't too cold to start. It caught, and after running roughly for a few seconds, revved smoothly.

No time for warmups, runups or checklists. Jesse shoved the throttle halfway in, and the airplane roared out of the hangar. Who could be in the car, he wondered; Coldwater and Casey couldn't have eluded the invading forces so easily. Could they? He stood on the right brake so hard that the airplane nearly spun back in the direction from which it had come.

The car was moving directly toward the airplane now, and if Jesse tried to taxi to the runway he would collide with it. Instead, he pointed the nose of the plane down the narrow taxiway and shoved the throttle to the firewall. The airplane began to pick up speed. Airplanes don't have rearview mirrors, so Jesse couldn't tell where the car was; instead of worrying about it, he flipped in the first notch of flaps and watched the airspeed indicator. He could fly at sixty knots.

Forty, then fifty, then the needle crept to fifty-five. Jesse was aware that headlights behind him were lighting his way. At sixty, he yanked back on the yoke, and the little airplane leapt into the air. As it did so, a car roared underneath it. Somebody had tried to ram him from behind.

He couldn't see the car now, because he was climbing too steeply. His airspeed was falling, and he pushed the yoke forward to let it rise again. As soon as he had eighty knots, he turned right ninety degrees; never mind waiting for the usual five hundred feet. He wondered if they were shooting at him, if they would somehow cripple the airplane.

He pushed the nose of the airplane down again, wanting to gain speed and put as much distance between him and the airport as possible. Trees rushed past him in the moonlight, fifty feet below, his recent reconnoitering made him feel safe, knowing that there were no high obstacles immediately to the south.

The GPS was still set to the St. Clair airport, so he could watch his distance increase on its screen. At five miles out, still at a hundred feet, he started to climb. He grabbed a headset from between the seats and handed one to Jenny.

"Are you and the girls all right?" he asked.

She pointed at the back seat. "I gave them each some bourbon in tea," she said.

Jesse looked back. The two little girls were sound asleep under a blanket. He went back to flying the airplane, establishing a cruise climb speed. When the climb was stabilized, he turned to the GPS and dialed in SLC, for Salt Lake City.

Jenny watched him do it. "How far is it to Salt Lake City?" she asked.

"Four hundred and eighteen miles," he said, pointing to the GPS.

"How long will it take us?"

"About three hours and a half, if there's no headwind. When we level off, the GPS will tell us exactly."

He continued climbing. His course was east of south now, so he needed an odd-numbered altitude, plus five hundred feet. He decided on eleven thousand five hundred, for the moment. Later, he'd have to climb to thirteen thousand five hundred, in order to clear the mountains south of St. Clair.

As he climbed, he made a ninety-degree right turn; it would take him off course, but he wanted to look back at the town.

As the airplane came around, he pointed toward St. Clair. "Look at that," he said.

The two of them stared at the conflagration atop the mountain. Occasionally a shell would cut an arc into the air, like a Roman candle.

"What is it?" Jenny asked.

"It's the end of Jack Gene Coldwater," Jesse replied, with some satisfaction. He turned the airplane back on course and dug behind the seat for a chart. Now he had to navigate them to Salt Lake City without coming to a sudden stop against a mountain.

CHAPTER

61

At dawn Jesse was yawning, trying to stay awake. He had expended so much adrenaline in the past few hours that he had precious little to get him through the remainder of the flight. He did an instrument scan to keep himself awake. They had a nice, twenty-knot quartering wind, he thought, since the ground speed on the GPS was that much faster than their airspeed, as shown on the gauge.

They were an hour out of Salt Lake City, and they had fuel for another two hours and twenty minutes of flight. They were in good shape. The only thing that worried him now was a thick layer of clouds about a thousand feet under them. He hoped that would break up before Salt Lake City, because he had no idea how to fly an instrument approach. He checked the back seat; the girls were still sound asleep.

Jenny stirred and opened her eyes. She was turned toward him, a blanket over her, and she pushed it away to have room to stretch.

"How are you feeling?" he asked.

"Okay, I think. I seem to have gotten some sleep." She reached over to kiss him on the neck.

As Jenny pulled back from him he smiled at her, and he saw her eyes widen. She put her headset on.

"What's the matter?" he asked.

She pointed past him. "Look," she said.

He swiveled in his seat and looked out the left side of the airplane. There, a mile and a half or two miles away, was a bright red shape.

"It's an airplane," Jenny said.

"You're right; I guess we're not alone up here, even at this hour of the day."

"What kind is it?" she asked, and she sounded worried.

Jesse squinted at the shape. "Low-winged, looks like a Piper." He looked back at her.

"Jack Gene has a Piper Commanche," she said. "And it's red."

Now the conversation about airplanes between Coldwater and the Reverend Packard came back to Jesse: Packard had the King Air, and Coldwater had said he owned a Commanche. Something else came back; in the big hangar at St. Clair, the airplane immediately behind the Cessna had been a red Piper. He looked back at the airplane, but the sun was now peeping above the clouds, and it blinded him.

Had the occupants of the Piper seen them? Certainly, the Cessna, given its position in relation to the sun, would be easy to see. Certainly, too, if Coldwater and Casey were in the Piper, they had figured out where he was going. Salt Lake City was certainly the logical airport, if the Cessna was heading south.

"It's Jack Gene, I know it," Jenny said. "What can we do?"

Jesse unfolded the chart in his lap. There were other airports he could head to, but they were smaller towns, without easy air connections to the coast. His eye fell on the southern tip of Nevada. Quickly, he

picked up the airport directory and looked up Las
Vegas. There were three airports; Las Vegas
International, for scheduled service, North Las Vegas,
which looked like the place where corporate jets might
go, and one other: Henderson Sky Harbor. Sky Harbor
was smaller than the other two, and a little farther
from the city; its only services were fuel and rental
cars. Jesse dialed the identifier, L15, into the GPS and
pushed the button twice. They were three hundred
and twenty-one miles from Sky Harbor, Las Vegas. He
tuned the course into the autopilot, and the airplane
turned right, then settled down on the new course.
Jesse waited until the ground speed settled down, then
checked the time to the airport. The new course did not
take as much advantage from the wind: two hours and
thirty-one minutes. He looked at the fuel computer for
their remaining flying time: two hours and sixteen
minutes.

"Oh, shit," Jesse muttered to himself.

"What did you say?"

"I said, we're going to Las Vegas," he said, reduc-
ing rpm's by a couple of hundred. He watched the fuel
computer recalculate: they now had two hours and
twenty minutes of flying time.

"Is everything all right?" Jenny asked.

"Everything's fine," Jesse lied. On their present
heading they would cross one of the emptiest deserts
in the United States, and Jesse didn't want to think
about being on foot out there. He switched the GPS to
its calculator mode; there was some sort of wind speed
function in there somewhere; he was sure he had read
about it. He found what he thought was the right function; he entered his true airspeed and heading, and the
computer showed the winds to be twenty-three knots
from 300 degrees. If the wind stayed where it was, they
would run out of fuel eleven minutes from the airport;
if the wind moved toward the west, ahead of them,

they would run out of fuel over an empty desert; if the wind moved to the north, behind them, they might make the airport. Jesse decided to gamble.

He searched his memory for discussions with his first flying instructor about airplanes. What sort of range did a Piper Commanche have? As much as a Cessna 182? More? Less? Jesse prayed that it had less range.

As he thought about this, he looked out the right side of the airplane. There, a mile or so away and slightly behind them, sat the red Piper. Jesse pored over the chart again. There was an airport called Morman Mesa, fifty or seventy-five miles northeast of Las Vegas. If, when he reached Morman Mesa, the fuel computer and the GPS told him he still didn't have enough fuel for Las Vegas, he could land there.

But it was a small place, and it could be a dead end for him. He leafed through the airport directory until he found Morman Mesa: there was a two-thousand foot dirt strip there, with fuel by prior arrangement, whatever that meant. Probably, you had to have an appointment with somebody. No rental cars. He did *not* want to land at Morman Mesa.

Jesse got the aircraft operator's manual out and read about fuel. The wings held thirty-eight gallons of usable fuel each, for a total of seventy-six. *Usable fuel*. There were another two gallons on each side that the FAA considered unusable, because it could not be depended upon, especially if the aircraft was maneuvering, as in a landing.

An hour and quarter passed. The red Piper remained a mile off their right wing. Slowly, tentatively, the wind swung to the north. Jesse recalculated the windspeed every five minutes. The Cessna's ground-speed inched up six knots. A comparison of the GPS and the fuel computer showed forty-four minutes of flying time left and forty-two minutes of fuel. Morman Mesa was looming ahead, and if Jesse was going to land there he had to make the decision now. He looked over at the Piper. "You first," he said.

As if the pilot had heard him, the red airplane began a descent. Jesse laughed aloud. "He doesn't have the fuel for Las Vegas," he said to Jenny. "He has to land at a jerkwater airport and try to find somebody to sell him fuel. Once we're in Vegas, he'd need an army of cops to find us."

Jesse consulted the GPS and the fuel computer again. Either of them could be wrong, he knew; his first instructor had told him often enough *never* to rely entirely on electronic equipment. He had made his decision. Sky Harbor, Las Vegas, even if it had to be on unusable fuel.

With thirty minutes of flying time showing on the fuel computer a light began to flash. "Low fuel," it said, over and over. Jesse couldn't find a way to turn the thing off.

62

Fifty miles out of Las Vegas, Jesse tuned in the unicom frequency for the airport. "Sky Harbor Unicom," he said, "This is November one, two, three Tango Foxtrot. Do you read?" Nothing. He repeated the transmission until, twenty miles out, he got an answer.

"Aircraft calling Sky Harbor," a voice with a thick foreign accent said.

"Sky Harbor, this is November one, two, three Tango Foxtrot. My name is Smith; I'm landing in fifteen minutes; can you arrange a rent-a-car for me?"

"Sure thing, Mr. Smith," the voice said. "The active runway is three-six."

Jenny had not noticed the blinking "low fuel" light, and Jesse saw no need to mention it to her. He began to get ready for his landing. He had descended to thirty-five hundred feet and reduced power when he spotted the airport at twelve o'clock. His instruments said he had four minutes to the airport and three minutes of fuel. He was approaching from the north, so in order to land on runway three-six he would have to fly around the airport and turn back to the north. The hell with runway three-six, he thought. I'm approaching from the north, and I'm going straight in to one-eight. He got on the radio. "Sky Harbor traffic, Sky Harbor traffic, this is November one, two, three, Tango Foxtrot. I am short of fuel, and I am straight in for runway one-eight."

A voice came back, "Tango Foxtrot, this is Whiskey Romeo; the active runway is three-six, and I'm already on base."

Jesse had the runway in sight now. "Whiskey Romeo and all Sky Harbor traffic, Tango Foxtrot is on three-mile final for three-six and short of fuel. I say again, short of fuel. I'm landing on one-eight, so get the hell out of my way."

There was a brief silence. "This is Whiskey Romeo; one-eight is all yours."

Over the runway numbers, Jesse began to breathe normally again. He taxied toward a row of tied-down airplanes and spotted a space between two other Cessnas. Camouflage, he thought. He turned into the space and stopped. As he reached for the mixture control to stop the engine, it stopped itself. The airplane was out of fuel.

"Okay, everybody, out of the airplane!" he cried.

Jenny woke the girls and, carrying their luggage, they walked to the terminal. Jesse kept a particularly tight grip on the plastic bag.

He persuaded the man at the counter to accept a five hundred-dollar cash deposit in lieu of a credit card, and a hundred-dollar bill for himself, in lieu of a driver's license. Jesse explained that he had left his wallet at home.

The car was filthy; it appeared never to have been washed, the ashtrays were full and it had eighty thousand miles on the speedometer, but Jesse loved it. No one would give it a second glance. On the drive into town, a happy thought occurred to him: they were in the one city in the United States where no one would bat an eye at the sight of large numbers of one-hundred-dollar bills.

They drove down the main drag, blinking in the desert sunlight and agog at all the neon. Jesse picked the biggest, gaudiest hotel he could see and pulled into the driveway.

"Checking in, sir?" a doorman asked.

"You bet." Jesse handed him the keys. "Take everything in the trunk, please." The man began removing their bags. "I'll carry this one," Jesse said, taking the plastic bag from him. As they were about to enter the hotel, there was a huge roar behind them. They turned and stood, transfixed, as a man-made volcano erupted before their eyes. "Only in America," Jesse said to the sleepy girls.

Jesse presented himself at the front desk. "I'd like a two-bedroom suite, something very nice," he said to the desk clerk.

The young man typed a few strokes on his computer keyboard. "I'm afraid we don't have anything at all, sir," he said, eyeing the rough-looking man in the sheepskin coat with the hillbilly accent.

Jesse placed the plastic bag on the counter, counted out ten banded stacks of hundred-dollar bills and stacked them on the counter. "And I'd like a hundred one-thousand-dollar chips," he said.

A sharp-eyed older man in an expensive suit practically elbowed the clerk out of the way. "Good morning, Mr. . . . ?"

"Churchill," Jesse said. "W. S. Churchill."

The man scribbled out a receipt for Jesse's money then hit a bell on the desk. A bellhop materialized. "Take the Churchill family up to the Frank Sinatra suite," he said to the man, then turned back to Jesse.

"Your accommodations and all your food and drink will be compliments of the house, Mr. Churchill. May I send your chips up to your suite?"

"Thank you, yes," Jesse said. They followed the bellman toward the elevators.

Jenny tugged at Jesse's sleeve. "Did that man mean everything is *free?*"

"Sweetheart, when you can afford to buy it, you often don't have to," Jesse replied.

"I don't understand this place at all," Jenny muttered as they got onto the elevator.

The following morning, they breakfasted *en famille* on their rooftop terrace. The living room was filled with boxes and tissue paper and luggage from their shopping, and there were one hundred and twelve one-thousand-dollar chips on the coffee table. Jesse had been down nineteen thousand dollars at one point, but he had come out ahead.

Jesse was transfixed by the *New York Times*. The story began on page one and was continued inside on two full pages. The explosion at St. Clair was being compared to Mount St. Helen. Troops were in charge of the town, hundreds of people were being questioned at the church and, in spite of sporadic gunfights, casualties were light, and there had been only two deaths, the guards on the mountaintop. Jack Gene Coldwater and his principal lieutenants were presumed dead in the explosion. He'd have to do something about that.

Jesse got up from the table and found the plastic bag. He emptied all the money into a new plastic briefcase, then took the papers from Coldwater's safe and spread them out on the coffee table. Jesse became short of breath. The documents were bank statements from all over the world, and, at a rough calculation, the balances totaled something over fifty million dollars in

Coldwater's accounts alone. Letters from the various banks contained the secret numbers for all the accounts—Coldwater, Casey and Ruger's.

It occurred to Jesse that he was now rich beyond his wildest dreams. If he wanted that. He thought about it for a while, then he put the documents in an envelope, along with the recorder he had worn, and scribbled an address. He picked up the phone and asked the hotel manager to come to his suite.

When the doorbell rang he cinched his new silk robe around his waist and went to answer it. The manager stood at the door. "Good morning, Mr. Churchill. You wished to see me?"

"Yes, please come in," Jesse replied.

The man removed an envelope from his breast pocket. "Incidentally, here are the air tickets to Los Angeles you requested."

"Thank you." Jesse had made Tokyo reservations from Los Angeles in their new name at a travel agent's. "Please have a seat." The two men sat in chairs on opposite sides of the coffee table.

"What else can I do for you, Mr. Churchill?" the manager asked.

Jesse set a plastic briefcase on the coffee table beside his chips. "I have a hundred and twelve thousand dollars in chips to cash in, and inside this case is another one million, four hundred thousand dollars in cash, all quite legal, I assure you. I probably shouldn't be carrying around this much cash, and I would like your advice as to what sorts of negotiable instruments I could exchange it for."

"Will you be traveling abroad?" the man asked.

"Possibly."

"I would suggest either gold certificates or bearer bonds," the manager said. "Either can be negotiated at any large bank in the world in a matter of hours, and I could arrange either for you by lunchtime."

Jesse scooped the chips into a large ashtray and handed them to the manager, along with the briefcase. "A million and a half in bearer bonds will do very nicely," he said. "I'm sure there will be some fees and commissions involved; the extra twelve thousand in chips should cover that."

"Oh, much more than cover it," the manager said.

"See that anything left over goes to your favorite charity," Jesse said.

"Thank you, sir," the man said, writing out a receipt for the funds. "Will there be anything else?"

Jesse held out his parking check. "Would you see that this rent-a-car is returned to Sky Harbor airport as soon as possible. There's a five-hundred-dollar cash deposit there; that can go to charity, too. And may we have your limousine for the airport at two o'clock?"

"Of course."

"One other thing." He handed the manager the large envelope containing Coldwater's banking documents. "I want to send a friend this package, and I don't want him to know where it came from; sort of a little joke."

"I understand," the manager said. "Perhaps I could forward it through our New York office."

"Excellent. Could you Federal Express it to them and have them take it to a FedEx office there and resend it?"

"Of course." The manager looked at the envelope and repeated the address. "Mr. Kipling Fuller, Nashua Building Products, 1010 Parkway, College Park, Maryland."

"That's it. And I think that's all you can do for me."

The manager stood. "May I say what a great pleasure it has been having you and your family as guests in our hotel? We hope you'll come back soon and often."

"Thank you very much. You may be sure that when we are in Las Vegas we will always stay with you."

At two o'clock, the Churchill family departed the hotel in the longest limousine Jesse had ever seen, even in Miami. Outside the terminal, Jesse dropped a paper bag containing his pistol in a trash can. The luggage was checked at the curb and the skycap handed Jesse his baggage tickets.

"Gate three, sir; you have thirty-five minutes before your flight."

Jesse gave the man twenty dollars and followed his family to the departure lounge. He had been there for ten minutes when a uniformed airline employee approached.

"Excuse me, Mr. Churchill, there's a problem with a piece of your luggage; could you follow me, please?"

"What sort of problem?" Jesse asked.

"They didn't say, but it should only take a moment."

Jesse turned to Jenny. "I'll be right back, but in any case, you get on that plane, you hear?" He handed her the briefcase containing the bearer bonds. "Take care of this."

She nodded.

Jesse got up and followed the man across the lounge and down a flight of stairs. "Down at the end, there," the man said, pausing at the bottom of the stairs and pointing at a door a hundred feet away.

"Thanks," Jesse said. He walked through the area, where baggage was being moved to and from airplanes, then came to a door marked, "M. Quentin, Baggage Manager."

Jesse stepped into the office. A man seated at a desk looked up.

"Hello, Jesse," Coldwater said.

CHAPTER

63

The door slammed behind Jesse, and he turned to see Pat Casey standing behind him. He noted that both Casey and Coldwater's pistols were equipped with silencers. When the time came they wouldn't have to worry about noise.

"You are a very great disappointment to me, Jesse," Coldwater said sadly.

"Jack Gene," Casey said, "why don't you just off him and get it over with?" He walked carefully around Jesse and stood in front of him as Coldwater came from behind the desk.

"He can't do that just yet, Pat," Jesse said. "He doesn't know what I've done with his banking documents; yours, too."

Casey turned to Coldwater. "What is he talking about?"

"Let me explain, Pat," Jesse said. "When I opened Jack Gene's safe and took the money, I took all the banking documents, too. They included the numbers to all the secret accounts, Jack Gene's, Kurt's and yours. You understand, don't you, Pat, that anybody with the account numbers has access to the accounts?"

Casey looked alarmed. "Jack Gene—"

"Shut up, Pat," Coldwater said. "Now Jesse, I'm prepared to do a deal; you give me the documents and you can keep the cash from the safe. That's enough for a fresh start somewhere, isn't it?"

Jesse managed a smile. "Not as fresh a start as with the sixty or seventy million in all those banks," he said. "What's the matter, Jack Gene, didn't you memorize the account numbers?" He turned to Casey. "You didn't think you would live to spend all that money, did you, Pat? Jack Gene had your account numbers, after all. He had Kurt's, too. He never planned on letting you keep it."

Casey stopped looking at Jesse and turned to Coldwater. "Listen to me, Jack Gene—"

Coldwater looked annoyed; he turned slightly and shot Casey once, in the forehead. Casey spun around and fell across a stack of suitcases, and his pistol landed at Jesse's feet. Jesse started to reach down for it, but Coldwater was too quick.

"No," Coldwater said, training his gun on Jesse. "You couldn't pick it up fast enough, believe me. Now think about it, Jesse, and you'll do the right thing."

"You mean, just hand over the documents and go on my merry way with your million and a half in cash?" Jesse reckoned his flight was boarding now. Time was short. "Could I trust you to do that, Jack Gene?"

"All I want is the documents, Jesse."

"Sure, Jack Gene. After I've just watched you execute your oldest and dearest friend? Why would you want to be so nice to me?" He had to get closer to Coldwater, or get Coldwater closer to him. He watched Coldwater thumb back the hammer on the pistol. "That's unnecessary, Jack Gene; that model is double action, after all."

"Jesse, you're wasting our time; we both have planes to catch."

"Come on, Jack Gene; there's a nationwide APB

out for you already; you wouldn't even get through airport security."

"Nobody's looking for my Comanche," Coldwater said, "and I've got the range for Mexico."

He was right, Jesse thought. In any case, Coldwater had more time to waste than he did. "Well, I guess you're in something of a quandary, Jack Gene. If you shoot me, you'll never get the documents and the money. You'll be right back where you started, twenty years ago. On the other hand, if you put down the gun, then that would make me feel that we could trust each other. I mean, the million and a half is already in a bank abroad; you couldn't take it away from me."

Coldwater gazed at him. "You have a point, Jesse." He kicked Casey's pistol away, then tossed his own onto the desk behind him. "All right, where are the documents?"

"At this moment," Jesse said, ''they're in the hands of a task force in the Justice Department, the same people that took your town last night." Jesse shifted his weight slightly and turned a shoulder toward Coldwater. "So, you see, you've never going to get your hands on a single dollar of that money. You're going to be a fugitive for the rest of your life, however short a time that may be."

Coldwater looked stunned and that quickly changed to anger. "You idiot," he said. "Do you think I need a weapon to kill you?"

"Yes," Jesse said. "You do."

Coldwater's fingers darted toward Jesse's eyes, but Jesse was ready. He caught the thrust on his left forearm, and, as hard as he could, he rammed his fist into Coldwater's throat. Coldwater grabbed at his neck with both hands, staggering backward toward the desk. Jesse kicked with his left foot and swept the bigger man's legs from under him.

Coldwater lay gasping for air, his eyes wide. Jesse

moved gingerly around him, pushed the desk out of the way and retrieved Casey's pistol.

"You have a minute or so before you lose consciousness," Jesse said to Coldwater. "And a little while after that before you expire. I learned about that from somebody in prison who tried to do it to me."

Coldwater's hands slipped away from his throat, but he continued to stare at Jesse.

"Of course, that kind of death would point to a third party," he said, "and I don't want anybody looking for me." He brought the pistol up. "This is for Jenny," he said, then fired a single shot into Coldwater's throat.

Jesse quickly removed the two men's wallets, then rearranged the bodies, wiped his fingerprints from the pistol and placed it in Coldwater's hand. A murder-suicide was the best he could manage on short notice. When everything looked right, he cracked the door to the office and looked around. He found a "do-not-disturb" sign hanging on the inside doorknob, transferred it to the outside and closed the door behind him.

He found Jenny where he had left her, and a voice was announcing final boarding for their flight. "Sorry to be so long," he said, picking up the briefcase. "Let's get aboard." He walked them toward the boarding gate, then, as they passed the ticket agent, he tugged at Jenny's elbow. "You take your seats; I'll be right with you."

"Jesse—" she said, alarmed.

"I'll be there in two minutes, I promise."

Reluctantly, she herded the girls down the gangway.

Jesse stepped a few paces aside and took the portable phone from his pocket. He dialed the number of the Justice Department in Washington. When the operator answered he said, "This is Dan Barker; patch me through to Kip Fuller, with the task force in Idaho."

There was a short delay, then a ringing.

"This is Fuller," he said. "This better be important."

"You busy, Kip?" he asked.

"Jesse! Where the hell are you?"

"I'm gone, Kip; I just wanted to say goodbye and to do you a favor or two."

"A favor? What are you talking about?"

"First of all, I've sent you a little package, care of Nashua, in College Park. I think you'll enjoy the contents."

"What is it?"

"Don't be impatient, Kip. Let me speak to Barker."

There was some mumbling, then Dan Barker came on the line. "Jesse?"

"Listen carefully, Dan. I can still blow you out of the water by releasing everything to the papers. I might even be able to get the investigation into my partner's death reopened. Do you understand me?" This was a bluff.

There was silence for a moment, then Barker folded. "Yes, I understand you."

"Good. Unless I read in the *New York Times* within ninety days that you've resigned from the Justice Department, I'll release everything. I have only to make a phone call. Do you understand me?"

"Yes," Barker said.

"Good; you have ninety days to think about it. Now put Kip back on the line."

"I'm here, Jesse," Kip said. "What was that all about?"

"Barker is considering early retirement."

"Listen, we found Ruger's body, along with Charley Bottoms. What happened?"

"The recorder is in the package; it will explain everything."

"What about Coldwater and Casey? Where are they?"

"Don't worry, they'll turn up. But believe me, they're not going to be a problem."

"Jesse, I can get you the pardon now; no problem."

"You hang on to it for me, Kip, in case I ever need it."

"If that's what you want."

"Tell Barker I'll be watching the papers, and take care of yourself."

Jesse broke the connection. He wiped the phone clean of fingerprints and dropped it in a trash receptacle, along with Coldwater and Casey's wallets, then he boarded the airplane.

EPILOGUE

AKAROA, SOUTH ISLAND, NEW ZEALAND,
FOUR MONTHS LATER

Jesse stopped into the village post office for his mail. Along with the usual utility bills and advertising circulars there was a letter from the home secretary's office in Wellington.

"Morning, Mr. Warren," the postmistress said. "Lovely day."

"Getting a bit chilly, though," he replied.

"Winter's coming."

Winter came in June in this country. "Suppose you're right."

"Think you'll like us as well in winter?"

"Seems an awfully nice place. I thought I'd look at some property." The postmistress was the local real estate broker, too.

"Glad to show you some; there's a very pretty place down on the point; bit pricey, though."

•
361

"I've got to run up to Christchurch today. Maybe we could look at it tomorrow."

"Glad to show it to you."

Jesse stepped out onto the porch of the post office. Behind him he heard the postmistress speak to another customer.

"That's Mr. Warren," she said. "American writer; pretty well known in the states, I hear. Been here for a couple of months, now; looks like he might stay."

Jesse opened the letter from the home secretary and read it. He, his wife, and his two daughters had been granted permanent residence status in New Zealand. Jesse smiled, put the letter into his pocket, got into the car and headed for Christchurch. It was his habit to drive up there once a week.

In the public library at Christchurch he read through the most recent copies of the *New York Times*. They were always at least a month old. On the national news page he found what he was looking for:

NEW APPOINTMENT AT JUSTICE

The White House press office announced today that Kipling Fuller has been named Assistant Attorney General for Law Enforcement. Fuller, who has been given credit by insiders for masterminding the successful raid on the Aryan Universe cult in Idaho, had been Deputy Assistant Attorney General, in charge of the department's special task force on dangerous cults, following the resignation of Daniel Barker, who retired last month.

The piece went on to recount Kip's background in law enforcement and his leading of the raid. Then, further down the page, Jesse saw something he had not expected.

DEATH AT ATLANTA PRISON

The Justice Department announced today that Jesse Warden, a former DEA agent who was serving a long sentence for the murder of another agent, died yesterday in the hospital of Atlanta Federal Prison, of injuries received in a fight with another prisoner in the exercise yard. Warden left no survivors.

Jesse closed the newspaper and returned it to the stacks. Well, he thought, it was almost as good as a presidential pardon.

He got into his car and drove back toward Akaroa. If he hurried, he would be in time for lunch.

Santa Fe, New Mexico, October 31, 1993

•

Here is an excerpt from

IMPERFECT STRANGERS

Published by HarperCollins*Publishers*
and available now wherever fine books are sold.

•

CHAPTER

1

As the sun rose over Berkeley Square, the May sunshine drifted through the blinds in the Mount Street flat, two blocks west. The rays fell across the face of Peter Kinsolving, waking him as if they had been the bell of an alarm clock. He lay on his back, naked, and blinked a couple of times. Oriented, he turned to his right and moved toward the woman next to him. He shaped himself to her back and pressed his groin against her soft buttocks, and he felt the stirring come.

She gave a soft moan and responded, pushing against him. In a moment she was wet, and he entered her, moving slowly, enjoying the early morning moment.

The phone rang, the loud, insistent jangling that only an older British phone could make. He cursed under his breath, and without stopping the motion, reached across her and lifted the receiver.

"Hello?" he said hoarsely.

"Peter, it's Joan." She waited for him to respond.

He still did not stop moving. "Yes," he said, finally, then he became more alert. "What time is it in New York?"

"Nearly two A.M."

"What's wrong?"

"Daddy has had a stroke."

He stopped moving, wilting like a violet in hot sun. "How bad?"

"They don't know, yet, but at his age . . ."

Jock Bailley was ninety-one. "I'll get myself on a flight as soon as the office opens. Where is he?"

"Lenox Hill. I'm calling from there."

"I'll let the New York office know what flight I'm on."

"Albert will meet you."

"You all right?"

"Tired."

"You'd better go home and sleep. There's nothing you can do there."

"I suppose you're right. Laddie and Myra are here, anyway."

"You should all go home and sleep."

"I will. I can't speak for Laddie."

"See you this afternoon."

She hung up without saying good-bye.

Peter replaced the receiver. A little ball of apprehension had made a tight knot in his belly.

"*Peter*," the woman said accusingly. "You stopped."

Peter rolled onto his back. "Sorry, luv. I've just been put out of commission."

"Bad news?"

"Yes, bad news. Illness in the family."

"I'm sorry."

"Thanks. I'd better get dressed. Do you mind breakfasting at home? I have to go to New York."

"Certainly, dear," she said, rising and heading for the bathroom. "I'll just get a quick shower."

"Thanks." Peter stared at his ceiling and tried to put a good face on all this. Jock wasn't dead, yet. That was something, at least.

Peter took the lift down at eight o'clock and let himself into Cornwall & Company, the wine shop on the ground floor. He stood for a moment and watched the sunbeams cut little swaths through the dust in the air, which was in the process of gathering on the hundreds of bottles that lined the walls of the large shop.

He walked to the rear of the shop and climbed the old circular staircase to the offices above. He set his briefcase on the desk in his little office and sat down heavily. As he did, the door from the first-floor landing opened and Maeve O'Brien stepped into the offices.

"Maeve," he called out.

She came to his office door. "Yes, Mr. Kinsolving?"

"Would you get me a seat on a flight to New York? The earlier the better."

"Of course. I thought you were staying until next week, though."

"Old Mr. Bailley has had a stroke."

"Oh, I'm sorry to hear it. I'll call the airlines." She hung up her coat and went to her desk.

A few minutes later, Maeve was back. "You're on the eleven o'clock; it was the earliest. I'll pick up your ticket from American Express, across the street."

Peter suddenly couldn't tolerate the office anymore. "I'll pick it up myself. I could use a walk."

"As you wish."

He let himself out the front door of the shop, locking it behind him and walked slowly past the Connaught Hotel and toward Berkeley Square. Even if Jock was still alive, at his age he couldn't come out of this whole. What would happen if he couldn't communicate, couldn't make his wishes known? Oh, Jesus.

He circumnavigated Berkeley Square and started back up the south side of Mount Street, past the poulterer's and the antique shops, past the tobacconist and the chemist, past his tailor's. He remembered he had a fitting that morning. He stopped at the little American Express office as the manager was letting herself in.

"Good morning, Mr. Kinsolving," she said pleasantly.

"I'd like to pick up a ticket for New York," he said. "The reservation's already made."

"Certainly. I won't be a moment."

He stood outside the agency and watched the morning light fill the elegant street, with its pink granite buildings, lately sandblasted of the decades of London grime, looking new in the moist air. He loved this street. He could get almost anything done within the block—have a suit made, lunch at the Connaught or Scott's, pick up a packet of condoms from the Indian chemist, then forget to use them, be measured for a brace of shotguns at Purdy's on the corner, or select a case of good port at Cornwall & Company, his London base. It jarred him that he was leaving this to go back to New York before the appointed time. He didn't know what awaited him there, and he didn't want to guess.

After a passable airline lunch, he ordered a single malt whiskey, uncharacteristic for him at this hour. He wasn't sleepy, but he wanted to be. An announcement came that the movie was about to start. He flipped up the little screen on the arm of his seat and adjusted the headset.

As he did, someone came forward and took the empty seat next to him. "My seatmate snores," a man's voice said. "Hope you don't mind."

"Not at all," Peter replied, smiling politely, not bothering to glance at the man.

The titles came up on the screen, and Peter prepared to lose himself in whatever the movie might be. It turned out to be the Alfred Hitchcock classic, *Strangers on a Train*.

CHAPTER

2

P eter folded away the screen and put away the headset, then accepted his third Scotch from the flight attendant. He turned to the man beside him out of automatic courtesy. "Join me?"

"Don't mind if I do," the man replied. "What is that you're drinking."

"Laphroaig."

"Oh, yes, the same for me, please."

Peter looked at his companion for the first time and found him to be very much like himself. Hardly identical in appearance, but about the same age, mid-forties, the same good clothes, good haircut, good teeth. His hair was sandy, going gray, as Peter's was dark, going gray. He noticed the three-button cuff at the end of the man's sleeve and knew that they went to the same shirtmaker. His accent was hard to place; something English in it, but not English; mid-Atlantic, maybe.

The man offered his hand. "I'm Alexander Martindale," he said. "Sandy will do."

"Peter Kinsolving." They shook hands.

"Not Pete, I hope."

"No. I had more than one fistfight over that as a kid. Never liked it."

Sandy's drink arrived. "Your good health, Peter," he said, raising his glass.

"And yours, Sandy." Both men drank.

"God, that's good! You can taste the peat. Too many of them wouldn't do your liver any good, though."

"Certainly wouldn't," Peter replied. "Not unless you were laboring very hard in the vineyard, sweating it out."

"And what vineyard do you labor in, Peter?"

"Wine. I buy and sell it. You?"

"Art. I buy and sell it. In San Francisco."

"I'm in New York and London. I can't place your accent."

"California Brit, I guess," Sandy said. "Born in Liverpool, been out on the coast for twenty years."

"How's the art business?"

"Good. And wine?"

"Good and getting better. I'm glad to see the recession behind us. I've got a lot of good claret in the cellars I'd like to have sold two or three years ago."

"But you can get more for it with the extra age, can't you?"

"Yes, but it's less nerve-wracking to sell it young, keep it moving."

"Your clothes are English, but your accent isn't."

"Grew up in Connecticut. Lived in or around New York all my life."

"School?"

"Amherst."

"I was at Oxford, probably about the same time."

"I envy you the experience. I tried for a Rhodes Scholarship, but didn't make it."

"You're the right age for Vietnam."

"Missed it. Had a wife and child by the time I left New Haven."

"What did you do right out of university?" Sandy asked.

"Went into advertising, like my father."

"When did the wine trade come along?"

"Not for some time. It was liquor, at first. My wife's father has had a large distributorship since Prohibition ended."

"Sounds like he might have been in the business before it ended," Sandy said, smiling.

"Right. His family were distillers in Scotland. He was the second son, so they shipped him to Canada, to see if he could move some of their goods to a thirsty America."

"And did he?"

"Oh, yes, and the goods of a lot of other distillers, too. By the time he was twenty-one, he was driving fast motorboats down the Bay of Fundy to the coast between Boston and Portsmouth. He knew Meyer Lansky, Lucky Luciano, the lot of them. They convinced him he should stick to importing, rather than distributing. They had that well in hand."

"So, when Prohibition ended, he went legal?"

"That's right. His father died about that time, and his older brother inherited. But he had the distribution rights to the family brands, and he was well connected with other distillers, as a result of his recent activities. He poured his illicit profits into the business, and pretty soon he was leading the pack."

"And how long did he run the business?"

"Right up until yesterday. He had a stroke last night."

"That's a long run. How old was he?"

"Ninety-one."

"So you'll take over, now?"

"That remains to be seen," Peter sighed. "Old Jock had a son and a daughter late in life. The son's in the business; I'm married to the daughter." He sighed again.

"You don't make it sound like the happiest of circumstances."

"I'm sorry. I didn't mean to whine."

"Oh, nothing like that, Peter, but I can see how that sort of family could be difficult to live in."

Peter pulled at the whiskey again and began to relax. He found he needed to talk, and he had the ear of a sympathetic stranger, someone he'd never see again after this flight.

"It was difficult at first," he said. "I married Joan the summer after my junior year at Amherst. She was at Mount Holyoke, and she was pregnant, if the truth be known, and I wanted to do the right thing."

"Were you in love with her?"

"Yes, and I was, oddly, very happy when she told me she was pregnant. Old Jock, her father, thought I was after his money, of course, so I made a point of not taking a penny from him. I worked two jobs my senior year, and we lived in a garage apartment. I don't think I've ever been happier."

"Why advertising? You said your father was in the business?"

"Yes, he was an old-timer at Young & Rubicam, and I joined the trainee program there. Did well, too. Jock had assumed I'd want a job with him, so I managed again not to meet his worst expectations. He liked that. Before long, he was insulted that I hadn't come to work for him, and he began to press me hard. When I thought I had played hard-to-get for long enough, I gave in. Since by that time, I was a successful account executive at Y&R, I thought he'd want me to take over his marketing." Peter laughed ruefully at the memory. "Let me tell you something, don't ever go to work for a Scotsman without a contract."

"I take it you did."

"I did. He put me to selling booze, and do you know what my territory was?"

"Not good?"

"The Bowery! One day I had a nice office and a secretary on Madison Avenue; the next, I was in and out of every gin joint from Eighth Street to Houston, in the regular company of what used to be called bums—that was before they became homeless."

"I don't guess you sold much single malt whiskey."

"Not much. Sixty percent of my sales were in cheap gin and rye. We weren't in the wine business in those days, so I didn't have to sell muscatel."

"Was it tough work?"

"I worked my ass off, and never made a squawk, either. Jock was waiting for that. Meantime, his son, John Junior, or Laddie, as he's always been called, was working the Upper East Side, lunching at 21 every day and getting his suits made at Dunhill's. If I'd showed up on the Bowery in a Dunhill suit, I wouldn't have lived through the first week. I worked in coveralls, out of a panel truck."

"I take it this didn't last forever."

"No. After two and a half years, Jock brought me uptown and put me in marketing—as *assistant* marketing manager, working for an old rummy who didn't know a third what I did about marketing and advertising."

"And how long did you take that particular form of abuse?"

"Not long. After about two weeks, I walked into Jock's office and, more or less, told him to go to hell. I told him I wouldn't work for him another day, that he didn't have sense enough to use talent where it would do some good."

"And what was his reaction?"

"I don't think anybody had ever talked to him that way before, but he took it surprisingly well. Cunningly, he asked if I had another offer somewhere. I told him the truth—I didn't, but I'd go out and make a job for myself. Advertising was in something of a depression at the time, and Jock knew it, but he knew I wasn't bluffing, either, so he surprised me."

"He gave you the marketing job?"

"No. He asked me what I'd like to do in the business."

"And what did you tell him?"

"I hadn't expected the question, so I didn't have a ready answer. Rather impulsively, I blurted out that I wanted to start a wine division. Jock didn't know anything about wine. I mean, he drank single malt Scotch with his meals. Not that I knew a hell of a lot about it, either, but I had the advantage of knowing more than Jock did, and to my surprise, he took me up on it. 'Okay,' he said, 'I'll give you a hundred thousand dollars of capital and a thousand square feet of warehouse space. Go start a wine division of Bailley & Son, and let me know how you do.'"

"That was quite an opportunity."

"I was flabbergasted, really. I walked out of his office in a daze. I don't think I slept for a week; I read every book about wine I could get my hands on, I visited every wine shop on the East Side, and I found an empty storefront on Madison Avenue and rented it. I invested most of my capital in California wines, and I took full-page ads in the *Times* and sold at steep discounts. It was my only way into the market, and it worked; I turned a twenty-thousand-dollar profit my first year, and I established some invaluable contacts with growers. The business grew rapidly.

"Then, three years ago, I heard from a friend that Cornwall & Company, an old established London shipper and retailer, was about to go on the block. The last Cornwall was on his deathbed, and he had not done a good job with the business when he was healthy. They had a golden reputation and a severe cash-flow problem, and I persuaded Jock to go for it. I bought it from the widow a week after Cornwall died, and it's been the most fun I ever had."

"That's great," Sandy said. "What happens now?"

Peter finished his drink and signaled for another. "I don't

know. If Jock had stayed healthy for another month, I'd have been a major stockholder in Bailley & Son."

"You mean you're not?"

"I own about three percent of the stock, but Jock was finally ready to do the right thing. The success of Cornwall finally convinced him that I was indispensible, I think, and he made me some extravagant promises."

"Which now, he may not be able to keep."

Peter started on the new drink. "Right. I don't know why I'm telling you all this."

"Can I make a guess about something? The marriage to Joan isn't what it once was."

"Hasn't been for, I don't know, twelve, fifteen years."

"And Jock has a grandson?"

"Our boy, Angus."

"Is he in the business?"

"No, he opted for medicine. He's a resident in cardiology at Lenox Hill Hospital."

"Is Joan in the business?"

"Not up to now," Peter replied.

"Suppose Jock dies tomorrow? What will Joan do?"

"She and her brother, Laddie, will inherit Bailley & Son. Except for my three percent, of course," he said ruefully. "And then I think it's likely that Joan will divorce me."

"Ahhhhh," Sandy moaned softly. "She's got you between a stone and a very firm surface, hasn't she?"

"She has."

"Well, you're not alone, Peter. I've been building my gallery for eighteen years, and it's become a regular cash cow. However, my wife of fifteen years has just announced her intention to divorce me and marry a painter that I made into a giant of the art world."

"I'm sorry, Sandy, that's a tough break."

"Tougher than you know. California is a community-property state."

Peter let out a short, ironic laugh. "Believe me, if New York were a community-property state, *I'd* divorce *Joan*."

"It gets worse," Sandy said. "Her new husband, the painter, will take most of my good artists with him, once the divorce and settlement are final. She'll take half the business, then, together, they'll gut my half."

The captain came onto the loudspeaker system and announced their approach into Kennedy Airport.

"Peter," Sandy said, "did you enjoy the movie?"

"*Strangers on a Train?* Loved it. I must have seen it half a dozen times."

"Tell me, what went wrong with Bruno's plan for him to murder Guy's wife and for Guy to murder Bruno's father?"

Peter thought for a moment. "Two things, I think; first of all, Guy didn't take Bruno's proposal seriously until it was too late, and second, and most important, Bruno was crazy."

"What do you think would have happened if Guy *had* taken Bruno's proposal seriously, and if Bruno *hadn't* been crazy?"

"Well, I think they would have pulled off two perfect murders." Peter stopped talking and looked at Sandy with new, if somewhat drunken awareness.

"Peter, do you think I'm crazy?" Sandy asked.

"I don't believe you are," Peter replied.

"Do you think I'm a serious person?"

Peter looked at Sandy for a long time. "I believe you are," he said, finally.

The airplane touched down and taxied to the gate before anyone spoke again.

Sandy stood up and stretched. "Perhaps we should talk again," he said.

"Perhaps we should," said Peter.

Shaun's heart started beating again.

"Someone broke in." He pulled off his dress shirt, wondering if his voice sounded normal.

"Who? Did you get the computer? Why are you undressing?"

"No. They have it. And I'm taking off my T-shirt to clean your face."

"Oh…" Coughing more vigorously, she tried to sit up, but he pushed her back down before pulling his shirt over his head. "Who's they?"

"I don't know. Do you always ask this many questions?" He didn't intend to answer so sharply, but he was still getting his equilibrium back at almost getting them both killed.

"No, I just… Sorry," she muttered.

He stopped and looked into her eyes. "No, Abigail, I'm the one who's sorry. I almost got you killed for the second time today."

Her eyes filled with tears. "I don't really see it that way, you know. I think you just saved my life for the second time."

KAY THOMAS

BULLETPROOF HEARTS

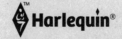

TORONTO NEW YORK LONDON
AMSTERDAM PARIS SYDNEY HAMBURG
STOCKHOLM ATHENS TOKYO MILAN MADRID
PRAGUE WARSAW BUDAPEST AUCKLAND

For Tom, for everything.

Recycling programs
for this product may
not exist in your area.

ISBN-13: 978-0-373-69541-6

BULLETPROOF HEARTS

Copyright © 2011 by Kay Thomas

www.eHarlequin.com

Printed in U.S.A.

ABOUT THE AUTHOR

Having grown up in the heart of the Mississippi Delta, Kay Thomas considers herself a "recovering" Southern belle. She attended Vanderbilt and graduated from Mississippi State University with a degree in educational psychology and an emphasis in English. Along the way to publication, she taught high school, worked in an advertising specialty agency and had a very brief stint in a lingerie store.

Kay met her husband in Dallas when they sat next to each other in a restaurant. Seven weeks later they were engaged. Twenty years later she claims the moral of that story is "When in Texas look the guy over before you sit next to him, because you may be eating dinner with him the rest of your life!" Today she still lives in Dallas with her Texan, their two children and a shockingly spoiled Boston terrier named Jack.

Kay is thrilled to be writing for Harlequin Intrigue and would love to hear from her readers. Visit her at her website, www.kaythomas.net, or drop her a line at P.O. Box 837321, Richardson, TX 75083.

Books by Kay Thomas

HARLEQUIN INTRIGUE

CAST OF CHARACTERS

Abigail Trevor—A professor of Southern literature attending her brother's funeral in Washington, D.C. When Abby finds out her brother's hit-and-run accident was murder, she is forced to trust a mysterious stranger to ensure her own safety.

Shaun Logan—Raised in Ireland, Shaun now works in the U.S. as a contract bodyguard security specialist for Zip Technologies. His job is to keep Abby safe, but can he do that and discover who really killed her brother?

Jason Trevor—Abby's brother and the creator of Zip-Net, a completely secure internet wireless protocol. Was he killed for it?

Michael Donner—CEO and founder of Zip Technologies, also Shaun's boss. Famous in the business world for his philanthropy and business sense, Michael is about to sign the deal of a lifetime if Shaun and Abby can find the answers he needs.

Karen Weathers—Abby's mentor and friend currently living in a Dallas rehab facility due to a stroke. Will she be used as a pawn while Abby and Shaun look for clues?

Harlan Jeffries—Shaun's best friend from Iraq. Can Harlan help Shaun keep Abby safe?

Hodges—Reports to Michael Donner. Shaun has worked with him before at Zip Technologies.

Chapter One

Watching the strangers scurry past her brother's grave, Abby Trevor felt blessedly numb everywhere...except her feet. The designer shoes she'd bought on a whim last spring with Jason hurt like crazy and pain was the only thing keeping her focused. The pinch in her right instep reminded her of the day she and her brother had shopped themselves silly in New York. At the moment that needle-like sensation was the way she knew the coffin in front of her was not some hideous nightmare as the rain fell in sheets from the dark morning sky.

If she let herself believe for one second the sea of black umbrellas around her was a dream, she'd stand up, kick off those wretched shoes and run screaming from the drowning cemetery. That would certainly set the tongues to wagging, especially here in Washington, D.C.

But she wouldn't disgrace her brother or his memory that way. Her mama's Southern belle training was too ingrained in her, despite the fact that she was one thousand miles from the Mississippi Delta and the small town that had been the cradle of her genteel upbringing.

Still, that home training—and her uncomfortable shoes—kept Abby's butt firmly planted in the soggy funeral home seat under the green awning. She'd never be able to stand the sight or scent of stargazer lilies again. Thunder rumbled in the distance, serving as another reminder that despite the surreal atmosphere, this was no dream.

Jason was dead. Killed by a hit-and-run driver while crossing the street on his lunch hour. D.C. police were still looking for the driver.

God, Jason, what happened?

She closed her eyes. When she opened them again, the rain was coming down in biblical proportions and almost everyone was gone. She wouldn't be surprised to see frogs falling from the sky soon. She felt nearly alone in the world. Nearly.

Estranged relatives in Mississippi didn't count. But Karen Weathers did. Even if her beloved mentor was in a nursing home in Dallas. Abby tried to imagine herself in happier days sitting in her old college professor's office at Southern Methodist University sipping tea and arguing about William Faulkner, anything to mentally take herself away from her present location. It didn't work. She was too aware of the rain. The overpowering scent of the lilies. The pain in her feet. And the temptation to run screaming from it all.

"Miss Trevor, I'm terribly sorry for your loss. Your brother will be missed." The deep voice had a rich Irish lilt to it.

The speaker was tall, wore a trench coat and held a massive golf umbrella against the dreary weather. Rain splattered his outstretched hand but she reached to take it anyway. His grasp was warm and wet.

"My name's Abigail but everyone calls me Abby." She glanced up with her practiced "polite funeral smile" in place only to get a distinct jolt when she stared into unusual blue-green eyes that reminded her of dark Caribbean waters that could change to a deep emerald when the light hit just so. She took a moment longer to study the man's Cary Grant cleft chin and high cheekbones. But that's where all similarity to her favorite movie star ended.

His aristocratic nose had been broken somewhere in the past and his dark hair, misted by the rain, was cut in a longer variation of a military "high and tight." The combination made him a bit dangerous looking, but his air was open and friendly. Overall, the nose kept him from being too pretty, otherwise he would have looked like a chiseled European model.

Somewhere in her perusal she found her voice again, glad to be shaken from her pity party and wild thoughts of running barefoot like a banshee from the cemetery. His grip was firm and he had a bandage on his index finger. She wondered what had happened to it.

She let go of his hand and asked, "How did you know Jason?"

"By reputation, initially. I was a great admirer of his work. My name is Shaun Logan. We became…friends later."

An admirer of Jason's work.

What a strange thing to say. She didn't think her brother's work was necessarily well-known. Jason was a concept development engineer, albeit a good one, for Zip Technologies. Zip Tech for short. A cyber-security start-up. And now the man was staring back at her in the oddest way. She had a feeling she was missing something significant.

She'd never thought of Jason as having admirers, unless… Ah, color her embarrassed. Of course.

Her brother was gay. And this lovely gentleman must be as well. Okay, so she'd missed that entirely. She'd been too busy checking him out herself.

"I had no idea." That covered such a multitude of things about her brother—his love life and her present gaffe.

Jason had been very open about his choices but not his lovers. And Abby had adored him—not judging, even when her parents had, to their own detriment.

She swallowed past the emotion clogging her throat. "Thank you for coming today. I appreciate it. I didn't know many of his…friends."

"'Tis my honor to be here. I only wish we could be meeting under more pleasant circumstances." His accent was like sliding into a warm comfortable coat on a cold day.

"Your brother was quite famous in the high-tech world," Shaun continued.

She shook her head, still at a loss to reconcile the Jason she'd known and to understand this aspect of his work.

"It's not something you would have been aware of if you weren't in the industry, especially as his sister. You just loved him for himself, aye?"

Again, Abby swallowed hard as sudden scalding tears burned the corners of her eyes. There were so many things she didn't know about Jason's life. Had he told this man all the details?

She sighed. "Jason never shared much with me about his job. It was so proprietary."

He nodded and offered her a neatly pressed handkerchief from his coat pocket. "Everyone at Zip Tech signs a nondisclosure agreement. Applies to family members, as well."

"Did he speak with you about his work?" she asked.

"Only in the most general of terms. He worked on some very interesting projects."

Abby tilted her head. That voice. Shaun Logan could charm snakes with it. She'd be completely intimidated if he wasn't gay. She looked directly at him and smiled. "Jason told me a little about the new security project—Zip-Net, I believe it's called? He was thrilled and so hopeful for the direction of the company. I can't quite believe he won't be here to—"

She stopped. She couldn't think about that now or she'd never make it through everything she had to do today and the rest of this week.

"It's an exciting concept. Everyone at Zip Tech is optimistic about the future and they owe your brother a great deal," said Shaun. "He was a wonderful man."

"He was a pretty terrific brother, too." She bowed her head and dabbed at her eyes with the handkerchief. It smelled like the same fabric softener she used herself. She was struck by the incongruity of that as she felt Shaun's hand on her shoulder.

"If there's anything I can do," he murmured.

She looked up. There was nothing to be done now but grieve, and there would be time for that later, in private.

"I'd missed several of his calls lately. I assumed he was traveling. We'd been playing phone tag for a couple of weeks and I hadn't been able to catch up with him." *Or hear about who he was seeing?*

"Right. He was traveling with lab testing all last month."

"I wondered why we kept missing each other." She thought of Jason's garbled voice-mail message a few days ago. She'd only caught the beginning because the connection was so bad. *Buttercup, how are you?*

She'd assumed his call was more decompressing about his schedule. While he couldn't tell her much about his actual work, he could bitch about the insane deadlines of a start-up company and the unique personalities involved—all while managing to make it sound entertaining. That was Jason. And that information wasn't proprietary. She'd always been willing to listen. He'd certainly listened to her enough.

She fervently hoped Jason had had others to listen as well and to give advice. Others perhaps like Shaun? He certainly seemed to know her brother.

Could he tell her more about Jason? They were alone now in the cemetery under the awning. Everyone had fled the rain except for the funeral director and the limo driver. She dove in without really thinking it through, especially as she assumed he "hit for the other team" so to speak.

"I won't keep you any longer in this horrible rain, but I've really enjoyed talking with you about Jason's work. I'd like to learn more about that part of his life. Do you have a business card? Could I perhaps email you?" she asked.

He reached into his pocket and handed her one. "Nothing would please me more."

"Thank you." She slid the calling card into her purse, disinclined to leave but knowing it was time.

"How long have you been in D.C.?" he asked.

"I got in the day before yesterday. Wait, I guess it was yesterday." She shook her head. "My internal clock is turned upside down. I flew in from London and I don't have my times figured out yet."

"Do you live in the U.K.?" He took her elbow, helping her through the rain to the limo. The golf umbrella was huge, yet the swirling rain still found them.

"I do now...for the past three months. I'm a professor at SMU. This semester I'm guest lecturing on Southern Literature at Cambridge University while one of their professors is teaching English literature in Dallas. We swap apartments and everything."

"What a fascinating way to see the world."

"It is. I've done this in Italy and France, as well."

"Where are you staying while you're here?" They'd reached the limo and he helped her inside.

"I'm at Jason's. I'll close his condo while I'm in D.C. Then—" She stopped and stared hard at her wet right shoe before she took a deep breath. "I suppose I haven't really gotten that far yet."

She glanced up at him. "Can I give you a lift to your car?" She was reluctant to leave him now. Hearing him talk, she wouldn't have cared if the Irishman was reading the phone book. She felt peaceful for the first time in four days, like she wasn't going to jump out of her skin. It felt for some reason as if she were letting her last ties with Jason go.

He shrugged. "No worries, I took a cab."

"Can I drop you somewhere? It's raining so, please… get in." She stopped again and blushed. "Oh, my, I'm not trying to pick you up at my brother's funeral. Not that you'd be interest—"

She stopped and shook her head, wishing suddenly for the earth to open and swallow her up. "I'm sorry. That's not what I meant at all."

She felt herself blushing, and suddenly she was back in Ms. Martin's seventh grade class, stammering through her "How to Make the Perfect Peanut Butter and Jelly Sandwich" demonstration speech. On top of spreading peanut butter on her speech notes instead of the bread, she'd dropped and shattered the strawberry jam jar in front of the entire classroom. That day, she'd wished for the world to end, as well—for an entirely different reason.

SHAUN COULDN'T HELP BUT SMILE as she flushed again, a pleasant pink, to the roots of her hair. It was lovely. He hadn't seen a woman who got embarrassed and blushed like that in a long time.

The part of his conscience that was still active was mildly bothered by the fact that he was deceiving a woman who had just buried her brother. That twinge of remorse surprised him. Intellectually he knew how she felt. But the remnants of his own grief and loss had been buried for so long, they no longer clouded his judgment.

Growing up in a country filled with centuries of violence had not produced an idyllic childhood, nor had losing both parents to "the Troubles" of his homeland in a bomb blast at the tender age of eight. Years of denial had worked in his favor at cementing a manhole cover of ice over that dark mental abyss. He shook off the old ghosts.

He hadn't planned to introduce himself at the funeral and certainly not as Jason Trevor's boyfriend. He'd been ordered to keep an eye on Abigail, possibly even protect her—as needed—from the background. He wasn't supposed to make contact yet. Donner needed this woman's cooperation but that wouldn't happen if Shaun spooked her first. He'd considered the funeral as more of a scouting opportunity, but this seemed too good an opportunity to pass up.

Getting her to lean on him, trust him was the job he'd been assigned. Abigail Trevor was clearly in pain. Plus, she was in an unfamiliar city with no family or friends close by. He'd been over and over how to play this the past three days. The problem was time and how little there was of it. Winning her trust in such a limited time frame called for a wee…creative manipulation of the truth. Such as concealing, for now, the fact that the female Trevor sibling was much more to his taste than her brother would have been.

Maybe he should have corrected Abigail's assumption and told her that he was definitely not gay. But he had to insinuate himself into her life as soon as possible. So he let her mistake stand as the quickest way to get under her defenses.

Shaun was just grateful he worked for Michael Donner now, instead of his old boss at Storm's Edge. He could trust Donner and his motives. In other words, he could lie with impunity.

There was certainly no one around to contradict him. No one knew him or could question whether Shaun had known Jason Trevor as a colleague, a lover, or if he'd never laid eyes on the man until today at the funeral home viewing.

Jason had kept his personal life extraordinarily private, and Shaun had seen the change in Abigail's eyes when she thought she'd put it together, so he didn't set her straight in any sense of the word.

Seeing Jason's coworkers hurry past, most not saying anything to her due in part to the torrential downpour, he realized that right now was the perfect time to approach her. She was off balance, grieving. Not evaluating or think-ing clearly. Any slipup he might make could be more easily covered. Letting himself be "talked into" a ride was the perfect setup.

Except when he felt that niggle of conscience and a real surge of attraction that was completely out of place here. Then she was talking and he almost missed what she was saying.

"…it's just I don't want to ride by myself and it seems a waste. I can drop you at a hotel in Georgetown at least. It'll be easier for you to grab a cab that way in this rain."

Shaun grinned. This would be okay. It would be splen-did, in fact. "Sure and I'd be a fool to turn down a lift from a lovely lady. Just drop me at the nearest metro station. I'll take the train home."

What could be more ideal?

ABBY MOVED OVER AS SHAUN climbed in beside her. He
was much bigger than she'd realized once he was seated
beside her—at least six foot three. He wasn't imposing
exactly but he was built like someone who worked out
a lot.

*Jason, even from the grave you snag the most amazing-
looking men. What is that about?*

At that moment Abby had a pang of longing for her
brother and all they had lost that was so intense, a tear
trickled down her cheek mixing with the raindrops. She
turned her head away to the opposite window and saw that
the limo driver had provided a couple of towels for her to
dry off with. She blotted her face and offered the other
hand linen to Shaun.

"Jason would have adored this," she murmured. "He
dearly loved a good thunderstorm. They always scared me
silly."

The limo driver swung around the gates of the cemetery
and paused a moment as a maintenance truck rolled past.
The plan was for her to be driven back to Jason's condo
in Arlington. Zip Tech had made all the arrangements.
She leaned forward to ask the driver to stop at a metro
station.

Breaking glass and a soft *svit* sound thumped the leather
seat behind her. The window beside her broke into a thousand tiny pieces, covering her back and hair.

"Get down!" Shaun tackled her, taking her to the floor-
board. Suddenly she was facedown underneath two hundred pounds of heavily muscled male, her nose pressed
into the taupe-colored carpet. All she could smell was
damp earth from their tromp across the cemetery and the
strange chemical scent of heavy-duty carpet cleaner.

More glass shattered.

"Damn it!" cried the driver, stomping on the brakes.

"Don't stop!" shouted Shaun. He raised up on one elbow and for a moment she could breathe. "Someone's shooting at us. We have to get away from here. Keep driving."

The back window imploded and showered across their bodies as the car swerved wildly before righting itself.

"Whatever happens," repeated Shaun, "don't stop driving."

"Which way do we go?" shouted the driver.

Shaun rattled off an address she'd never heard of in a heavier Irish brogue, adding to the surreal feel of everything.

Then he lowered his head again, covering her body with his and once again, she couldn't get any air. His hair tickled her cheek, then his lips were right beside her ear. She was light-headed from the lack of oxygen—and more. It was chillingly bizarre, yet intimate at the same time.

"Are you okay?" he whispered.

Words stuck in her throat. "No...no, I'm not. Why is someone shooting at us? Are they following us?"

"We're going somewhere safe."

He shifted his weight to pull out a cell phone and started texting.

"You didn't answer my question. What's going on?" Was this guy some kind of criminal that people were shooting at him in her car? "Why are they shooting at you?" She heard the rising panic in her own voice.

"Abigail, *I'm* not the person they're shooting at."

"I don't understand what's happening here. What are you doing?" she demanded.

"I'm trying to get us some help."

"By texting?" She didn't try to hide the sarcasm in her voice. Fear made her snarky. "I don't understand. Why are you texting someone instead of calling 9-1-1?"

"I need you to calm down."

"Calm down when there are people shooting at us, at me? And I can't…I can't breathe."

She was serious about that part. For some reason her asthma was kicking into overdrive and she was going to have to use her inhaler as soon as possible or she would be in serious trouble.

He shifted his weight, once again reminding her that regardless of his sexual orientation, he was a man and he had her pinned to the ground.

"Your driver is doing a fine job of getting us away from the situation. I'm making sure we have help when we get to where he is taking us."

"You haven't told me who you really are, have you?"

He ignored her question and called to the driver instead. "You doing okay up there?"

The guy nodded.

"What's your name?" asked Shaun. They were speeding along Rock Creek Parkway now.

"I'm Carl."

"Carl, I'm Shaun and you're doing great. Donner briefed you, right?"

"Yes, sir."

"Okay, I need you to take us to that address I gave you."

Carl nodded.

"What's going on? Why won't you tell me? Carl?" She turned her head to meet Shaun's eyes. "Where are we going? To the police?"

They were nose to nose and she could see a tiny scar under his chin. His eyes seemed darker up close than she'd originally thought, with deep green flecks in the irises. She stared, determined not to look away or back down till she got answers.

"No police. But 'tis a safe place, where we're going," Shaun answered.

"Why no police?"

"Because I'm not sure they can help you right now."

"And you can? Who are you?" she asked again. Fear was giving way to anger.

"A friend." The snake charmer was long gone; he was cool and businesslike.

She shook her head and turned back to face the carpet. Some friend. No one had started shooting till she met him and up until two minutes ago, Carl had been *her* driver.

"Why should I believe that?" she whispered.

Chapter Two

Shaun heard the whisper of her voice but couldn't catch what she'd said as he contemplated the back of Abigail's blond head. She was so small, he had to be crushing her beneath him. Yet he felt compelled to physically shield her until he was absolutely certain that danger had passed. He rose up and checked out the window before hunkering down again. Carl had left behind whoever was shooting at them, but Shaun was still buzzing from the adrenaline rush.

In his mind's eye he could see a bullet whizzing through the door. If Abigail Trevor hadn't leaned forward when she did, he'd be dealing with another dead body.

He couldn't think about that. He was surprised that someone had tried to kill her. He was expecting bribes, threats, intimidation. That was what his assignment brief had covered. The situation wasn't supposed to turn violent—not yet, not without any warning first to make it clear to Abigail what was at stake. This was more dangerous than he had realized, which made it all the more imperative that he keep her safe.

"Can you get off me, please? I can't breathe. I'm not kidding. I have asthma." Her voice was thin but firm.

Ah, Christ. It wouldn't do to save her from bullets only to have her die of asphyxiation. Careful of the glass, he rolled to the side and helped her turn over without cutting herself.

She took a wheezing gulp of air, sat up and coughed.

"Do you have one of those inhaler things?" he asked.

She rubbed the back of her neck. "I'm not sure. Probably not."

"Why not?" His tone was sharper than he'd intended.

She glared. "Because I changed purses this morning and I didn't think to put the emergency inhaler in my bag. I was burying my brother. I was not expecting to get crushed by a giant."

Her voice had a distinct edge to it now, but her eyes glistened with tears. She was more upset than angry. This had to be a nightmare for her and surprisingly, he felt bad for her. Again his conscience was taking him unawares.

He didn't have time for the demons of his own remorse and he couldn't do anything about her hurt feelings. Instead, he took her miniscule purse from the seat and dumped it on the floor of the limo. The time for being polite or charming was long past. What mattered now was looking after her as best he could.

"Hey," she wheezed.

Hairbrush, wallet, lipstick, cell phone, compact—nothing resembling an inhaler. *Damn.*

"I could've just reached in and looked for it," she protested. Another coughing fit racked her small frame.

"Quicker this way," he muttered. He tried to fit everything back in the impossibly tiny bag and was alarmed by the ferocity of her coughs. Naturally, the contents wouldn't fit.

Women's purses. He'd been all over the world, faced exotic things that had made grown men gawk while he stood unmoved. Still, a woman's purse seemed just a bit forbidden and slightly mysterious.

He quit trying to shove in the hairbrush and pulled his cell phone back from his pocket. At this point, he'd be better off doing something he was capable of—letting Donner know about the new wrinkle in their situation.

"What kind of inhaler do you use?" he asked.

"Huh?"

"What kind of meds do you need for your asthma?"

"Who are you?" she repeated, breathless with confusion and discomfort.

"I'm someone who's here to protect you and right now I'm your pharmacist. What kind of meds do you need?"

"An albuterol nebulizer and Symbicort." She gave him the milligrams. "I think I could use an EpiPen, too."

"All right." He typed the instructions into his phone.

Donner replied immediately and Shaun grimaced.

He studied Trevor's sister as she leaned her head back against the carpet. With all the shards of glass scattered about, it was easier for her to stay on the floor where she'd been originally. Her eyes were closed but he remembered their unusual color—like a single malt scotch.

He took the time to study her smooth, porcelain white skin. She had an exotic mole above her upper lip à la Cindy Crawford and features that were so delicate; she looked like a china doll—except for the wheezing that was growing progressively louder. He focused on her lips for any signs of asphyxia but they were still healthy and pink, not the slightest tinge of blue. Very soft looking, too. He looked away. Now was not the time to get distracted by a very kissable set of lips.

He debated explaining a bit more about what was going on but decided against it. She was struggling to breathe and she needed to be able to concentrate to understand the Pandora's box that had been opened with her brother's death. He settled for taking care of her instead. Over the years he'd found that actions tended to speak much louder than words, anyway.

"Do you need to see a doctor?" he asked.

She didn't open her eyes. "If I get my meds, I'll be fine."

He wasn't so sure about that. He reached for her wrist. "I want to take your pulse."

She didn't argue and that concerned him more than anything. He took her hand in his. It was small like the rest of her and her nails were free of polish. Her wrist felt impossibly fragile as he counted the frantic beats. Her eyes were still closed and he took the opportunity to stare at her once more.

Her black skirt was pulled up to midthigh; she obviously hadn't realized that yet. He couldn't pretend he wasn't getting an eyeful. He was so distracted by the fact that she wore stockings and a garter belt instead of traditional panty hose that initially he didn't realize he was gaping. He contemplated the red lace straps attached to gossamer nylons while he tried to take her pulse and glanced back at her face to find her staring straight at him.

Busted. He dropped her hand with a plop.

What was wrong with him? He didn't get distracted, especially in the middle of work. Of course in the midst of being shot at, he didn't usually see women in red garter belts with beautiful legs, either. Abigail Trevor was his own personal fantasy come true. Too bad it had to be happening in the middle of a job gone completely sideways.

"Your resting pulse is 120. That's pretty high."

"It's not a resting pulse rate when someone's shooting at you," she snapped, pulling her skirt down to hide his tantalizing view. "Can I sit up now?"

He moved back carefully to make room for her. "Sure, if you feel like it."

"I'll be able to breathe better that way." Avoiding the glass, she propped herself up on an elbow.

He was mindful not to focus on her legs or the way her outfit, that wasn't made for crawling around on the floor of a limo, strained across her chest.

"Please tell me what's going on." Her breathing intensified when she hauled herself to a sitting position.

"I'm here to protect you, that's a promise."

"You said that. And I suppose if you meant me harm, you wouldn't be ordering asthma meds."

He nodded as she continued to wheeze and his phone vibrated. Donner was sending more instructions. Shaun leaned forward to give Carl the new directions.

"Once you get your medicine, we'll talk."

"I'm gonna hold you to that," she muttered but again she didn't argue and given her earlier behavior, that ratcheted up his concern.

Moments later Carl pulled up in front of the Washington Marriott Wardman Park. Shaun wondered if he could get a severely asthmatic woman through the lobby without attracting attention.

The valet opened the door, no comment beyond a raised eyebrow to find both passengers seated on the carpet surrounded by the remnants of broken windows. Who knew what the man thought? He'd probably seen it all. Shaun and Abigail looked as if they'd been having sex on the floor of the limo, except for the glass bits all around them. Shaun tipped the doorman two twenties as he crawled out.

Glass skittered to the ground when he stood. He reached back to help Abigail get brushed off and out of the car. More shards fell to the pavement with tiny *chinking* sounds. Carl drove off as soon as the door closed behind her.

Abigail coughed and her eyes widened ever so slightly when she saw where they were. Squaring her shoulders, she walked with him toward a side entrance from the valet stand.

"How you doing?" he asked.

She nodded but didn't speak. Instead she held tightly to his arm, seemingly focused on making it through the door and down a long corridor filled with elegant chairs arranged in private seating areas. Opulent oriental rugs muffled their steps in this older wing of the hotel.

No one else was waiting for an elevator. Once inside the wood-paneled car, she leaned heavily against him and took more deep wheezing breaths. He was glad they were almost there. Her lips were no longer the healthy pink they'd been in the limo.

Shaun hung on to her when they exited and she almost made it to the door of their suite before her knees buckled. He pulled out the key card he'd been given earlier in case a "safe house" was needed, unlocked the door and carried her the final few steps across the threshold into the richly appointed living room. The master bedroom had a large balcony and sliding glass doors with a spectacular view of the National Zoo. The far more interesting sight was the large white pharmacy package beside the bed and the nebulizer that was already assembled.

Donner's second team was fast and Shaun was grateful. He'd sent the text only twenty minutes ago. Normally he himself was the one racing around like a bat out of hell, setting this stuff up. He wasn't sure how Donner had this task executed so quickly unless he'd known Abigail was asthmatic. But then, Donner was known for being prepared for every eventuality.

Maybe Shaun's job wasn't quite as secure as he'd thought. He saved that happy thought for another time and tore open the bag.

Inside were all the requested medications including an

EpiPen. Abigail was reaching for it and had the wrapper off before he said anything. She pressed the auto-injector to her thigh above the top of that stocking that had so fascinated him earlier and reached for the other items, as well.

She opened the emergency albuterol inhaler, using it twice before speaking. "I'll do a treatment with the machine, too."

She picked up the mouthpiece for the nebulizer and flipped the switch. A tiny stream of smoke poured out. Putting her mouth over the vapor-filled end, she started breathing in the medication. It looked as if she was smoking a hookah.

"You want something to drink?" he asked, feeling a bit like a voyeur.

"Water would be great. Thanks," she murmured between puffs. The change in her breathing from moments before was remarkable. He left her and texted his boss from the kitchen to tell him that they'd arrived and to take the heat for blowing his cover so soon.

His phone rang immediately. "What happened?" asked Donner. "I didn't even think you were going to talk to her at the funeral."

"It was too good an opportunity to pass up."

"I'll trust your judgment on that," said Donner.

"'Tis what you pay me for." Shaun wasn't absolutely sure he trusted himself on this, but he wasn't telling Donner that now. "Are you coming to explain the situation, or shall I?"

"I'll be there in fifteen."

Shaun snagged two bottles of water from the fridge. He started to go back in the bedroom, but Abigail's nebulizer was still puffing like a steam engine. Within a few minutes he heard it stop and her heels clicked on the hardwood of the bedroom floor. He stood. Abigail didn't strike him as the kind of woman who was going to wait long for answers once she was back on her feet. Better to meet her head-on. Maybe that way, he could stall until Donner got there.

He met her in the living room doorway. "I brought your water. You sure you don't want to lie down?"

She unscrewed the bottle cap and sipped the drink before spearing him with those whiskey-colored eyes. "No thanks. I'd rather talk in here."

"Let's sit."

"This is all very civilized." Her deep Southern accent came pouring out with no trace of the wheeze in her voice, but there was plenty of sarcasm. "However, I'd prefer we cut to the chase. Who are you and what's going on?"

Chapter Three

Abby stared hard at him, daring him to lie to her. Her breathing was stable and for now she was holding it together but she knew she didn't have a lot of time before the adrenaline surge wore off, jet lag kicked in and the day came crashing down on her. Still, as long as she was able, she was going for answers and right now she wanted the truth about what had just happened.

"I'll tell you everything I can." He took a long sip of his own water and met her gaze without looking away.

For a moment she lost herself in his stare. His blue-green eyes were that mesmerizing, changing from emerald green to Caribbean blue depending on the light. Then she remembered admiring his face when she'd first met him and he'd implied he was a "friend" of Jason's.

Had he lied about everything?

She glared, her blood heating for a completely different reason. Yeah, she was pretty sure he had. "Do you know who was shooting at us?" she asked.

"I have no idea."

"What's your real name?"

"Shaun Logan."

"What are you doing here?" she asked.

"I'm trying to protect you."

"From whom?"

"From those who would do you harm."

"Why does someone want to *harm* me?" She began to settle in her seat as she slipped off her shoes and tucked her aching feet underneath her.

"I'm not at liberty to sa—"

"Oh, bull." He didn't rise to the bait.

"Did you even know my brother?" she asked a moment later.

"I'd met him." He took another pull on the bottle.

"Did you sleep with him?"

He coughed and sputtered, the question obviously taking him by surprise. "I don't see what that has to do with anything."

"I want to know. He was my brother. You approached me claiming you were friends. I want to know how much of that was a lie." Her voice broke on that last word as she felt the loss and toll of the day begin to catch up with her.

"All I said was that I was an admirer of his work. That much is true. But if you need to know, then no, I didn't sleep with your brother. For the record, I'm straight, not gay."

Right. She'd pretty much guessed that when she'd caught him checking out her legs in the limo, but she'd wanted to know for sure. She studied him like a bug under glass, and to his credit he didn't flinch beyond that initial splutter with the water. Instead, he leaned back into the plush sofa.

"Some people might find your line of questioning offensive," he added.

"You said you'd tell me everything you could."

He shook his head and narrowed his own stare for a moment. Other men might have raked their eyes down her body to make their point, but his eyes never left hers.

He looked deeply into her face, reading her and letting Abby clearly see that yes, he'd been aware of everything—just as she had in the limo. He'd felt her body beneath his, he'd enjoyed it and he wouldn't mind repeating the experience—minus the flying bullets.

She wasn't unused to being examined in what seemed such a personal way, but it had been a while. She was fascinated and uncomfortable at the same time. She didn't want to think about how this made her feel. Certainly not now. She moved on to a new topic.

"Who do you work for?" she asked.

"Zip Tech."

She snorted. "The same company as Jason. I don't know that I believe that."

"Why not?"

"You're definitely not an engineer."

"There are other jobs at the company."

There was a knock at the door and he stood to answer it. Abby didn't know what to expect—certainly not for the CEO of Zip Tech to walk into the hotel suite. She'd seen Donner's picture before in *Newsweek*. Today he wore an expensive Italian suit and shoes that she guessed had cost more than her own designer ones.

"Hello, Miss Trevor. I'm Michael Donner. I'm terribly sorry to meet you under these circumstances. How are you feeling?" He reached out to shake her hand then sat across from her without any preamble. He was tall and almost as big as Shaun but fair-haired and not quite as buff.

She noticed that Shaun had snapped to attention when he walked in. Was this who Shaun had been texting from the limo? Come to think of it, she remembered him saying something to the driver about Donner, but she'd been too distracted by trying to breathe to notice at the time.

"I've been better, thanks. So what am I doing here *under these circumstances?*" she asked.

"You're Jason's sister and you're in danger. We want to help you."

"Why am I in danger?" This was feeling more and more like Alice down the rabbit hole by the minute.

"Your brother's work was very valuable," said Donner.

"I know nothing about Jason's work. He took those nondisclosure agreements very seriously and didn't share technical details with me. Not that I'd have understood them, anyway."

Donner nodded. "It's not just a question of what he might have told you, though. Our concern is what he left behind. You're his sole beneficiary—and the only one who might be able to access the files putting you at risk."

"I'm sorry. You've completely lost me."

"Jason was our top engineer on a wireless security project. His hardware and software designs were at the heart of Zip Technologies's newest product, Zip-Net. I believe his security protocol will revolutionize cell phone capabilities."

She nodded. Jason had been so excited about his job. She hadn't realized the magnitude of its significance till now. "But that still doesn't explain why someone was shooting at me."

"We believe the shooter wants something from you. Something that Jason wasn't willing to hand over. Something that may have been responsible for his accident."

"I thought my brother's hit-and-run was random."

"We're not so sure."

"I don't understand. What do you mean? And who's *we?*"

"Shaun and I. We don't think your brother's death was an accident. We think he was murdered."

"MURDERED?" ONCE MORE ABBY felt the world tilt. "What? Do the police know about this? Are they investigating?"

"Yes," said Donner. "The police are investigating as much as they intend to. We are as well."

"I don't understand. Why you? Why aren't you letting the authorities handle it all?"

"Because they don't want to believe there's more here than a simple hit-and-run. It's a delicate situation. Allow me to explain. May I call you Abigail?"

"Please...everyone calls me Abby."

"My name's Michael."

She nodded impatiently. "Delicate how, Michael?" Her voice rose on that last word as her composure slipped over the edge of the cliff.

"Like I said, your brother created a new kind of security protocol that's quite unique. I believe he's changed how all cellular and data networks will be designed and secured from now going forward. I also think he may have been harmed because of his work."

"Harmed?" She shot a look at Shaun. "You're using that word, too. *Harmed* is getting your arm broken, Mr. Donn—Michael. My brother was hit by a car going at least fifty miles an hour through a crosswalk in Dupont Circle. He was dead before he hit the pavement. *Harmed* is not the word I would choose to describe that, especially if, as you suggest, it was done deliberately."

Donner had the grace to look embarrassed as she continued. "I don't understand why you believe it was murder. Isn't the product he created already in use? The design is out there and you have a patent, I'm sure? What reason would anyone have to hurt Jason over a product he's already completed?"

Donner nodded. "While we've already rolled out the first generation of the product and it's working quite well for our initial customer, it's not entirely accurate to say that Jason's work was done."

"Why is that?"

Donner glanced at Shaun before answering. "We have another client who has asked for an exclusive contract for the first five years. Normally we wouldn't award a relatively new technology with such potential to an exclusive customer, but this is a special case because of who the client is."

"Well, who is it?" she asked.

Donner cut his eyes back toward Shaun then again to her. "The Department of Homeland Security. They want the exclusive in order to use Zip-Net for all their cellular communications security. It's an amazing opportunity. It would fast-track this technology into the stratosphere. Millions of dollars are at stake. Company growth will skyrocket. Assembly line jobs will boom just to keep up with the demand. And as the cherry on top, our national security will be better served than ever before. It's a win-win for everyone."

She watched him as he talked and could see why he was considered to be so charismatic. Despite her confusion she felt pulled in by the force of his personality—his mannerisms, his gestures. Mentally she shook herself.

"Your brother was handling some debugging issues for the program the morning he died. You can imagine with an operation this large, it can get 'glitchy' at times, especially when it's just going online. He was about to install upgrades to take care of that."

"Sure." Abby nodded. She didn't have a lot of computer expertise but she knew how easy it was for her own PC to get "glitchy."

"Up until then Jason hadn't been sharing the software upgrade plans or file on the company network and frankly,

I didn't require him to. Industrial espionage is rampant in this industry and after checking to make sure he had firewalls in place on his home computer, we let him safekeep the information the best way he saw fit. The fewer people with access the better. I see now that was a huge error on my part. We never expected anyone to resort to murder."

"But how can you be sure it was murder? The police seem convinced it was an accident."

"If it was an accident that your brother died right before turning in the updates, that would be quite a coincidence— don't you think? If we can't make those upgrades, the government contract won't go through. The consequences for not delivering the product would be catastrophic to Zip Tech and to this new protocol because of the blow it will be to our company's credibility. Any 'accidents' at this time would make me suspicious, but then for you to be attacked at the funeral? Bullets aren't an accident, Abby. Someone fired those shots on purpose."

"And your competitors would kill me and my brother to see that technology fail?"

"Unfortunately, some would. We're talking about a billion-dollar security industry that's about to be turned on its ear."

"I don't understand." But she did; she just didn't want to believe it. Her stomach threatened to rebel and her skin grew clammy. Everything felt so surreal. Jason was a lovable, geeky guy, and this all sounded like something out of a spy novel. How did he turn into a target? How did *she* turn in to a target?

"The next generation of cell phone traffic will be carried exclusively over the internet. Security isn't just one of the issues in cell phone communication, it's the *only* issue. Your brother designed an exceptionally unique product with an unbreakable code that keeps cellular traffic completely confidential. Unhackable. Homeland Security is so confident in the technology that they are willing to contract exclusively with Zip Technologies for security services. But in order for that to happen, we need the upgrade file, and we need to find it fast. There's an issue of a delivery deadline. We have four days to get the updates installed or this contract with Homeland Security is dead in the water."

"What kind of updates are you talking about? It sounds like more of a major flaw in the system," she observed.

Now it was Shaun glancing at Donner. The CEO nodded.

"The bugs in the system right now aren't just glitches, they're showstoppers," Shaun explained. "We must find the fix Jason created the morning he died, going in through the back door."

"What do you mean by *back door?*" she asked.

"'Tis technical."

"Make me understand," she argued.

"Many engineers put special signatures on their work. It used to be a vanity piece. Now it's a way into the system they've created so they can tweak things if necessary without having to go through all the security after production. It's a shortcut. We've got a major bug that needs modification and the only way to fix it is if we can have access to that 'back door' Jason created."

"What kind of bugs are we talking about?" she asked.

"The kind that will make the system fail…catastrophically."

"Oh." Her eyes widened as understanding dawned.

Donner spoke up. "Here's where it gets tricky and highly confidential. Zip Tech is due to sign that contract with Homeland Security and pass over control of the system at midnight in four days' time. Once we sign, we'll no longer be able to modify the program, even through that back door. Zip Tech must have your brother's security upgrades to make the changes beforehand—afterward, we won't have access. Once DHS signs off on the contract, government engineers with the necessary security clearances take over and we step away. Without those upgrades from your brother, the DHS network will be vulnerable to hacking."

He paused a moment, no doubt to let the implication sink in. A Homeland Security network that wasn't secure.

"Why not just tell Homeland Security the truth?" she asked.

Donner stood. "Zip Tech can and will tell if we can't get the updates in time. But once we do, the company loses everything. Not just a government contract. We're 'all in' at this point. When negotiations began with Homeland Security about Zip-Net, our company made certain modifications to the design based on the government's specifications. Based on those specifications, Zip-Net is no longer viable for anyone but that first client and Homeland Security unless other large companies with broad user bases also adopt the technology. Which is definitely what we're hoping for, but it would take time."

Donner stepped into the kitchen area and poured himself a glass of water as he continued. "In this industry, six months is like three years. We'd lose our market advantage completely. Not to mention our investors. If this contract doesn't go through, the company is finished."

"I know this is overwhelming and a lot to take in," said Shaun. "But you deserve to know the truth about what happened to Jason—why he was killed. Why you could be next."

"You're saying my brother was murdered to stop this DHS contract from going through?"

Donner nodded. "People have died for less."

Abby sighed. "That doesn't explain why someone was shooting at me. I don't have this upgrade file you're speaking of." She looked at Shaun as she spoke but he said nothing else. He just leaned against the living room side of the kitchen counter sipping his own bottled water.

"Are you sure about that?" asked Donner.

Chapter Four

"What do you mean?" asked Abby.

"I think you might know more than you realize," said Donner.

She didn't answer but her blood began to boil as he continued.

"You have access to all your brother's papers and files in his home office at his condo. As his only relative, you'll soon have access to his safety deposit box, as well."

"Yes." She tried to tamp down her temper and the growing disbelief that he could possibly be asking for this, today of all days. But a part of her was grateful for the anger that was snapping her out of the grief and overwhelming hopelessness of the situation. She put on her best Southern belle smile even as the acid in her stomach burned. "What do you really need, Michael?" she asked.

"Access to your brother's laptop. The upgrade file must be there somewhere. Specifically we need the password. Our people have been at it for several days now and haven't been able to come up with anything that works. His personal security system on the computer will erase all the data if we keep trying incorrect passwords.

"For everyone's sake, we desperately need those upgrade plans. We've been through Jason's files at Zip Tech's offices but we can't find the information we're looking for anywhere. Once the product is complete, you'll no longer be a target. Until then, we can protect you. But none of this can end until you help us find those upgrades."

As he explained, the ugly truth became obvious. Zip Tech had already been in Jason's condo looking for the file. Though he tried to twist things to sound as if this was all in her best interest, the man clearly had no qualms about blackmailing her to get what he needed.

"Surely he has a backup for all this valuable data? I mean otherwise couldn't a competitor just type in the wrong password until they wiped the system?"

"Yes, I'm sure he did have a backup…somewhere. Unfortunately, we can't find that, either. Believe me, our people have looked. That's why we need your help."

"So you've already been in his condo? Uninvited?" She smiled a particularly sugary grin and felt her blood pressure spike up a notch.

Michael smiled back, a sheepish quality to it that she knew was meant to be endearing. Under other circumstances, he might have been considered charming. He knew he'd been caught but he still didn't realize how badly he'd screwed up.

Her literature students could have told Michael Donner that he was about to be pulverized. She might look and sound like a pushover, but she had a reputation as one of those professors you did not tick off unless you had a death wish for your GPA. And you did not lie to Abby Trevor under any circumstances. Grad students called her "the carnivorous steel magnolia."

She'd fostered that notoriety in her teaching.

She could be a pit bull and once she was angry, even *she* knew it was a long, difficult road back into her good graces.

The way she saw it, Michael was all about Zip Technologies needing her brother's upgrade file. Oh, he tried to frame it as a step for the greater good—even for her own protection—but she was smart enough to read between the lines. He cared much less for her safety than he did for the success of his company. If he was truly concerned about her, he would have come to her from the beginning instead of waiting for the attacks to start so he could hold her safety hostage against the guarantee of her cooperation. Additionally, the way his people had broken into Jason's condo made her hopping mad and slightly ill at the same time.

Well, to hell with Donner. She didn't care what happened with Zip Technologies's contract with Homeland Security. As for her safety…well, that's what the police were for. Whether or not they believed the hit-and-run that killed her brother was deliberate, surely they couldn't claim the shots fired were accidental.

"He signed a waiver fo—"

Donner was talking but she didn't let him finish.

"Tell me, did that agreement say you could waltz into his home and take *anything* you wanted *whenever* you wanted in the event of his death?" she asked.

Donner looked a bit taken aback at being interrupted. After all, he'd graced the covers of *Forbes* and *Newsweek*. She had a feeling he wasn't used to women *not* falling all over him.

"Jason signed nondisclosure agreements and proprietary information clauses at Zip Tech."

"But no agreements to allow you a search and seizure in his home after his death? You're a high-tech company, not the Gestapo, but that's what this feels like."

"Ms. Trevor…Abby, I—"

She kept talking, just like she did in her lectures when

a student tried to interrupt her before she was finished making her point.

"I'm distinctly uneasy with what you are asking and what you've already undertaken without permission. Until I speak with an attorney, I'm not comfortable with you or any other employees of Zip Technologies entering my brother's home. I won't press charges at this point—but do it again and I'll have your people arrested."

"I don't understand, Abby. Someone was just shooting at you."

"That's right. And I have no idea who they were. It could have been your competition. Could have been you for all I know, trying to scare me into trusting you just to get into Jason's condo. I do have a question though. If Jason was so valuable, why didn't you have security with him while he was doing this upgrade work? You were awfully complacent to have such a valuable employee climbing in his car and driving away every night with the future of your company on his laptop in a briefcase. Seems you might have seen this coming. And if you couldn't protect him, why should I believe you'll be able to protect me? I'd be more comfortable with the authorities handling this. Why can't we call the police about Jason?"

"I have," said Donner as he came to sit across from her again. "They don't think your brother's accident was anything more than that."

"But surely after today's shooting in the cemetery, the police will reconsider?" She stared hard at them both, her anger still fizzing.

"Perhaps." Donner didn't sound very hopeful. "I've been dealing with a Detective Diaz. It might help if you spoke with him."

"I'd very much like to do that, I'll just get my phone. It's in the bedroom."

"Use mine," offered Donner. "I have Detective Diaz's direct number in my contacts." He handed her his cell. "He's the officer in charge of your brother's case."

"That's not who I spoke to when I identified his body," said Abby.

"There are many layers there at the department," reassured Donner. "We'll step outside, if you'd like some privacy."

"No, I'll go." She stood and walked barefooted onto the balcony that overlooked the city.

As soon as she was out of earshot, Donner turned to Shaun. "You're sure you've got this under control? She can't be left alone."

Shaun nodded. "Of course. Though I want to know what the devil happened in the cemetery. That was insanity."

Donner shrugged. "I agree but I don't know if even this will convince Diaz to investigate Jason's death as anything more than an accident. I have no idea what he'll say about this latest incident but it will definitely be better coming from her than me. He already thinks I control too much."

Shaun raised an eyebrow. "You don't say?"

Abigail returned from the balcony a few moments later, shaking her head in confusion. The angry look on her face told Shaun exactly how the conversation had gone.

"Diaz says there's been quite a bit of recent gang-related activity in the area around the cemetery. He thinks that's what happened and I was just in the wrong place at the wrong time. He's sending out an officer to investigate at the cemetery, but he doesn't think the shooting is in any way related to Jason's accident."

She handed Donner's phone back to him. "I don't like this," she mumbled.

Shaun started to say something but Donner spoke first, pushing the advantage like the business shark he was. "Will you let Zip Tech help? We can offer you protection that no one else can. And if you help us find the file, you can resolve the situation for all of us at the same time."

"I don't want to but I don't see that I have much of a choice. Tell me why I should help you besides the fact that you're offering protection as a kind of blackmail?" she asked. "If I can even locate the upgrades how do I know that will make the attacks end?"

Shaun spoke up. "There are no guarantees. But Abigail, I'm certain the shooting in the cemetery was related to your brother's file. I'm also certain that someone has already searched your brother's home without you knowing it."

"Someone besides Zip Tech? Sounds like there should be a revolving door on Jason's condo." She sounded angry and he couldn't blame her. She had to be scared and completely exhausted at this point.

Unfortunately that was exactly how he needed her. He didn't want her thinking she could take care of herself alone. And since she didn't appear to know anyone else in town, he had to make himself indispensable. Still, it was obvious she didn't trust Donner and right now the jury was still out on how she felt about him. It wouldn't be easy to bring her around—and would it actually pay off in the end?

The biggest question was did she even know her brother's computer password?

Either way, she was clearly too upset with Donner right now to share any information she might have. Shaun signaled for his boss to leave, and Donner stood to walk out. He'd given his explanations, as unwelcome as they were, and was leaving Shaun to deal with the consequences. That was his job, after all.

"Abby, regardless of what you decide to do, I think it best if you let Shaun stay. He won't let anything happen to you. This is what he does."

Donner's hand was on the doorknob but Shaun could tell Abigail wasn't buying it. And Shaun was staying out of it until Michael Donner was on his way. He could tell she was on the verge of throwing something at his boss's head whether Donner realized it or not.

"I didn't ask for your help," she said to Donner's retreating back.

He was halfway out the door but snapped around to answer. "No, you didn't. But I'm giving it anyway. Please, let Shaun look after you. No matter what you think of me, I'm not burying two Trevors in one week. I won't be put in that position." Then he was gone, closing the door behind him with a barely audible click.

She turned on Shaun as the door closed. "How long is this suite paid for?"

"It's reserved for the entire week."

"I'll stay tonight. Alone. I don't want you here. I'm fine by myself. I want Zip Tech out of my life."

Shaun revised his thoughts about her similarity to the china doll. She was marble. Cool and unmovable. But was she unbreakable? Time would tell.

She needed more time or as much as he could spare before he'd know the answer to that. Donner was usually smoother and Shaun wasn't sure if there was any recovery for his boss practically admitting they'd broken into her brother's condo. Giving Abigail space was the first step, and being as honest as he could be. He felt the now familiar stab of conscience. So…telling the truth would be a stretch for him. "Right. I can understand why you want me out—"

"You don't understand a damn thing, Shaun Logan. If

you did you wouldn't have fed me that crappy story at the cemetery about knowing Jason and admiring his work. Earlier you said you had met him. Did you really? Had you ever even seen him before the viewing today in that casket?"

Shaun nodded. "Yes, I met him at a corporate function last month. And I rode in an elevator with him two weeks ago."

She stared at him and a crack appeared in her marble façade as a lone tear streaked down her cheek. She brushed the moisture away.

"Are you going to find who killed him?"

"I'm going to try, but my priority is to keep you safe."

"Okay. You're still not getting near his papers because I don't give a rip about Zip Tech's problems, and I don't want you anywhere near me. But thank you for looking into his death. Now, I want you out of here."

"I don't want to leave you by yourself."

"I'm a big girl—I'll be fine."

He raised an eyebrow as she stood. Yes, he had to agree, Abigail was very fine indeed. Unfortunately, he had no choice but to walk to the door or get into a tussling match with her. And while that might be fun under other circumstances, now was definitely not the time. He wasn't going to point out that there were two rooms here in the suite.

He'd just go downstairs and get the room across the hall from her if it was available and sit with his door open. And if it wasn't available, he'd set himself up outside the suite as her personal bodyguard. She'd never know he was there. He doubted she planned to go anywhere tonight.

At the door she surprised him with another question. "Donner said this is what you do. What did he mean? What do you really do for Zip Tech?"

He'd never felt queasy explaining his job, but under her

penetrating stare, he did. He knew he had to tell her the truth. It was the first test for him here. But how? Hard and fast like ripping off a Band-Aid or with finesse?

He took a guess along with a deep breath and gave it to her straight. Finesse would be wasted, anyway. There wasn't really a polite way to describe what he did. "I'm a fixer."

"Pardon me?"

"I fix problems. You know. Company vice president's son gets a DUI, I help keep him out of jail and make sure it doesn't get in the papers. An executive's mistress threatens to tell the Mrs. about their affair, I pay the woman off. I keep Donner, his company executives and their families looking happy and prosperous for all the world to see and examine."

Shaun trusted Donner and up until this morning he'd always done the job without a qualm of conscience but with this woman, he was uncomfortable. It was a unique and unpleasant experience. He had no idea where those feelings were coming from, he just knew he didn't like them. She studied his eyes, seemingly not nearly as put off by his job description as he had expected her to be.

"So now you get to try and fix me?" she asked, challenging him with her open gaze, all but inviting him to fight back.

For the first time today he allowed himself to really look at her, not just sneaking glances when she wasn't aware of him. It was different from earlier when she'd asked him about his sexual orientation. She'd practically been begging him to look at her then. So of course he hadn't.

But now, he started at her feet and raked his eyes up her body, deliberately lingering at her hips and chest.

Her cheeks were flaming when he finally reached her face. He knew he'd been baited and it was profoundly unprofessional but he couldn't regret what he'd permitted himself to do, particularly as it wouldn't be happening again.

Still, he had to swallow before he spoke. "There's not a damn thing wrong with you, Abigail. Not that I can see."

Chapter Five

She glared at him and shook her head. Oh, he was a "fixer" all right. Good thing she'd had a big brother who'd taught her a thing or two about men. Tears burned the back of her eyes as she fought to stifle a sniff. No way would she cry in front of this man.

"I would imagine you are quite good at your job, Shaun Logan. But don't think you're going to charm yourself into my brother's condo or laptop that easily." She shooed him out the door.

The expression on his face would have been comical if she hadn't been hurting so badly. Suddenly she was spoiling for a fight. One part of her knew she was putting off the inevitable—being alone with her dismal thoughts and overwhelming sorrow. Hearing about Jason's work, the importance of what he'd been doing, just drove home the heartache of his death.

Her brother hadn't told her about the government contract, but she'd known he was hoping for something like this kind of opportunity when he took the job. He wouldn't have worked his brains out without the hope of a fantastic payday or substantial job security. Zip Technologies had been his life for three years but everything that Shaun was saying rang true.

If Zip Tech failed because of something Jason had left

undone, even inadvertently, it would be another tragedy to compound his death. But she couldn't let go of her anger at the disrespect Donner had shown to Jason's memory by searching his condo. She wasn't sure she could ever trust him after that. Could she trust Shaun? She remembered the way he'd reacted when the shots had been fired, protecting her with his body. Was it wrong to want to trust the safety he'd provided?

With that in mind she dove into questioning Shaun as he stood in the hall. "Have you always worked for Michael Donner?" she asked.

"No."

"What did you do before?"

"Same type of work," he responded.

"And do you really think I have a role in this mess? I barely even knew about Zip-Net before today."

He pinned her with those unusual eyes of his and she had the uncomfortable feeling she was being sized up even though she was the one asking all the questions. "Depends on you," was his response.

"What does that mean?" she asked.

He moved toward the doorway and she fought against taking a step back into the suite, angry at herself and at him that she felt the need to retreat.

"Like Donner said, I believe you have information. Something you may not know you have from your brother. I need your cooperation to figure out what that is."

"But I don't have any information."

"I think you may have access to the password to his computer or the location of the upgrade file and not realize it."

She shook her head *no* but at the same time thought of last summer and using Jason's laptop. She did have an idea about the password but she wasn't sure she wanted to help and didn't know how to respond without outright lying. She'd known that she could assist earlier when Donner had spoken of needing the password, but she'd been so incensed about his having gone into Jason's home without permission she hadn't considered it.

She didn't want to consider it now.

So she did the only thing she could. She closed the door.

Or tried to. Shaun slid his foot neatly inside the door frame to stop her.

Angry, stalling and studying him at the same time, she was puzzling out what to say when the day completely crashed in on her—the funeral, the asthma attack, the shooting, the wild ride to the hotel and the awful revelation that Jason had been murdered. Plus she was starving on top of everything else—her body's defense mechanism when stress took over.

Food. She wanted it. Now. Almost as badly as she wanted him gone.

"May I take you to dinner?" he asked.

"I can't do this anymore, Shaun. I can't think about this situation right now. Please move your foot." Her stomach growled, betraying her and punctuating the request.

She tried to close the door again and only meant to glance at him a final time because now she was exhausted on top of being irritated. But those uniquely colored eyes bored into hers, more emerald than blue-green now, and surprisingly her irritation turned to frank interest as her resistance melted like a snowball on a hot sidewalk.

"I'm ordering room service," she declared, more to convince herself than him.

Forcefully breaking eye contact, she gave in to the toll of the day's events. She was totally out of emotional and physical energy to spend on this…on him. She didn't shut the door. She just let go of the handle and walked back to the sofa.

He followed her inside the suite. "Why don't you rest while I make arrangements for dinner?" he offered.

"If I go to sleep now I won't wake up for a month. I'd rather eat first."

"Of course." He nodded and picked up the room service menu from the coffee table. "What would you prefer?" His question, spoken in that lovely rhythmic cadence hung in the air as thunder rumbled outside. Rain pummeled the window and suddenly everything here felt too intimate, too close. Abby didn't want to be alone in a room with this man who set her libido to buzzing simply by talking and looking at her. In her diminished state of resistance that could be very bad.

"I think I'd rather go to the restaurant downstairs. Can we do that?"

"Whatever you'd like."

Whatever she'd like was a loaded phrase and one she wasn't going to dwell on. What she'd like was this man's hands on her body, a huge glass of Merlot, ten hours of sleep and most of all…Jason. Laughing, joking, taking her shopping. Alive.

But none of that was going to happen. Her brother was buried in a grave less than ten miles from where she stood. He was never coming back. The people who killed him might be coming for her next, and she had no idea who to trust, who to believe. As comforting as oblivion might be, if she had a glass of wine right now on an empty stomach, she'd fall asleep on the spot or do something incredibly foolish with her new bodyguard.

No way was she going to bed with Shaun Logan. Not after everything she'd learned today. And definitely not after he'd lied to her.

"I'M FINE WITH WATER." Abby sat across from Shaun in an opulent dining room overlooking the Capitol and watching it rain. She was desperately trying not to get comfortable with him. With that Irish charm, he was pressing a glass of wine on her—despite her objections. And it was only four in the afternoon.

"You just buried your brother and someone tried to shoot you. Have a drink, Abigail."

And whose fault was Jason's death? Shaun's? Donner's? Some mysterious competitor's? A terrorist trying to derail DHS? How could she know? That initial question more than anything had her sipping the Merlot more quickly than was prudent as Shaun drank iced tea. She was even ordering another glass after the salad, when she should have waited on the main course.

Lightning flashed and thunder rumbled, putting on a display that many would have paid to see. The food arrived when she was halfway through the second glass of wine.

"What was it like growing up in Mississippi?" Shaun asked.

She shrugged, wary of his attempts to make her open up. She'd shut him down earlier when he'd brought up the possibility of going to Jason's tonight.

She didn't want to talk to him about her childhood. She'd spent a lot of money and time in a therapist's office dealing with it. Lord knows after her parents' upbringing, she'd needed the help.

"I'm not sure what to compare it to," she finally answered. "My brother and I were very close. My parents and I weren't. And while part of my childhood was quite wonderful...my teenage years were not."

"Care to elaborate?"

She sighed. "My home was a difficult place to grow up in."

She knew she should keep her mouth closed or better yet, take another bite of the luscious steak in front of her and chew till the urge to talk had passed. But she didn't. Later she'd blame it on that second glass of Merlot.

"My parents always said we could tell them anything and they'd love us no matter what. They lied. When my brother came out of the closet, my parents disowned him. It was the spring semester of his senior year in college. I was sixteen years old. After Jason told them he was gay, they cut him off without a penny. I begged my father not to do it, but he wouldn't listen. Jason barely scraped by that last semester, but he graduated with honors and never set foot in our house again until their funeral. I never forgave my parents for that."

She wasn't sure what she expected but Shaun was listening with rapt attention, his own plate ignored as she spoke. It felt good to be able to talk, really talk about Jason to someone who wasn't being paid to listen.

"He'd been planning to get a doctorate, but he couldn't afford to after they took everything. One day he had an apartment paid for, a car, insurance, a future. The next, he had nothing. My parents even emptied his savings account. They called it practicing tough love. In reality, it was monstrous."

"You must have been devastated."

She nodded, took another sip of wine. This was better than therapy, better than yoga, better than jogging on that damn treadmill at the gym.

"I wanted to run away but Jason made me promise not to. He said I had to get a degree or I wouldn't be able to stand on my own without their help. He got a job in Dallas and when I graduated from high school, I applied to SMU. I only went home when I had to."

"Did your parents realize how badly they'd screwed up?"

She shrugged again. "They must have, but they wouldn't admit it. We couldn't talk about him without having horrific arguments. I'd always end up grounded or making my mother cry when I was still living at home, so the topic of my brother became the three-hundred-pound gorilla in the living room that no one would discuss. After I left for college my visits were so rare, we never spoke of him. It was as if Jason didn't exist for either of them anymore. They died in a car crash a couple of years ago and left the house to both of us. So while I do think they had finally figured out some of their mistakes, by then it was too late."

"You weren't exaggerating about a difficult place to grow up, were you?"

She nodded. "Everyone has hot buttons surrounding their childhood. As a result of mine, I don't like to be lied to. Ever."

"I'll keep that in mind."

"Do that." She smiled to soften the warning and took another sip of wine. "Enough about me. What about you? Where did you grow up? I've made this crazy assumption it was Ireland."

The corners of his mouth turned up slightly and he nodded. "I was born in Dublin."

"What was that like? Do you have family there still?"

He looked startled for a moment—staring at the glass in her hand, his expression unreadable before he recovered and met her gaze. "Well now, that's a conversation for another evening and another bottle of wine. On second thought, we'll definitely need something stronger to drink if we're going to discuss my formative years."

He smiled broadly but the expression didn't quite reach

his eyes. She took the hint. He obviously didn't want to talk about his childhood.

That brought her up short but it was just as well. She was getting too comfortable with him. Sharing too much. Becoming entirely too vulnerable. This could only lead to bad things.

"Could you excuse me for a moment?" She stood to leave the table and Shaun rose. "You don't have to follow me," she said.

"Nay, but I do have to stand. Surely you remember that from where you grew up, Abigail?"

She laughed and felt the blush blooming across her face even as she turned away. Southern manners with an Irish twist. Too bad she couldn't trust him. Even if she hadn't had that second glass of Merlot she'd be charmed. Exhausted and slightly buzzed, she hoped she wasn't weaving as she made her way through the tables to the ladies' room.

She pulled the powder room door closed behind her with the realization that she was weakening toward Shaun and needed to rally her defenses back around her. She couldn't let herself be sucked in by his appeal. Until she found out who was really responsible for Jason's death, she wasn't sure who she could trust. No matter how lovely the accent.

The problem was, in order to figure out who'd killed her brother, she'd need Shaun to recover that file. Although working with Shaun right now wasn't exactly a hardship, particularly when he was giving her the full-court "charm offensive" press.

And besides, recovering that file was the right thing to do. She might not like Zip Tech's founder, Michael Donner, but to keep the company afloat and to keep a lot of people from losing their jobs, Zip Tech needed her brother's file. Other employees' families' livelihoods, their lives as they knew them in this economy, were at stake. Jason wouldn't have stood for that. He'd known what it was to have everything ripped away.

She was washing her hands in the sink and looked up when a well-dressed woman in a lovely designer jacket walked into the restroom. Glancing up, Abby met the woman's eyes in the mirror, before going back to rinsing. Designer Jacket Woman smiled, then turned to lock the main restroom door behind her before opening her bag and pulling out the largest handgun Abby had ever seen.

Abby felt the blood drain from her face and knew if she looked back in the mirror, she'd see a pale reflection of herself. "Who are you?" she whispered.

"A messenger."

"From whom? What do you want?"

"It's not important who I work for. But my message is. No one gets Jason Trevor's upgrade file. You retrieve the updates however you like but Zip Technologies doesn't get them."

"I don't know what you're talking about. Who are you?"

"Someone who knows everything about you, Miss Trevor." The woman pulled out a photo envelope and dropped it on the counter beside Abby. Water droplets covered the marble top where Abby's hands had dripped, but it didn't matter when the paper sleeve opened and pictures spilled out.

Inside were photos of Abby in London, shopping at the market, walking alone on campus. Nothing very remarkable but the last three pictures made her blood run cold.

Karen Weathers in a hospital bed.

The woman who'd been more of a mother to Abby than her own after she'd fled her home as a freshman in college. Karen, who had helped Abby figure out what she was going to do with her life. Who'd been a university advisor, then a mentor, now a friend, and who'd been photographed in her rehab hospital room, all alone.

"I believe Miss Weathers has recently suffered a stroke?" said Designer Jacket. The question was more a statement.

Abby nodded woodenly, her thoughts a jumble. She'd just talked to Karen last night. Karen was fine. Abby was planning to see her in Dallas, after settling all of Jason's affairs here.

"Tricky things, strokes. A patient can be recovering beautifully, then turn for the worse so quickly and you never know why. It'd be a shame for something to happen to a bright woman like that."

Abby went from fear to white-hot fury. "How dare you threaten Karen. She had nothing to do with any of this."

"But that's where you're wrong. Everyone connected to you is now connected to Zip Tech. I'm only the messenger, Miss Trevor. Stay away from Michael Donner and his company before anyone gets hurt." She stroked a hand over Karen's picture. "It'd be such a shame for anything to happen. Get into your brother's files and destroy them. If the Zip-Net sale to Homeland Security goes through with your brother's upgrades, you won't like the result. I'll be in touch."

"Or?"

"Well, you saw what happened to Jason, no?"

Abby had known the words were coming even before Designer Jacket said them. Still they hit with a chilling finality. Nothing more was necessary as the well-dressed woman slid the gun into her purse, unlocked the door and slipped away, leaving the pictures on the damp counter.

Abby studied the soggy photos and looked up into

the mirror hardly recognizing the face that stared back at her.

What was she supposed to do now?

SHE RIPPED OPEN HER PURSE and pulled out her cell phone, frantic to hear Karen's voice. When they'd talked last night Karen had been okay—just wanting to be here with Abby so badly, though it simply wasn't possible.

If anything had happened to her... Abby couldn't think about that. Karen was like family. No, Karen *was* family.

The older woman answered on the third ring. "I've been thinking about you all day. How did the service go?"

Abby gasped in relief. "Karen, oh, God. Are you all right?"

"Honey, I'm fine. What's going on? Are you crying?"

Abby couldn't, wouldn't go into everything now. She'd talk to security at Karen's rehab facility after she hung up and let them know to keep an extra watch out. Upsetting the patient would serve no purpose except to increase the woman's blood pressure. Something they were trying to avoid at all costs.

So Abby told a different version of the events of the day, leaving out a few details and emphasizing the ones she knew would distract Karen from the funeral itself. And if Abby elaborated on a few particulars, it was all in the name of positive thoughts being good medicine.

She had to get into Jason's condo, into his computer and into his files without Shaun seeing her. Jason's upgrade file was her only bargaining chip, and she needed to get her hands on it. How could she do that? Her mind was reeling so, she almost missed Karen's words.

"So this new Irish friend of Jason's, is he panty-meltingly handsome?"

Abby gasped a laugh, struck by the incongruity of her thoughts and Karen's words.

"Yes. You could say that. He's definitely too handsome for my peace of mind."

"Good. I'd say you could use a diversion about now," said Karen.

A diversion? Of course. That's exactly what she needed. Abby knew one way of keeping Shaun distracted so she could get Jason's file without him noticing, but could she really go through with it? He had certainly acted more than a little interested earlier.

She wasn't answering Karen.

"I'll keep that in mind, but don't hold your breath," said Abby. "I'll see you in few days. Okay?"

"Of course. Whenever you get done there in D.C., I'll be right here or so they tell me. I'm catching up on all that reading I've been putting off for years." Karen's voice sounded wistful.

"You're staying positive, that's important."

"There's no other way to look at this. I'll be back and I'll be better than ever. Now I've got to run—or rather, wheel—to my next therapy appointment. I'll see you when you get here. Go enjoy your Irishman."

If only, thought Abby.

"Jason wouldn't fault you that," said Karen, and hung up before Abby could argue.

"Goodbye," Abby murmured to the dead air, staring into the mirror for several long moments before coming to a decision. She reached into her bag for her compact, lipstick and hairbrush, carefully applying the lip color and smoothing her hair. Could she actually do this right now? Seduce this man, this practical stranger, all in the interest of pulling the wool over his eyes?

For Karen, she would do it. She was the only family Abby had left. Zip Tech would not get that file.

"WHAT THE HELL HAPPENED in the cemetery?" demanded Donner, stepping into the light of the bare bulb.

"I'm…I don't know." The younger man was practically shivering in fear. Hodges had been an employee for eighteen months, but he lacked Logan's experience.

Donner smiled inwardly as his expensive shoes scraped loudly against the concrete. The abandoned warehouse had been a good place to meet. He much preferred dealing with people in this raw, direct way. Just cut to the chase. Much easier. Too bad he couldn't do it more often.

Hodges's voice was unsteady. "The rain was so heavy, I couldn't see, sir. She moved, and my aim was…off," he finished weakly.

Donner raised an eyebrow. "If your aim had been anymore 'on,' this party would have been over before it began. You almost killed the woman. What in God's name were you thinking?"

"I wanted to make sure she was scared. That she got the message. Just like you said."

"Oh, she got the message all right. Thanks to you, she thinks someone is out to kill her."

"That's what you wanted, right, sir?"

"Correct. That's exactly what I was after." Donner studied the man and felt the weight of the handgun in his leather jacket.

He really hated to do this, but it couldn't be helped. The police were involved now. As soon as Abby had made the call to Diaz, it was a foregone conclusion. This man could not be questioned by anyone else. Most likely there were casings left at the cemetery. Hodges had certainly been too nervous after seeing his very near miss to have gathered them all up.

Donner sighed. He was glad he'd had the foresight to treat the carpet in the limo with those special chemicals. Abby Trevor's asthma had kicked in just as he'd hoped, causing her to need them—specifically to need Logan. Everything was going as planned.

He grimaced. Or as well as this disaster recovery plan could go. He wondered if he had enough time to use Hodges for one more job before he had to be eliminated. There was a risk because the shooter could be linked back to him. But after his misstep at the cemetery, Hodges would be eager to make amends. Motivated employees were difficult to find.

Surprisingly his stomach felt a bit queasy at the thought. Still, he'd known this was the road he was taking when he had ordered the cemetery diversion. Hell, he'd known it long before then but this particular track had been necessary to ensure Abby Trevor's cooperation. Bad luck for Hodges, though. Bad luck for Logan, too. He would remain completely out of the loop on this deal.

Donner's phone indicated an incoming text. Reading it, he was glad he'd waited to decide the shooter's fate. The competition was sniffing around. There was one more thing that needed to be attended to.

"Despite these issues, I have another assignment," said Donner.

"Yes?" Hodges's voice was so hopeful it was slightly pathetic. Donner detailed the grim job. Hodges was most anxious to accept even though it was obviously above his level of expertise. The young sharpshooter had no idea he'd never get to spend a dime of the money being promised him.

"Same terms as before. Wait for my call," ordered Donner.

Chapter Six

Abigail hurried to the table and Shaun stood as she sat. She looked a little pale to him, not at all like the blushing woman who'd just left a few moments before. "I'd like you to take me to Jason's condo."

He held his surprise in check. "Of course. We'll finish eating and be on our way."

"No, I want you to take me now."

"I can't do that." He didn't have his backup team in place. When she'd refused earlier, he'd told his people to go to dinner themselves.

"Can't or won't? I thought you were all ready to do this immediately."

He studied her. Something in her expression gave him pause. Her makeup was flawless and there wasn't a hair out of place. Still, her eyes were glittering and he wasn't sure if it was from tears or fear. "Does it matter if we go immediately or in a couple of hours?" he finally asked.

"Yes, it does. You were so hot to do this earlier. What's changed?"

"Nothing has changed. But I don't want anything to happen to you while we're there and I don't have my team ready to go with us."

"What makes you think something would happen?"

He shook his head and laughed but there was no humor

in it. "Given everything that's gone on today, I'd have to say there's a fair chance your brother's condo is being watched."

"Are you scared to do this?" She locked her whiskey gaze with his own, challenging him with what he would have thought was a sexual come-on if he'd been in any other situation.

"What's going on, Abigail?"

"I need to go to Jason's condo. Right away." No doubt about it. There was a tremor in her voice.

"Okay." He studied her eyes again. Determined not to miss anything this time. "We'll go."

"Now?"

He nodded and she leaned forward, staring boldly back at him. Her eyes caressed his chest and moved lower, egging him on almost. But why? He'd agreed to do what she asked.

His body tightened in a surprising response.

This was all wrong.

He was aroused and trying to figure out what in hell was going on at the same time. Something had obviously changed her mind between the time she'd left the table and come back, but damned if he knew what it was.

"We're going but let's head to the room first. You need to get your inhaler and other meds. We're not leaving without those. And I need to make one or two calls—to let Donner know what's going on and to get some people in place so we aren't going in unprotected."

"Of course. Thank you." She stood and brushed past him, her shoulder touching his as they walked along the corridor to the elevators. The ride up to their room was crowded. Her breasts touched his back as they slid out of the paneled car. He took a deep breath. An hour and a half ago, she'd all but told him to go to hell when he'd suggested they go to her brother's—and he'd have laid odds on her decking him if he'd looked at her the wrong way.

There'd certainly been no sexual overtones to their conversation at dinner. Now she was determined that they go to Jason's tonight. She was absolutely coming on to him with her smoldering glances and casual but deliberate touches. It was bizarre. She hadn't had that much to drink.

While everyone responded differently to grief, he wasn't buying a sudden sexual urge as an explanation for her behavior. While he'd have been happy to oblige, Abigail didn't strike him as a woman who dealt with sorrow that way—more's the pity.

He followed her to the suite, determined to figure out what was spinning in that lovely head of hers before they left for her brother's condo. He wasn't about to take her into a situation where they could be shot at again when he didn't know all the variables. The way to unravel it was to follow her seductive lead, and while the process would be a pleasure, the aftermath wouldn't be pretty. She would despise him for it later.

ABBY WALKED INTO THE ROOM in front of Shaun, careful to brush against him again as he held the door. She hated what she was doing, but this certainly seemed the most expedient way. She had to distract him.

It wasn't as if she planned to have sex with him. She just had to flirt, heavily. And Abby had an A+ in flirting, thanks to her upbringing.

She turned as they came into the suite and was startled to find Shaun standing directly behind her. She suppressed a small yelp of surprise. He really was "panty-meltingly" handsome, just as Karen had said. But handsome or not, she wasn't sure how far she would have to take the "distraction charade."

The problem was, she couldn't have Shaun looking over her shoulder when she searched for that file in Jason's computer. She had a password and she wanted to try it. But Shaun had to get her safely to Jason's condo while giving her space, too. She needed him to willing let her do whatever she wanted with that upgrade file when the time came. So right now, she needed him malleable, which meant she had to seduce him. But this was only for the sake of the plan.

The plan she'd come up with on the way from the powder room to the dinner table. Once inside Jason's computer—if his old password still worked—she'd forward herself the file then delete it from his laptop…if she could. Lots of *ifs*. She wasn't sure if she'd be able to get that much accomplished or not but the first thing was finding out *if* there was anything even on the computer. And the only way she could do this was to get Shaun on her side. And the best way to get him on her side…

Well, most men's trigger was pretty simple. At least most men she knew. And she was fairly certain Shaun was attracted to her. So this was all going exactly as she'd planned, wasn't it?

"You're determined to go to Jason's right away, aren't you?" he asked.

"Yes, yes, I am." He was so close she could see that scar under his chin again.

"You're sure you don't want to wait a few hours?"

She felt his breath on her skin. "I'd really rather go now."

"I see." He stood gazing into her face and waited a beat. "Better get your stuff then. I've got a couple of phone calls to make."

She nodded and started to turn away before he reached out to her. "C'mere. You've got something." He touched the shoulder of her dress to remove a thread that had been stuck there most likely from their time on the floor of the limo.

He smiled. "There." He gently brushed her shoulder and she stood perfectly still as the touch turned to a caress.

She stared into those blue-green eyes, watching them heat, feeling herself drawn in.

Yes. This was what she wanted and needed…for her plan to work, of course. She reached up to touch his hand on her shoulder. Her gaze never left his.

He clasped her fingers, slowly bringing their hands to his lips. She reached up with her other hand to touch his cheek. She could feel the light stubble of his beard against her palm.

He let go of her fingers, leaning down to kiss her face and she was lost in the sensation—his lips against hers, his hands pulling her closer. She forgot for a moment about what she was supposed to be doing. And she no longer cared about the plan as he slid his tongue past her lips. He tasted like coffee and the crème brûlée they'd had for dessert. It had been a long time since she'd indulged herself.

She drank him in, wrapping her free arm around his back and pressing her body to his. Her other hand was still caught tightly against his chest. He explored her backside, pulling her to him.

She tilted her head, taking the kiss deeper and when he pressed her against the counter, she leaned back and wrapped an ankle around his calf. He ran a hand along her side, caressing her breast through the thin material of her dress.

He set her on the kitchen counter and she opened her thighs for him to step closer. When he pulled himself fully against her, tiny alarms starting going off in the back of her head. But his breath on her cheek felt warm and she ignored the warning as she melted into him.

He unbuttoned the front of her dress. One hand was on the front clasp of her bra and the other was sliding past her garter and up against the silken material of her panties when the alarms in her head started clanging in earnest.

She felt like a fool when she realized what she'd almost done. This was not what she'd intended. Not exactly part of the plan.

Distract him? Yes. Have sex with him on the suite's kitchen countertop? No.

She put her hands on his shoulders and gently pushed herself away. "No. I'm not doing this. I'm sorry. I got carried away."

"Right." He backed off immediately and she forced herself to meet his eyes.

Abby wasn't sure what she'd been expecting. Chagrin. Frustration. Irritation, at the least.

She'd been wrong to let this go as far as it had and she'd understand if he was annoyed with her for stopping. But his face was completely blank—totally cool and collected.

No passion. No irritation. Nothing.

It was as if a curtain had been lowered over the heat that had been boiling a moment before and she could have been refusing his offer for a coffee refill for all the emotion he now displayed.

Instead of being relieved, Abby felt let down. She liked to think she made a bigger impact than that. Her body was still crying out for more, yet Shaun appeared as if he didn't even need a glass of water to cool the flames.

She leaned back for a moment and swallowed audibly. "I…um…this was not what I was expecting."

He raised an eyebrow but didn't say a word. The silence stretched out. It was obvious he wasn't going to say anything.

The flush of embarrassment crept up on her and now she was the one who was irritated. Damn it, she hadn't ended up on this countertop alone. So why did she suddenly feel like a whore at the church picnic?

A little voice in the back of her head reminded her that perhaps it was because she'd set out to do to Shaun exactly what he'd done to her.

But instead of rattling him, he'd rattled her. Badly.

She barely stopped herself from shaking her head in disgust. *What goes around comes around.*

Karen could have told her that—wise sage that she was. So much for Abby's grand plan of distracting the man.

She'd managed to catch herself in her own trap. She snuck another glance at him. He looked completely unaffected. She needed the cold shower, not him.

Well, she could act that way, too. The past five minutes had never happened. He hadn't just had his tongue down her throat or his hands on her butt. She'd pick right up like they'd been in the restaurant.

"So what kind of calls do you have to make before we can go?" she asked, sliding off the counter and buttoning her dress as if this happened all the time.

"Are you okay?" he asked.

She ignored the burning in her cheeks. "We're not going to talk about this," she said and shot him another glance.

He shrugged. "Talking can be overrated." His soft Irish vowels and hard consonants made that loaded statement sound lyrical but she ignored the sexual tug. From now on she was immune to accents.

"Who do you need to call before we leave?" she repeated.

"Just a couple of people. I need to let Donner know

where we'll be. Plus I want my backup team there watching us. You ready once you get your inhaler?" he asked, studying her as she buttoned the top closure of her dress.

She nodded, refusing to let herself blush again under his perusal.

Donner had left them a car and the doorman brought it around. The drive took twenty minutes in the steadily falling rain. The scenery sped by but Abby didn't see it.

At Jason's condo she stepped from the SUV before Shaun could come around and open her door. As soon as she exited the vehicle she realized she'd left her purse on the seat but since she'd already gotten out the keys to the condo, decided against going back for it. She was nervous about this whole enterprise, plus Shaun's old world manners got to her. He used them to a terrible advantage— when he wasn't throwing her to the floor of limos or kissing her senseless on kitchen countertops.

Opening doors and standing when a woman left the table—those common courtesies reminded her of home and she missed them. Manners mattered to her and were sorely lacking in lots of places she'd lived since leaving the South.

Still, she had to resist the comfort Shaun's inviting demeanor offered. Besides, she'd learned from her parents that charm and manners didn't necessarily equate with trustworthiness. They'd abandoned Jason when they were embarrassed by his lifestyle and her parents had been two of the most charming people one would ever hope to meet.

While she unlocked the condo door, Shaun stood close beside her, without touching, under a big golf umbrella. The air smelled of Pinion. Jason burned the special wood all the time and the faint piney scent clung to everything even though it had to have been at least five days now since a fire had been lit.

She'd spent last night here, but everything was different now. A light sheen of sweat beaded her upper lip. Were there people watching now? Had anyone been there this morning after she left for the funeral home?

Once inside she walked straight to Jason's office and Shaun followed.

"I've got some ideas about the password." Abby sat at the computer.

"What are you thinking?"

"I'm hoping he hasn't changed it since I used his computer last year." She didn't look at him as she opened the laptop and powered it up.

"You knew what his password was at the hotel?" Shaun pulled up a chair beside her.

She stared at the blinking cursor, unable to ignore his question or the tone of accusation in it. "I visited last summer and Jason gave me a password to let me check my email. How many more tries do we have here before the hard drive wipes?"

"Don't think about that," said Shaun.

"But the hard drive erases itself if I'm wrong. We'll lose everything," she argued. Her palms felt moist against the keyboard.

"And if you don't try, we don't have access. Either way, we're screwed here unless you make an attempt." His words were harsh but still delivered in that lilting cadence. There was no arguing with his reasoning.

Mentally crossing her fingers, she typed *837321* and *BUTTERCUP* into the appropriate boxes—Jason's gym locker combo from high school and his nickname for her from their favorite movie, *The Princess Bride*. Together she and Shaun watched the screen.

Nothing happened.

The machine made a whirring sound. Could she have typed in the password wrong? Her heart sank as the screen went ominously blank.

Chapter Seven

As they both stared at the computer, Abby became hyper-aware of Shaun standing over her—his breath in her hair, the citrusy tones of his aftershave. She was turning her head, about to ask him to move back a step when a screen-saver photo opened of her and Jason together standing atop the Empire State Building at midnight.

She exhaled the breath she'd been holding—then stared at the picture and let herself remember. The lights of New York spread behind her and Jason like a glowing picnic blanket. Her brother had his arms wrapped around her waist and a tremendous grin on his face. She remembered exactly how she'd felt when that photograph was taken. Tired, exhausted in fact, but so happy.

Shaun took several steps back. She heard him dialing his phone as she continued to gaze at the picture. "We're in, Donner. What do you want?"

He cruised into the other room leaving her alone with the computer. She was a little surprised and had no idea how much time she'd have before he came back. It was now or never. Someone else would be taking over soon. Once Donner got hold of this computer, Abby would probably never see it or the file she needed again. She wasn't sure where to begin but clicked on the mail icon for lack of a better idea.

It was rather overwhelming.

There were more than five hundred messages in the inbox. Some personal, some business. Painful as it was, she scrolled down to the day Jason died. There were a hundred emails from that day alone, along with one undeliverable message—a bounce back.

Maybe because it was easiest, she decided to start with that one. What had Jason been sending that day? Who had he been emailing? Donner said he'd been working on fixing the "glitch." Could he have sent a copy of "the fix" to someone before he'd made that fateful trip to the office?

Shaun's voice was still a low rumble in the kitchen.

Clicking on the email, she read through the bounce code to get another shock.

The message was originally addressed to her. Sent at 11:02 a.m. on April 10, less than two hours before he was hit by the car. This had to have been one of the last messages he'd sent before shutting down his computer and leaving the condo.

There was a video file attached and she clicked on it. Jason filled the screen.

"Hey, Buttercup, it's me. Sorry we keep missing each other. Thought this might be the best way to catch up."

Instantly her eyes filled and she brushed the tears away. Just days ago, he'd been sitting right here at his desk and recording the video clip on his computer, alive and well.

"Next week we close the deal to sell Zip-Net to…
God, I can't tell you where yet, but it's huge. Told
ya it would be."

He grinned before leaning back in the chair.

"I've been thinking I should tweak part of the
program, and today I realized…there's something weird going on. Abby, it scared me. When
I got inside messing with things, there was code
that I didn't write in multiple places. I'm pretty
sure it's spyware."

He shook his head and leaned into the camera.

"I know you have no idea what I'm talking about,
but this is really bad. Zip-Net is supposed to
be—hell it *is*—the most secure product that's
ever been written. It's going somewhere that
absolutely must be secure and someone has put
spyware inside the program."

He was playing with a yo-yo as he talked—throwing
the toy back and forth and then spinning it. The same
yo-yo was in front of her now. She picked it up as he kept
talking.

"I don't know how they did it, but this morning
I've isolated the spyware and put a lock on it, so
whoever was doing this can't get to anything in
the contracted package. These malware codes
were buried so deep. No one was ever supposed
to find them. And the timing on this is so close to
the deadline for the sale. It's bad. Only someone

from my team could have done this. Nobody else knows the program well enough."

He was nervous. She could tell from the way he tossed the plastic neon toy as he talked. He wasn't looking at the camera anymore.

"This kind of spyware would enable one to listen in on every phone call made from the protected Zip-Net customer. When you realize where this will be installed, it's just crazy insane. Now with my lock on it, no one can get into any part of the program but me. I basically made a coded key for the whole thing and I'm freaked out enough to know I have to do something with it. I'm still trying to get my head wrapped around all this."

Outside the wind had picked up again and thunder rolled. She wanted to close the video clip and stop listening but she couldn't. Instead she watched her brother toss the yo-yo, then spin it out before tossing it back and forth to spin it again.

"I'm going in to talk to Donner today. He thinks I've only been working on security updates. He'll have a cow when he realizes the entire program is locked down. In case I get hit by a bus or something on the way to work today, I'm sending you the security upgrade file and the key. Just for insurance."

Abby drew in a sharp breath and almost doubled over in shock. He flashed her his trademark grin as he finally looked up again at the camera. She fought to focus and keep everything around her from going dim. If she stopped to think about the hideous irony of his being hit by a car less than two hours after he had recorded this, she'd collapse in a ball of misery.

Shaun walked up behind her. She hadn't intended for him to see any of this but she was too stunned to turn it off. So many unanswered questions swirled in her head. Some things made sense and some made less sense than ever.

She concentrated on Jason's voice.

"I put the file someplace special and deleted it from my computer in case someone else gets to my laptop before you. I haven't actually sent the file to you. You'll figure it out. You were so good at imagining things and you always were a helluva domino player. Remember the last time we talked about this?"

She keyed in on the last part of his message. She knew exactly where he meant. The only time she'd ever played the game. It was one of the few happy memories she had of their family together. Jason had beaten them all quite handily at the kitchen table. Her father had been so sure his son had the makings of a great mathematical genius. Daddy hadn't been that far off the mark.

On screen, Jason laughed.

"I'm talking like you'll actually have to sort this out. Don't worry, it's all gonna be okay. Call me when you get this email. We'll talk. Even if it's in code. Um...that's a joke, Buttercup. Love you."

The screen went blank as hot tears ran down her cheeks and she gripped the yo-yo in her hand. She hadn't realized she was crying till now. She still couldn't believe Jason was gone.

Pain clawed at her chest but she fought back against all she'd lost in burying him today. All they'd never share together, laugh over together, cry over together.

Someone at Zip Technologies was responsible for killing her brother. She was sure of that now—and certain that no one could be trusted. Not even Shaun.

"Where did you play dominoes?" Shaun asked, handing her a tissue.

"What?"

"I need to know where he sent the file."

She glared at him through her tears, a combination of fury and devastation behind her gaze. "I'm not sure." Even she recognized the lie in her voice.

Still he held her stare, refusing to challenge her on the obvious deceit.

"Donner has a lot more explaining to do before I tell you anything else," she said, growing uncomfortable under his scrutiny. "Like what the hell is going on inside his company. Someone at Zip Tech murdered my brother. Donner has a serious problem."

"That's why he needs Jason's file."

She turned away. She couldn't do this right now. She wasn't sure how much of the video Shaun had seen.

She knew he'd walked up behind her at some point but had he been listening from across the room when Jason talked about the spyware? Did he know that Jason had locked down Zip-Net? Maybe he did. Maybe that's why Jason had been killed.

She needed time to process it all. "Well, he's not going to get—"

The lights flickered out as something bumped against the wall on the back porch with such force that it rattled the window.

Shaun was on his feet in an instant.

"What was that?" she asked.

"I don't know. Be quiet." Shaun pulled out his cell phone and started punching away. The screen illuminated things enough that she spotted a candle on the shelf above the desk. She reached for it, feeling around in Jason's desk drawer for the matches she knew he'd kept with his emergency stash of cigarettes.

"Stay here," Shaun said, walking away from her into the darkness.

He was still punching numbers on his cell as he went. Jason's office was in the center of the condo. Abby stared into the inky blackness after him as her hand closed around a square unopened package in the desk. She'd be glad her brother hadn't given up smoking, despite all her harassing, if only she could find what he'd used to light them with.

She reached farther into the drawer, finally locating a book of matches among Jason's pens, pencils and paper clips. She peered into the darkness after Shaun, unsure if it was okay to light that candle or not. Her night vision was awful and her eyes weren't adjusting very well. She struck a match, lit the candle and suddenly Shaun was there standing beside her.

She stifled a gasp. He was so quiet; she hadn't heard a thing.

"What did you find?" she asked.

"Nothing good. My backup is gone."

ABBY LOOKED UP AT SHAUN looming over her in the darkness. The candle threw strange shadows on the wall behind him, reminding her of an old-fashioned cartoon character where the villain is looming over the victim and about to pounce on the victim.

"Gone as in 'left' or gone as in 'you can't get them to pick up their phones'?" she asked.

"Both. They're not answering and when I look out the window, I don't see their cars anymore. This group of condos appears to be the only ones with no electricity. Everyone else at least has a front porch light on."

She swallowed hard. "You're right, doesn't look good. What do we do next?"

They were whispering but the rain had increased to such an intensity, he had to put his lips directly against her ear to be heard. "We need to take your brother's laptop and get out of here."

She nodded, ignoring the tingles of awareness that shimmied down her spine. "Let me get something to cover it with before we take it into the rain." She grabbed the candle and crouched under the desk to scrounge for a bag of some sort. Shattering glass had her startling and bumping her head against the kneehole. Something or someone was breaking through the patio door.

"Stay down," commanded Shaun, pressing her to the floor with his hand on the small of her back. He leaned over her, a gun in the other hand. His body heat seeped through the thin material of her dress. She could smell his aftershave again or maybe it was a shampoo he used that made up the scent that was uniquely his. This all had a sense of eerie familiarity, like today in the limo.

"Stay here. Blow out that candle. I'll be one minute." His hand left her back and she felt strangely bereft.

Still clutching Jason's yo-yo, she'd gone to her knees with no protest but just as she about to snuff out the light, she spied a plastic grocery bag tucked under a box of printer paper, perfect for protecting the laptop from the rain. She tugged on the sack, determined to pull it from under the forty-pound carton.

More glass broke. She took a breath to blow out the candle when she sensed someone behind her.

She had time to turn, look up and scream before the crash came down against her head and everything went black.

Chapter Eight

Shaun heard Abigail's scream from the kitchen and his blood ran cold. He sprinted to Jason's office to find her on her back in the middle of the floor. The cubbyhole under the desk was on fire; the papers there were completely consumed.

What the hell had happened?

He pulled her away from the flames and checked her pulse. Her heart rate was steady and she was breathing fine. He turned to beat out the flames, hoping that would only take a moment—otherwise the building would burn down around them. But then he spied the blood in her hairline. He ripped off his jacket, no longer torn between dealing with the fire or her injuries.

He heard a noise behind him and turned to find two men in ski masks. Both held guns. One also held Jason's laptop.

Shaun slowly raised his hands. "What do you want?"

The man with the laptop spoke. "Get the woman out or die. Your choice."

Shaun couldn't be sure with the smoke, the masks and the noise from the fire, but the voice sounded familiar.

"Who do you work for?" Shaun asked.

"You don't need to know that. You just need to know you have the chance to live."

Shaun stared at both guns pointed directly at his chest and felt the increasing intensity of the flames behind him. Unchecked, the desk and drapes were fully involved. The fire had moved so fast. There had to be an accelerant involved.

It didn't matter anymore if Shaun recognized this guy. He and Abigail would die here if they didn't move soon. If it had just been one man with a gun he might have tried to stop this madness, but two?

He wasn't crazy. He had to get her out. He had no idea how serious that head injury was. Nothing here was worth dying over.

As he picked her up, a plastic yo-yo fell from her hand. Ignoring it, he carried her through the front door into the pouring rain without a backward glance, stopping only when they were well away from the condo under the overhang of the complex's clubhouse across the parking lot. She was still out cold as he gently placed her in an Adirondack chair on the covered porch.

A cold ball of dread settled in his stomach as water poured from the sky on all three sides, cutting them off from the world with a silver curtain. He knelt beside her, rechecking her vitals. They were both soaked.

Why wasn't she coming to? She should be awake by now.

He sat back and took a moment to pull himself together. Why was he so panicked by this? Why did she mean so much? She was only supposed to be a job.

Sirens blared in the distance, saving him from dwelling on that thought.

Who had called the cops already? Neighbors or his missing team? Whoever it was, he was grateful.

Abigail's eyes fluttered open. "What…what happened?"

His heart started beating again.

He was so screwed.

"Someone broke in." He pulled off his dress shirt, wondering if his voice sounded normal.

"Who? Did you get the computer? Why are you undressing?" She peppered him with questions between coughs as he tried to check her eyes for any signs of a concussion.

"No. They have it. And I'm taking off my T-shirt to clean your face."

"Oh…" Coughing more vigorously, she tried to sit up but he pushed her gently back into the chair before pulling his white cotton tee over his head. "Who's *they?*"

"I don't know. Do you always ask this many questions?" He didn't intend to speak so sharply but he was dabbing at the blood trickling down her cheek and still getting his own equilibrium back after almost getting them both shot in what was feeling like a bad case of déjà vu.

"No, I just… Sorry," she muttered.

The sirens were getting closer.

He stopped and looked in her eyes. "No, Abigail, I'm the one who's sorry. I almost got you killed for the second time today."

Her eyes filled with tears. "I don't really see it that way, you know. I think you just saved my life for the second time." She stared back and something passed between them. He wasn't sure what but he was in danger of drowning in her seemingly bottomless amber eyes.

A fire truck and an ambulance both barreled up the quiet street saving him from himself. Despite the torrential rain, the condo was now fully engulfed in the flames. Other residents were emerging from their units, as well. Umbrellas dotted the sidewalk.

Paramedics and firemen leaped into action but it still looked as if Jason's unit would be a total loss. Shaun located a medic and brought her over to check on Abigail and give her oxygen. The asthma had him worried and he told the EMT about it. The uniformed female put them in the ambulance out of the rain to get a good look at Abigail's head injury. Her hair was rain soaked but it had a lot of blood in it, too.

"It's almost certain you have a concussion." The EMT stitched up the cut as she spoke to Abby. "You need a nebulizer treatment as well for that asthma."

Abigail nodded as the woman prepared a treatment. "But your chest is still going to be tight for the next few days. You should probably come to the hospital tonight to be checked out," continued the paramedic.

Abigail started to shake her head *no,* but stopped abruptly and pulled away the mask. "I don't want to do that. What can they do for me there that I can't do for myself?"

"Is there someone who can stay with you? You can sleep but you need to be woken up every couple of hours to make sure you are okay. And if you start vomiting, or having any kind of vision disturbances or tingling sensations in your limbs, you absolutely must get to an E.R. right away."

Abigail turned to meet Shaun's eyes. "I don't want to go to a hospital. Can you help me at the hotel?"

He had a choice to make. If he said yes, he was signing up for more than just helping her with the concussion. He was signing up to bend his rules, as well.

That little charade he'd played with Abigail earlier in the hotel room on the kitchen counter had been a serious miscalculation on his part. He'd meant to scare her into telling him what was going on, not turn himself on to the point where all he could think of was how to get his hands on her again. If he went back to the hotel with her, he'd be looking for a reason to do just that. Something about

Abigail Trevor got under his skin in a way that had him throwing all his personal precepts out the window. Even though he knew emotional involvement on the job was a recipe for disaster.

She was still staring at him waiting on his answer. There was nothing he could say but "Of course I will…if you'll keep that mask on until she finishes giving you the nebulizer treatment."

Abigail nodded gingerly this time and slid the mask back up. The EMT didn't look entirely pleased but she'd seen enough to keep her mouth shut. "Okay, here's the paperwork you have to sign. Where's your hotel?"

"Here in Arlington," Shaun lied. He wasn't entirely sure it was safe to go back to the Wardman. But he wasn't telling anyone where they were really staying. Not that he had other options now. But the one he was considering was a little insane.

"I'll be right back," he told the EMT and Abigail. While she was taking her asthma treatment, he slipped out of the ambulance and made a dash for his car. Working for a security company like Zip Tech, he'd been thoroughly trained in the technique he was about to employ. It took less than three minutes for him to pop the fuse from under the dash and disengage the company's GPS system, thereby removing them from Zip Tech's tracking capabilities. He stared at the fuse box in his hand.

How had he ended up here?

Shaun never got involved personally or physically with the principals. It would have meant exposing himself in too many ways. Not that there hadn't been plenty of opportunities in the time he'd been working for Donner. With his particular occupation, there were always beautiful, unhappy women around.

While he'd been with Zip Tech, Shaun had been

propositioned by several. It was a bit of a job hazard, not that many men would call it that. But he'd never treated those women with anything other than the utmost respect, even as he was telling them *no*.

His mantra had always been, when a woman was part of an assignment, she was off limits and was to be treated like glass. Otherwise, it was just too damn complicated and very likely to lose him his very lucrative position. Yet, here he was disabling the company car's GPS system, and about to sign off on paperwork to take Abigail exactly where he knew they shouldn't go.

Had he lost his mind?

Apparently so. He pocketed the fuse and ran back to the ambulance.

Twenty minutes later, the nebulizer treatment was done and the EMT was putting away her equipment and giving them directions to the nearest hospital.

Abigail didn't say a word. She just slid off the gurney, bumping into Shaun as she did so. Her chest hit him squarely in the back. He would have moved forward but there was no place to go and turning to face her wasn't a good idea. But then he felt her swaying on her feet.

She was so close he could smell the perfume she'd been wearing earlier. He turned. There was blood on the front of her blouse. He immediately quit thinking about how sexy she was when he was reminded of how close she'd come to getting killed.

The EMT shut the ambulance door and left them standing on the condo's office steps just out of the rain. Shaun slid his arm around her waist and they made their way to the car, getting soaked yet again in the process.

"You don't trust anyone, do you?" she asked, fastening her seat belt over soggy clothes.

He startled, unsure if he was ready to fully explain the

why of everything he'd just done. It took him a moment to realize she wasn't asking about the GPS.

"I trust a few," he murmured. "But there was no reason to tell the EMT where we were really staying, now was there?"

"I don't suppose so. Are we going back to our hotel?"

"No. I don't understand how those men knew we were going to your brother's tonight unless they were watching his condo already. But just in case they followed us from the hotel, I don't think we should make it any easier for them." He drove out of the neighborhood.

"Do you believe me when I say the person who killed Jason works for Donner?"

"I don't know. Everything is on the table for now. It's important to reexamine what we know so far."

"You aren't sure?"

"Abigail, even if I was sure, I don't know who did it. So I can't just dive in without evidence."

"Where are you taking us?" she asked.

"Shopping." He pulled into the parking lot of a Walmart.

"What are we doing here?" she asked.

"Getting you new clothes. From the skin out. We look like we just climbed out of a swimming pool and we smell like smoke. I've got some extra things where we're going, but you don't." He wasn't going to mention her perfume. "I don't think you want me picking out your bra and panties, do you?" He wouldn't have minded. She'd be surprised to know how skilled he was at that particular job, as well. He'd sized several women in his work for Zip Tech.

He opened her door and she stared at him a moment, clearly at a loss for words.

"All right, Abigail, unless you want me to pick out your *polyester* pants, too, you better come in."

That got the result he was hoping for.

She straightened from her huddled position. "I prefer the entire leisure suit, thank you," she countered and scrambled out to follow him across the parking lot.

Chapter Nine

Since everything she'd brought with her to D.C. had been in a suitcase in Jason's condo, Abigail had to start over from scratch. Forty minutes later, Shaun was hauling multiple bags to the parking lot—groceries, jeans, two T-shirts, underwear, bra, pajamas plus a pair of tennis shoes along with toiletries, makeup and a duffel bag to keep everything in—compliments of his company credit card.

Thankfully she'd left her purse in the car when they'd gone into her brother's home. That saved her I.D. and phone from the fire, but Shaun didn't allow her to use her own money. He worried that whoever was after her might be trying to trace her credit card activity. His cards should be safe enough—he refused to share her suspicions that Zip Tech was responsible for the attacks against them. She was off the radar and secure for now.

"Where are we going?" she asked.

"Someplace safe."

She didn't ask anything else, which meant she either trusted him or she was exhausted. He was a realist and assumed it was the latter. He drove steadily through the downpour, grateful for a reprieve from her questions. Donner didn't even realize Shaun still owned this property. It'd be easy enough to figure out through tax records, but one would have to be hunting for the connection. It would do for what they needed tonight.

Rain dripped from the tall oaks while he wound his way through the deeply wooded lot. The storm seemed to be subsiding at last. The two-story house loomed in the darkness as he drove past the circular drive around back to the garage. He parked the car and punched in his code on the electronic panel by the door. The automatic metal door rose silently and a single light came on.

Abigail was quiet when they walked through the empty garage and into an enormous kitchen.

"What is this place?"

"Like I said…a safe haven."

"A what?"

"No one knows about it. At least, no one looking for us tonight."

"How are you so sure?"

"It's mine. But everyone thinks I sold it…last year. Even I thought so."

She smiled and raised an eyebrow, leaning wearily against an oversize marble-topped island. "How does that work exactly?"

"I signed the papers and moved out, only to come back from an overseas business trip to find that the deal had fallen through. I'd remodeled it myself and couldn't stand the thought of putting the property back on the market with the housing prices so dismal. I love this place."

He paused a moment, surprised he'd just said that out loud. He'd never spoken the words to anyone.

"I still own it but Donner and the people I work with assume I sold it. I've never told them differently."

She raised the eyebrow higher and he shrugged.

"This is not because I don't trust them. 'Tis just…I don't

really share my financial issues with people. They'd heard
I was selling and assumed it was a done deal."

"Where do you live now?" she asked.

"Donner provides an apartment in D.C. as part of my
salary, so this place is almost empty except for a few odd
pieces of furniture." He steered her toward the living room
while they spoke.

"The master bedroom is still partially furnished and this
room, too." He pointed to the large sofa and entertainment
center. "I keep some essentials here for when I need to get
away from work for a bit."

He looked around and took inventory of the living area
along with her. There was a large coffee table, a matching
love seat for the couch and an end table. But she wasn't
studying the decorating. She seemed to be hunting for
something instead.

"What do you need?" he asked.

"*We* need to talk about what happened tonight at Jason's—and earlier."

Earlier. She couldn't possibly mean what had happened
in the hotel suite? She looked directly at him, seeming to
challenge him with her eyes. He couldn't help but notice
how pretty she was, even with soot on her cheek.

"Do you want to get cleaned up first?" he asked.

"No." She crossed her arms and stood in the middle of
the room. "Who were those men at Jason's?"

"I have no idea."

She watched him for a moment. "I don't believe you. I
think they were people you work with at Zip Tech. They're
the only ones who knew we were going to my brother's.
You called Donner and told them we were going."

"That's a big leap." Even as he said the words, he knew it
wasn't a leap at all. But that didn't mean it was the only ex-

planation. As he'd said before, someone could have trailed them from the hotel, or been staking out the condo.

"No, it's not. I think your boss is responsible for my brother's death and you know it. You just…" Her voice cracked on the unshed tears. "You just don't want to admit it."

He wasn't immune to her distress but he couldn't let that affect his judgment. He had to analyze all the facts before he came to any conclusions. That was how he operated. "I don't know anything of the sort. But I'm going to find out. Please, trust me just a little longer."

"Trust you? The company you work for is making that extremely difficult. Jason said on the tape that only someone on his te—" She stopped.

"What did Jason say? On the video? Tell me, Abigail. I can't figure this out or help you if you don't tell me what's going on."

"How can I trust you?" She stared at him for a long time before seeming to come to a conclusion. "I'm wondering if you already know. Someone at Zip Technologies is responsible for the problems within Zip-Net. Jason thought it was someone on his team. He found spyware in the Zip-Net program. That's what he was working on right before he was killed. Not upgrades."

"He said this on the video?"

"Yes."

"What else did he say? I need to know," said Shaun.

"There was code there in the program that Jason had not written himself, embedded within Zip-Net. Jason said it looked like spyware and that he'd locked it all down until he could figure out what was going on."

"Is that what's in the file he talked about sending you?"

She nodded. "He sent me the updates that you and

Donner wanted along with a key code to unlock the entire Zip-Net program. He locked it down the morning he found out about the spyware in Zip-Net. Apparently that was right before he…died. He was on his way to talk to Donner about it and…" Her voice trailed off.

"Where did he send it?"

She studied him again. "I'm not ready to tell you."

"That's fair enough." He kept his voice calm but acid burned his stomach.

She was right to be cautious. He'd almost gotten her killed tonight. As much as he hated to admit Zip Tech could be behind this, there wasn't another explanation, not if Jason was correct. It opened up a whole new area of ugly possibilities that didn't make a whole lot of sense right now.

The company was depending on the Zip-Net product being unhackable and Donner was invested to his eyeballs in the new technology. If there was spyware embedded inside the program, there was a serious problem. What had Donner really been after on Jason's computer?

Updates? A key code? Both?

Shaun was ruminating over the possibilities when Abigail said, "I was in the ladies' room at the restaurant and something happened."

"What do you mean 'something happened'?"

"A woman came in with a gun and told me if I gave Jason's file to Zip Technologies, she'd hurt…someone close to me."

"Who?" His voice was sharp. A boyfriend? He was clenching his teeth so hard that his jaw hurt.

"Karen Weathers. She's a dear friend who had a stroke a few weeks ago. She's more like family really. She's in a rehab home in Dallas."

He took a deep breath. "Why didn't you tell me this earlier?"

"I didn't trust you earlier."

No, she'd just tried to seduce him in the hotel room to lull him into doing whatever she wanted. At least now he had an explanation for her sudden change in behavior on the hotel suite's kitchen counter.

"And now?" he asked. "How do you feel about things at this point?"

"Now, I don't have a choice. I have to trust you whether I want to or not. Retrieving that file is the only way I can keep Karen out of harm's way and get justice for my brother. I need your help to do both those things."

She stared at him, seemingly unashamed of her admission or her earlier behavior. "I don't think I'd trust you under normal circumstances, but I know you can keep me safe."

His training kept him from flinching. She'd only known him about ten hours and had him figured out pretty well, describing his temperament so perfectly it was painful. He wasn't someone you normally trusted but he could keep you alive or he should be able to. Unfortunately it hadn't always worked that way.

Gregor Williams and the scandal surrounding Storm's Edge were in the past but they still affected his present. Mentally he shook off the black pall. He didn't have time for that nightmare stroll down memory lane.

"So what do you want me to do?" he asked. He needed her to spell it out. He wanted her to ask him. For some reason it would make it easier to bend—no break—that blessed rule of his if it was at her request.

"I want you to help me recover Jason's file and the key code," she said.

"Do you know where they are?"

"I think so. Will you come with me to get them?" she asked.

"All right."

"Just like that? You'll come with me? No questions?" she asked.

He looked at her. Knowing what he was going to say long before the word left his lips. "Yes."

"Because it's your job to get the file?"

"No. Because it's my job to keep you out of harm's way," he answered.

There was a beat of silence. "I have one condition," she said.

"Name it."

She cocked her head at his tone. "You can't communicate with Donner or anyone else at Zip Tech until we get back with the upgrade file and the key code. That's nonnegotiable."

He bit his lip against what he really wanted to say and she raised her hand to stop any debate. "No argument. You want to come with me. Those are my terms. Otherwise, I go on my own."

"You really think Donner is responsible for Jason's death?" he asked.

"Someone at Zip Tech murdered my brother. Donner *is* Zip Tech. Either he was involved directly, or he let it happen under his nose, and did nothing. In my eyes, that makes him just as culpable." Her eyes were liquid but her voice was firm.

"That's a serious accusation. I've known Michael Donner for two years."

"I want justice for Jason. You and I both know the only way I'm going to accomplish that is to get the file before someone at Zip Tech does."

"What'll you do with the file and code when you recover

them?" he asked. "Some in your place might be tempted to seek revenge rather than justice."

"I honestly haven't gotten that far yet, but give me time. First I have to make sure Karen is safe. I'll probably turn the file and key code over to the authorities. But right now, I just want to sleep. I've had a helluva day. I buried my brother, got shot at and brained in his condo after being held at gunpoint in a bathroom, then got stuck in a burning building."

She did look exhausted. He knew that despite her tough talk, she was at the end of her emotional and physical rope. Still, he had to make one thing clear.

"Right. We'll do it your way. No Donner. No Zip Tech. But if I get in a situation where I think you're in danger beyond what I can handle, all deals are off. I'll do what's necessary to keep you safe and call whomever I need. No bargain we've struck is going to stop me. You agree to that going forward?" He was staring at her, working hard to keep his gaze impersonal.

"Who would you call?" she asked.

He shook his head, never breaking eye contact. "Not telling, but you can trust whomever I bring in."

She nodded. "If we find ourselves in that kind of danger, I would be pretty stupid not to, wouldn't I?"

He barely managed to pull himself from her whiskey-colored gaze before doing something completely insane.

Unbidden, his mind flashed on what they'd very nearly done on the kitchen counter earlier. He could almost feel her skin beneath his hands. His body tightened as he imagined what it would be like to have her on the sofa behind them now—her body pressed against him, his hands tunneled in her silken hair that had fallen loose earlier.

He shook his head again—this time to clear the erotic images. "Dumber things have happened," he muttered. "Believe me."

Chapter Ten

Abby watched him watching her and decided it was time to take a shower. A cold one. This attraction to Shaun Logan was the very last thing she needed. She was vulnerable, exhausted and hurting while he was charming, beautiful and trouble with a capital *T*. Sinking into him for some mindless oblivion would be entirely too easy.

She broke eye contact and gathered her purchases from Walmart. "I need to get cleaned up. Where can I bathe?"

Shaun pointed to a staircase and led the way. She followed, entirely too aware of the way he filled out his slacks and damp dress shirt. At the top of the stairs, they passed two empty rooms. He stopped at the end of the hall before a bedroom that was fully furnished with a four-poster bed, mirrored dresser, captain's desk and an overstuffed chair.

The bathroom was like something out of a luxury hotel with a six-foot Jacuzzi tub and a television built into the opposite wall. Abby felt her eyebrows hitting her hairline.

"Wow, Shaun. This is pretty amazing. You don't exactly strike me as the Jacuzzi type."

The corner of his mouth tilted up in a smile. "That bathtub is a long story. I lost a bet but discovered I didn't mind that much. Truth be told, 'tis rather tremendous, actually."

He laughed and shook his head in what appeared to be genuine disbelief. "Who'd have thought? Make yourself at home. There are towels, shampoo and such. I keep a few essentials here. Just let me get some dry clothes and it's all yours. I'll shower in one of the others."

"But this is your room," she argued.

"It's yours tonight. I'll take the sofa downstairs. Feel free to use anything you need." He cruised into the walk-in closet while she looked around the palatial bathroom. "The EMT said you can't sleep for a while but there's no reason you can't be comfortable."

He left her and fifteen minutes later she was chin deep in the Jacuzzi's frothing bubbles. Getting her hair clean had been a challenge. She'd had to lather it up three times in the high-tech shower to rid herself of the smoke smell but now she was watching sandalwood-scented water swirl about in a tub the size of an Olympic swimming pool. She leaned against a padded bath pillow, closed her eyes and smiled—trying to imagine Shaun lounging in the water like this. That must have been some bet he'd lost.

Instantly the mental picture was there. Dripping wet biceps and washboard abs covered in swirling water. For a few moments she let her mind wander…everywhere. Sexual fantasies might not be the answer to her problems, but they were a lovely escape. At least for a little while.

What was she doing here and how in the world had she ended up in Shaun Logan's pimped-out bathtub?

Eleven hours ago she'd been at her brother's funeral and hadn't known Shaun existed. Ten hours ago someone had been shooting at her. Nine hours ago she'd been recovering from an asthma attack and talking with Michael Donner. Three hours ago she'd been in a burning condo.

Now no one knew where she was. No one knew what had become of her. When had everything slipped so completely out of her control?

SHAUN STOOD UNDER THE STEAMING hot spray and wondered how everything had slipped so completely out of his control. There was no doubt about when it had happened. At the same moment he'd started bending his rules. Here was further proof of how far he'd fallen down the slippery slope.

He never brought assets home. This was his last place of utter peace. Now there was one in his bedroom, in his bathtub for God's sake. He finished his shower quickly. He wasn't bending his rules, he was shattering them. As he stepped out of the marble enclosure to towel off, his cell phone rang—Donner's special ringtone.

The man paid Shaun's considerable salary and Shaun wasn't going to ignore his boss, despite what he'd said to Abigail. He wasn't ready to break that rule, as well. You told the principal whatever they wanted to hear in order to gain their cooperation, or that's how Shaun justified himself as he once again ignored his conscience and knotted the bath sheet around his waist before answering the phone.

Donner normally didn't get rattled but he was now.

"Logan, what the hell is going on? Where are you? Is Abby Trevor with you?"

Shaun still didn't want to believe Donner had anything to do with Jason's death but he couldn't ignore the fact that when he'd told his boss and backup where they were going, Abby'd ended up knocked unconscious and he'd had two guns pointed at his chest. That was why he had disengaged the GPS before they left Trevor's parking lot.

"Abigail's with me. She's okay. We're just back from her

brother's condo." He explained about the break-in, the fire and his missing team.

"Interesting that she knew the password all along," said Donner.

A chill slid down Shaun's spine when he didn't ask about the fire, the missing backup or those men who'd held them at gunpoint. Was that because Donner already knew or because he didn't care? Either explanation was a fairly serious indictment of the man.

"She accessed a video from Jason."

"A video? What did it say?" asked Donner.

"I don't know. I only heard the end of it when Jason was telling her where the upgrade file was. Apparently he was worried someone might get to his computer and to the email he'd sent her so he crafted a bit of a scavenger hunt. He was giving her clues on the video right before the break-in."

He wasn't sure why he didn't confront Donner right then about the spyware. Maybe because he'd promised Abigail he wouldn't talk to the man at all, but he consciously chose not to go into the spyware or key code issue. It felt important to keep that information to himself.

"I have to have that file, Shaun. Now it's more important than ever. We can't fix Zip-Net and this contract with Homeland Security is dead in the water if we don't."

"I understand."

"Does the woman know where the upgrade file is?"

"Yes, but she's not telling. Like I said, Jason hid them somewhere. She's convinced someone at Zip Tech is responsible for her brother's murder."

"Well, you know that's bull."

"Do I?" asked Shaun.

"Of course." Donner's voice was smooth and convincing. "I need you to unwind the puzzle, man. You're my fixer and this is what I pay you for. Work your magic on that woman and do whatever it takes. I don't care about consequences. I need that file."

Whatever it takes? This wasn't the Michael Donner that Shaun knew.

Shaun didn't use people; he never had. And despite his job description, Donner had never asked him to forget consequences. Shaun's whole purpose at Zip Tech was about avoiding consequences. That's why he'd been hired. What was going on?

Michael was always conscious of his public image. This felt like Storm's Edge and the disaster in Iraq all over again. Shaun couldn't believe the irony. Didn't want to accept it. Donner hadn't even mentioned the key code or Jason having locked down Zip-Net. He had to know about the lock, so why wasn't he asking about the key code? It all seemed very wrong. The key code was more important than the upgrade file at this point.

Was Abigail right? Was Donner responsible for Jason's death or was he completely clueless about everything going on? Shaun had to buy time to figure it out. He couldn't lie directly to his boss but there was no way he was mentioning the spyware now.

Still, he was about to start a very dangerous game. If he was guilty, Donner had far too many resources and fail-safes for Shaun to outrun him. He had more bells and whistles in wireless communication than Shaun could ever hope to understand. If Donner thought he was being played, he could have them hunted down and crushed if he wanted to. Shaun and Abigail would never know what hit them if they started without marshaling their own resources and aroused Donner's suspicion.

But Shaun had some of his own resources he could

call on, as well. He'd play along until he had everything unwound.

"Okay, Michael. But she doesn't want me contacting you while I'm with her. She doesn't trust you." He heard Donner's low chuckle over the phone.

"And you couldn't convince her I'm completely trustworthy? I'm surprised at you."

Shaun forced a levity into his voice he didn't feel. "There's just so much I can do before I start sounding like your fan club president. I'll contact you when I can to let you know where we are. For now it'd be better if you backed off and gave us room. I don't want her spooked anymore than she already is. Why don't you work the police on your end to find out about the fire? I got her out of there before the cops could start asking a lot of questions."

There was a pause and Shaun knew in his gut—his boss wasn't going to contact the authorities. He'd been so mistaken about Donner.

About everything.

Suddenly it seemed extraordinarily important to get off the phone as quickly as possible. Donner hated being out of the loop and could be tracing this call right now just to satisfy his curiosity about where Shaun and Abigail were spending the night.

The knowledge had him reeling. He was back in a long hallway hearing a girl's screams, the clinical smells and sounds of a hospital. Fire, explosions, darkness and pain.

Later finding that she'd disappeared completely off the face of the earth. He'd known then what the people he respected were capable of and he'd never forgotten the way it had made him feel. Betrayed, grasping for something to hold on to. Something to believe in.

Donner's voice brought him back to the present nightmare. "All right, but you stay in touch. I need that file ASAP. Remember, we sign the contract in four days."

How could he forget?

Shaun hit End and pulled on his clothes, feeling as if the top of his head was about to fly off. Four days to figure out why a man he trusted and looked up to had possibly had one of his own employees killed. It didn't make sense. Donner stood more to lose than anyone if the Homeland Security contract fell through for Zip-Net.

How did Shaun talk to Abigail about the conversation he'd just had? She'd asked him not to communicate with Donner at all if he wanted to come with her to get the file. Telling her that he'd just told his boss almost everything seemed like a good way to get his ass booted to the curb, even if he told her the conversation had convinced him that she'd been right.

He had a sick feeling that Donner was indeed responsible for Jason's death. But nothing about it made sense. He still didn't know what was going on or why. And the last thing he wanted was for her to fly off the handle and run off on her own, as she'd threatened.

So, for now, he'd say nothing to her. That might be a mistake as well, but this seemed to be his day for screwing up his life and breaking all his own rules.

Besides, words had never meant much to him; it had always been what you did that made the difference. How you stood for what you said you cared about. It defined who you were. People trusted what they saw you do, not what you said you'd do. If someone didn't trust him, he'd always found that showing them rather than telling them was more important.

That could work both ways here. He'd have to show her that she could trust him and hope that she really knew where Jason's file and the key code were. If not, they were both in more trouble than his considerable skills could deliver them from.

Chapter Eleven

Barefooted, Shaun wandered downstairs to the fridge. He wasn't hungry but he opened the stainless door anyway. He had beer, wine, Gatorade and one can of soda. The beer was tempting but that wasn't a possibility when he was working.

Deciding on a pot of coffee instead, he turned when Abigail came into the kitchen. Her hair was damp and piled high on her head in a clip, drying in wild curls around her cheeks. She'd put on his robe over her new pj's. He fought against staring at how the silk garment enveloped her while still accentuating her generous curves. Forgotten till now, the designer robe had been hanging on the back of his master bathroom door—a gift from a former lover who hadn't known his tastes very well.

"I didn't want to put on my new clothes since I was going to need them tomorrow," she explained. "I took you at your word and borrowed this."

How was it that the robe swallowed her but still managed to get him hot at the same time? That was simple. He'd been on top of her more than once today plus the interlude with her on that damn kitchen counter he was going to dream about. It wasn't much of a leap to imagine exactly how she'd feel against him if she wasn't wearing anything at all.

He turned abruptly to the refrigerator again. Bringing her home with him had been a horrible idea. "Can I get you something to drink?" he asked, opening the freezer compartment. "I'm about to make coffee, it's caffeinated."

"No, just water for now. My throat is terribly dry from the smoke."

"Of course." He should probably have some ice water himself. He could just dump it down the front of his jeans.

"How's your head feeling?" He got her a glass.

She wobbled her hand back and forth. "So-so. Do you have any ibuprofen?"

"I don't know. I may have cleaned out all that kind of thing when I was moving the first time. I'll check and see."

She nodded, rubbing the back of her neck and shoulders. "What's up with your neck?"

"I don't know…I think I twisted something funny when I was under the desk, just before I got hit." She tried to sidle onto a bar stool but winced as she sat.

He handed her the water and walked behind her. Placing his palms on her shoulders under the robe, he felt a knot in the muscles along with the heat from her skin.

Putting his hands on her like this was probably a mistake too, but he could just add it to the list of mistakes he seemed to be making where Abigail was concerned. Besides, she was hurting and he could fix it. He'd had the training. And he desperately needed to fix something about this crazy, screwed up day.

He pressed his thumbs along each side of her spinal column starting at her hairline.

She moaned out loud. "Ohhh, that feels amazing."

Yes, it does.

Her skin was just as smooth as he'd imagined. Slowly

he turned her head from side to side before kneading the muscles along the base of her neck and back into her scalp. The knot was loosening already.

He pushed harder. The soft sounds she made had his mouth going dry and his body tensing up. He closed his eyes and took a deep breath as she sank into the bar stool armrest. The back of her head was almost touching the middle of his chest.

He could smell his bath soap on her. The scent was different on her body—or maybe it was just her scent in general. She made little mewing sounds in her throat as he rubbed her neck. He knew it had nothing to do with sex in her mind but she was definitely turning him on.

This was such a huge mistake.

He dropped his hands. "I think that's got you taken care of."

She sat up slowly, turning her head this way and that. "Yes. It is…much better. Thanks so much. That's…that's remarkable."

She swiveled on the seat to face him, but he turned away to busy himself with the coffee before he did anything insane like bury his head in her hair or pull her into his arms.

"No problem," he muttered.

"So how are we going to do this?" Abigail asked, sliding off the bar stool.

"Pardon me?" Shaun's one-track mind was still reeling in the wrong direction.

"How are we going to stay awake?"

"Oh. You don't have to. The EMT said you could sleep, you just have to be woken up every couple of hours. I'll be setting an alarm."

"That doesn't seem very fair for you to have to stay awake while I'm sleeping." She stifled a yawn, stretching as she spoke. His robe, too big for her, gapped open to reveal a lacy camisole underneath. He suddenly had a whole new appreciation for the lingerie department at Walmart.

"It's okay. I'll doze. I don't need a lot of sleep. Besides, you're practically out on your feet. Your head will feel better this way, too. Go on up and I'll look for that ibuprofen."

He followed her, grateful she would be upstairs. After his conversation with Donner, he felt so mixed up, so upside down. The farther away he was from Abigail right now the better.

He rifled through the medicine cabinet, spied the pain reliever and found her at the bedroom window, staring into the night. The drapes were open, moonlight bursting through the clouds into the room. Abigail's hair glowed an unearthly white.

He watched her a moment, wishing she were here under different circumstances. Wishing he'd met her anywhere else—a bar, hell, even at one of Donner's charity events. He shook the bottle, effectively breaking the spell he felt himself falling under.

"Found some," he murmured. She swiped her cheeks as she turned to face him. So he pretended to ignore her tears, trying to give her the privacy she obviously craved. He had to get out…now. He wanted, needed something to ground himself in, but it couldn't be this woman. Not here, not under these circumstances.

"I'm downstairs if you need anything."

She nodded. He handed her the bottle, her fingertips accidentally brushing his.

"Thank you." Her voice was soft.

He quashed the urge to reach out to her. To hold her and tell her it would be okay.

"I—"

"Yes?" he asked.

She stared at him a long moment and something passed between them in the moonlight. She didn't say anything; she just stood, looking at him. He could have reached out to her then and had her. Taking her to the bed behind them would have been so easy and both of them could have forgotten about the hellacious day that had just passed… for a while. But that wouldn't have been fair. Not tonight. The day she'd had was the very reason he wouldn't do it.

He waited. Watched her and wished again he'd met her somewhere, anywhere else.

"Nothing. I'd better get to sleep," she murmured.

"I'll be back to check on you in a couple of hours."

He left before he could do or say anything crazy. That would only compound the disaster that this particular job had become. He couldn't exactly pinpont when it had gone off the rails. But…he now had a woman in his bedroom who was a principal asset. His boss was most likely crooked. Perhaps a murderer. Getting physically involved with Abigail Trevor would take it from disaster to Armageddon.

Even knowing that, he had a feeling that Armageddon was inevitable.

Now he knew where he'd gone off track. Their kiss in the kitchen of the hotel suite. That was where everything has slipped out of his control and this whole downhill slide had begun.

Could he stop it from rolling completely off the cliff? Could he just stay away?

Probably not. Biggest reason—he didn't want to.

That was the problem.

He flicked on the television trying to escape his dismal thoughts. A late edition of the news prattled away. Fire trucks and police cars filled the screen. He recognized

Jason's condo immediately. At first he thought it was only a report of the fire.

The reporter was speaking earnestly into the microphone as a shrouded gurney was wheeled down the steps.

"Firefighters made a grim discovery several hours after starting to fight the blaze. The body of a woman was discovered in the condo at the epicenter of the fire. She has been identified as Therese Mattagon."

A picture of an attractive woman who could have been anywhere between thirty-five and fifty-five years old depending on her plastic surgeon flashed on the screen.

"Police are searching for two individuals at the scene who are material witnesses and wanted for questioning. Abby Trevor and Shaun Logan."

Shaun heard Abigail gasp on the stairs behind him. "No. That's the woman from the bathroom at the restaurant."

Aww. Jesus. Despite his best efforts, Armageddon had begun.

Chapter Twelve

Shaun was riveted to the television. How had he missed a body in Jason's apartment? He hadn't searched the entire place; there hadn't been time before everything went haywire. But still, who was Therese Mattagon?

Abigail stood frozen on the stairs, her face as pale as the moonlight streaming in the windows.

"Good Lord, what happened in that condo after we left?" she whispered.

He went to her. "It could have happened before we got there. That's really the only way it could have happened."

"But why would she be at Jason's? I mean obviously she wanted the file but why would someone kill her? She didn't have it." Abigail shook her head.

"Maybe those men we ran into didn't know that," he suggested. "Maybe she beat them there and they thought she had the file. Maybe she fought back too hard."

He didn't say the worst of what he was thinking. Maybe Therese Mattagon wasn't dead before the fire. She could have just been tied up in a closet he hadn't checked. That thought would haunt him for a very long time.

He swallowed hard. "Let's think this through. She leaves you in the ladies' room and goes directly to Jason's to look for the file herself. If someone else was there, maybe watching the condo, waiting…"

"For me? Oh, no! They thought she was me and killed her instead?"

For Therese Mattagon's sake, he hoped they had at least knocked her out cold or, God forgive him, that she'd been killed before the fire. The horror of being awake and tied up in a closet and then dying of smoke inhalation was the stuff of nightmares.

He refocused on Abigail who now looked stricken. Even though he hadn't said it, she'd figured it out. "Oh, no. Maybe Therese Mattagon wasn't dead before the fire."

She took in a deep gulp of air. "I can't… That's too horrible to think about. I… Oh, God…" Her voice broke and she started to cry, sinking to the steps.

He reached out to grab her, wrapping her in his arms. As she held on to him, he fought against the very strong desire to bury his face in her hair. Instead he focused on talking to her softly, gently. Rubbing his hand up and down her back, as he'd do to soothe a troubled child.

"We don't know anything yet," he said. "That may not be what happened at all. I checked upstairs, not every closet, but it was very quiet in that condo. If she was conscious, I've got to think I would have heard something." He was trying to reassure himself as well as Abigail.

She burrowed deeper into his embrace and he struggled to keep it impersonal but there were some things he wasn't going to be able to hide much longer. Unfortunately his body didn't know that it wasn't supposed to be responding to the woman he'd been fantasizing about having sex with and who was now, finally, in his arms.

She took a steadying breath and the storm of tears seemed to pass. She needed comfort. Any second she was going to realize that wasn't exactly what he was offering. But disentangling himself wasn't an option at this point.

She sank further into his chest and stopped.

Right. That's exactly what she thought it was. He was that happy to see her. He waited for her to say something, to push him away. At the very least to step back, but she didn't.

She sighed and tilted her head up—the tears still wet on her cheek. "Do you want me?"

"I think it's obvious. More than is proper after the day you've had."

He started to back away himself but she held his arm and kept talking. "I don't believe Emily Post could possibly cover what's happened in the past twelve hours. What I really need is to forget about today. It's been horrid on every level. I want to lose myself in you. To forget." She looked up at him then, the intensity in her amber gaze taking him by surprise.

"You're serious," he whispered.

She didn't say anything. Instead, she stood on her tiptoes and tilted his head down so she could press her lips to his.

He could taste the toothpaste she'd used earlier that belonged to him. Smell the shampoo she'd borrowed from him, as well. Running his hands over her butt, he pulled her closer and parted her lips with his tongue. He kissed her so she'd have no doubt about him wanting her.

She pulled back to look him in the eye again. "Yes, I am serious. I don't want to dream about limos with shattered glass, or people holding guns on me in powder rooms or burning condos. And I especially don't want to dream about my brother. I just want to lose myself for a while."

In mindless sex were the unspoken words.

The part of his conscience he'd truly thought was buried

till he'd met this woman earlier today made him ask, "And tomorrow? You won't be sorry?"

"I don't know. I might be…but I'm a big girl. I can handle it."

And just like that he knew what he had to do. His body was going to hate him and Abigail was, too. But he wouldn't pile on morning-after regrets to the horrors of the day she'd just endured.

"Ah, well. You might be able to handle it, Abigail darling, but I'm not sure I can." He reached up, and though it absolutely destroyed him, he unclasped her arms from around his neck. "I just don't think that my heart could stand it."

She stood there with her mouth slightly agape, her lips forming a silent *Oh*.

He prattled on, filling the deathly silence, knowing he was going to have to push further for the reaction he needed. "Yeah. Sorry. I just don't think this is a good idea for tonight. I'm supposed to protect you, not screw you."

"Oh?" This time she said it aloud and in a tone that let him know he'd hit the mark. Her voice actually ratcheting up just a bit. She drew back and he saw fire in her eyes.

There now, that was exactly what she needed. As much as he hated it. Rage would keep her going far better than falling into bed with him. At least that's what he was going to tell himself tonight when he was trying to sleep on his sofa that really wasn't very comfortable at all.

"Well, I certainly wouldn't want to interfere with you doing your job," she said.

No danger of her rethinking this idea. He watched, as she wiped her face and gathered a cool cloak of anger about her, seemingly dismissing what had just happened between them like she had those scorching kisses in the hotel suite earlier.

"It'll be better this way." He patted her shoulder in a brotherly way, despite the fact he was feeling anything but brotherly. "You'll see. So tomorrow morning—" he began.

"Shouldn't we call the police?" she asked.

He cocked his head. "We can do that tonight if you want. But you know what they're going to say, don't you?"

"No. What?" Her voice was colder than an arctic wind.

"As a person of interest, you won't be able to leave town. Our trip to get the file will be postponed."

She glared at him, weighing her options, then glanced at the television. "My God, who *didn't* break into Jason's condo today?" She shook her head. "Why haven't the police called you or me on our cell phones? That EMT took your number."

"I may have transposed a number—or three."

"Just like you told them we were staying at a hotel in Arlington?"

"Something like that," he said.

"So if you hadn't turned on this newscast, we'd have no idea they were searching for us?"

"That's right."

"And there's no way they can prove whether we'd seen it or not?"

"Uh-huh."

"So we can just go along like we'd never heard about any of this?"

"Abigail Trevor, are you suggesting that we don't go to the police?"

She shook her head. "It's not like they've been a lot of help so far. And if what you say is true, now all they'll do is keep me from doing the one thing that might actually help catch my brother's killer. So yes, that's exactly what I'm suggesting."

He would take successes where he could get them at this point. "Right. So we won't call them. We'll leave in the morning like we never saw the news."

"What about your boss?" she asked.

"Donner? What about him?"

"Won't he wonder about all this? Why you aren't calling?"

And let that be a lesson to him. Don't count successes when the bigger challenge was just around the corner waiting to bite you in the ass.

Here it was. His moment of truth. He should just say it: I've already spoken to him. Donner called while you were in the shower. I think he may be trying to trace my calls.

But he didn't. Not after what he'd just done to her.

She'd leave his butt here in the morning and never look back if he admitted he'd talked to Donner less than ninety minutes after promising not to—no matter what his justification was for doing so. He had to lie to her, no matter what happened later. He couldn't let her go out on her own. She'd be in too much danger.

Plus he'd never see that file or the key code.

He took a deep breath. "Because talking to Donner is a deal breaker, right?"

"Absolutely. I thought I was real clear about that."

He smiled and nodded. "The topic's closed then. So what direction are we headed tomorrow? Are you at least going to tell me that much?"

She glared at him, obviously still mad over his rejection. He longed to run a hand down her face but that would completely undo the anger he'd stoked up here.

"South."

He nodded. "How far south?"

"Pack a bag."

"You telling me any more than that?"

She gave an unladylike snort. "I still don't know if I can trust you."

He waited. That was fair. He'd definitely yanked her chain tonight.

"We're going to Clarksdale, Mississippi—the town where I grew up."

She turned for the stairs and he watched her walk back up to his room. He would have to wake her every two hours but between all he'd just found out and thinking of her lying alone in his bed, he wasn't going to sleep much between now and then anyway.

He waited until he heard the door snap shut before pulling out his cell phone. It was time to call in some favors.

He hoped like hell that Harlan was home.

HARLAN JEFFRIES ANSWERED on the third ring.

"H?"

"Yeah."

"'Tis me. Shaun."

"How are you? I didn't recognize this number. What's going on?"

"Long story. Are you going to be home tomorrow night?" asked Shaun, glancing at the newscaster now muted in front of a large weather map.

"Sure."

"I need a favor. Can you meet me?"

"Of course. You know that. Anything," replied Harlan.

Shaun explained an abbreviated version of the Zip-Net issue and asked for his help in checking out Abigail's family home in Clarksdale.

"Where are you right now?" asked Harlan.

"At my house in Tyson's Corner. We'll be in Mississippi tomorrow night. It'll be late."

"No problem. But that's a long drive for one day. Have you seen the weather report?"

Shaun focused on the television to see computerized bolts of lightning and clouds covering the southeastern half of the map. "Yeah. It's on right now."

"Tomorrow is going to be ugly. Be careful, and call me when you know what time you'll be getting in. You're welcome to stay with us here in Starkville. Gina'd be glad to see you. We'll put you up."

"Thank you but no. I've got…problems. I won't bring them to your house."

"Shaun? After everything you did for Gina, Adam and me? Spiriting us out of Texas and letting us stay at your house when everyone and their dog was looking for us? You know we're here if you need anything."

Harlan was a friend who really cared and understood. One of the only people in his life who knew about the fiasco in Iraq with Gregor and Storm's Edge. Excepting Harlan, Shaun had acquaintances only. And there were parts of himself that he'd buried so deeply, he'd forgotten. Forgotten what it felt like to have a friend who knew all the dark places inside and still reached out.

"Right. I know. I just…I'll meet you. It'll probably be very late when I call, H."

"S'okay. Gina's not sleeping anyway. Baby's due any day now—she hasn't been able to get comfortable. I'll talk to you tomorrow."

Shaun hung up. Encouraged for the first time in a long time. Maybe, just maybe, this was going to be okay.

Chapter Thirteen

Day Two—Evening

Abby sat in the passenger seat trying to get comfortable. They'd been on the road for ten hours now and she needed to stop and stretch her legs. It had started raining cats and dogs as Shaun was changing a flat outside Blacksburg, Virginia. They'd been making horrible time ever since.

Clarksdale was still at least ten hours away, even if Shaun drove like a bat out of hell, which he wouldn't do because of the slick road conditions. They should probably just stop. She'd slept horribly the night before—staring at the ceiling after being woken every two hours by Shaun, then waiting for him to come back and do it again. To top if off, this day seemed never ending. She vacillated between fury and mortification.

In retrospect, asking him to take her to bed because she wanted to forget had been a wretched idea and not very flattering to either of them. She was overwhelmingly relieved that he'd turned her down—unable to imagine this interminable car ride after a pity screw.

Earlier she'd swallowed her anger and attempted conversation but he wasn't in a chatting mood. He'd completely shut her down when she'd asked him again about growing up in Ireland. He didn't want her help with driving, either.

Feeling raw and prickly herself, at the last stop for gas, she'd finally given up and bought a romance novel along with a tiny reading light in the Stop and Shop for something to keep her mind occupied. Still, she couldn't keep from glancing at his hands on the steering wheel as he drove. Remembering how those hands had felt on her neck and shoulders last night, she stole a glance at his legs encased in the dark denim jeans. She shook her head to erase the images that conjured up, choosing instead to bury her head in the book.

At ten-thirty they were pulling into another truck stop with an attached restaurant when she looked up from reading and realized they were no longer on I-40W.

"Where are we?" She turned to him on the seat. "Shouldn't we be headed to Memphis to get to Clarksdale?"

"Yes, but we're taking a detour first."

"Through Alabama?"

"Do you remember when I said if I couldn't keep you safe, all agreements were off in regard to who I asked for help?"

She nodded.

"I think we need someone watching our backs when we go look for the file."

She started to say something but when he turned to her and she saw the expression in his eyes, the protest died on her lips.

"I've got a friend who is going to help us. I can't look for the file and look out for you, too. Harlan and I were together in Iraq. I'd trust him with my life. He's trusted me with his and with his family's safety in the past. Harlan's going to come and help us when we go to Clarksdale."

"Why didn't you tell me about this earlier?" she asked.

"I didn't want to argue and I was worried you wouldn't like it."

"You're right, I don't like it."

"Abigail, my job has always depended on my understanding and accepting my own strengths and weaknesses. I can't protect you and do what has to be done if someone is following us. I don't know what is going on here with Therese Mattagon's and your brother's murders but it's obvious people are after you now. You need to understand and accept the implications of that."

She listened to the steady *swish swish* of the windshield wipers even though they were parked in front of the restaurant.

"I'm not going to argue with you, Shaun. I don't even know what town I'm in. I've nothing to my name here but a duffle bag of clothes that you bought for me at Walmart. I may be hardheaded but I'm not a fool."

"You're taking this better than I expected."

She shook her head. "Not really. I'm frustrated that you didn't trust me enough to tell me earlier. That's the reason I don't like this, but I do understand why you want help."

The wipers continued to beat against the windshield.

"Where does your friend live?" she asked.

"Starkville. The plan was to meet him there tonight and go on tomorrow to Clarksdale. But we've made bad time today with the weather. There's no way we'll get there before two or three a.m."

For the first time since she'd met him, he sounded tired. There was no way he'd slept last night, either. While she'd been struggling to fall back asleep after he'd woken her every two hours, she suspected he'd stayed up long after— watching over her. Plus he'd driven the entire way today in this unrelenting rain. As tired as she was, he had to be completely wiped. He wouldn't stop for himself, but she knew he'd do it for her. And she had a good idea of how to make that happen.

"I'm exhausted. Can we stop for the night here? Would your friend be okay with meeting us tomorrow in Clarksdale instead?"

He was staring straight ahead at an old phone booth in front of their car before he turned to her, pinning her with his gaze. She didn't back down.

He had to get some sleep and if convincing him that she needed to rest was the only way to make him stop, then so be it. She was still irritated at him for not telling her about his plan sooner, but she wasn't rash and it would be dangerous for him to keep driving as worn out as he was.

"How's your head?" His arm was stretched along the back of the seat and his fingertips brushed her shoulder. She struggled not to startle. His touch surprised her. So much so that she didn't think before answering.

"A little achy, that's all." She wasn't lying, she didn't feel bad, but she was weary. Did he know she was asking for him, more than for herself? It didn't matter as long as he agreed.

He rubbed her shoulder absently, his mind obviously somewhere else as he stared at the phone booth. "Okay. I'm beat, too. We'll find a hotel. But let's eat first."

THEY DASHED THROUGH THE RAIN together huddled under an umbrella that provided less than adequate protection. "It's a monsoon!" Abigail grabbed his arm for balance as they slipped and slid through the restaurant door, their shoes making squishy noises on the linoleum floor.

Shaun shook his head and droplets of water flew. "My Gran would have called this little sprinkle a 'soft old night' back home." He smiled faintly at the memory of his late grandmother as Abigail tried to brush the water from her clothing and shoes.

"Soft old night? It's raining like mad out there." But she was laughing as she said it.

He shrugged, returning a grin. "We're a hardy lot."

"Indeed." She made a beeline for the restroom. "I guess us Southern girls melt in this kind of precipitation. I'm hoping they have one of those auto hand dryers for my tennis shoes. I stepped in a huge puddle. Back in a minute," she called over her shoulder.

He waited till she was around the corner and felt his own smile fade. Did he have enough time to make a phone call to Donner? He looked down at his wet clothes.

It wouldn't be noticeable if he got any wetter. Besides this was going to be a short conversation. He didn't trust his boss. Donner had too many gadgets and tracking abilities at his command. Even though Shaun wasn't going to talk long enough to let him trace their location, Donner would still want to hear something. And Shaun still had to play along as if he was keeping Donner in the loop. If Shaun didn't call, Donner would get antsy. And an ansty Donner was not a good thing. The man tended to act impulsively.

He opened the umbrella and jogged back outside to the dilapidated phone booth, hoping the phone was still operational. The glass door was cracked and the dial tone was fuzzy but the phone itself worked and the roof wasn't leaking. All good signs.

Donner answered on the first ring. "Where in God's name are you?" he demanded in lieu of a greeting.

"On the road. In the rain. Somewhere between D.C. and Florida." Did Donner know he was lying? Shaun had no way of being sure.

"Where you headed?"

"She's not telling me. Just giving me directions as we

go. I'll keep you posted, but I wanted to check in. What's up with the police? Any word about the fire or the woman who died there—Therese Mattagon?"

"You and Abby Trevor are wanted for questioning about the fire."

"I know. I saw the news report last night before we left town. Who was that woman? She cornered Abigail in the bathroom at the hotel restaurant before we went to Jason's condo. I didn't find out till later."

Donner uttered a foul expletive. "She worked R & D for our competition. According to our preliminary research her background was quite similar to Jason's."

"Dig deeper," urged Shaun. "She carried a gun. I'd venture to say at least part of her background was quite different from Jason Trevor's. Find who hired her and you may find who killed your engineer." Shaun checked his watch and looked at the large plate glass restaurant window.

Was Abigail back from the restroom yet? It was time to hang up.

Donner was talking again. "Possibly. Or we may just find someone else trying to sink us. I'll check with my contacts."

"I've got to go. Remember, I told Abigail I wouldn't talk to you. This may be hard for you to believe, but she doesn't trust you."

"Hmm. Sounds like this could be interesting. Keep in touch."

"I've got to go, Donner."

"I know that but you just remember. I hired you to do a job. You're my 'fixer' and I expect you to deliver, no matter what."

"Right. I'm on it."

Chapter Fourteen

Shaun hung up the phone with a sick feeling in the pit of his stomach. How long had he been on the call? Could they have traced it? He didn't think so, but Donner had all kinds of new prototypes and products that weren't on the market yet. Good thing he'd disconnected the car's GPS.

Sprinting through the rain, he slid into a booth just as Abigail stepped out of the ladies' room. He couldn't look her in the eye. He knew he was screwing up by not telling her about Donner but he was too far down that road to admit it. Even though he wasn't telling Michael where they were, lying to Abigail was eating him up. When had that happened? Why couldn't he just tell her about talking to Donner?

The woman who brought their food was a talker and when Abigail asked if there were any bed-and-breakfasts or hotels in town, the waitress gave them the rundown and three phone numbers. The first two places were full thanks to some kind of local festival that was going on but with the third call, they got lucky. A last-minute cancellation due to the weather…but one room only.

Abigail put her hand over the cell phone and raised an eyebrow. "You okay with that?"

"Yeah. I'm so tired, I'm going to pass out once my head hits the pillow."

She moved her hand. "We'll take it."

He stared at her as she disconnected the call.

"What?"

"You sure you're okay with sharing a room?" he asked.

"Why wouldn't I be? Last night I asked you to sleep with me, didn't I?" Her eyes never left his. "You don't snore, do you?"

It took him a moment to realize she was joking. He forced himself not to look away as he answered. "No. I've never been told I snore." He didn't add that might be because he rarely stayed with a woman long enough after they'd had sex for her to know if he snored or not.

"Great. Me neither. We'll be fine." She turned away to gather her purse, never acknowledging the gauntlet thrown down between them.

He swallowed hard. Last night it had taken all of his self-restraint to let her walk away after she'd asked him to make love with her. He wasn't going to kid himself that he could do that again.

Sitting beside her today in the car he'd been hyperaware of every movement, every sound she'd made. It had made him positively surly. Being so close to what he knew he shouldn't touch. Not talking to her hadn't helped as much as he would have thought.

The last thing he'd meant to do was be rude, but she'd kept asking questions, and then he couldn't seem to stop himself from snapping at her. What was it about this woman?

Before he had met Abigail, he'd always been able to stay in control, to bite his tongue if necessary and use his charm to get what he needed from people—to see the job done. But that ability to stay cool and unaffected seemed to have deserted him. A couple of hours ago she'd gotten so mad at him, she'd finally quit trying to talk and started to read; at least he'd been able to breathe a little easier.

But then he caught himself rubbing her shoulder when they stopped in front of this restaurant. It was a completely unconscious move. He was shocked at how easy it was to reach for her. He no longer trusted himself where she was concerned.

There better be a sofa in the room or he was going up in flames. No way could he sleep in the same bed with her and not touch her.

ABBY SURVEYED THE VICTORIAN bed-and-breakfast, complete with a porch swing. The innkeeper checking them in looked like a grandmother from a Norman Rockwell print. The living room was filled with doilies, lace and two couples having drinks watching a big screen TV. She wished she could enjoy this—the wood burning fireplace, the lovely oak paneling, the ambiance.

Normally she loved B and Bs but for all her nonchalance, she didn't want to share a room with Shaun. She reached for her duffle bag and his hand closed over hers at the same time. She jumped and almost yelped as she yanked her hand away.

He made her extremely nervous. Correction. She made herself nervous around him.

Why was she freaking out over the idea of sharing a room with him? It was crazy. He so obviously felt nothing toward her but "obligation." Of course, that thought was depressing as hell.

She tried to focus on the lovely surroundings while Shaun carried both bags up the large staircase to their sumptuously furnished room. Located at the end of a long hall, the Hawthorne Suite had a private bath with a tremendous claw-footed tub and shower combo containing exotic toiletries, plush towels and sweet-smelling candles. Noth-

ing would feel as good as a long soak in that tub—after
Shaun was dead asleep.

The bedroom itself held a cozy sitting area with a love
seat, coffee table and overstuffed chair along with an antique armoire. There were luscious draperies covering the
windows and a bed…the size of a postage stamp.

Actually it was a double. She desperately wished it was
a queen or better yet a king, so there'd be no chance of her
touching him accidentally in the night. She might sponta-
neously combust.

He shut the door and suddenly she was acutely aware
of everything about him. How he filled the room. How his
stillness made her conscious of every movement she made.
As she watched, he seemed to unwind a bit. It struck her
that in addition to everything else, he had been on hyper-
alert the entire day. Perhaps now he could relax, too.

Surely they were safe here. They'd paid in cash and he'd
used a different name on the registry. It sounded like he
might be going to sleep immediately. She sincerely hoped
so.

"Do you want to grab a shower first?" she asked. "I'd
like to take a long soak in that tub. I'm happy to wait."

He looked up from the small love seat he was staring
at. His eyes were unreadable. "Sure, I'll be quick and you
can soak away."

"That way you can go ahead and get to sleep. I don't
want to keep you up."

"Right." He hustled into the bathroom, shutting the
door rather firmly and thirty seconds later she heard water
running.

As she unpacked her meager belongings, there was a
knock on the door. It was the grandmotherly innkeeper
with a carafe, a plate of fruit and chocolate.

"I brought you two some wine, a Shiraz. It's compli-

mentary on check-in. After your long drive, I didn't know
if you'd be coming down or not."

"Thank you, this is lovely," said Abby. "We appreciate
it."

"You're welcome. I also wanted to let you know I just
heard the weather report. It's going to get nasty tonight.
Terrible thunderstorms and such. If we lose power, there
are matches in that bedside table and you see the candles
all around, of course." She pointed to various pillars and
tapers throughout the room.

"Yes, thank you."

The elderly woman nodded. "Nothing like a booming
thunderstorm for good sleeping. See you in the morning."

They'd made the right call in stopping. Driving in this
weather would have been terrible. But no electricity, just
candlelight? That would *not* calm her nerves.

She poured herself some wine. She could only hope
Shaun was asleep before the lights went out.

The shower shut off and she gulped a large sip of the
Shiraz before refilling her glass. On second thought, stopping here had been a terrible idea. Surely they could have
driven farther.

Five minutes later Shaun stepped out in black knit bas-
ketball shorts and a tight fitting T-shirt. She struggled not
to stare. How could she have ever thought this man was a
software engineer?

He was so obviously...fit. His shoulders and thighs
were huge. He looked bigger standing here in the romantic bedroom than he had anywhere else before now. She
stuttered, explaining about the storm and the wine before
finally escaping into the bathroom with her own full glass.
The wind was moaning like a woman in labor when she
emerged twenty-five minutes later and found him under
the covers, his eyes closed. She wasn't sure he was really

asleep but she was grateful he was pretending to be even if he wasn't.

The lights flickered once when she was in the tub and she had a feeling the electricity wasn't going to last much longer. Thunder crackled and her nerves zinged in time with each lightning flash. Putting off the inevitable, she poured the last of the wine, filling her glass again to the top. She noticed he'd had some, too, and she grabbed a chocolate as well, not caring that she'd brushed her teeth moments ago. She needed the comfort as well as the liquid courage before climbing into a bed that now appeared to be the size of a pool float.

Her Walmart pj's consisted of a cotton camisole and shorts and left her feeling overexposed. She hadn't been expecting to attend a pajama party when she'd selected them. Last night she'd been shopping for comfortable not concealing. But if she'd known about this, she'd have gone for the flannel granny gown.

To hell with Karen and her comment about "panty-melting" Irishmen. With what she *didn't* have on here, there was too much opportunity to bump into Shaun and all his lovely skin on that mattress that appeared to be shrinking by the second. Just thinking about it made her sweat.

She could blame the overheated feeling on the bathwater having been too warm, but she wasn't going to lie to herself. Ever since she'd kissed him in D.C., she'd been trying to avoid thinking about what it'd be like to sleep with Shaun. This was not exactly what she'd imagined. Still, crawling into bed with him was unavoidable at this point.

Taking another cleansing breath and a deeper sip of the wine, she turned toward the bed with the chocolate in her mouth. Thunder and lightning crashed together, shaking the windows. The lights flickered once…twice and went out for good.

"Well, hell," she muttered around the chocolate. "That's just perfect."

Chapter Fifteen

Immediately Shaun was up and moving, drawn toward her like a magnet. He'd done the best he could to give her some privacy when she came out of the bathroom, keeping his eyes closed and pretending to sleep even though he'd peeked just a little when she was roaming about the room. That hadn't been one of his better ideas.

Her barely there pajama shorts and top were now forever emblazoned on his brain along with her silky smooth legs. He'd been fantasizing about her body all day while she'd ridden beside him in that car. Now he didn't have to imagine anymore. To have her uncovered and exposed like this was a combination of torture and delight.

"You okay?" He walked toward her in the darkness.

"I'm fine. I…I can't see anything though. It's so dark."

"Right, just stand still. Your eyes will adjust in a few seconds." He was several feet from her at the end of the bed.

"I'm not scared but I am holding a very full glass of red wine and I'm going to spill it all over myself and the floor if I try to move." There was a tremor in her voice.

"Then don't." He was beside her now, gently touching her shoulder. He told himself that was to orient his body in the darkness but it was a lie. He wanted the excuse to touch her. Her skin was just as soft as he remembered from the neck rub and the night before. It took an effort not to stroke his hand across her back.

"Wine, we can take care of. Want to share?" he asked.

"That I can manage." Her arm accidentally brushed against his but he remained completely still.

Slowly he took the glass and drank deeply. Rain pelted the window with the curtains drawn loosely against the storm. He felt her straining to see him through the darkness. She was standing so close. Her body, still warm from the shower, threw off heat and smelled like flowers and chocolate. His own body responded and he took another sip of the Shiraz before wrapping her fingers around the goblet's crystal stem.

"Your turn." He moved his palm to her waist to steady her and heard a sharp intake of breath. He visualized her hands wrapped around him and worked not to tense his grip on her.

Lightning flashed outside and he caught a glimpse of her standing before him. Her head tilted back as she sipped the wine. So close. If they'd been lovers he would have leaned forward and kissed the hollow in her neck and worked his way downward from there.

"Were you asleep?" she asked.

"Not yet."

"All that thunder, I guess I'm not surprised." She took another sip. "Just a 'soft old night,' no?"

He could tell from her voice that she was smiling.

"Indeed. Some would call it that," he murmured. The moment stretched out. The sound of the rain surrounded them.

"I'm not sure I can drink all this," she finally said.

"That's because you're not sharing."

"You're right." She held out the crystal goblet and his fingers wrapped around hers again.

He didn't take the glass from her this time, instead he took her hand, still holding the goblet, to his mouth. He was torturing himself but he didn't care. He wanted her and this way he could look at her in the darkness and not have to hide what he was feeling.

He kept hold of her waist. If he took one more step, she'd be in his arms. Outside lightning slashed across the sky and thunder roared, shaking the windows again.

She shivered. He tightened his grip ever so slightly without pulling her to him.

"It's okay. You're safe here," he murmured.

He needed to stop touching her. But then she put her hand on his shoulder, steadying herself in the dark, drawing herself in.

Surprised he wasn't burning her with his stare, he drained the wine glass and reached around her to put it on the table behind them. Her breasts brushed his chest. An electric hum charged the air that had nothing to do with the storm outside.

"Do you want to go to sleep now?" he asked.

She didn't answer and for a moment he thought he'd finally spooked her. Then she rested her head on his chest and he was lost.

"No, that's not what I want." She tilted her head up and part of him wished for the lights to see her while the other part was grateful it was dark because he knew this wouldn't be happening if the lights were on. Darkness was making her braver than she would have been otherwise. What she would have seen in his face right now would have frightened both of them.

"I want you to take me to bed." Her words, spoken barely above a whisper, shocked him.

For a split second he wasn't sure he'd heard her correctly. Then she kissed the side of his neck and he didn't need any more encouragement as he ran a hand under her camisole, up her back and his other hand down her hip, pulling her into him so there was no doubt that he was completely on board with her idea.

"You're sure?" he asked.

She nodded and put her palms on his cheeks before pulling his face down to hers.

"Yes."

He kissed her then, tasting the Shiraz and chocolate on her tongue. She melted into him as he slid both his hands under the elastic of her pajama shorts and pulled her completely against his erection. Kissing his way down her neck and chest like he'd imagined earlier, he walked her backward toward the bed, his hands on her soft curvy ass.

When the mattress hit the back of her thighs, she landed on silky sheets and he caught himself before falling on top of her. She started to giggle and they both ended up laughing as they untangled themselves. Then she was helping him out of his shirt and his shorts while he pulled off her top and those barely there shorts he'd never gotten a real good look at.

His night vision was shot to hell with the flashes of lightning followed by pitch black, but he didn't need it as he forgot himself in her. She had her hands on the hard length of him and she was nipping at his lower lip. She began moving down his body in the dark. Tasting and touching him everywhere. "Abigail, what are you doing to me?" he murmured.

"Do I need to explain?" she asked and once more he could hear the smile in her voice.

The laugh rumbled in his chest. "No, it's just...you make

me forget…" But that wasn't it. She made him *hope* for the first time in such a long time. How had she done that?

She lay her head on his thigh waiting for him to finish the thought.

"That's a good thing, right?" She was touching him again and he was definitely losing his train of thought.

"Right…it's all good." He quit talking and put his hands in her hair as she took him away. Outside the rain fell and the thunder crashed but he no longer cared. It was just this room, this woman and the darkness.

ABBY WOKE WRAPPED IN SHAUN'S arms with her face tucked against his shoulder. Thunder rumbled in the distance and rain beat against the roof, though not as ferociously as it had earlier. She wasn't sure how long she'd slept but the lights were back on and the digital clock on the bedside table was blinking red at 12:00 a.m. Could be 2:00 a.m., could be 6:00 a.m. She had no idea. She started to raise her head but realized she would wake Shaun when she moved.

How had she ended up here? The last time she'd woken up in bed with a man had been over a year ago in Rome. She'd been leaving within a month, so the Italian history professor had been safe.

She looked down at the body of the man she was sprawled across. The sheet was bunched at his hips and she took the opportunity to study him like she hadn't been able to the night before.

Shaun was many things. But *safe* was not the first word that sprang to mind. His shoulders were impossibly broad and he had an intricate Celtic cross tattooed on his left biceps. The circular portion of the design was so detailed, it almost looked three dimensional even though everything was in black ink. Truly a work of art.

A wicked-looking star-shaped scar was at his waist. She leaned forward, ever so slightly. Was that a gunshot wound?

She stared at the uneven skin tone—obviously a severe injury—and wondered what had happened to him. She noted other marks, too. A jagged line ran along his shoulder and another mottled spot marked his collarbone. Aside from references to his grandmother, he'd avoided mentioning his past life, except that one veiled reference at dinner the first night and needing more wine to discuss it.

His words hadn't indicated an idyllic childhood. He'd only told her what he did now for Donner, and that he'd done the "same type" of work in the past, but these marks indicated something more than fixing DUI arrests and paying off mistresses.

Like perhaps a war wound? She examined the tattoo again and gently traced the scar at his side, re-evaluating what precious little he'd told her about himself.

He certainly hadn't minded her touching him there or anywhere else last night. Abby wasn't shy about her sexuality, still, Shaun was overwhelming in his intensity, plus he could switch it on and off with such control. The passion had seemingly come from out of nowhere. He'd turned her down cold at his home in Virginia and ignored her all day long in the car.

She'd have thought he was completely unaffected by her, even after their episode in the hotel suite, up until he inhaled her last night. She hadn't been able to read him beyond the overt physical reactions because it was dark. Then she hadn't cared anymore, staggered as she was by the power and desire he exerted—whispering to her in what she assumed was Gaelic while he made love to her with such ferocity.

But now she wondered. Before, he'd been so very private

with her. So closed and cool except for that one remark about his Gran and the weather. Charming, of course, but he could turn that charm on and off like a faucet—just like he could his physical reactions to her. And she was all too familiar with the secrets charm could hide. So far, he hadn't been willing to share anything of himself except his body.

That she understood. Failed relationships were her forte and she always made sure she had her own getaway built in. Her Italian history professor last year was a case in point.

She'd known all along she was coming back to the U.S. within six months so she'd had a natural escape hatch with her job assignment. Any relationship she started there couldn't be anything more than a short-term fling. In the end the professor had wanted her to consider staying in Europe but she'd refused. He'd been hurt, but she'd been unmoved.

She'd read enough to know her mother and father's horrific choices had a great deal to do with her approach to intimate relationships. But there came a point when you couldn't blame your parents or your past anymore for your present failures. She still couldn't figure out how she'd ended up making love with Shaun last night but she wasn't going to panic. This could still work.

He was protecting her until the threat was over, so it was only short-term. The trust issue here wasn't about anything intimate between them, even though the stakes were quite grave. The trust was about something much more basic. She just needed to quit thinking and she'd be fine.

She looked across his perfectly sculpted chest and decided she'd worry about her escape route later. Tiny crinkle lines were at the outer corners of his eyes and deeper laugh lines bracketed his mouth. She put her hand up to touch the faint scar under his chin. The one she'd noticed that first day in the limo when he'd been on top of her. She was bolder now that she'd been studying him for a while.

His mouth turned up at the corners and she drew back. "See anything you like?" he whispered, his voice wrapping around her like a warm blanket.

"You're awake."

He opened his eyes and grinned.

"Why didn't you say something?" she asked.

He sat up on an elbow and deliberately looked her up and down, scorching her with his Caribbean blue-green gaze. She pulled the sheet closer and willed herself not to scoot away in the bed.

"You seemed to be a lot more comfortable thinking I was asleep." He moved closer, reaching for her and leaving no doubt as to what he had in mind. "I assure you, I'm not sleeping."

"So I, um—" she laughed, her eyes darting downward for a moment "—see."

She went into his arms willingly. Unsure as to why she felt shy after last night except that she was thinking again and it was no longer dark.

He held her loosely in his arms. "You okay with this?"

Her head was once more against his chest—his heart-beat loud in her ear, the sound of it resonating in her own body, even over the rain. "I think so. Dunno, honestly. This is all happening so fast."

He pressed a kiss to the top of her head and pulled away from her slightly. "So…we'll slow it down a bit."

"Don't." She pulled back as well, propping herself up to stare into his face. "That's definitely not what I want." She levered herself on top of him and felt what was undeniably a sign that he did not want her stopping.

Then his hands were on her butt and she was kissing his

neck and working her way across his chest to a flat rounded nipple. She circled it with her tongue and heard his sharp hiss of breath when she nibbled at it with her teeth. "This is what I want," she said.

"Abigail…"

His voice was lost in the sounds of the storm outside.

"Shh…" she murmured. "I never thought I'd say this because I love to hear your accent but sometimes you talk too much."

He laughed and said nothing more as the storm played itself out.

Chapter Sixteen

Day Three—Late Morning

Shaun shut Abigail's car door with more force than necessary and made his way to the driver's side. If he could, he'd have kicked himself to the vehicle. How had he allowed this to happen?

Sleeping with her had been a huge mistake—an awesome, earthshaking, rock-his-world mistake he'd like to repeat as soon as possible.

He'd never had morning-after regrets, not because he hadn't slept around but because he'd always been careful about who he slept with. He avoided women he could see himself with beyond the short-term. His job and lifestyle were not conducive to long-term commitment.

That had all changed this morning when he woke up fantasizing about a life with Abigail after this was over. He had pillow shock for a completely different reason than the typical reaction to a one-night stand. Because when he'd been lying there, running his hand along Abigail's waist, still half-asleep, he'd started thinking maybe they could have a future together.

Maybe she'd want to be with him.

Maybe this relationship could be different.

Then he'd turned his head, spied his gun on the bedside table and reality had bitch slapped him in the face.

Abigail didn't want him. She needed his protection until this was over. Then she'd be gone. Especially when she discovered that he'd been talking to Donner since that first night, after she'd made him promise not to. He couldn't forget he had started this whole relationship based on lies. That wasn't likely to go over well when she found out.

Indeed. He was screwed—in every sense of the word.

So for now he had to get back to business.

He slammed his own door and the rich aroma of the B and B's gourmet ground coffee surrounded him. The innkeeper had fortified them with a hearty breakfast and "to go" cups before they'd checked out. He took a scorching sip of the brew to put off facing the inevitable.

Now that he'd slept with Abigail, his objectivity was out the window. There was no unringing that bell. He hadn't said much to her since they'd showered together in that massive claw-footed tub and he assumed she had to be confused since he was confusing the hell out of himself.

That was the problem to be addressed right now. He adjusted his seat belt and shoved his keys into the ignition. He only hoped their night together wouldn't make things awkward when they met the addition to their "field trip."

"Time to head out," he said.

"Yeah?" She turned from the window and smiled cautiously. "How about we go to Mexico instead of Mississippi?" She was a trouper, he'd give her that, trying to lighten his obviously bad mood.

He forced a smile himself. "Not today. But don't forget, we're meeting that friend of mine."

She stopped with her coffee in midsip. "That's right. I'd forgotten. Um…I'm not sure about this, Shaun. It makes me nervous."

He cleared his throat. "I understand your concern but believe me, you can trust him."

"No, *I* can't. *I* don't know him."

"Abigail, don't do this."

"Do what? Argue? Tell you the truth? Tell you how I feel about this, even though you're obviously holding things back from me and slamming doors and skulking about like a child?"

"No, just don't make this harder than it has to be."

She didn't answer but simply glared as they sat, still parked in front of the bed-and-breakfast.

"Do you trust me?" he asked.

"I don't know. You're making it difficult."

He laughed. "That's the smartest thing you've said to date. I'm not a safe bet."

"Yes, but I've already placed my bet, haven't I?" She didn't say it but the unspoken words were: *I did that last night.*

"Besides, it's more about trust right now than anything. It'd be easier for me to say I love you than I trust you," she continued.

He felt his face form a mask of disbelief. Then she laughed, but there was a trace of underlying bitterness in the sound.

"Don't worry, that's not what I'm saying," she explained. "I've always had a difficult time with trust. My parents said they'd love my brother and me no matter what. Unconditionally. But they didn't. When Jason told them that he was gay, they cut him out of their lives irrevocably. After all this time, I still can't believe they lied to us." She shook her head. "I've slept with you. That's as close to trust as I can give you."

He stared at her a moment. She'd told him about her parents at dinner two nights earlier and he'd known they'd left her with trust issues, but he hadn't realized they ran this deep. He'd made a serious miscalculation lying to her about his phone calls to Donner but he couldn't let her know. So he turned on the charm and smiled instead. "All right, Abigail, but please, don't sleep with Harlan. His wife wouldn't like it."

When she laughed, he heard the edge to it. He started the car and backed out of the B and B—a sense of dread spreading through his body. He got out of town and onto the highway as quickly as possible.

Could he tell her the truth now?

He glanced at her, trying to figure out how to start the conversation.

She was settling into the seat, tucking her legs underneath her butt. Her eyes were closed and she'd leaned back against the headrest. She was probably five minutes from being asleep.

He could do this. But how to explain?

He just had to say it:

I've been talking to Donner. I knew he would suspect we were up to something if I didn't stay in contact and I was worried he would send people after us to track us. This way we've stayed out in front of him.

That sounded reasonable. Hopefully it would work. At least it was a start. He considered pulling over but decided a high rate of speed was a better plan. She'd have to at least sit and listen to his whole explanation even if she was angry. He glanced her way, opened his mouth to speak and her phone started ringing.

Her eyes flew open and she fumbled in her bag to answer. "Karen? Hey, how you doing? Everything okay? No…no, calm down, I'm fine."

He tried to ignore the sense of relief he felt at having been spared his confession for the time being.

"Right. Well, no, I'm not in D.C. right now. We're going to my family's house. Yes, with him. It's…complicated. I'm okay. Please don't worry. I'm in good hands. No, I wouldn't go quite that far. Hmm…details, right."

Was she talking about him? He got a weird feeling in his gut as he listened to the one-sided conversation. His earlier relief was short-lived.

"Wait, Karen. Slow down. Who was there? What kind of questions were they asking?"

He sat up in his seat.

"Okay…no, you did exactly the right thing." She put her hand over the receiver to explain. "Someone's been at the facility asking questions about me and you." She went back to the phone conversation.

His mind raced. Someone had made contact and was asking Karen questions? It could have been Therese Mattagon's people or Donner's. Either way it was bad news.

"You know that's always been my biggest issue but I do believe he's…um…trustworthy in this sense."

He glanced at her phone and the uneasy feeling multiplied exponentially. She'd used Donner's phone in that hotel suite. His boss had practically insisted. That meant Donner could be using some new voice recognition software to keep a bead on Abigail, too. It didn't prove he was dirty, although that was most likely the case. At this point, there was no time to waste if they wanted to stay off his radar. If her cell phone was already on the grid, they'd be watching for any incoming or outgoing calls. Donner could be tracking as well as tapping her line through this call. The reason didn't matter.

He knew what he had to do. The one upside was even if he was wrong about the line tapping, he could solve multiple problems at once. Unfortunately, there was no time for explanations or charm. He reached for her cell phone, his hand closing over her fingers and the speaker. "Finish it now. I think that call can be traced."

Her eyes grew wide. "Karen, I've got to go. I'll get in touch when I can. Don't worry about me and don't call me back. I'll—"

He punched End.

"—call you." Her voice trailed off, her eyes wide with hurt and uncertainty. "Why did you do that? Karen will worry about me now."

"Why? Because every second you spent on the phone was time someone could have been tapping your line, knowing exactly what was being said, as well as tracing our precise location."

It took a moment for the implication to register. Her mouth opened in an understanding *oh*.

"Do we have any idea who was questioning Karen?" he asked.

She shook her head. "They showed up last night wanting to know if she'd heard from me. Asking if she knew you."

"What did she say?"

"She played dumb. Told them she'd talked to me the day of the funeral but that was all. Said she had no idea who you were. Do you really think Donner is tracing or tapping calls?"

He shrugged. "I don't know, honestly. I believe he's capable of it from a technical standpoint. If he is, it might just be because he can't stand to not know where we are and what we're doing. You met him, I'm sure you could tell that he doesn't like being left out of the show."

"And if you believe that…" She rolled her eyes and he glanced down at her phone, coming to a decision. If he hadn't been so worried for her, he would have been kinder.

"No more incoming or outgoing calls." Keeping his eyes on the road, he rolled down the window, slipped the battery off and tossed the lithium ion wafer.

He handed her the useless phone and she exploded. "Why did you do that?"

"No more temptation."

"I wouldn't have called anyone! All you had to do was trust me to turn it off."

He hesitated a moment before glancing her way and answering. "You just got through telling me that you weren't sure you trusted me. I can't take the risk right now."

The anger in her eyes told him that he'd solved more than one problem. She was cut off from everyone and everything she knew with the added bonus of being completely furious with him. She'd never let him close enough to get in her bed again.

Mission accomplished.

She was safe on all fronts. So why did he feel like a failure?

THE RAIN DID LITTLE to cool Abby's anger as they ran into the Burger King on Highway 61 in Clarksdale. Shaun had stopped at a pay phone and arranged to meet his friend there. He wasn't making any more calls on his cell, either. He had turned his off after tossing her battery out the car window. He and Abby had barely spoken in the six hours since. It was like last night had never happened. She knew she was going to have to be a lot more Zen about the situation but she wasn't there yet.

Still, her mother would have been proud of her manners as Shaun introduced her to Harlan Jeffries. She was polite and they grabbed a bite to eat while she got her first look at the man Shaun had called to help them.

He was huge, obviously from working out. He was taller

than Shaun and had a fishhook scar above his eyebrow that made him almost scary looking because of his size. He was wearing all black, including a baseball cap, and he would have appeared downright menacing if she hadn't seen the hat's embroidered multicolored ribbon divided into puzzle pieces with the stitched logo that read I love someone with Autism. It was difficult to be intimidated by him when he was wearing that cap.

Shaun asked after his wife, Gina, and their adopted son, Adam. When Harlan Jeffries smiled, she wondered why she'd ever thought the man scary at all. She ate her food trying not to be charmed by him and the familiar comfort of his Southern boy manners.

She excused herself to the ladies' room and when she returned they were deep in conversation. She didn't mean to eavesdrop but Harlan's words stopped her in her tracks.

"Did you ever have to testify?" he asked.

Shaun shook his head. "No. Gregor got himself killed before it ever went to trial."

"Well. That was good of him. The one decent thing he did," said Harlan.

Shaun stared at his unfinished burger. "Small favors, I suppose." He looked up and saw Abby standing there. She wasn't sure what she'd just heard but she knew it hadn't been intended for her ears.

"I'm sorry," she said. "I didn't mean to—" The words stuck in her throat. That wasn't true. Of course she'd meant to. She was desperate to know what Shaun was about.

Harlan glanced up at her but his eyes were kind. "Think I'll grab a refill and give Gina a call before we leave."

Harlan left Abby standing there and she watched him walk toward the counter. Sounds of the restaurant echoed around her. Children laughed. A baby cried. Workers bustled about behind the counter among various bells and timers going off.

She stared after Harlan a moment longer, tying to figure out how she'd ended up here alone with Shaun again. He so obviously didn't want to talk with her about this.

"I'm sorry—" she repeated.

He held up his hand to stop her from speaking. "You must be wondering. I worked for a civilian company that did security for contractors and troops in Iraq—Storm's Edge."

Abby couldn't prevent the sharp intake of breath. Everyone had heard of Storm's Edge. It had been all over the newspapers when the largest civilian security contractor in the Middle East had declared bankruptcy and ceased its operations overnight.

"I see you're familiar with the company. My boss, one of the founders, raped an Iraqi woman—a girl, really—and then tried to cover it up. It was ugly."

He took a sip of his soda before continuing. "When it happened, I tried to help her. Her parents didn't understand what was going on until it was too late. And that was a nightmare. I'm pretty sure the girl's entire family died in the process. Gregor tried to kill me in Iraq, too. He was back here about to be indicted on some other charges last year when he got himself killed."

"Oh, God," whispered Abby. "I heard about that. He died outside Murphy's Point on the river, didn't he?"

Shaun nodded. "I met Harlan in Iraq. He pulled me from the wreckage of what was apparently an IED explosion. I was on my way to report the rape incident to the military command when my SUV exploded."

He was rubbing his arm now. "I was never sure if it was an actual IED or a bomb in the car itself. Harlan got me to a hospital and—since he was military—to people who didn't fall under my boss's influence. Baghdad is an easy place to get yourself killed if someone wants you dead."

"What did you do?" she asked.

"I survived. Came back to the U.S. to heal." He looked up at her and his eyes broke her heart. He shrugged. "Apparently, a bit of a lost cause, that. Maybe I'm just a little too broken to put back together completely. I started doing private security work. That's how I met Donner."

No longer angry, she was starting to understand his frustration of trying to protect someone and not being able to do it.

"We've got a problem." Harlan hurried to the table, with a cell phone to his ear.

"What is it?" asked Shaun.

"Have y'all looked at the TV news lately?" asked Harlan.

"No," replied Abby.

"Not since the night before last," said Shaun. "The electricity went out at our bed-and-breakfast right after we checked in." He was so smooth, no one would ever guess what they'd done when the lights had gone out. Abby struggled to pull her attention back to the Burger King and the problem at hand.

"Gina tells me that you're both making your debuts in a big way on the national news." He slid into the booth beside Abby so they could be more discreet.

"What? I thought it would just be in the D.C. area," said Abby.

Harlan raised a shoulder. "You've graduated. You're wanted for questioning in the death of Therese Mattagon. Your pictures are being shown and there's a crawl across the bottom of the screen."

"But why? I don't understand," said Abby.

"We were in the condo the woman was pulled out of, so we're suspects," explained Shaun.

"What do we do? Call the police and explain?"

"I wouldn't advise that," said Harlan drily.

"It's almost six o'clock. I think we should head over to your folks' house and have a look before we run out of time and daylight here," said Shaun.

"You mean just ignore this?" asked Abby.

"For now," replied Shaun.

"But we can't take your car anymore," said Harlan. "I'm surprised you haven't been picked up yet in it. Let's take mine."

"Agreed," said Shaun. They grabbed their luggage and put everything in Harlan's Jeep.

Abby's childhood home was palatial by any standard and located about twenty minutes outside of Clarksdale. With Jason, it had been a magical place to grow up. But once her brother was gone, she had felt as if the walls were closing in on her. Today, she tried to remember the happier times without the bitter aftertaste—holidays around the Christmas tree in the living room, family games at the kitchen table, swimming in the backyard with friends from school. It was difficult to separate that ache of missing Jason from the good times they'd had together before he was banished.

The house was built in a Colonial Revival style—two stories, brick, shutters, columns, very spacious. Surrounded by cotton fields, it was set back from the road. The family farming the land had been doing so for years.

Since her parents' accident, the management company maintaining the property had been encouraging her and Jason to put their childhood home on the market. Even in this current economy, the area known as the original *birthplace of the blues* was growing. Year-round, Clarksdale hosted various music and arts festivals and people from all over the world passed through to see blues landmarks.

She and her brother had been putting off selling for various reasons—the biggest being they hadn't wanted to face going through all their parents' personal effects.

"I don't have a key with me to get in. We'll have to call the property management company," said Abby. "Let me get my purse. Their phone number is in my address book. I left in it the Jeep."

Shaun glanced at Harlan. "That won't be necessary," he said.

"Are you going to break in?"

"Technically, no. You're the owner and since you'll be standing right beside me when I open the door, it won't be breaking in. It will simply be getting you into a house that you are locked out of," explained Shaun.

She could see him skirting that gray area that she suspected he operated in a great deal of the time. They were on the front porch and Harlan was commenting on the massive oak trees in the driveway as Shaun knelt on one knee. She ignored them both and glanced at the empty brass mailbox beside the front door.

She wasn't sure exactly where to start looking for Jason's mysterious file. She supposed the kitchen. That was the last place they'd played dominoes together. Before she realized what he'd done, Shaun was swinging the massive front door open. She tried not to gasp but it was impossible.

Everything had been destroyed.

Chapter Seventeen

The house was completely trashed—recently, from the looks of it. Pictures were ripped from the walls, sofas gutted with stuffing and feathers from pillows littering the floor. Subflooring had been wrenched up in a few places as well and this was only in the living room just inside the entry.

Whoever had done this was obviously looking for something. Shaun immediately stepped in front of Abby and Harlan stood with his back to her, both acting as shields and pulling handguns. She hadn't realized either man was armed.

Slowly they made their way toward the back of the house where the destruction became more intense. Tables were overturned, mattresses shredded, even bathroom mirrors shattered. She could only assume whoever had done this had grown more frantic while making their search and coming up empty.

In the kitchen, a stainless faucet had been torn from the granite countertop. Several cabinet fronts had been ripped from the hinges. The destruction was as pointless as it was devastating.

A lifetime of memories was in tatters around them. Her life here may not have been idyllic but this had been her childhood home. Tears burned at the corners of her eyes.

She brushed them away in frustration and headed for the large table in the breakfast nook—the site of the dominoes game.

Deep gouges marred the surface of the burled wood—as if someone had taken a knife to the top in frustration. Her mother had loved this old antique. She'd purchased it at an auction when Abby and Jason were very young. They'd made tents out of it as children and lay on their backs staring at the underside—imagining themselves under the stars and hiding from Indians, in a mountain cave stealing dragon treasure and their favorite fantasy—in a castle living the life of a knight and princess. The tears stung and threatened to overflow as memories swamped her.

She realized she'd never told Shaun about what she'd seen in Jason's email video about being here, and it was past time she did. He and Harlan listened as she explained the particulars of why this table would be significant. Both nodded when she was done.

"But it's bothered me since I first saw the video clip. If Jason only sent the file and key code the morning of his death, how could they be inside the house? He wasn't here that day to hide them himself, and he didn't have time to do anything from long distance. The only places a package could have been delivered to were the mailbox or the front porch with UPS type deliveries. I don't think anything like that came. If the people who did all this found a package, why trash the house?"

She shook her head in defeat—her brother's words running through her head.

You were always so good at imagining things and you always were a helluva domino player. Remember the last time we talked about this?

In a last-ditch effort, she got down on her knees and lay on her back looking at the bottom of the table. Nothing was there but the underside of a ninety-year-old antique with the stamp of the furniture maker on it.

Faulkner Fine Furniture.

Faulkner. Faulkner.

William Faulkner had been the subject of Abby's thesis. Karen had been her college advisor for her thesis…*the last time we talked about this…*

"Oh, God," said Abby. *Karen?*

"What is it?" asked Shaun.

Abby almost banged her head getting out from under the table but she didn't answer. Instead, she sat in one of the dining chairs and stared at the marred top.

Karen had been at her parents' funeral. She'd been sitting at this table afterward talking with Jason. Had they mentioned dominoes? Abby honestly couldn't remember.

She had been too tired, too angry and too sad to focus that particular day. But her brother and Karen had talked and talked and talked about all sorts of things. The good memories he'd had about growing up in this house.

They must have talked dominoes at some point. Abby did remember Jason talking to Karen about lying underneath this table and their silly childhood imaginary stories.

God, she'd been slow.

Could he have sent the information to Karen in Dallas?

Abby only hoped she wasn't too late.

SHAUN TURNED HER TO FACE HIM, a question in his eyes.

"Abigail, what is it?" he asked.

"The upgrade file and key code are in Dallas."

"You sound pretty sure."

"I'm positive." She explained to both men why she thought Jason had mailed everything to Karen.

"There's only one way to know for certain," said Shaun. "Do you have Karen's number memorized?"

She glared, the memory of her tossed battery still raw. "As a matter of fact, I do."

"H, can she use your phone? I'm concerned that ours can be tapped when we make calls."

Harlan raised an eyebrow but handed his cell phone over.

Shaun grimaced. "Okay, yes. Calls from your line can eventually be traced and tapped, as well. But your number isn't on anyone's radar yet, so using it will slow down any tracking considerably."

"Who's doing it?" asked Harlan.

"Jury's still out on that."

"Humpf," groused Abby.

"Put your friend on speaker," suggested Shaun.

Karen answered on the second ring. Abby didn't even get to ask the question before Karen interrupted her. "I've been trying to reach you for a couple of hours. I know you told me not to call but I've gotten some kind of package from Jason. It was mailed the day he died and got held up at the reception desk here because it needed a signature. I have no idea what this is but I definitely think you should have it."

A frisson of excitement and concern danced along Abby's spine. "Karen, does anyone else there know who the package was from?"

"I'm not sure. There's only a return address. No name. The FedEx sat at the desk downstairs for several days then at the nurse's station on the floor here for a few hours. If anyone was curious, I can assume they know *where* it came from but not necessarily from *whom*."

Shaun reached out and muted the phone. "Ask her not

to tell anyone else about it. Tell her that we'll be there as soon as we can but it will probably be tomorrow."

She nodded.

"How long would it take us to drive from here to Dallas?" asked Shaun.

"Seven to nine hours," said Harlan. "Depends on how fast you drive." He paused for a moment. "It'll take you seven." He grinned.

"We'll have to get another car before we can go," said Shaun.

"Take mine," said Harlan

Shaun was shaking his head. "I can't do that."

"Sure you can. What else are you gonna do?" asked Harlan.

"Hey, can you guys argue about this in a minute?" The two men swung back to face her. Abby still had the phone muted but to her ear. "Look, I'm glad to tell her I'm coming, but I can't scare her. She's had a stroke."

"Abigail, what do you think these people would do to Karen for that package?" Shaun asked, pinning her with his intense stare. The truth was frightening to face and she looked away to Harlan who nodded sadly.

"They'd…they'd kill her," she said.

"So scaring her just a little isn't such a bad thing, if it'll keep her safe, is it?"

She shook her head.

Karen was talking, too. "Abby, what's going on? Are you in trouble?"

"No. I'm fine, Karen." Her conscience only zinged her slightly for lying and she told herself it was for Karen's own good. "I'm sorry I can't explain over the phone but I'm coming to see you right now and I'll tell you everything then. I promise."

"Do you have your Irishman with you?"

Abby glanced up at Shaun and felt the blush bloom across her cheekbones. "He's right here."

"Good. Don't you do this by yourself."

"Yes, ma'am. See you in a few hours." She hung up and looked at Shaun and Harlan together. "So, we're going to Dallas."

Shaun nodded. "We are but Harlan's not. We're dropping him at a car rental place on the way."

Harlan cheerfully slapped him on the back. "Hey, buddy, standing right here. Am I suddenly invisible?"

"Not hardly," said Shaun, but he was laughing as he said it.

"How 'bout I come with you? How do you know these guys aren't on their way to Dallas, too?" asked Harlan.

"We don't," replied Shaun. "But you've got a very pregnant wife and I'm not taking you eight hours away from her this close to her due date. Gina would have my head on a stick."

"No, she wouldn't."

Shaun chuckled. "Never underestimate the power of a pregnant, hormonal woman, Harlan. I can't believe you haven't figured that out yet."

"Gina's not that way."

"Maybe not, but I'm still not doing it. I want to be invited to dinner when I come to town," said Shaun.

Abby smiled. "I see you haven't crossed her yet when she's been having a chocolate craving."

Harlan grinned. "Well, hell, any idiot knows not to do that."

"You'd be surprised." She laughed and it felt good.

They were headed for the front door, Harlan in the lead, his hand on the knob.

There was no warning. The front door simply imploded inward. Abby was knocked flat as Harlan flew backward, his head hitting the foyer wall with a hollow sounding thud. Shaun fell on top of her as flames burst from the kitchen behind them. Shaun was sitting up before she realized what had occurred.

Harlan wasn't moving; a trickle of blood oozed from his forehead. Flames raced along the ceiling. It was happening so fast. The air was on fire. This was Jason's condo all over again. A bizarre sense of déjà vu overwhelmed her.

"You okay?" Shaun asked, running his hands down her arms.

She nodded, still shaken, and glanced over at Harlan. "I'm fine. Check on him." Shaun's friend was too still and his arm was twisted at a funny angle.

He nodded and moved to Harlan, looking him over as Abby tried to stand up. "What happened?" she asked, still trying to clear the fog from her head. Everything was so loud.

"I don't know. Gas leak, maybe," yelled Shaun. "We've got to get out of here." He pulled her to her feet, pushing her toward the opening that had been the front door, then turned for Harlan. She struggled over flaming debris around the threshold and looked back. Shaun had Harlan in a fireman's hold, hauling him out behind her.

She'd made it to the first step on the porch when fragments of brick exploded around her. It took a moment to recognize what she was hearing over the sounds of the fire. More shards of brick flew up beside her.

Gunshots!

She looked up but couldn't see anything in the darkness. Her eyes were still adjusting from the light of the fire behind her. She headed back up the steps meeting Shaun along the way.

"Someone's shooting at us!" she shouted.

Chapter Eighteen

Shaun didn't hesitate. Still holding Harlan, he turned and headed back into the inferno. They raced through the living room, dodging flaming debris along the way. Smoke thickened the air. Abby could feel the pressure of it forcing the oxygen from her lungs. She was going to start wheezing any second.

The carnage from the break-in—flipped tables, chairs, lamps, torn books, magazines and pillows—coupled with the destruction from the explosion made it difficult to get past. The electricity was out but orange flames lit the way.

"If they're waiting at the front door, they may be waiting at the back door, too," said Shaun.

"What do we do?" she asked through her coughs. Smoke was growing thicker by the second. She dropped to her knees seeking clearer air, but it was useless. Her eyes burned and watered as her throat began to close.

"Is there a window?" he asked.

No longer wasting oxygen on speaking, she nodded, heading for the floor-to-ceiling casement behind an overturned sofa.

"Get down as you open it," directed Shaun.

Abby nodded again. Using the couch as a shield, she unlocked the window and pushed it open from a squatting position. For a moment, bilious smoke poured forth and the flames gusted toward the night air, seeking more oxygen for fuel. Then she was falling into the Indian Hawthorne bushes and Shaun was right behind her, lowering Harlan's body into the branches. They lay in the landscaping for a moment, gulping clean air and waiting to see if more gunshots were forthcoming.

She was sweating and heard a slight whistling in her own breathing. Willing the imminent asthma attack to hold off, she crawled forward as Shaun pulled Harlan along under cover of darkness. Seconds later they were in another clump of bushes fifteen yards away watching two men silhouetted in the flames. A third joined them and together the three circled the house, walking toward the back. Shaun had been right.

"We need Harlan's keys," he whispered. "They're in one of his pockets. Find them and we can get out of here."

"Okay." With a silent apology to his wife whom she hadn't yet met, Abby started dipping into Harlan's front jeans pockets as Shaun searched through his jacket. On her second foray into his Levi's, her fingers closed around a key chain. Harlan's eyelids fluttered.

"Gina?" he murmured.

"Nope, just me," she muttered under her breath. "Got 'em," she wheezed aloud.

"Great." Shaun pulled Harlan to his feet and half carried half dragged him to the Jeep. A blue sedan was parked beside it.

No doubt about it, she was having another full-blown asthma attack now. It was like trying to suck in air through a coffee stirrer. At the Jeep, Shaun was shoving Harlan in with the obvious intent for her to drive since she knew how to get to the E.R.

She'd barely shoved the keys into the ignition when

her hands quit working. "Gotta have meds," she managed between labored breaths.

Shaun stopped at the sound of her voice, recognizing what was going on. "Where are they?" he asked.

"Duffel…bag."

He didn't comment on her not carrying the rescue inhaler on her person. He just rustled around in the back of the car for fifteen seconds and came up with her medication, steering her to sit in the passenger seat as he shoved the plastic case in her hands.

She puffed on the inhaler as her butt eased back into the bucket seat. He stared into her face for five full seconds and without a word, left her to dash around the blue sedan beside them. She couldn't see what he was doing as he bent down beside the tires. She wasn't sure she wanted to.

She tried to relax, to concentrate on breathing through her nose and letting the meds do their thing. But watching her childhood home burn and "relaxing" were mutually exclusive.

No sirens sounded in the distance. It was too late for that, anyway. It had been too late from the beginning. The house was a lost cause.

She turned to look at Harlan, wondering if she should climb in back with him. His face was so pale but his chest rose and fell at a steady rate. His eyes fluttered once more. "Gina," he murmured again.

"It's okay, Harlan. Hang on."

Come on, Shaun, we've got to go. Those men would be coming back to the front of the house any moment.

Harlan was thrashing around in the backseat. His eyes were open now. "Jeez. What happened?" he asked.

"House blew. You got…whacked…in…head." Speaking wasn't any easier yet, but she was getting more air. The one positive in all this.

SHAUN LEAPED INTO THE DRIVER'S seat, shoving a pocket knife into his back pocket. "We're gone."

He cranked the engine and floored it, his heart racing as he studied the side mirrors. He'd cut it very close on time.

"What did you do?" she asked.

He was quiet, speeding down the drive and switching his gaze between the road in front of him, the rearview mirror beside him and the burning house. The three men were running toward them, but they were too far away to shoot…he hoped.

He stared out the back a bit longer.

"Shaun?"

He turned to her, shaken from his reverie. "I slowed them down. Slashed their tires. That'll give us a head start."

Her eyes widened and Shaun glanced back at Harlan. "Hey, H, welcome back. How's your head?"

"Hurts like hell, so does my arm."

"You took quite a hit. Your arm may be broken."

"We're taking him to the hospital, right?" asked Abby.

"Right," said Shaun.

"Wrong," said Harlan at the same time.

"You need to get checked out," argued Shaun. "You can call Gina from there to come get you."

"No," said Harlan through gritted teeth.

"Come on, Harlan, you're killing me here."

"What? Are you crazy? That'll scare Gina to death. No way."

"I'll call her myself if you don't go. You got thrown against a wall and you passed out. You go to the E.R. No arguing. Come on, man, don't be stubborn about this. You've had head injuries before. Besides, it helps us with the whole getting-to-Dallas-quicker issue, if you want to be pragmatic about it. I don't have to worry about how to get you home while I'm taking your car. You're getting what you wanted after all. Let's report it stolen now so you and Gina are completely out of this."

"Well, when you put it like that," Harlan relented just as Shaun knew he would. Keeping his family safe trumped everything—as well it should.

"Don't forget to swap out the license plates though," reminded Harlan. "Any big shopping center parking lot is a good spot for it, in case you're wondering. Look for one on the way to the E.R."

Shaun laughed. "Thanks for the tip, Clyde Barrow."

"I've learned a few things. It'd be bad if Clarksdale's finest picked you up before you got out of town."

"Won't they…find…yours and Harlan's connection?" asked Abby, still struggling for air.

"Yeah, but not right away. They'll be more focused on the stolen vehicle report than our association," explained Harlan.

It was much easier to do the swap than Shaun expected. They simply sat in a grocery store parking lot and watched someone deposit their car in a far corner. Shaun walked over and did the deed in less than five minutes. Thanks to Harlan's tool kit in the back of the Jeep, they were in the parking lot less than ten minutes. Harlan could now report his vehicle as stolen and get his family separated from this mess as quickly as possible.

Shaun climbed back in the car and turned to his friend. "You happy?"

"Ecstatic. Um… One more thing. I'm not calling Gina till after I'm checked out of the E.R.," Harlan said.

Shaun's blood turned icy. "No, I can't just leave you. I won't do that."

"Don't worry about it. You're dropping me and I'm

calling Gina after I check out. I'll tell the E.R. folks I fell off a ladder and a buddy gave me a ride. It's easy."

Shaun felt slightly nauseated. "You know why I don't want to do this."

"Yeah, I know and there's nothing to be done for it," argued Harlan. "I can take care of myself. I'm a grown man, not a teenage girl. You're not deserting me or letting me down. Don't worry." They were five minutes from the E.R. entrance, but Shaun and Abby couldn't risk either of them being seen in public with their pictures everywhere.

"You're sure?" Shaun asked.

"Yes," said Harlan. "We just went to a lot of trouble to sever my association from you. I mean this in the nicest way possible but I don't want you near me right now, okay? Besides, words a pregnant woman does not need to hear are *I'm fine but I'm on my way to the E.R.* She'll still be upset but much safer with *Come get me, baby. I'm okay. I just checked out of the E.R.*"

"I see your point," said Shaun. As much as he hated this, it couldn't be helped.

"If she's pissed, I'd rather have her pissed and driving the speed limit. And you," Harlan said, addressing Abigail and him, "are invited to dinner anytime. I'll be more than happy to see you when this is over."

Swallowing his unhappiness with the situation, Shaun smiled. "Ah, now. Don't be saying that 'less you mean it. You know I'll be taking you up on one of Gina's home-cooked meals."

He parked in the E.R. entrance where he hoped he was not in security camera range and got out to watch as Harlan spoke earnestly to Abigail. He couldn't hear a word through the window. He guessed they were talking about him if her gaze on him was any indication. Shaun opened the back door in time to hear Harlan say, "Believe me."

Abigail looked serious and so did Harlan. Lightening the mood was definitely in order. "Believe you?" joked Shaun. "Why, you're the most well-practiced liar I know, Harlan. And I have the poker stories and empty wallet to prove it."

Harlan looked up and grinned, cradling his arm. "No worries. I just told her that you believed in leprechauns and the fae."

Shaun smiled. "Of course I do. Always have. Can you get inside?"

Harlan stood and hissed in a deep breath as he jostled that injured arm. "I can manage. Trust me."

Shaun cocked an eyebrow. "On this one point, I don't. But I'm going to have to, aren't I?"

Harlan was turning back to Abigail when Shaun overheard something he knew wasn't intended for him. "Remember what I told you," said Harlan. "He's a good man. The best. He'll take care of you." Harlan clasped her hand before limping over to the curb.

Inwardly Shaun cringed. He knew he wasn't a good man. Not really—"well-practiced liar" was the more apt description. Harlan didn't know that Shaun had been lying to Abigail basically since he'd met her. He wondered what else Harlan had said about him, but he didn't have time to go into it out here it the open.

"I'll be in touch about the car. Thank you for everything, H. I don't know how to begin to repay you."

Harlan shook his head. "There's no need. You know that."

Shaun couldn't shake Harlan's hand because that was the arm that was broken. Instead he patted Harlan on the opposite shoulder and watched him do an awkward hobble-shuffle through the E.R. entrance. He didn't have another friend like Harlan. Shaun only hoped Gina would forgive him for putting her husband at risk, then leaving him here in the hospital alone. He waited till the sliding doors closed and Harlan disappeared into the building before getting back into the Jeep.

Shaun now had a whole new host of problems.

Abigail's asthma, for starters. Was he making a huge mistake in not leaving her at the E.R., too?

An hour ago he would have taken her in to be seen there before going on, but now he couldn't. That option was entirely too dangerous. It didn't matter what Abigail thought of him or Harlan or what he even thought of himself. He was the only one who could keep her safe.

That was the truth he had to concentrate on.

Everything had changed when he'd seen who was racing across the lawn with guns blazing at her parents' house. It had been a shock, especially as he'd worked side by side with the man before.

Donner wasn't just tracking him and Abigail as Shaun had feared. One of his security detail was trying to kill the two of them.

Chapter Nineteen

What was Hodges doing here trying to kill them?

It didn't make sense.

Shaun wasn't surprised that the man had found them. He'd known in his gut since their conversation after the condo fire that Donner was dirty. He just hadn't fully embraced it then. Hadn't wanted to believe he could be so wrong about everything…again. Wrong like he was in Iraq with Storm's Edge and Gregor. But there was no denying it now.

Shaun had seen the solid proof in his rearview mirror less than an hour ago. It had been Hodges racing after them. Shooting at them. Hodges, who was part of Donner's security detail. Hodges, who'd had military training as a sniper.

Christ. Had Hodges actually been the one shooting at Abigail in the cemetery?

There was no denying Donner was responsible for all of this. Hodges wouldn't be taking orders from anyone but him. And Shaun knew now that Hodges had been the one holding the gun in Jason's condo, too. Shaun had thought the voice sounded familiar. Hodges had probably even taken care of Therese Mattagon—though for the life of him, Shaun had no idea why.

It wasn't logical. With Jason dead and the file missing,

the sale to Homeland Security couldn't go through. The backups and bugs Jason had originally gone in to update and repair weren't fixed yet and now that Zip Technologies was locked out of Zip-Net? Donner had to have Jason's key code or the entire program was worthless. Abigail was their only link. Donner couldn't kill her before getting the file. The bigger question was: Why had they killed Jason to begin with, without that key code for the spyware?

Unless, they'd killed him before they knew he'd locked them out of Zip-Net.

That was the only thing that made sense.

Jason had found the spyware issue in the morning, locked down Zip-Net, emailed Abigail and overnighted the key code information and the upgrade file to Karen Weathers, then got himself killed on his way to tell Donner all about it.

Jason must have unknowingly talked to a colleague who was in on the scheme before he met with Donner—or he could have mentioned it to Donner on the phone when they set up their lunch appointment that day. The lunch appointment Jason never got to. Donner must have had apoplexy when he realized Jason had essentially locked them out of the kingdom and thrown away the key.

But where did Therese Mattagon come in? She had only threatened Abigail about the original updates. Most likely she had been spying on Jason before his death and just switched to Abigail afterward—looking for that upgrade file to block the sale and Zip-Net's success. Therese was part of the cutthroat competition.

But why kill her in Jason's apartment—unless Donner wanted to keep Abigail from going to the police? He'd known Shaun would discourage her from seeking out the authorities. And Shaun had played right into it. After the condo fire, it had been easy to frame them for Therese's death.

In Donner eyes, it had been a win-win situation. Framing Abigail and Shaun kept them dependent on him, reporting to him. Or if they chose to strike out on their own, Donner had all kinds of means to help the police catch them.

He glanced at Abigail. He had to tell her. She'd been right. Donner was rotten to the core, planning to screw Homeland Security with spyware in their new wireless system so he could sell classified information to the highest bidder once he got his hands on that key code and Jason's file.

Shaun drove on, knowing he had to tell her about this latest twist. Dreading what she was going to say. Her worst suspicions confirmed. Would she believe he'd been trying to tell to her for at least twenty-four hours that he believed the same thing?

He'd been so wrong not to confess to the earlier on-going conversations with Donner. Now there was no way to convince her that he hadn't been lying about everything, especially once he'd slept with her.

How had he made such a mess of this?

"Abigail, there's something we've got to talk about."

"Yeah?"

"Back there. One of those men at your house. I recognized him from Zip Tech. He works there." He glanced at her, saw how pale she'd gone and he murmured words he hadn't used in front of a woman in a very long time.

She completely surprised him by laughing out loud. "You know I was starting to wonder if you ever cursed. I mean serious sailor kind of cussing."

"Much to my grandmother's chagrin. She claimed I turned her hair gray when I was younger. I try to restrain myself now."

She nodded. "Your Gran sounds like a pistol."

"She was. I liked that about her, when she wasn't washing my mouth out with soap."

She laughed once more. "I would have paid to have seen that."

"She would have enjoyed knowing you." He looked her way again. The color in her cheeks was coming back. He forced himself to go on—hating to break the lighter mood, hating what he had to tell her next.

"The man I saw. 'Tis worse. He works—worked—for me on Donner's security detail."

She didn't reply at first but stared out the window into the night. Finally she asked, "So are you convinced now that Donner is responsible for Jason's death?"

He drove on. Knowing what he needed to tell her but unable to make himself say it all…so he compromised. In the interest of keeping her safe. She'd leave him if she knew the truth and that wasn't a safe alternative.

"Yes, I think it's true. I didn't want to believe it, but I do now. I'm sorry."

"You're sure?"

He could only nod. He couldn't force himself to speak the rest of it. The truth. So he lied by omission. *I know because I've been talking to him almost every day since we left D.C., and everything he's said has made my suspicions grow.*

She'd leave him if he told her that, and Donner's men would kill her. Once he had the upgrade file and key code safely in the hands of the proper authorities, she'd be safe and of no further interest to Donner.

So he was going to lie just a little longer, even as it took a bit of his soul to do it. Lying hadn't bothered him at all in the past. Now it made him feel like hell.

Once she found out he'd deceived her—and she was

going to, that was inevitable—their short-term relationship would be over. So not coming clean right away had at least one thing going for it: he could be with her till she found out the truth and told him to drop dead.

Day Three—Late Evening

"WHAT THE HELL HAPPENED?" demanded Donner. He punched the accelerator on his Porsche, speeding along the Parkway to the airport and his private jet.

"We lost them, sir." Hodges's voice trembled.

"You what?"

"We lost them," the younger man repeated.

"Let me get this straight. You had the house surrounded with three armed men. You blew it up with the woman and Logan inside after I expressly said I wanted them alive, and then you lost them?"

"Yes, sir."

"How long ago did this happen?" demanded Donner.

"Three hours."

"How in God's name did they get a three-hour head start on you?"

"Logan disabled our vehicle and there's sketchy cell coverage out here. We're walking to town."

Donner said something foul and scathing before taking a deep breath. "The irony of that statement is not lost on me, Hodges. Nevertheless I must have the updates and that damn key or this entire sale is lost. At midnight tomorrow we're supposed to turn over complete control to the Department of Homeland Security and right now we can't even turn Zip-Net on, much less get our window inside."

"Give me another chance, sir. We know where they're going." His voice was particularly deferential. Donner liked that in his employees.

"Why should I do that? You've screwed up multiple aspects of this job already. We won't even talk about what happened to Jason Trevor in Dupont Circle."

"An unfortunate miscommunication, sir. I did not receive the text to abort until after I'd completed the job."

"Hodges, a miscommunication is ordering anchovies on my pizza when I ask for pepperoni. Killing someone before I have a chance to ascertain if they have relevant information is not a friggin' miscommunication." He slowed as he approached the airport entrance.

"Yes, sir."

Donner sighed. Hodges was an idiot and a suck-up but he was loyal. Certainly more so than Shaun Logan. Besides, Donner was out of options until his plane landed.

"Don't misunderstand me. I want that upgrade file and the key code. I don't know for certain if the woman in Dallas has them, but all indications are she has something of value from Jason Trevor. He sent something to her the day he died. We just got the info from our corporate FedEx account this afternoon. So we'll start with Karen Weathers. If nothing else, she can be leverage, if those pictures we found in Therese Mattagon's briefcase are any indication."

Therese Mattagon had been the one aspect of this matter that had gone precisely as planned. Mattagon's corporate spying had put her in exactly the wrong place at exactly the right time to suit Donner's needs. Her death had served multiple purposes, including keeping Shaun and Abby off balance and looking to Donner for information as the police zeroed in on them as suspects in her death. In addition, Mattagon left a briefcase that held invaluable information on Abby's family background, some of which Donner had never seen before, even though he'd employed her brother for several years.

Hodges cleared his throat. "I'm on it, sir."

"Excellent. Don't screw up this time."

SHAUN AND ABBY DROVE ALL night, arriving in Dallas as the sun's rays peeked over the gold-mirrored buildings on Central Expressway. Abby yawned when they pulled into a Starbucks in a strip shopping center off Mockingbird Lane.

"Do you want to grab some coffee and something to eat before we see your friend or go straight to the rehab facility?" asked Shaun.

"It's not even seven o'clock yet. I hate to wake her up. Let's eat fast and grab something for her too, perhaps? She likes banana nut anything from here."

The temperature had dropped unexpectedly and the gauge in the Jeep read forty degrees. Typical for Texas in April. It could be eighty degrees one day and forty the next. Abby was shivering by the time they got into the coffee shop and missed her Walmart sweater that had been trashed in the fire. Shaun put his arm around her as they stood in line.

She ordered a latte and a scone for herself along with Karen's beloved banana bread. It felt perfectly natural for Shaun to have his arm encircling her waist—like they were "together," but something was off. Maybe it was the days of road grunge she was dealing with. After placing the order she took a detour by the bathroom to wash her face and give her hair a once-over. It wasn't much of an improvement but better than nothing.

When she came out of the ladies' room, Shaun was no-where to be found. She assumed he was in the bathroom, as well. There was a barista-in-training behind the counter and a long line in front, so their coffee wasn't ready yet and she settled into a comfy chair. Five minutes later Shaun came in the front door with a plastic bag in hand. He sat across from her and slipped a gray Dallas Cowboys hoodie from the sack along with a new phone battery and charger combo.

"I bought it next door at Stop, Gas and Save. You were cold, and I owed you a battery," he explained, sliding the ever-present pocketknife from his jeans to cut the tiny plastic hook away from the sweatshirt jacket and slip it around her shoulders.

"They had phone batteries?"

"It's an urban truck stop. They have a little of everything."

"Thank you," she murmured, undone that he would have thought to buy her the hoodie.

"We'll get the battery charged up in the car. After you get Jason's file and key code turned over to the authorities, it won't matter what Donner taps into."

"How is he doing it?"

"I'm not sure but Zip Technologies has all kinds of experimental prototypes that were created in the development of Zip-Net. Illegal as hell to use outside the lab, but I doubt that's stopping Michael right now."

She nodded and he rested the back of his palm on her cheek, then her forehead. "Your asthma, it's getting worse isn't it?"

She shrugged. "I'll be okay once I'm out of the city." Of course, this was spring in Dallas with every pollen known to man plus some they'd never heard of—the worst place for allergies on earth.

"I think you're being overly optimistic," he replied, shaking his head and surprising her completely by leaning forward and kissing her so thoroughly she forgot they were in the middle of Starbucks.

He pulled away first and for a moment there was such

despair in his eyes. She couldn't understand why. Then the barista was calling their orders, and his eyes changed to a cool blue-green in the early morning light and she wondered if she'd imagined that sadness.

He came back with their coffee and pastries and kissed her again before sitting across from her in an overstuffed chair. He tasted like a double shot espresso and she stared at him as he settled into his seat. Had something changed? He was more deliberate in his attention, more demonstrative. More direct.

What was it? Were they both less tense now that they were so close to getting the file and key code? She had no idea.

Yet when he took her hand on the way to the car, she had the oddest sense—it was as if it were for the last time.

Chapter Twenty

Day Four—Midmorning

Karen's rehab center was located near White Rock Lake, a few blocks from the Dallas Arboretum and its sixty-six acres of botanical gardens. Once out of the car, Abby looked across the shimmering water where a couple of sailboats were out along with a few kayaks. She shivered in the cool morning breeze despite her new hoodie.

Forest green awnings dotted windows on the tan brick building behind her. Balconies facing the lake were filled with plants and wind chimes. It was comforting to know that Karen had such lovely surroundings for her recovery.

Shaun slipped his jacket around her shoulders and took her hand, twining his fingers with hers as they crossed the parking lot and entered the rehab facility. When they found Karen's room, a nurse informed them that she was at physical therapy and should be back anytime.

A few minutes later Karen was rolled inside in a wheel-chair and stretched out her arms for a hug. "Abby, honey, how are you? I'm so glad to finally see you. So sorry it's like this."

Abby nodded, pulling back and feeling the tears behind

her eyes. "I'm glad to see you, too. I'm better now that I'm here."

Shaun started backing out of the room. But Abby held out her hand and he took it again. "Wait." She pulled him to her side. "I want you to meet someone."

Karen's eyes twinkled. "So this is your Irishman."

Shaun took her offered palm. "'Tis a pleasure to meet you."

"Abby's told me just enough about you to make me very curious."

He smiled and Abby watched as he proceeded to charm her friend.

"You have the package from Jason?" Abby eventually prompted.

Karen handed over a FedEx envelope that had been opened. Inside was a manila envelope addressed to Abby. She ripped it open, as well. Inside were two flash drives and several sheets of paper filled with computer code.

"I have no idea what I'm looking at." She glanced back at Shaun.

He was inspecting the contents over her shoulder. "Me either, but we don't have to understand it." He scrutinized the top page. "These have to be the upgrade file and key code printed out. Is there anything else?"

She turned the packaging upside down. Another sealed envelope fell out. Her name was scrawled across the front in Jason's handwriting. She stared at it for a moment, felt those tears well again and knew she didn't want to open this in front of an audience.

"I'll be back in a bit," she said, stuffing the thumb drives in her hoodie pocket and carrying the printouts with her. She walked from the room down the hall to a small living area set up for the residents with a television and a telephone.

A half wall with a long row of potted plants on it formed a hidden corner that appeared to be for reading or just a little privacy from the general hustle and bustle. A small window provided a view across the parking lot to the Arboretum. There was an emergency exit door with a crash bar that she assumed led to stairs and a sign with a warning about an alarm sounding if the door opened. She took refuge there beneath the plants on a small sofa, out of sight to read her letter—tearing open the envelope and taking a deep breath, unsure of what she'd find.

Hey, Buttercup,

If you're reading this…I'm sorry. I assume I screwed up and I guess it was pretty bad. You must have gone on quite the treasure hunt to get this package. But I need you to do one more thing before we're done with all this.

Take these two thumb drives and the papers to Rob Kenny. He's an old friend from school who works for the FBI now and lives in Dallas. You met him once. Remember? His cell number is 555-759-5601.

If it's gone this far, he'll know what to do and how to contact the proper authorities. And, Abby, whatever you do, don't trust anyone with Zip Tech.

Whatever is going on, whatever happened to me, they're behind it.

God, it feels so melodramatic writing that. But if you're holding this letter, it means I wasn't there to retrieve the package from Karen—so it's true.

Damn, there is stuff I still want to do with my life. Things I wanted for both of us.

Be happy, Abby. Make every minute count. Thank

you for standing by me when Mother and Father wouldn't.

   I love you, baby girl.
   Jason

She swallowed hard. Breathing hurt. She struggled to hold the tears back but lost the battle as she closed the letter. At least in her corner no one could see her. Completely hidden with a box of tissue beside her from the end table, she let go and silently wept—closing out the sights and sounds of the world around her.

Long moments later, she sat with her head down—exhausted but better. The noises of the facility gradually seeped back into her consciousness. A television set was turned up a bit too loud in the rec room across the hallway. Nurses worked at their station a few feet away. The traffic bustled outside the window beside her.

Cutting through all that, she recognized the hushed tones of Shaun's lilting speech. Obviously he was on a phone call. She started to get up and go to him. She could use a strong shoulder right now, but something held her back.

What was it?

The tone of his voice?

The warning in Jason's letter?

Shaun was, after all, part of Zip Tech. But surely she could trust him? She'd trusted him enough to sleep with him.

"I said I'd do the job and fix things, Donner. I've done all you've asked and more. Every day we've talked. She trusts me. Why don't you?" His words faded as he walked toward the rec room.

Air tore at her throat as it left her lungs in a whoosh. She felt like she was going to be sick. She wanted to scream.

Shaun had talked to Donner every day?

Had everything been a lie?

How could she have been such a fool? She'd thought he felt something for her beyond obligation. But he'd only slept with her, lied to her, used her the whole time to get Jason's upgrades and key code.

The realization sank in as an elephant sat down on her chest. She reached for her rescue inhaler in a vain attempt to nudge the crushing weight off and took a quick hit of albuterol. It wasn't much use. Her lungs had been punished to the point of persecution over the past four days.

Damn it. She could not have another asthma attack.

She had to get out of here. Afterward, she could rage and die of humiliation, but right now there was no time. She had to leave before he saw her.

She looked around her little niche for a way to escape. The emergency exit was rigged with an alarm. Didn't matter. She had the thumb drives, the printouts and her brother's letter. She had to vanish. Now.

But Karen...

As if on cue, she spied a nurse wheeling her friend down the hall to what Abby assumed had to be another of her therapy appointments. Abby hunkered down farther to insure she couldn't be seen.

Karen was safe and Shaun was across the hall as he finished that phone call. She couldn't believe it had come to this. She tried to take another deep breath and felt the air ripping at her throat.

She wasn't going to be able to run away from him. She was going to have to "cab it." Or hide. Physically running was beyond her. It wasn't going to be feasible to even walk a long distance at anything more than a sedate pace.

She huddled in Shaun's jacket, alternately staring out the window at the gardens across the street and at the emergency exit door. Sliding her hands into the pockets of his Windbreaker, her fingers closed around…car keys?

Her heart leapt a little as she pulled them out to make sure that they were indeed the keys to Harlan's Jeep in the parking lot. Shaun had left them in his jacket, not thinking he'd be separated from her.

This was perfect. If she could just get to the vehicle, she'd be home free. She could lose herself in the city and call Jason's FBI friend to come get the upgrades and key code.

She pulled out her inhaler, took another puff and glanced over her shoulder. Shaun was still talking and standing in the doorway to the rec room.

She picked up Jason's papers and letter, quietly folding them, and put them in her jeans pocket alongside her albuterol. With one final exhalation through her nose she headed for the door—fearing that if she looked back, and met Shaun's piercing gaze, she'd turn to stone.

The screeching alarm shattered the quiet of the facility but she stayed calm.

Keep walking. Like you're supposed to be here. Don't panic.

If her luck held, everyone, including Shaun, would assume it was a resident making an unauthorized exit instead of her. But try as she might, she couldn't resist looking over her shoulder as she shut the door.

She didn't turn to stone. It might have been preferable. Instead, adrenaline coursed through her bloodstream when she made direct eye contact with him. Shaun's blue-green eyes were clouded by confusion then hardened into something dark and dangerous she hadn't seen directed at her before now. That "something" she hadn't wanted to believe he was really capable of.

Too late she realized her mistake. Her careful plan for

walking calmly down the stairs flew out the window. She saw a dead bolt toggle and locked it. Ignoring her tortured breathing and pinched lungs, she ran.

Chapter Twenty-One

Shaun broke off his argument with Donner in time to see Abigail slip through the emergency exit.

What the hell?

He ran for the door and made it just in time to hear a dead bolt lock into place.

Huh?

Then he realized. Hospitals and psych wards. Dead bolts were sometimes on the outer side of emergency exits for the patients with Alzheimer's.

The sign indicated another stairwell without an alarm by the elevators. He headed for it, knowing instantly why she'd run. She'd overheard him arguing with Donner.

He'd been getting calls throughout the night from his boss and he'd known he had to contact him. Convincing Donner that Shaun thought he still worked for him was necessary but only for a little longer. Shaun knew he should have gone downstairs to make the call, but he hadn't wanted to get too far away from Abigail or Karen.

What she'd heard sounded bad. Like he'd been working for Donner the whole time he'd been with her—driving her from Washington, helping her in Clarksdale, making love to her in the bed-and-breakfast in Alabama. Not telling her the truth had finally caught up to him.

He should have explained two days ago and certainly

yesterday. Now he had no idea if she'd even talk to him, but he had to try. Although first he had to catch her.

He found the stairs and was on the ground floor in less than sixty seconds. She couldn't be that far ahead. The woman was asthmatic and possibly running a fever, judging by the way she'd been shivering earlier.

He'd put his coat on her to—*shit*.

The Jeep keys were in his coat pocket. That was why she'd taken off like that. She'd known if she could just get to the car she'd be gone.

Damn it to hell.

He poured on the speed, bursting through the front doors in time to see her peeling out of the parking place. He sprinted across the asphalt, knowing it was too late but making a supreme effort anyway. He watched her fishtail out of the lot and into the traffic before barreling away. She didn't look back.

So this was the price he must pay for lying. Except he wasn't the one who would pay. Abigail would…with her life.

ABBY KEPT DRIVING EVEN AS she saw Shaun racing out of the entrance to the rehab center. She was coughing from her dash down the stairs—the constriction around her chest so tight she was becoming light-headed. If she could only get a few blocks away, she'd pull over and catch her breath. Then she'd be fine.

Rounding the corner, she saw a long ivy-covered fence topped every couple hundred feet by huge planters filled with blooming exotics. She peered through the leaves as she drove past a full parking lot. A massive sign stretched across the road announcing Dallas Blooms, the Dallas Arboretum's annual spring flower festival. A long line of cars headed inside. This appeared to be the perfect place to get lost for the afternoon and regain her strength.

Shaun would never guess she'd driven less than a mile away from the rehab center. Her other asthma meds were in the backseat. She could do a breathing treatment in a bathroom if she had to.

Stalled in slow-moving traffic, she was set to pull into the parking lot when her phone started ringing. Glancing at the caller ID, she was grateful that she'd plugged in her new battery to charge before they'd gone up to see Karen at the rehab center. She recognized Shaun's number from when he'd had her program it in earlier on their trek from D.C. He'd insisted in case they got separated. Well, this sure as hell counted as separation.

She took in as much air as she could and answered.

"Abigai—" he began.

She cut him off. "Why do you keep calling me that? Everyone calls me Abby."

Why that was the first thing that popped out when there were so many other pressing things to be asked, she had no idea.

"Never mind," she snapped. "Don't answer that. There's nothing you can say that will convince me that you're not scum."

"I understand you're angry. But what you overheard is not what it seems."

She coughed a sarcastic laugh. "Oh, really? So you haven't been in constant contact with Michael Donner the entire time we've been on our way here?"

"Yes, but it wasn't because I wanted to help him, you have to believe that. It was because I knew that if I said *no*, he'd just send someone else to follow you. Someone who would hurt you."

"I don't have to believe anything you say. But I am

curious. Is that why you had sex with me? To keep me compliant?" *My God, I was a fool.*

"No. I made love to you because I couldn't stop myself. I'm sorry I hurt you. I've never let myself get so involved with someone I was supposed to be protecting. I've never let them get this close. It's always been my unbreakable rule. Afterward, I couldn't tell you about Donner because I was afraid of this happening. I knew you'd leave and I couldn't let you go out on your own, unprotected. He'd have access to you then. You'd be vulnerable like you are now."

"Why didn't you say something back in D.C. or before we ever slept together?" she asked.

"Because I didn't know what you'd do. If Donner had thought I wasn't on board with the plan to keep in touch with him, he would have crushed us before we ever left town. He has those kinds of resources. I know I was wrong. I did it all wrong. But you have to believe this one thing. I never meant to hurt you." His Irish lilt was thicker over the phone—or it seemed that way when all she had to focus on was his voice.

"How can I believe anything else you ever tell me? You talked with him every day. You told him where we were. You told those men where we were going so they could burn my house down. You probably told them that we were going to Karen's to get the package and that I have it now."

"No, Abigail. No. I didn't."

"You told me that you were too broken to be fixed. That's the one thing you got right, Shaun." She knew she shouldn't be on the line any longer or the call could be traced. According to what Shaun said yesterday, Donner might even be recording her words. She snapped the phone shut before he could reply, slipping the cell into her bag as she pulled into the entrance for the gardens.

She needed a place to disappear for a while more than ever and the crowds were perfect cover.

She moved through the ticket line stopping only to ask about pay phones. The clerk behind the counter told her there was a phone bank at the concession stand in the middle of the property.

The warm spring day shone down on her as she walked with young parents, children and the elderly along the central walkway—the Paseo de Flores—then on through the main area of the gardens. Wiped out from her asthmatic sprint from the rehab facility, she wandered till she found a shady secluded corner to plop down in. She had to rest while she figured this out.

She used Shaun's waded up jacket and her new hoodie for a pillow and lay back on the grass. Slipping on sunglasses, she kept careful watch as she tried to wrap her mind around all she'd just learned.

Who could she turn to? She fingered Jason's letter and thought about the friend he'd mentioned. Could Rob Kenny be trusted? With Donner's capabilities it might be a risk to even use a pay phone, but this was her only option now. She'd take the chance.

Making her decision, she left her spot in the shade and walked toward the concession pavilion. The phone booths were around back and out in the sun. She pulled out her letter from Jason and dialed Rob's number. He picked up on the first ring.

"Rob, it's Abby Trevor, Jason's sister."

"Abby, of course. Great to hear from you. I haven't talked to Jason in a while. He left me a message last week and I haven't been able to catch up with him."

She pictured Rob with his all-American grin and blond-haired good looks. She'd had a terrible crush on him at one time. It was hard to believe he was an FBI agent now. And as much as she might desperately wish this was just a social hey-I'm-in-town-let's-get-together call, there was no way to beat around the bush.

"Jason died last week in a hit-and-run accident."

Rob gasped and started to give her condolences but she interrupted. "Only, it wasn't an accident. He was murdered. I have some information he left that he instructed be sent to you. When can we meet?"

It was so quiet that for a moment she thought the line had gone dead. "I'm very sorry for your loss. Jason was a good man."

"I appreciate that. Can you help me? I need to see you as soon as possible."

Her mother would have rolled in her grave at Abby's bluntness but Rob was unfazed. "Of course, I'll meet you," he said. "Where are you and what do you need?" All pretense of a casual conversation was over.

She wheezed a sigh of relief. "I'm at the Arboretum at White Rock Lake. How soon can you get here?"

"I'm in Arlington right now. With the traffic, it shouldn't take me more than about an hour or maybe a little over. Can you hang on till then?"

"I think so. I can hide if necessary," she said.

"Hopefully it won't come to that. But if you have to, hunker down and sit tight."

"All right, but you need to know there are people after me for this information. You could be in some danger, too, if you help."

"Don't worry about me, Abby. I can take care of myself. You just hold on."

Tears were threatening again. "Okay, I will. Thank you, I didn't know what else to do." She hung up and realized she wasn't getting much air. She'd been holding her breath on the phone. She leaned her head against the booth as dark spots danced in front of her eyes.

Crap. She pulled out the rescue inhaler and took another shot. The sun no longer felt pleasantly warm but hot. She needed something cool to drink. This was nerves most likely, but it didn't really matter. She could pass out just as easily from nerves as from a real asthma attack at this point.

She moved to the concession pavilion where it was marginally cooler. Taking slow breaths, she tried to calm her rising panic. Everything would be okay.

Rob would be here in an hour.

She could do anything for an hour.

Chapter Twenty-Two

Shaun paced in the lobby of the rehab center going slightly out of his mind. The situation was so much like Iraq he thought he was hallucinating—even down to the girl running away when he tried to explain he was helping her and her family get safely away from his boss.

Because Shaun had been on the phone with him when she ran, Donner knew Abigail was missing. To further enhance the nightmarish quality of the experience, Shaun had to act like none of this mattered when he talked to Donner a second time and heard the boss's plan. One of Zip Technologies's latest toys was just now up and running— privately and illegally tapping into the local phone lines and monitoring the airwaves for Abigail's voice using a brand-new protocol for voice recognition. If she used any phone in the area, the new program would find her, recording everything said by and to her.

Or Donner could also have her location as soon as Shaun called her back and talked long enough for a trace. With this new system, the process would only take about twenty seconds—a blindingly fast speed for a trace, much faster than anything developed to date. Thank God this new prototype hadn't been operational thirty minutes earlier when she'd hung up on Shaun. Donner would have had her location while Shaun would not.

There was no way around it. To save her, Shaun had to call her again and convince her to tell him where she was. But in calling her, he'd be betraying her at the same time because Donner would have the location, as well. And Shaun wasn't convinced Donner would tell him where she was if she wouldn't tell Shaun herself on the phone call.

Shaun had to convince Abigail he was telling the truth and then afterward he had to lie so well that Donner would be fooled. Lying would be so much easier, but if Abigail figured it out and bolted, she was dead. She could smell the lies on Shaun now, even over a cell connection.

But first he had to get her to pick up the phone.

Right…should be easy.

The desk clerk at the rehab let him use the office line to make the call since the clerk believed Shaun's phone to be out of battery power. Caller ID worked in his favor and Abigail picked up on the first ring. "Karen, are you okay?" she asked.

"Abigail, 'tis me. Don't hang up, Karen's fine. I used this phone so you'd answer. Please just listen."

He could only hear a slight wheezing and for the first time he was grateful for her asthma because he knew she was still on the line.

He took a deep breath and went for the whole truth.

"Donner can tap and trace calls…quite fast. He'll be able to get a trace on this call because he got your voice recorded when you used his phone in the hotel suite in D.C. And he has your cell number in the system now. He'll have people on their way to wherever you are. I can help. I can get to you first, but you've got to trust me."

Nothing but silence.

"Abigail?" He heard the strain in his own voice. He had to stay calm, but she had to talk to him and tell him where she was. Donner would have the information any second.

"Trust you?" She laughed bitterly. "Is this a new tack you're taking? Baffle the little woman with bull?"

"No, I…it's true."

"How can I possibly trust you? You've lied to me about everything."

He didn't know what to say. Donner had the trace by now but Shaun had no clue where she was. He could hear something in the background. Children squealing…a park maybe?

The truth was his only option.

"There's not a single reason I can think of as to why you should trust me. But I'm asking you to anyway," he said.

No sound. Then in the silence a faraway voice.

"Today at the Dallas Arboretum, we're proud to be hosting the North Texas winners of the Junior High National Strings Competition in a public concert. Join us on the concert lawn for the free performance starting in ten minutes."

She was at the Arboretum.

"I can help, Abigail. Please. Wait, don't hang up—"

The line went dead.

I can help.

Sure he could. Like he'd helped her right into bed and into this mess. Abby snapped her phone shut and stood.

How much of that announcement had he heard?

No way to know.

She should assume he'd heard it all and leave now. But where? Rob wasn't here yet. Should she wait on him?

Taking the car was no longer an option. If Donner's people had tapped any of her earlier calls, then they could already be on their way to the Arboretum looking for her.

It didn't matter anymore if she used her phone. Donner knew everything.

The only thing she could do was call Rob and warn him. She couldn't have him walking into this blind. She dialed his number but got voice mail.

"Rob, it's me. I'm still here but they know where I am. I'm in some trouble. I think they're tapping and tracing my calls. I can't say any more."

She headed back toward the *Paseo* intending to head to the parking lot but two men were on their way down the path hurrying along with the flow of concert traffic. They hadn't spotted her yet but one looked vaguely familiar.

Was that the man from her parents' house or was she imagining things? They'd gotten here so fast.

She took a hard left instead of going for the exit. She wasn't sure what she'd just seen but turning around to stare seemed a bad idea. Picking up her pace through the crowd that had suddenly grown rather dense, the constriction around her lungs grew tighter with each hurried step. The thought of Donner's men behind her had the elephant plunking its butt firmly down on her chest again.

"Join us on the concert lawn for the free performance starting in ten minutes." The recorded voice making the announcement had a clipped British accent, striking her as highly ironic given the circumstances and her location here in the heart of Texas.

She needed a place to hide till Rob came. She walked, studying the map given to her on the way in. A concert crowd could be the solution but she had no idea what kind of numbers were attending. Could she blend in?

The north side of the gardens appeared to have a sort of bamboo forest that wasn't even on the colorful graph of the grounds. That could be the ideal cover. She paused to casually sip from her water bottle and look over her shoulder.

The men were still behind her and the taller one was definitely the man from the fire. She was about to turn back to the path when she recognized another man talking on a phone behind the first two.

Michael Donner was here.

Blood rushed to her face. She froze and that's when they saw her. Tall Guy pointed and started for her. Donner's other man pulled a gun. She rushed along the path toward the bamboo forest, opposite the line of people headed for the concert.

Her breath was coming in wheezing gasps as dense stalks thirty and forty feet tall rose in front of her. The contrast was startling there on the edge of the well-groomed gardens and appeared to go on forever or at least to the edges of the property—like something you'd imagine on an Asian continent. She didn't hesitate or even glance over her shoulder, she just barreled off the sidewalk into the bamboo.

SHAUN'S CELL RANG AS SOON AS Abigail hung up. He knew who it was without looking at caller I.D. He was jogging toward the Arboretum but it was several blocks away.

"Sounds like you struck out, Logan." Donner's voice was cool, clinical.

"I had to go with the truth, Donner. She would have recognized anything less. You understand that. And it did the job of keeping her on the line. Did you get the location?" Shaun was at the curb waiting for a break in the traffic. The huge sign for Dallas Blooms was right above his head.

"Yeah, we got it."

Shaun stood perfectly still and took a calming breath.

He had to play this just right and sound calmer than he was. "So tell me where. I'll go, get the stuff and get out. Where is she exactly?"

He heard a low chuckle but it wasn't a pleasant sound. "I'm not sure you need to know. Hodges can handle things from here. I'll see you back in D.C. if you're so inclined to still work for me."

Damn. He tried counting to ten and made it to three.

"Christ, Michael, what's the deal? What do I have to do to prove myself to you?" His palms were slick on the phone. He had to get to the Arboretum now but it was a huge friggin' place. He needed to know where she was in there. He peered down the street waiting for the light to turn.

"Nothing, Shaun. That's the beautiful thing. Do nothing at all. Go home. Leave her be. Your work here's done. That's never been an issue for you before. Is it going to be now?"

Well, hell yes it was but he wasn't about to tell Donner that. Shaun forced himself to laugh. "Of course not. See you in D.C. I'll be driving back so it'll be a few days."

"No rush."

"Right. See you next week." Shaun shoved the phone in his pocket, saw a break in the traffic and ran.

STUMBLING INTO THE BAMBOO forest, Abby immediately felt cut off from the world even though she could still see the manicured grounds behind her. The men were racing along the path toward her—taking a shortcut across the lawn despite numerous plaques warning of dire consequences for those who walked on the grass.

She took one last look over her shoulder and started running herself. It was tough going through the heavy bamboo. Downed stalks blocked her path and darkness closed in for a moment before her eyes adjusted. Fallen branches caught in the oversized stems tore at her clothes and slapped at her face.

She pushed forward until she could no longer see the gardens behind her. Dried bamboo leaves crackled as she moved through the forest. She had to get to a hiding place and stop or they'd hear her.

How big was this thing? She stopped to get her bearings but it was difficult in the dim light. Only by looking straight up could she see the sun as it filtered through the branches and leaves. Her breathing was labored and her vision went dark around the edges. She sank to the ground with a plop.

Then she heard them, crashing through the brush somewhere off to the left and behind her.

"Hodges, where is she? You see her?"

"No. Split up. She can't go far. The woman's got asthma, for God's sake. There's no way she can run fast or go quietly."

The man called Hodges was right. They'd find her soon. Unfortunately she couldn't be completely quiet. Her breathing was going to give her away.

She dug her hand into the ground to get up and move forward. The sandy loam fell through her fingers and like that, she knew what she had to do.

She grabbed a small branch that had blown in from some other type of tree, got to her knees and began digging. It wouldn't have to be a deep hole but she needed a marker. Then she needed to move.

"Hodges, you in here?"

Her heart stuttered and her hands stilled as she recognized the Irish cadence in the words.

"Yeah, we're here. Where did you come from?" asked Hodges.

"Rehab center across the street," said Shaun. "Have you spoken to Donner?"

"Not since we got here. Thought you were on your way to D.C. Are you here to help?"

She held her breath. The moment of truth. Had everything Shaun told her been a lie?

He was within ten feet of her when he answered.

Shaun stepped into a slight clearing. "Sure, I just don't want to get shot at or blown up this time." There was a distinct edge to his voice.

"Sorry 'bout that." Hodges laughed but it had a rather nasty sound, indicating he wasn't very sorry at all. "How'd you know where we were?"

"Figured it out."

"Huh?"

"You leave a trail a blind man could follow in this bamboo."

The other, taller man barked a laugh.

"Screw you, Logan."

Shaun laughed. "Not that kind of guy, Hodges. Besides, security's on their way. You and your buddy there…chasing a woman across the Arboretum. Folks notice."

Hodges uttered a foul but creative string of expletives.

Abby clamped down on her lip till she tasted blood. Shaun had to know she was close by and listening to every word. Was he trying to tell her something? He'd asked her to trust him, but how could she?

"You've got to get out," urged Shaun. "I have a hard copy of everything Jason sent Karen Weathers. We don't need the sister. We don't have time to find her while she's hiding."

But Shaun didn't have the hard copy or the thumb drives. She had them. She'd specifically taken the printouts of the upgrade file and the key code with her into that waiting room to read Jason's letter. He knew that.

She wanted to assume he was lying to Hodges to protect her. The other option was too horrifying.

"This place will be crawling with security soon," said Shaun. "Maybe even cops."

"Feds or local?" asked Hodges.

"Does it matter? Get Donner and get out of here. He can't be part of this."

"What about the woman?" asked Hodges.

"Leave her to me," said Shaun.

Chapter Twenty-Three

Leave her to me.

What did that mean? Was Shaun going to kill her or save her? She hoped it was the latter and that she hadn't just made the biggest mistake of her life in the pick-a-good-man contest. Abby dug faster and as quietly as possible. She could still taste the blood where she'd practically bitten through her lip to keep from gasping when Shaun showed up and started talking. Sweat ran down the back of her ear as she pushed sandy dirt out of the hole.

Hodges sneered at Shaun. "You're the reason we're here now, Logan. You've screwed this up from the get-go."

"It was part of the cover. How was I supposed to get the information if I didn't go along with her? You wouldn't have gotten this far without me. Call Donner if you feel the need. But hurry. If cops get involved, you've got some explaining to do about the past week, don't you?"

"More than you know," murmured Tall Guy.

"Hodges, were you hiding in the cemetery?" asked Shaun.

She stopped digging to listen.

"Donner's orders." Hodges's tone made it clear he was proud to have been following them.

"You almost killed her. You almost killed me. I know Donner didn't tell you to do that," said Shaun.

She could hear the strain in his voice now. She'd noticed it over the past four days but hadn't recognized it for what it was till now. His accent thickened when he was stressed; the consonants were harder, the vowels softer.

"I was improvising. Besides, the bitch moved in time, didn't she? She's okay, so why are you whining?" Hodges was irritated and getting louder. Abby beat back the slick, oily coating of fear inside her belly.

"Well, hell, man, while I'm thankful for small favors, I'd appreciate it if you'd go to the practice range when we get home. I don't fancy having to hide whenever you strap on a gun. Now go fetch the boss."

She started digging again. The hole was almost big enough.

"Are you sure?" asked Hodges.

"Yes, I'm sure. I'll take care of her. Hodges, do you *want* to go to federal prison? There's no place to hide there."

Hide. Shaun had used that word multiple times. Message received. She prayed she was understanding him correctly and finished burying the flash drives and papers as the two men crashed away from her in the underbrush. That last comment about prison had gotten them moving.

A soft spring breeze stirred the bamboo but she didn't let the seemingly peaceful surroundings fool her. Shaun was here. Waiting to "take care of her."

She covered the hole and marked it with a small pile of branches before crawling silently away.

"Abigail darling, where are you? We've got to go now, before they find out I haven't spoken to Donner about anything we discussed here and come back."

Could she trust him?

Did she really have a choice? Of course she did. She huddled in the shadows, just out of sight and made her decision.

She knew this man. He was one of the good guys. He'd saved her on multiple occasions over the past four days. He was going to save her this time. She was betting her life on it.

"I'm here," she said softly, stepping into the dappled light.

HIS THROAT TIGHTENED AS SHE moved toward him. Her face was too pale and her lip was bleeding. There were scratches on her chin and her clothes were disheveled but she was alive. He intended to keep her that way. It was an effort to keep from reaching out to her.

"Did you hide the stuff?" he asked.

She nodded.

"Good. Don't tell me where."

He didn't want to know. Didn't want her to think he wanted the information. He'd let her tell the cops. He was out of this part of it.

He was watching her with all those thoughts running through his mind then she was in his arms. She was crying softly; he was kissing her hair and despite the danger, it just felt so right. She fit so right. He'd never thought he was going to hold her again.

He wanted to imagine for just a moment that she could be in his life for always. But he knew that was insanity. She'd never want him after all he'd put her through. Now was not the moment to be worrying about this—time was ticking away. He pulled back.

"Abigail, I'm sorry. I…I have a lot of things to answer for. I know that. But we've got to get out of here. Afterward, I'll tell you anything you want to know. Can you trust me till then?"

Her amber eyes were huge pools of fear and uncertainty. He couldn't blame her. He'd lied to her from the beginning.

But somewhere along the way, he'd stopped doing a job and started caring about her. Started dreaming of an impossible future with her.

Her lips turned up in a small smile. "Yes, I trust you."

He didn't deserve that but he was grateful. Pulling her closer, he kissed her softly before taking her hand. She was wheezing as he tugged her along through the bamboo and the undergrowth but he had no choice. They had to hurry.

Minutes later they were on the Paseo headed to the main gate with no crowds for cover. The first shot came from out of nowhere, going wide and striking a pot on the sidewalk beside them filled with ivy and flowing blossoms.

The clay container shattered into a million pieces, mixing with the dirt and flowers to litter the finely groomed grass and sidewalk like confetti. Shaun pushed Abigail ahead of him, shielding her as they ran. He could see the ticket kiosks up ahead but they were still thirty yards away.

Four more shots hit the sidewalk. Chips of concrete blew in the air, stinging his arms and face. They weren't going to make it. He pushed her toward a huge oak tree, just off the path. He was running behind her, making sure he was between her and the shooters. He was almost there and she was behind the tree when the sixth bullet hit its mark.

It was like being hit with a baseball bat.

He went down. Hard.

ABBY HEARD THE SICKENING sound of a bullet hitting flesh and turned from the cover of a massive oak to see Shaun fall and roll. He landed on his side just off the Paseo in a bed of white begonias.

He was conscious but unmoving. She reversed direction,

grabbed him under his armpits and pulled him behind the tree, blood oozing on the plants in their path.

"Are you okay?" That was a ridiculous question. Of course he wasn't. He was bleeding all over the white flowers they were sitting in, and trying to pull a gun from his shoulder holster at the same time. Then he was shoving the weapon into her hands. The hard steel felt cold and clinical here in the gardens. This was all happening too fast and she was wheezing like mad.

"Use this, now."

The gunmen were coming toward her. She could hear Hodges shouting directions to his partner.

"Oh, God," she murmured. "I don't know how. You… you're bleeding so much."

"Don't worry about that. Concentrate, Abigail. Look at me. I need you to focus on this." He pinned her with those remarkable blue-green eyes, filled now with pain and determination.

"The safety clicks off here." His fingers were shaking but he was showing her. She vaguely recalled hunting lessons with her dad from ages ago. She grabbed the gun, gripping it in both hands and stood—pointing it in front of her in a traditional shooter's pose.

Behind her she heard the *whop whop whop* of helicopter blades and sirens in the distance. The cavalry was coming. The only thing she didn't know was if the helicopter belonged to Donner or the authorities.

"Stop!" she shouted at the approaching gunmen. "Right there or I shoot."

"Abby." It was Donner, walking toward her empty-handed as he continued to speak. "You don't want to do this."

"Oh, don't I?" She didn't have air to say much else.

The sirens were closer. She aimed and pulled the trigger. Dirt flew up at Donner's feet and he stopped walking.

"I don't have a gun, Abby. Would you shoot an unarmed man?"

"You really want me to answer that?" she wheezed.

"All right, we'll just stand here and talk for a moment. Where are the thumb drives?"

Maybe they'd go away if she told them the truth. "Don't…have them…anymore."

"What did you do with them?"

She listened to the sounds of the approaching helicopter. The police sirens were closer than she'd originally thought. Good thing. Her vision was getting spotty with the lack of oxygen. Adrenaline was the only thing keeping her upright.

"They're hidden. Can't get to them now and…you don't have time to make me before that…helicopter lands."

Shaun shouted over the cacophony. "'Tis over, Donner. You have to choose. Get out of here and maybe escape or stay and everything turns to dust. If you shoot us, who wins?"

"Shaun, I thought you knew me better. I always have a plan and I always win. If I can't have a happy ending, no one will." Donner shrugged. "It's my helicopter." He turned to Hodges who was still holding his gun on both of them and nodded.

Hodges smiled and raised his gun to take aim as another shot cracked across the garden. Blood bloomed on Hodges's white knit shirt and the gun fell from his hand. He looked down in surprise as a red stream poured from his left side and he crumpled like a pile of dirty laundry.

Abby looked over her shoulder to see blue-jacketed officers with FBI emblazoned across their chests running toward them. It registered with her that Rob Kenny really could take care of himself and he'd brought backup to prove it.

Donner raced for the helicopter landing on the lawn.

He was seconds from making it into the cockpit but the agents were faster and there were more of them. They surrounded the aircraft, pointing their weapons at the pilot.

Donner had lost.

Four agents were surrounding Abby, as well. She dropped the gun and sank to her knees beside Shaun. His eyes were open but his breathing sounded horribly labored.

"Please, he needs help," she gasped, her own airway quite compromised by now. She held her hands open so the agents could see that they were empty before pressing them against the wound. His blood pulsed warm against her fingers and even more of the flower blooms were stained red instead of white beneath him. She stared into his eyes, praying it wasn't for the last time.

"Don't you dare…leave me. You've got entirely too much explaining to do. Please, Shaun… Hang on." Her breath came in ragged gulps now.

The corners of his mouth turned up in the ghost of a smile but his eyelids fluttered closed as the agents surrounding them tried to take over.

One started to pull her away but another said, "Give her a moment. The EMTs are almost here."

"Shaun?" She grasped his hand and he squeezed it faintly. "Please…I need you. I'm here."

She was out of air as tears streamed down her face. She didn't want to move away but realized fighting with the agents would only interfere with getting Shaun the attention he needed.

"Ma'am, we'll take care of him," insisted the first agent. Then the EMTs were there and they were putting him on a gurney and she couldn't help it, she started to weep in earnest. Something inside her tore as they were wheeling Shaun away.

"Abby?" Another blue-coated agent came out of the crowd. It was Rob.

The tears came faster then and she couldn't breathe at all. He nodded sympathetically, patting her shoulder, mistaking her wheezing for tearful grieving.

"Please, Rob, let me…go with him, I…" She couldn't go on. Her own vision was going dark around the edges.

Rob nodded, not realizing the real physical distress she was in. "They're going to take care of him, Abby. I promise. And I'll take you to the hospital to be with him."

That would be good. She was going to need a hospital herself. That was her last lucid thought. Rob's voice was coming from a long way away. The elephant had moved from sitting on her chest to jumping up and down on it.

"Abby, are you all right?"

She nodded slowly but she wasn't sure what she was agreeing to anymore.

"Abby? What's wrong? Are you hit? Hey, someone get me an EMT."

If she could only exhale it would be okay but she couldn't because that damn elephant wouldn't budge. Rob was talking to her again but she couldn't understand a word. Then the ground was coming up to meet her and she knew nothing more.

Chapter Twenty-Four

Shaun lay in bed listening to the rain and watching the storm through the miniblinds. It was a half hour before he got more pain medication and he was counting the minutes.

He hurt.

Bad.

But he'd been damned lucky. If that ambulance hadn't been in route from another accident, he'd have bled to death, right there in the Arboretum. As it was, he was looking at a long recovery.

When he wasn't conscious he was dreaming wildly erotic dreams of Abigail or dark, violent ones of Donner, Hodges and Iraq—all thanks to his IV pain meds. He vacillated between not wanting to have them administered because he dreaded what they did to his head and craving the relief they offered.

Forty-eight hours since the shooting and he'd been conscious for a grand total of ten—all by himself except for the hospital staff and a visit from his friendly FBI agent, Rob Kenny. It had been a debriefing of sorts, bizarre and not a little awkward. Kenny obviously felt quite protective of Abigail and seemed determined to ascertain Shaun's intentions toward her.

Trouble was Shaun had no idea of his own intentions.

Before their tête-à-tête was over, Shaun had to wonder if
Kenny was in love with Abigail himself. The idea of her
being with someone like the blond-haired, blue-eyed FBI
agent made him more than uncomfortable and irritable. He
was just coherent enough to recognize his own jealousy.

Even after talking with Kenny, Shaun still had no
idea where Abigail was. When he'd asked, the FBI agent
had gone from friendly and forthcoming to hostile and
tight-lipped, saying he wasn't at liberty to divulge any information. Official double-speak for I'm-not-going-to-tell-
you-because-you're-the-last-one-who-needs-to-know.

Kenny was willing to share that Donner was in custody
and the thumb drives had been recovered. The agent had
called in backup after getting Abigail's second panicked
call, hence the large number of both local and federal
agents at the Arboretum. Since he was dealing with a
Homeland Security issue, Shaun was surprised he'd been
told that much.

The cable business channels were an even bigger source
of information than the FBI on Michael Donner. The boss's
arrest was huge news, even though Zip Technologies was
a privately held company. Not surprisingly, the contract
for Zip-Net to Homeland Security had been delayed in-
definitely, but the venture capital investors and executive
board for Zip Technologies had moved quickly to separate
themselves from Donner and the scandal.

Being arrested by the FBI put you on a fast track out of
the boardroom. Within twenty-four hours they had a new
CEO and president. There was even talk of the start-up
being acquired. Perhaps all those jobs at Zip Tech wouldn't
be lost after all.

However on the subject of Abigail, Shaun was kept completely in the dark. Maybe she'd decided he really was too

broken to deal with and was cutting her losses. He couldn't blame her.

But for as long as he lived, he'd remember her hanging on to his hand—begging him not to leave her there in the gardens in the Arboretum. She'd given him the will to hang on as he bled out all over those flowers. Or could that have just been one of his drug-induced hallucinations, too?

He'd lied to her so much. Surely she'd had enough and had taken herself back to England and her books. She was likely on a plane bound for London right now—to pick up the pieces of her life in academia.

He'd wanted it to be something different. Abigail was something he hadn't let himself hope for since...

Hope.

In a bed-and-breakfast in Alabama, she'd actually made him hope for the first time in so long.

How had he expected it to end? It didn't matter how good the sex was. She'd said from the beginning, *don't lie to me.*

So what had he done?

Lied to her at every turn, pretty much sabotaging everything from the very beginning before he'd even realized what she would come to mean to him.

Because it wasn't about sex. He was in love with her. And now he was alone.

Mother of God, when had this happened?

His shoulder throbbed mightily and he grimaced against the pain. What a time to figure things out. After the girl was gone and he couldn't go after her.

He squeezed the bridge of his nose in an attempt to stop his eyes from watering. Didn't work. He was going to lose it and cry, just like a preschooler, and it wasn't from the pain in his gut.

He glanced at the clock again, using words no three-year-old should know as the minute hand seemed to move backward.

There was a soft knock on the door.

Perfect, someone was here for his untouched dinner tray and about to see him in all his weeping glory.

"Come in," he murmured, wiping his eyes with the back of his hand.

Abigail stuck her head around the corner and his breath caught in his throat. He couldn't believe it. She carried a large bouquet of flowers but she was also wearing a hospital robe herself.

"Hey there," she said, shuffling into the room in hot pink leopard slippers. Her hair was piled on her head in a clip with a riot of curls around her too pale face. She looked amazing.

"I see you've been shopping without me." He found his voice but it cracked on the word *shopping*.

She smiled as she slid into the chair beside his bed, giving him a great view of her lovely legs and those sassy slippers. "Rob got them for me, to keep my feet warm on these linoleum floors. I had an asthma attack, a big one, in the gardens. They've just now taken me off oxygen."

He tried to ignore how the comment about Rob shopping for her slippers made him feel queasy and angry at the same time.

"Are you okay?" he asked.

"Yeah. They're discharging me tomorrow. Between all the smoke inhalation from the house and Jason's condo burning, plus running through the gardens and not taking my meds, I did a number on myself."

He nodded. "I'm sorry, Abigail. I didn't take very good care of you."

"What? Are you kidding? I'm not the one who got shot. How are you feeling?"

"I'm fine—" He stopped himself. "Actually, I hurt like hell. But I'm much better now that you're here. I appreciate your stopping by—"

He stopped talking. Her eyes glistened with unshed tears.

She stared at him a moment and finally said, "Rob explained a lot of things to me but I want…I need to know why. Why did Michael Donner do this? He had a product that was going to make him millions. Why did he kill my brother?"

"I don't know for certain. Greed? Ambition? There's always someone who wants more and there are so many out there who are willing to pay for information. For what it's worth, I don't think it was all about the money. I've known Michael Donner for two years and frankly, money isn't that big of a motivator for him."

Shaun shook his head and continued. "But power. Ah, now, that's huge. The man can't stand to lose at anything. With the spyware, he would have wielded remarkable influence. But he had to have the key code so he could sell that 'window into Homeland Security' to the highest bidder after the Zip-Net product was installed. Jason took that all away from him. And Donner didn't even realize it until after he'd had him killed."

She nodded, slowly absorbing all the information. "I don't know what I would have done if you hadn't been there."

He stared at the flowers she'd brought, unable to meet her eyes. "When I found out Donner knew your location there at the Arboretum, I was going crazy trying to find you."

"Thank you for everything. That sounds so inadequate. I wanted to visit earlier but the doctors wouldn't let me off my floor till today."

He broke his gaze from the flowers to glance at her. "No worries. You didn't have to come."

She cocked her head and looked at him strangely. "Well, you did save my life. Multiple times. It's the least I can do." She smiled as she said that last part.

He didn't smile back. *Damn Rob Kenny, even if he was just explaining things.* Shaun stared, unable to look away. "I don't want you to feel obligated in any way, Abigail."

An awkward silence descended as a new nurse breezed in after a quick knock. "Oh, you have company. I'll be quick. I'm here with your pain medication."

"Can that wait?" he asked, hating the interruption and desperately needing a clear head for this conversation.

"No. You don't want to let that pain get ahead of you now, do you?" Before he could say he really didn't give a damn about that at the moment, she'd injected the narcotic into his IV.

He tried not to glare but he certainly did not want to have this discussion half-looped.

"Would you like me to put those flowers in water?" the nurse asked, unaware of what she'd done.

"Sure, thanks," muttered Shaun, suddenly utterly miserable. *Anything, but leave. Please.* The woman had just nuked his chances of having a coherent discussion with Abigail for the next six hours. She'd be long gone when he was lucid again.

The nurse took the bouquet, finally seeming to realize she was interfering with something important, and said nothing else other than a cheery, "Be back later."

Like I'll be awake then.

Abby stood and he thought she was leaving, too.

"Don't go," he said.

She sank to the edge of the bed, her expression inscrutable. "Shaun, I wasn't going anywhere and I need you to know I don't feel obligated to be here because you saved my life. I'm here because…I'm in love with you."

For a moment he thought he'd imagined her words. But it was too soon for the drugs to be kicking in. He gave a small shake of his head. "How is that possible?"

Her eyes widened. "So not the response I was hoping for." She stood up again.

"Wait." He reached for her hand, taking it firmly in his, hoping he made it through this conversation before the meds took effect. "I'm sorry. You really mess with my head and—"

Her expression grew cooler.

"God, I'm saying this all wrong. I've never felt like this, Abigail. I just figured it out before you walked in here. When I thought I'd lost you and the chance to tell you."

His eyes filled and he took her other hand. *Damn.* This was not how he wanted to tell her but she had to know, had to see what was really inside him with no walls. No more hiding behind that cool exterior he'd always shown to everyone when his emotions threatened to get in the way.

Taking a deep breath, he dove in. "I love you and I don't know how to go on without you. But after all I've put you through, I'm just wondering how you could feel the same way about me."

She laughed aloud, in genuine relief, and he felt…hope. It was still too fast for the meds to be making him feel woozy, so this sense of promise had to be real.

He raised an eyebrow. "I need you to explain. Really."

Her cheeks turned pink and he remembered meeting her for the first time—how lovely it had been seeing a woman who blushed.

She squeezed his hand. "For some reason I feel like I'm in fourth grade telling a boy I like him. I trust you and I never thought I'd say that. Your past doesn't scare me. You're a good man."

He didn't deserve this or her. "I'm not good. You don't really know me. You said it yourself. I'm too broken—"

She put a fingertip to his lips and smiled. "I was wrong to say that and I'm sorry. I don't know everything about you but I know enough. Enough to know I'm not looking for a way out or an escape hatch." She focused on his eyes. "Are you?"

He shook his head. This wasn't a dream. She wanted him. "You're it for me," he murmured.

She smiled and lifted her hand to wipe a tear from his cheek. "Then that's all there is. I love you, period. No conditions."

She was leaning toward him when he felt the first hazy bump of pain medication wash over him. Then she was kissing him and he felt her breath against his face but this was still real. He was done with trying to talk her out of it and he wasn't tempting fate anymore. Hadn't he given her fair warning? He no longer wanted to talk her out of anything, except maybe a few articles of her clothing.

She leaned in again, avoiding all the IV lines as he reached for her—touching her hair, longing to freeze this moment in time. He heard one of her slippers hit the floor.

"You really want this, don't you? You want me." He was caught in the wonder, even as his voice was slurring. The IV narcotic was definitely kicking in.

She grinned and nodded at the same. "Yes, I do. But I think I may have to tell you again when you wake up."

"Nope, I'll remember. I may even get to dream the good stuff now."

"What does that mean?"

"Tell you later. I'm knackered," he whispered, squeezing

her hand, knowing he was wearing a ridiculously goofy grin. His eyes drifted closed but he fought it hard. This was entirely too important.

"I'm all in, Abigail. I'm not letting you go...ever. Trust me."

"I do."

"And fifty years from now, you remember to tell our grandkids—I tried to warn you off but you wanted me anyway."

"I'll do that." She crossed her legs, a bare foot catching his eye before she kissed him again and his eyes drifted closed.

She'd be here when he woke up. He knew it with a certainty he hadn't felt in...never. Abigail would be here today, tomorrow and tomorrow. Life would never be the same.

* * * * *

Harlequin®

INTRIGUE®

COMING NEXT MONTH

Available May 10, 2011

#1275 BABY BOOTCAMP
Daddy Corps
Mallory Kane

#1276 BRANDED
Whitehorse, Montana: Chisholm Cattle Company
B.J. Daniels

#1277 DAMAGED
Colby Agency: The New Equalizers
Debra Webb

#1278 THE MAN FROM GOSSAMER RIDGE
Cooper Justice: Cold Case Investigation
Paula Graves

#1279 UNFORGETTABLE
Cassie Miles

#1280 BEAR CLAW CONSPIRACY
Bear Claw Creek Crime Lab
Jessica Andersen

You can find more information on upcoming
Harlequin® titles, free excerpts and more at
www.HarlequinInsideRomance.com.

HICNM0411

REQUEST YOUR FREE BOOKS!
2 FREE NOVELS PLUS 2 FREE GIFTS!

BREATHTAKING ROMANTIC SUSPENSE

HI11

*With an evil force hell-bent on destruction,
two enemies must unite to find a truth that turns
all-too-personal when passions collide.*

*Enjoy a sneak peek in Jenna Kernan's next installment
in her original* TRACKER *series, GHOST STALKER,
available in May, only from Harlequin Nocturne.*

"Who are you?" he snarled.

Jessie lifted her chin. "Your better."

His smile was cold. "Such arrogance could only come from a Niyanoka."

She nodded. "Why are you here?"

"I don't know." He glanced about her room. "I asked the birds to take me to a healer."

"And they have done so. Is that *all* you asked?"

"No. To lead them away from my friends." His eyes fluttered and she saw them roll over white.

Jessie straightened, preparing to flee, but he roused himself and mastered the momentary weakness. His eyes snapped open, locking on her.

Her heart hammered as she inched back.

"Lead who away?" she whispered, suddenly afraid of the answer.

"The ghosts. Nagi sent them to attack me so I would bring them to her."

The wolf must be deranged because Nagi did not send ghosts to attack living creatures. He captured the evil ones after their death if they refused to walk the Way of Souls, forcing them to face judgment.

"Her? The healer you seek is also female?"

"Michaela. She's Niyanoka, like you. The last Seer of Souls and Nagi wants her dead."

Jessie fell back to her seat on the carpet as the possibility of this ricocheted in her brain. Could it be true?

"Why should I believe you?" But she knew why. His black aura, the part that said he had been touched by death. Only a ghost could do that. But it made no sense.

Why would Nagi hunt one of her people and why would a Skinwalker want to protect her? She had been trained from birth to hate the Skinwalkers, to consider them a threat.

His intent blue eyes pinned her. Jessie felt her mouth go dry as she considered the impossible. Could the trickster be speaking the truth? Great Mystery, what evil was this?

She stared in astonishment. There was only one way to find her answers. But she had never even met a Skinwalker before and so did not even know if they dreamed.

But if he dreamed, she would have her chance to learn the truth.

Look for GHOST STALKER by Jenna Kernan,
available May only from Harlequin Nocturne,
wherever books and ebooks are sold.

INTRIGUE®

**WILL THE QUEST FOR THE KILLERS BE
TOO MUCH FOR THIS TOWN TO HANDLE?**

**FIND OUT IN THE NEWEST MINISERIES
BY *USA TODAY* BESTSELLING AUTHOR**

B.J. DANIELS

WHITEHORSE MONTANA

Chisholm Cattle Company

Colton Chisholm has lived with the guilt
of not helping his high-school sweetheart
when she needed him most. Fourteen years
later, he's committed to finding out what
happened to her the night she disappeared.
The same night he stood her up.

BRANDED

May 2011

Five more titles to follow....

—— www.eHarlequin.com ——

Fan favorite author
TINA LEONARD
is back with
an exciting new miniseries.

Six bachelor brothers are given a challenge—
get married, start a big family and whoever does
so first will inherit the famed Rancho Diablo.
Too bad none of these cowboys is marriage material!

Callahan Cowboys:
Catch one if you can!

www.eHarlequin.com

HAR75358